Highest Praise for
John Lutz

"John Lutz knows how to make you shiver."
—Harlan Coben

"Lutz offers up a heart-pounding roller coaster
of a tale."
—Jeffery Deaver

"John Lutz is one of the masters of the police novel."
—Ridley Pearson

"John Lutz is a major talent."
—John Lescroart

"I've been a fan for years."
—T. Jefferson Parker

"John Lutz just keeps getting better and better."
—Tony Hillerman

"Lutz ranks with such vintage masters
of big-city murder
as Lawrence Block and Ed McBain."
—*St. Louis Post-Dispatch*

"Lutz is among the best."
—*San Diego Union*

"Lutz knows how to seize and hold the
reader's imagination."
—*Cleveland Plain Dealer*

"It's easy to see why he's won an Edgar
and two Shamuses."
—*Publishers Weekly*

Twist

"One of the top ten mystery novels of 2013."
—*The Strand Magazine*

Pulse

"Grisly murders seen through the eyes of killer and victim; crime scenes from which clues slowly accumulate; a determined killer . . . compelling."
—*Booklist*

"One of the ten best books of the year."
—*The Strand Magazine*

Serial

"Wow, oh wow, oh wow . . . that's as simple as I can put it. You gotta read this one."
—*True Crime Book Reviews*

Mister X

"A page-turner to the nail-biting end . . . twisty, creepy whodunit."
—*Publishers Weekly* (starred review)

Night Kills

"Lutz's skill will keep you glued to this thick thriller."
—*St. Louis Post-Dispatch*

ALSO BY JOHN LUTZ

*Carnage: The Prequel to "Frenzy" (e-short)

*Twist

*Pulse

*Switch (e-short)

*Serial

*Mister X

*Urge to Kill

*Night Kills

*In for the Kill

Chill of Night

Fear the Night

*Darker Than Night

Night Victims

The Night Watcher

The Night Caller

Final Seconds (with David August)

The Ex

Single White Female

*featuring Frank Quinn

Available from Kensington Publishing Corp. and
Pinnacle Books

JOHN LUTZ

FRENZY

PINNACLE BOOKS
Kensington Publishing Corp.
www.kensingtonbooks.com

PINNACLE BOOKS are published by

Kensington Publishing Corp.
119 West 40th Street
New York, NY 10018

All Kensington titles, imprints, and distributed lines are available at special quantity discounts for bulk purchases for sales promotions, premiums, fund-raising, educational, or institutional use. Special book excerpts or customized printings can also be created to fit specific needs. For details, write or phone the office of the Kensington special sales manager: Kensington Publishing Corp., 119 West 40th Street, New York, NY 10018, attn: Special Sales Department; phone 1-800-221-2647.

This book is a work of fiction. Names, characters, businesses, organizations, places, events, and incidents either are the product of the author's imagination or are used fictitiously. Any resemblance to actual persons, living or dead, events, or locales is entirely coincidental.

PINNACLE BOOKS and the Pinnacle logo are Reg. U.S. Pat. & TM Off.

ISBN-13: 978-0-7860-2830-6
ISBN-10: 0-7860-2830-0

First printing: October 2014

10 9 8 7 6 5 4 3 2 1

Printed in the United States of America

First electronic edition: October 2014

ISBN-13: 978-0-7860-3548-9
ISBN-10: 0-7860-3548-X

For Wendy

Love always

PART ONE

These be
Three silent things:
The falling snow . . . the hour
Before the dawn . . . the mouth of one
Just dead.

—ADELAIDE CRAPSEY, "Triad"

1

Gasping for air, Quinn tried to lengthen his stride but couldn't. He swallowed, accepted the pain. Kept running.

The killer was far enough ahead of him that he couldn't be seen through the trees, but occasionally Quinn could hear him crashing through the brush in his flight for freedom. The noise of the killer's desperate dash seemed to be getting louder.

Quinn was gaining. Some of the others were, too, he was sure. But he had laid out everything he had in the beginning, putting every fiber and muscle he had into the chase. Now he was paying for it, but he was closest.

Quinn was closest, and closing.

It was like a fox hunt, and he was the fox.

The killer, whose grisly calling card read simply D.O.A., pressed on through the rustle and crackle of last year's dead leaves, listening to the barking dogs, the occasional human shouts. His pursuers were gaining on him. It was as if they were actually having fun with him. With *him!*

He was out of breath, and almost out of options. But *almost* could be the most important word in the English language.

The ground was gradually falling away. He could see it beginning to slope, and he could feel it in the fronts of his thighs. He knew from the grade that he was approaching water.

Almost there!

The hectic barking of the dogs was getting louder. More frantic. He wondered what kind of dogs they were. The animals sounded as if they were in a frenzy, as if they wanted to kill him.

And maybe that was the game.

The killer glimpsed a blue-green plane of water through the foliage ahead, and his hope surged. *The lake!*

The question was, where along the shoreline was he going to emerge from the woods? Where would his sudden appearance *not* draw attention and bullets?

This can still work! It can still work!

He put on what in his mind was a burst of speed, but was in reality simply a great deal of thrashing around, like an exhausted long distance runner approaching the tape.

Almost there!
Almost!

2

"Dwayney!"

The house where it happened was at the edge of the water. The green lawn sloped gently away from the house, to an Olympic-sized swimming pool that appeared to merge with the bay. It made for an interesting illusion.

"Dwayney, honey?"

Maude Evans was lying posed on a webbed lounger at the edge of the rectangular pool, looking oddly as if she were floating on an invisible horizon. Every half minute or so she stretched her lithe, tanned body so she could reach her whiskey sour, take a sip, then replace the glass on a small white table. Towels were folded carefully beneath her so the lounger's webbing wouldn't make temporary ugly marks on her sleek body.

"Dwayney, fetch me another drink!" Maude called.

Dwayne's body jerked. He'd been half dozing in the late-morning Florida sun. He peered over at Maude above the dark frames of his sunglasses. Looking back at him, Maude held up her drink and swished around what was left in the bottom of the glass. A clear signal and command.

He obediently went inside to the kitchen and carefully made a whiskey sour the way he'd been taught. Dwayne personally didn't like whiskey sours. For that matter, what limited experience he'd had suggested to him that he'd never like alcoholic drinks. But after building Maude's drink he sipped it to make sure it tasted the way she wanted it to taste.

More like demanded.

When he went back outside and handed the glass to Maude, she seemed to notice him only barely. Dwayne thought she smelled wonderful, of mingled scents of lotion and perspiration that gleamed on her smooth tan skin.

He left poolside and stood on the rear deck of the house, where he could observe his soon-to-be stepmother. He'd just turned fourteen, and he couldn't help but be enthralled by Maude. Not that she minded. She would secretly urge him on, smiling and winking at him behind his father's back.

Well, not so secretly. They were both amused by Dwayne's discomfort, by his inability to conceal the erection he would often get in Maude's presence. This embarrassed Dwayne so that he blushed a vivid pink, provoking their laughter. Sometimes, to tame and reduce the erection, Dwayne would think about his late mother. About how he'd hated her.

She and Dwayne's father had used him in ways he hadn't imagined possible. Ways he despised, and that made him despise them and himself.

When Dwayne's mother died nine months ago, Dwayne hadn't known how to feel. He did know the nighttime visits would stop, the gin breath and the giggling, his pain that his parents so enjoyed. His father had objected to hurting him that way at first, then his mother had convinced him that it didn't matter. That Dwayne actually enjoyed what they were doing. She had figured out various ways to prove it.

When she died from heart failure that was somehow connected with the white powder she and her husband used, Dwayne had to pretend to mourn convincingly enough to fool the phony friends and business associates who came to pay their respects. He got pretty good at it.

What was life but playing a series of roles?

There had never been mention of where his father had obtained Maude Evans. She'd simply shown up a few weeks after his mother's death. His mother's life.

Maude smoothly replaced the life part with her own version.

Dwayne's own life slipped into a routine. He was supposedly being homeschooled. A strict tutor, Mrs. Jacoby, would arrive at nine o'clock every weekday and stay until one o'clock. She was a broad, middle-aged woman with a perpetual scowl. There was no need for him to know her first name, as long as he learned his prime numbers and Latin roots. She took no crap from Dwayne.

Mrs. Jacoby and Maude seemed barely to notice each other. Or maybe that was just in Dwayne's presence.

At precisely nine o'clock, when Mrs. Jacoby arrived, was when his father would go to work at his property procurement and management office. The company owned prime beach front property all over Florida, and some in the Carolinas. Money was no problem. Money allowed for the regular, sun-drenched routine. It was something taken for granted.

After the conversation Dwayne overheard between Maude and Bill Phoenix, the man who came every other day to service the pool, Dwayne knew that money was all that had attracted Maude to his father. Phoenix was a tall, rangy guy with friendly brown eyes, muscles that rippled, and curly black hair on his head and chest. He looked like he'd make a great James Bond in the movies. Maude and money had attracted Bill Phoenix.

Dwayne knew that Maude and the swimming pool guy had plans.

3

Creighton, two years ago

Quinn kept up a rough but steady pace parallel to the shoreline, casting a sharp eye in all directions as he ran. He knew the dogs were slightly ahead of him and to his left. To his right was the lake. Directly ahead of him was the killer. It was like a steadily narrowing isosceles triangle, gradually bringing killer and pursuers together at its narrow point. The killer could keep going the way he was and stay in the squeeze. Or he could break to his left and try to get out ahead of the dogs and their handlers. Or he could break to his right and start swimming.

Quinn figured the killer would stay on course, and when he ran out of safe ground, he would run out of freedom or life.

Maybe that was the way he planned it.

No way to know that for sure now. No point in worrying about it.

They'd almost had the bastard back at the lodge, where he'd just taken his latest victim, after torturing her with dozens of knife cuts and cigarette burns, and gradual disembowelment. An anonymous phone call, proclaiming that someone was being murdered at the lodge, hadn't come in time to save the victim.

The killer had seen their approach. He'd fled the scene after making the phone call, not realizing how quickly they would respond, how close Quinn was on his heels. Now he found himself in a running gun battle with Quinn and the county sheriff.

Quinn was sure that the sheriff, a slim, gray haired man named Carl Chalmers, had been badly wounded. The last Quinn saw of him, he was sitting on the ground, talking on what Quinn assumed was a cell phone, and waving his free arm at Quinn, urging him to continue the chase. Chalmers had come late to the hunt, joining Quinn after Quinn had followed a trail of dead bodies from New York City to Maine.

There was a lot of blood around the sheriff.

And here Quinn was, in the chase and with unexpected help. He knew now that the sheriff had called in the dogs as well as the state police.

Quinn also suspected that the anonymous phone call had been made by the killer to him alone, to lure him to the scene of the murder, to trick him into a futile chase.

This was the kind of asshole who played that kind of game.

Now, unless the killer had a boat stashed somewhere, the chase might not be futile after all. The dogs, forcing a hard and close pursuit, might be the difference. The killer might not have planned on the dogs.

Suddenly the flat plane of the lake appeared through the trees to Quinn's right, exactly where it was supposed to be. Quinn slowed and veered in that direction, coming out at the edge of the woods, and near a long and dilapidated wooden dock that poked like an accusing finger out toward the opposite shore.

Quinn stopped running and bent forward to catch his breath, leaning his rifle against a nearby tree.

He knew now how the killer planned to escape. He also knew the killer had outsmarted and outmaneuvered him.

But not out-lucked him.

Quinn had the bastard!

The killer could see the level blue-green surface, and knew he was almost on the mud bank. He slowed down and glanced right and left to get his bearings. The trees thinned. There was a subtle but unmistakable scent that rose from flotsam and algae and acres of still water.

He hadn't been running blind. He had some sense of where he was and had to be close to the dock.

He glimpsed movement through the trees and stopped running immediately, standing stock still and trying to quiet his breathing.

Ahead of him, his back to the water, was Quinn!

Regret and anger flashed through the killer's mind: It had all gone as planned, except for the damned sheriff. If he hadn't come along with Quinn, and somehow remained alive long enough to call in a nearby tracker with dogs, this would all be working out very well.

Then he saw that his luck wasn't all bad. Quinn was bent over with his hands on his knees, out of breath. His rifle was leaning against a tree, beyond his immediate reach.

The killer watched Quinn straighten up and stretch,

raising his arms high and twisting his body so he momentarily faced the lake. As if he couldn't resist another glance back at the rickety pier, where the last thing he expected was docked.

Then he turned back to look around on shore, no doubt to find shelter from which to ambush his prey. Obviously, he assumed he'd won the race to the lake.

Excellent! If the killer's first shot didn't hit home, he had time to pump another bullet into Quinn before the doomed cop could reach his rifle. He moved to the base of a large tree where he'd be difficult to spot, even after firing at Quinn.

The killer couldn't help smiling slightly and thinking, *Checkmate.*

4

The cabana with the blue-and-white striped sides was off to the east, so it didn't spoil the view from the house.

Dwayne, if he was careful, could make his way through trimmed shrubbery and around to the back of the cabana. The way the bay curved, he could only be seen from the water, and that didn't pose much of a problem. He could crouch unseen there and listen to nearby conversation, and whatever sounds filtered through the cabana's thin wall.

It was almost sunset, and he waited for it to get dark before he went to his spot behind the cabana. Now not even someone out on the bay on a boat, with a telescope or binoculars, was likely to notice him.

His father was in Augusta on business, and Dwayne was supposed to be bent over his homework. Maude and her lover, Bill Phoenix, wouldn't suspect that Dwayne wasn't in his room, but behind the cabana's back wall. Dwayne knew from experience that they would talk to each other inside the cabana, thinking that outside the sound might carry over water. Not to mention that Bill Phoenix had voiced a fear of being observed and eavesdropped on by the neighbors.

Dwayne suspected it wasn't really the neighbors Phoenix worried about. Not them personally, anyway. But they might gossip, and he *was* doing things with the wife-to-be of one of the richest, most powerful men in Florida. The kind of man who might hire detectives.

Or worse.

Maude was not only rich, she was sizzling hot. Phoenix was a guy who maintained swimming pools for the rich.

Figure it out.

Dwayne, who knew about his father, was sure he didn't suspect Maude of seeing another man, especially at their home. Not many men would be so stupid.

But Maude had a way about her.

Dwayne nestled closer to the cabana wall. Even pressed his ear to it.

"I've talked him into setting a date," Maude was saying, her voice easily understandable on the other side of the thin wall. "When we get back to town, we'll tell people we're married. Maybe we'll even throw a big party."

"Jesus!" Bill Phoenix said. "Next week."

"It's gotta be that way. There's a window of opportunity and we gotta get through it. The old windbag is in a trance that won't last forever. With his wife dead, he's gonna make a new will, and his *new* wife—that would be me—will be the beneficiary of his fortune."

"What about the kid?"

"The *entire* fortune."

"I don't follow. He'll still want the kid to have some of it."

"Being dead, he won't have a say in it. He'll trust me to give a fair share to Dwayne. He really thinks I love the little prick. That I'm like his actual mother. Anyway, I've got him convinced the kid is mentally deficient, according to his tutor. Just can't learn. Might never learn how to handle real money. We've already made arrangements for a private school in Kentucky to take him. Big surprise for the kid."

"What about the tutor? She go along with this?"

"She'll get hers."

"But won't she hold it over us?"

"Not when she realizes what we've done, and that she's done it with us. She'll take her reasonable commission and lose herself."

"And the kid?"

"Don't make me laugh."

"He might make trouble, Maude."

"Not to worry. I'll take care of it. I took care of the wife, didn't I? Cokehead bitch got the biggest and last heroin trip of her life."

Dwayne knew what she meant. His mother had been murdered. No doubt about it. His body began to shake so hard he feared they might hear him.

Then a calm came over him, like a cool breeze off the sea. He was in a real predicament. But Mrs. Jacoby herself had taught him how he should keep his head and not be overwhelmed by the facts. He should stay calm and *think*.

Think.

After all, he wasn't sorry his mother was dead. He

didn't have to pretend otherwise, even to himself, after the things she'd done to him. Especially he didn't have to pretend to himself. He wasn't sorry she was dead. That her death wasn't an accident didn't make that much difference, did it? Maude was planning on marrying his father and then killing him so Maude could inherit his fortune. Then Maude and Bill Phoenix would be rich and live happily ever after.

That wasn't all bad either, was it?

It didn't have to be.

Not if you turned it this way and that in your mind, like Mrs. Jacoby had preached. Dwayne was grateful to Mrs. Jacoby, even if she was going to take money from Maude and Bill Phoenix to help lie to him and put him in a prison-like distant public school.

She thought.

Dwayne scooted back away from the cabana. Careful to keep to the shadows of the shrubbery, he made his way back to the house.

He lay in bed most of the night without sleeping, thinking about what he'd heard.

Next week. Like Bill Phoenix had said, that wasn't much time. Dwayne was sure that if Maude wanted his father to take her to Las Vegas and marry her, that's what his father would do.

Then what?

Dwayne refused to be trapped again in the games adults played.

He knew Maude, and knew his father. He didn't want to go to a private school where life would be miserable.

And he knew that when his father and Maude were married, and Maude was sleeping in the bed where Dwayne's mother had slept, things would eventually become the same as when Dwayne's real mother was alive.

Then, after a long enough time that it wouldn't seem too suspicious, Dwayne's father would die.

That was how it seemed to work.

The family would be together again, at least for a while.

5

New York, the present

When Andria Bell opened the door of her suite in the Fairchild Hotel in New York, she expected maid service or a bellhop. Instead, she found herself face-to-face with the worst thing she could have imagined.

She'd seen the man talking to Grace in the Museum of Modern Art earlier that day, and there'd been something about the way he was looking at Grace, the subtle smile, the lean of his body toward hers, that suggested predator and prey.

And here was the predator at her door.

Still standing in the hotel hall, he looked beyond Andria. She saw a quick movement of his head and darting of his eyes, to make sure they were alone.

His eyes.

The predator again.

Then he showed her a gun, which he drew out from beneath his light jacket that was still spotted with rain from the drizzle outside.

It was a stubby gun of the sort operated with both

hands, and it had what Andria had heard referred to as a banana clip. An automatic rifle, she believed. *Rat-a-tat-tat . . .*

She knew little about guns, but she understood that the carnage could be astounding.

Andria had never had a gun pointed at her. She taught art, not war. Her legs went rubbery as she stared into the black hole at the end of the muzzle. It was hypnotic, the way the gun's dark bore seemed like an eye gazing back at her with malicious meaning.

She retreated as if in a trance when the man pushed his way in and closed the door softly behind him. He raised a forefinger to his smiling lips in a signal—a warning—for her to remain silent. Then he clicked the gun onto a clasp on his belt so it dangled pointed forward. He smiled with his head cocked to the side, and shrugged while displaying turned up palms, as if to say, *See. No problem here. Nothing to be scared of, lady.*

And like that, he had her by the neck.

She knew immediately that she was in the hands of an expert, but it wasn't a comforting thought. He knew exactly where to squeeze, and how hard. The room darkened, and Andria was aware that her hands had become fluttering, useless objects, as she clawed feebly at his iron fingers. She began to weaken, began losing consciousness. She knew she might never return to this world. This was it. The end of her life.

Her left hand closed on the gun and fumbled at it, played feebly with the immovable trigger to no avail. She had no mastery over her fingers. There would be a safety somewhere, but even if she found it she wouldn't recognize what it was, wouldn't be able to move it.

The darkness deepened.

Andria was aware that her assailant was still smiling at her, as if they were friends and this was pleasant discourse. He leaned in even closer to her and she smelled his fetid breath as he whispered, "Good-bye for a while . . ." He almost sang the words. She inanely thought the tune was the theme song of an old TV show.

His grip on her neck tightened painfully, and she became incredibly light-headed, as if she might rise like a balloon into a dark sky.

So this is how it is . . .

She became aware of movement, and as she lost consciousness saw that Grace had come in from the suite's bedroom where the girls, her students, were watching TV before preparing to sleep on two double beds and a rollaway. She was wearing jeans and a T-shirt that left her midriff bare.

Grace . . . Grace . . . Grace . . .

Grace was standing frozen, her slender figure caught in an awkward pose, her wide blue gaze fixed in horror. Her right fist was raised to her mouth so that she was gnawing on a knuckle.

Andria had never seen anyone look so terrified.

As the darkness engulfed her, she felt that somehow she would remember Grace that way forever.

The killer unfastened his AK-47 from its belt clasp and kept it aimed at the thin blond girl from the museum. With careful conversational prodding, she'd told him all he needed to know—who the group was, why they were in the city, where they were staying.

The teacher leading the group was interesting, but

not as much as the blond girl, Grace, who stood now in the doorway staring at him as if he were the tarantula at the party.

"Stay calm, Grace," he said. "Remember me? We talked at the museum."

"I remember," she said in a barely audible tight voice. The throat tended to clench at times like this.

Grace had seen his face, so he had no choice other than to make her cease to exist. The killer really didn't mind that there was no choice.

"Let's go back into the bedroom," he said. He tickled her navel with the tip of the gun barrel and made her gasp and bend at the waist.

"We'll make it a kind of party."

With the scary AK-47, the girls were easy to manage. Two of them lost control and dampness appeared in the crotches of their jeans. Those two should be the least likely to present problems. Fortunately, they all wore jogging shoes—recommended for walking around the concrete city—with long sturdy laces.

At his direction, Grace tied the wrists and ankles of her four friends tightly with their shoelaces, left lace for wrists, right for ankles. Then he tied Grace, and used the girls' panties, which he stretched and sliced away from them, as gags that he stuffed tightly into their mouths. They could work such gags loose with their tongues after a few hours, but they didn't have a few hours.

Well, maybe. He should make the most of this rare gift from fate.

After making sure the girls were all firmly bound, he began to remove his clothes.

Andria could see the clock by the bed, but it was blurry.

Not just the green numerals were blurry, but the entire clock.

How in God's name . . .

Then the realization of where she was, how she'd gotten there, what had *happened,* fell on her like an avalanche. It was like waking up the morning after someone you knew and loved had unexpectedly died. At first the recollection wasn't real—then it was way too real.

My girls! My God, what's happened to my girls?

Andria was on her back and still couldn't move. Her throat was burning as if she'd swallowed acid, and her breath was ragged and loud.

She fixed her gaze again on the clock, and the phone next to it.

She had to get to that phone.

The clock's liquid-diode figures did come into focus. Forty-eight minutes had passed since the killer had entered the suite.

He's probably gone. Thought I was dead and left. Please make him be gone!

Andria rolled onto her left side, marveling at how every inch of her body ached. It took her almost ten minutes, but she managed to maneuver herself onto her hands and knees.

Where should she go now?

The door? The bedroom? The phone?

"There you are," he said pleasantly. As if he'd momentarily misplaced her.

At the sound of his voice she dropped to her side again, drew her body into the fetal position, and squeezed her eyes shut.

"I'm particularly interested in chatting with you."

She heard soft footsteps on the carpet.

Opened her eyes.

There he was, nude except for white rubber gloves, smiling, holding a large knife in his right hand. There was blood on the knife. There was blood on him.

"I was sure you could be brought around again by now," he said, "but you made it back so fast on your own. That shows real determination. You should be proud."

He came closer, and she saw that he had something in his left hand. It looked like a wad of shoelaces.

"C'mon over here," he said, and bent and lifted her as if she were weightless. He was careful not to penetrate her with the knife.

She tried to scream but could only croak.

"Careful," he said. "We wouldn't want you to lose your voice completely."

He laid her on her back on the hard walnut coffee table, then used the shoelaces to bind her arms and legs to the four table legs. Her head was off the table, lolling backward. She couldn't control it. Her neck muscles were putty.

Like the rest of her. Painful putty.

He sat on the sofa by the table, leaned forward, and showed her the large, bloody knife. She saw that it had a yellowed bone handle.

"We need to talk," he said. With surprising ease, he

used the bloody knife to cut button after button from her blouse. "The only way you can get out of this mess is to talk your way out of it." There went the front of her slacks. Then her panties. The sharp knife blade so close to her flesh. "You'll need to tell me the truth. That won't be as difficult as you might imagine. What they say about the truth setting you free . . . well, it's true. At least in this case."

She knew he was lying, but she wanted so much to believe him. His words were her only hope, and she couldn't help but cling to them. That was the way it worked. He knew that.

The bastard knows that!

He also knows he doesn't have the vital truth.

He'd heard part of what he wanted to know from Grace, at MoMA. Grace could tell him part because that was all she knew, all that Andria had told her. But Grace had revealed where the rest of the story might be found—with Andria.

Andria and the killer both understood that, at this point, understanding how fear and hope would work against her didn't make much difference. He was sure she had a truth to trade, and they both knew that in exchange for even the slightest chance to live, she would trade it.

And he would renege.

6

"The maid came in this morning and found them," New York Police Commissioner Harley Renz said. "I figured this was one for you."

Former homicide captain Frank Quinn, now with his own investigative agency, Quinn and Associates Investigations (Q&A), simply nodded. His old friend and enemy the commissioner sometimes contracted Q&A in work-for-hire arrangements with the NYPD. Quinn was perfect to lead especially sensitive and perilous investigations. Cases that might do political harm to the ambitious and avidly unscrupulous commissioner.

Quinn did recognize that Harley Renz harbored a twisted kind of honesty. He not only ass-kissed and blackmailed his way up the bureaucratic ladder, he was proud of it. In fact, he cheerfully bragged about his abhorrent behavior, rolled in and reveled in his corruption.

Greed of every sort had helped to make Renz fifty pounds overweight. He was wearing his artfully tailored commissioner's uniform this morning, knowing there'd be plenty of photographs and maybe a TV spot.

The pink flesh of his neck ballooned over his stiff white shirt collar, lending him multiple chins.

Quinn, though he was the same age as Renz, was still lean and muscular, with a face so homely it was handsome, and unruly straight brown hair parted at the side. He appeared as if he needed a haircut, even immediately after a haircut. With his height, broad shoulders, plate-sized rough hands, and nose broken one time more than it had been set, he came across as a thug. Until you took a second look into his steady green eyes, at the intelligence that lived there. Intelligence and something else that most people didn't want to look at too closely.

"They were all killed the same way," a nasty nasal voice said. It belonged to Dr. Julius Nift, the medical examiner. He was a short, fashion plate of a man, best described as Napoleonic. He used some sort of a shiny steel instrument to poke at the end girl on the bed, a slender redhead who looked about sixteen years old. Most of all the girls' clothes had been cut away, some of the remnants used to cover where their throats had been cut, to minimize arterial blood being splashed around during their death throes. "Same knife, and probably its point was used for the torture leading up to their deaths."

"Same knife used to slice the initials in their foreheads?" Quinn asked. The letters *D.O.A.* had been neatly carved into the foreheads of all the victims.

"Don't know for sure, but probably."

"Old friend of yours," Renz said to Quinn, and just like that Quinn was back at the lake in Maine, listening to—feeling—the reverberation of a rifle shot.

The scar where the bullet had ripped into the right

side of his back began to burn, as it often did when he thought of that day at the lake. Unfinished business. It drove a man like Quinn. He often revisited Creighton Lake in his memory.

Memory was a powerful engine that drove him. He would never forget, but there was one way to lessen the pain.

"My dead friend, we hope," he said. "This could be a copycat killer, a secret admirer."

Nift glanced at the row of dead, all-but-nude young women. "He left the good parts alone, anyway."

Quinn felt a surge of anger but pushed it away. It was Nift's impulse to try getting under people's skin. "What about the victim in the other room?" Quinn asked. "Why was she tied down on the coffee table?"

"Maybe the killer just ran out of room on the bed," Renz said.

"No," Quinn said. "She got special attention."

Nift was grinning at him lewdly. "You have a good eye." There were stories about Nift, about his attitude toward the dead. Especially if they'd been attractive women. Quinn thought some of the stories were probably true. "She was older, too," Nift said.

"Thirty-seven," Renz said. "According to her Ohio driver's license."

"You got all the IDs?" Quinn asked.

"Yeah. The special one on the table was Andria Bell. She was chaperone and guide for the others. The young girls were art students at some academy in Cleveland."

"Andria was an artist?"

"A teacher, anyway." Renz propped his fists on his hips and shook his head in dismay. "Damn it all. Those young girls, never had much of a chance to get to know life. Imagine how the news media's gonna be all over this mess. High school yearbook photos of those girls, beautiful and smiling. Interviews with the families. Awkward questions. The media assholes will pull out all the stops."

"Why shouldn't they?" Quinn said.

"Oh, no reason in the world. The bastards are doing exactly what I'd do. Only there's only one of me. They're like a pack of wild dogs, gonna ravage everything and everybody in the way of a juicy story. A police commissioner who can't catch a killer who's like a local Richard Speck who's been on vacation, and now he's back. Now there's a story. All it needs is some poor sacrificial schmuck to rip to pieces on news programs and in the papers."

"There are five dead women here," Harley said. "Plus we've got two killed in Maine, plus at least four in New York prior to Maine. And you're feeling sorry for yourself."

"Isn't that just the point? I'm still alive."

And still wants to be mayor someday.

Quinn pushed the thought from his mind. He knew Renz was right. The voracious New York news media would make the most of what was a sensational story anyway. The dead women would get more than their fifteen minutes of fame, and then, except for the memories of those who'd loved them, they would be forgotten.

He looked around at the carnage. "Any computers?"

"If there were any," Renz said, "the killer took them with him. But that's doubtful."

"Why?"

"Everybody here has an iPhone, or something like

one. Damned things are like little computers themselves."

Renz gave Quinn a steady look with his flesh-padded
eyes. The commissioner has a busy day ahead of him,
the look said. It was time to make it official. "Are you
on this one, Quinn? Usual arrangement?"

"Yes and yes," Quinn said. No hesitation.

"It's yours, then. Keep me apprised, and I'll handle
the media unless I tell you otherwise."

*So I can take the serious media shots and be blamed
for every day the killer isn't caught.* "Of course," Quinn
said. He'd known the second he saw the letters carved
on the victims' foreheads that this was his case, whatever the painful memories and dark deceptions.

He'd been chosen, and not only by Renz.

Renz moved toward the door. "I'll get the papers to
you to sign. And appoint some kind of liaison."

Quinn nodded.

Liaison. Another word for informer. Just what Quinn
needed.

A man in white coveralls appeared in the doorway.
The crime scene unit had arrived. Usually they arrived
at crime scenes about the same time as the ME. Quinn
wondered if Renz had purposely delayed them so
Quinn could get a better look at the victims. Make him
really *want* this case. Quinn knew that was the way
Renz thought. Always there was more than one reason
for whatever he did.

"Where's Pearl?" Nift asked. Working the love-hate
thing they had going but without the love.

"She'll be here," Quinn said. "It'd be a good idea if
you were gone by then."

Nift grinned. He was too insensitive to scare. "A threat?"

"Yeah. You'd be surprised what Pearl's capable of if you piss her off."

There was something to that, and Nift knew it. He began putting away his instruments in a compartment of his black valise where they'd be separated from those that were still sterile. "Tell Pearl I said hello. I'm done here, anyway. Got a hot date with all these beautiful ladies, down at the morgue." He shrugged. "Well, not so hot."

Quinn didn't bother answering.

"Let's get some breakfast," Renz said. "Let the CSU do its thing without us in the way."

"I already ate breakfast," Nift said.

"Good," Quinn and Renz said simultaneously.

Nift didn't seem to notice their obvious gratefulness that he wouldn't be joining them.

"One thing," Quinn said. "I want any iPhones, regular cell phones, or anything else that's tech, set aside for Jerry Lido."

Lido was the alcoholic but brilliant tech analyst for Q&A.

"No problem," Renz said. "So let's go get some waffles."

"I'm gonna wait for Pearl," Quinn said.

"Soon as the CSU people and photographer give the word, I'll send these dead folks to the morgue," Nift said. "If that's how you wanna do it."

"That's how," Quinn said. He'd looked enough at the dead women.

"Or I could wait around for Pearl with you," Nift said.

Quinn gave him a look. "I think not," he said.

He went outside with Renz and watched the corpulent and corrupt commissioner lower himself into the back of his personal limo. Watched as the long black vehicle drove to the end of the cordoned-off block. A uniform moved a blue wooden sawhorse to make room for the limo to glide through and continue on its way.

Quinn stood in the sunlight and leaned against the stone face of the Fairchild Hotel, waiting for Pearl.

He thought about the *D.O.A.* initials carved in the victims' foreheads. The same bloody initials had been the "signature" of the infamous D.O.A. killer who'd murdered four young women in Manhattan two years ago.

That killer was the one that had flown away from Quinn. Had shot him and left him for dead beside a lake in Maine. And then died himself when his plane went down.

That had been the assumption.

Now the killer—or a copycat—was back. That was why Renz was so sure Quinn would take the case. That Quinn would jump at it.

With Renz the case was political. With Quinn it was personal.

Quinn caught familiar movement among the knot of pedestrians crossing with the signal down at the corner. He pushed away from the sun warmed stone wall and his day immediately brightened.

Here came Pearl.

Pearl saw Quinn right away, standing in front of the Fairchild Hotel. When she strode closer to him, she could see the look on his face, and she knew why it was there and what it meant. It took a lot to make Quinn look like that. Like a Mt. Rushmore figure only pissed off.

She'd heard what was upstairs in the hotel. And she knew what it would mean to Quinn. "The last time you and this killer met, he almost made you one of his victims," she said.

"Almost," Quinn said.

"I don't want that to happen," Pearl said.

Quinn smiled. "Neither do I."

"Would it do any good to beg you not to get involved with this killer again?"

"In all honesty, no," he said. And then, "I'm sorry."

She knew that he was. Which made her want to curse him and cling to him and kiss him all at the same time. "You know you're obsessive," she said.

"Persevering."

"Obsessive."

"You've been talking to Renz."

"Of course I have. He doesn't mind if you get yourself killed."

"More than you might think."

Pearl felt herself approaching the point where frustration would become ire. *Men!* she thought. *Some men!*

"I'm going upstairs to the crime scene," she said.

For a second she thought he was going to advise her against that, for her own good. Forbid it, in fact. But he knew her better than that.

"Nift is still up there," he said.

"So are maggots."

"Pearl . . ."

"Screw Nift."

Pearl pushed through the tinted glass revolving door, somehow not missing a step, as if dancing in concert with its myriad moving images.

She noticed how cool the lobby was.

Like the morgue.

7

The day could hardly be bleaker. There was blood on the uniform of British Expeditionary Force Corporal Henry Tucker. He checked carefully with hurried hands and decided with immense relief that none of it was his own.

He looked up and down the beach and saw people running and diving for cover.

The German Stuka dive bombers hadn't gone away. He could see them as tiny dark specks in the sky out over the channel, wheeling in formation so they could take another strafing run at the beach.

His heart raced and he began to run. Everyone on the beach was running.

Tucker saw the Stukas, much closer now, awkward and dangerous looking even without the bombs slung beneath them. The planes went into a dive to come in low over the beach. Their "Jericho Horns" began to scream, scaring the hell out of people on the ground, which was their purpose. Tucker was sure as hell scared. He knew that any second machine gun bullets from the planes would start chewing up the beach, and anyone in the line of fire.

Scared as a human being could get, that's what Corporal Tucker was, and not too proud to admit it. From the east, German troops and tanks were closing in, and would soon push the BEF, including Corporal Henry Tucker, into the channel. Death by bullet or drowning waited there.

Gathered at and around the damaged docks along the beach were boats of various kinds and sizes, not military ships, but private craft. Little by little, they were moving the British, and some of the French, troops across the channel to England. It was a terrible gamble. Those who didn't die on the beach, or when the boats they were on were strafed, bombed, and sank, were the lucky ones who got out of France alive.

Tucker prayed to be in their number.

He saw sand kick up from the impact of bullets. Watched an abandoned troop truck shudder as heavy-caliber rounds tore into it. In the corner of his vision a woman was waving at him, frantically beckoning him.

She was standing next to a small, damaged beach cottage with two stucco and concrete walls still standing in a crooked L-shape that provided some cover.

The first trio of Stukas was past, flying almost wing to wing. A second grouping was on the way, flying even lower than the first.

Tucker heard the scream of their approach as he sprinted toward the wrecked cottage. The woman, tall, with long brown hair, motioned for him to follow her behind the protective walls jutting from sand soil. There was no decision to be made by Tucker. What was left of the house was the only cover around.

The Stukas' screams reached a crescendo, then Tucker was around the corner and comparatively safe in the crook of the house. Sand flew as machine gun bullets from the Stukas raked the beach where he'd been only seconds ago.

The woman was on her knees, yelling something Tucker couldn't hear. Not that it mattered. She was speaking French.

The planes were gone suddenly, reduced to a distant drone becoming fainter by the second.

Then there was silence. At least for a while.

Tucker, who'd dived for cover behind the chipped concrete walls, sat up and saw that he wasn't alone with the woman. A dirty-faced blond child in her early teens was there, looking more dazed than frightened. And a sturdy man with a huge stomach and with dark hair and a darker mustache. He was wearing baggy gray trousers, with some kind of blue sash for a belt.

"They'll come back," the woman said, in English but with a French accent. She sounded terrified.

Tucker nodded. "Don't I know it, love."

The woman stared at him.

"She doesn't understand English," the rotund man said, "just speaks it."

That seemed odd to Tucker. The teenage girl observed him silently, her eyes huge.

"I speak the English," the man said.

"Ah!" Tucker said.

The man grinned with very white teeth beneath his black mustache. "We need of you a favor."

"You've already done *me* a favor," Tucker said, looking at the woman, noticing for the first time that cleaned up, with her wild dark hair combed, she would be attractive. "Saved my bloody life, is all."

The man reached behind him and dragged a tan canvas backpack around so it lay between him and Tucker. He shoved it forward so it was only inches from Tucker, and grinned again, though he looked afraid and serious.

"This," he said, "is the favor. Take it to England with you. There is a note inside with a London address on it. And a name. There will be money for you at the other end." He reached forward and nudged the backpack even closer to Tucker. "Jeanette saved your life, no? Yes. So, a favor returned."

Tucker hoisted the backpack and found it surprisingly heavy.

"Is what I'm doing legal?" he asked.

Mustache laughed. The woman, Jeanette, smiled.

"We have to trust you," the man said.

Sirens in the sky began yowling. Jericho sirens. The Stukas were back, diving toward the beach. Tucker knew they would soon flatten out their dives and trigger their machine guns.

But these were different planes and hadn't yet dropped their bombs. One of them attacked the already shot-up troop carrier that probably looked intact from high above.

The screaming sirens grew deafening and there was a tremendous explosion. Shrapnel, something, slammed into the remains of the cottage's walls. Something flew over Tucker's head. He thought it might be the woman who'd invited him to share her shelter.

Henry Tucker placed his hands over his ears and squeezed his eyes shut.

* * *

When Tucker opened his eyes he was alone. He would think what just happened was a dream, a hallucination brought on by all he'd seen during the three weeks he'd spent in France. The madness on the beach whenever a boat of any kind might be boarded for an escape across the channel to England.

Tucker looked all around him. What had happened to the woman, child, and man? Had they been blown to bits? Had they simply run from the bombers and were now cowering somewhere else? They must have left him here, alone. Maybe they thought he was dead.

He started to sit up higher to peek over what was left of the cottage's only remaining wall. And his arm bumped the backpack.

His hearing, which had been temporarily blocked, returned. There was a commotion on the beach, voices yelling.

Tucker raised himself higher to look toward the beach.

Amazing! There were two small boats at the dock. That they'd made it across the rough, gray channel was unbelievable. The larger of the two looked like somebody's personal yacht. It was listing badly. The other was a small fishing boat. It had SONDRA painted in black letters on its bow.

There didn't seem to be any planes in the sky at the moment.

Tucker got shakily to his feet and started to run toward the nearer of the boats, the little fishing boat *Sondra*. Then he stopped and turned back, grabbed up the backpack, and continued his dash toward the small boat. It was in close enough that he wouldn't have to try to swim. As he ran, he tossed aside everything other than his rifle and the backpack.

Miraculously, he made it to the dock when the boat was only about half full of British and French troops. He splashed through water up to his waist, then was grabbed by people already aboard and hauled up onto the deck. On the way up, he dropped his rifle into the water. But he hung on to the backpack.

On deck, he scrambled away from the rail and leaned sitting against the wheelhouse. The boat smelled like fish, like the open sea. It smelled great to Tucker.

Voices kept shouting for everyone, for everything, to hurry, hurry. Move faster, faster, so they could get the boat away from the dock, where any German bombing or strafing attack would be concentrated.

It seemed impossible to Tucker that *Sondra* would ever make it back across the channel to England before everyone on board was killed.

But the boat did reverse its engines and did turn its bow toward open water. As it left the dock two men were clinging to the rails, trying to scramble aboard the already teeming deck. One of them made it, the other fell into the water. Tucker thought the exhausted man was too far from shore to make it back.

Poor bastard . . .

Tucker pressed the back of his head against the sun-warmed wheelhouse, closed his eyes, and thought of England.

There was no talking now, no sounds other than the steady thrum of the engines and the waves slapping against the hull.

Tucker finally dared to admit it to himself. It was possible, maybe even probable, that he would again see home.

Just past mid-channel, German planes appeared on the horizon.

8

The media went bonkers, and why shouldn't they? Six dead women, five of them still in their teens. it was a grisly sensation.

National news picked up on the story. Fox News did a special. The media argued with itself over who was covering the story too much or not enough. The muddled and misguided came forward and confessed to the horrible crime at the rate of a dozen a day. A man in Oregon sent Quinn a written confession complete with photographs. That one was taken seriously until the police lab determined that the grisly photos were shots of published NYPD photographs. Surprise, surprise. Someone in the department was leaking.

That was Renz's problem.

The rest was mostly Quinn's. He knew that if there wasn't another D.O.A. murder the papers and TV news eventually would stop running photos of him and bits of the video of his only press conference. But only if the killer ceased in his gruesome harvest.

And of course there were some who would never stop.

Quinn's answers to the media wolves' barrage of questions hadn't been satisfactory, and he knew they'd be after him for more. Minnie Miner, whose talk show *Minnie Miner ASAP* ran daily on local television, was the most persistent of the media types. And the call-in segment of her show was keeping New Yorkers not only interested, but afraid. Minnie was to New York what a mixer was to a milk shake.

Quinn did owe Minnie a favor. But then almost everyone newsworthy in New York owed Minnie a favor. She saw to that. Favors were the currency of her realm. Hers and Quinn's.

Renz held his own press conferences, often defending his decision to pit Quinn and the killer against each other a second time. It hadn't worked out so well the first time, which only added to this time's dramatic impact. Yet Renz's press conferences weren't as lively and well attended as Quinn's. Quinn, with his bony thug's countenance and perpetually shaggy haircut, simply made for better television than Renz, and that was that. Renz had to live with it.

Which Renz did for a while. Then he forbade Quinn to waste any more time on the media; he was to concentrate on the investigation. He, Renz, would be the link between the investigation and the media. If he needed more charisma he would grow some.

" 'Bout time," Pearl said, when she learned of Renz's instructions.

Quinn thought so, too. "You know how he is," he said.

"Yeah. Renz waited for you to take all the heat and

test the waters. Now he's ready to jump in and hog the publicity and whatever glory might come to pass."

"That's Renz," Quinn said, in his mind seeing Renz do a cannonball into a small pool.

Quinn and Pearl were sitting in the Q&A office on West 79th Street. It was arranged almost like a precinct squad room, with desks out in the open, some of them facing each other. There were fiberboard panels that could be moved around when privacy of a sort was required, but right now they were stacked back near the half bath.

Both Quinn and Pearl knew what the other was thinking. If Q&A didn't locate or apprehend the killer this second time around, it might result in losses of reputation and business. In no more Q&A.

Add to that the fact that this killer was prey that tended to morph into predator. A lot was on the line here.

"What's Renz?" Larry Fedderman asked, having caught the tail end of Quinn and Pearl's conversation. He was standing by Mr. Coffee, pouring some of the steaming liquid into his mug. His white shirt cuff, which usually came unbuttoned because of the way he gripped pen or pencil, was still fastened, indicating that the day was young and he hadn't yet made any notes.

"I think we all know the answer to that," Pearl said.

Quinn went over and poured a mug of coffee for himself. Added some cream and stirred longer than was necessary. He was waiting for Sal Vitali and Harold Mishkin to arrive, the detectives who had worked so long as a team in the NYPD, and now were employed by Q&A. It was almost nine o'clock. Time for the morning meet, at which they all shared knowledge. Quinn was determined that everyone knew the same version of what was going on. It prevented a lot of wasted time and effort.

As Quinn took a careful, painful sip of the near-boiling coffee, Sal and Harold arrived. Sal, short and stocky and full of decisive movement, had a full head of wavy black hair just beginning to gray, and a voice that sounded like gravel in a bucket. His partner Harold was slender and balding, with a slight forward lean and a bushy gray mustache. He looked more like an actor who should be playing Mr. Chips in a movie than a cop. Sometimes Harold was difficult to figure out, especially for Sal. Both men were carrying flat white boxes with grease stains that somehow hadn't gotten on their clothes.

"We got doughnuts," Sal rasped.

Over by the coffee machine, Fedderman said, "We got coffee."

"We got cholesterol," Harold said.

Sal glared at him. "Don't be crass, Harold."

Pearl said, "Do you have something with cream filling?"

"We did," Sal said. "Also with chocolate icing. Harold ate it."

"Why?" Fedderman asked, sounding angry and puzzled. "He's the one concerned about cholesterol."

"I'll compensate at lunch," Harold said.

"You should have slapped it out of his hand," Pearl said to Sal.

Quinn listened quietly. He knew that for whatever reason the ongoing angst among his detectives aided in their collective thought process. They were like oysters who needed agitation to produce pearls. They all knew that, but none of them would admit it except to him or herself. Better to maintain the productive balancing act.

Quinn walked over and leaned with his haunches on his desk. Crossed his arms. Pearl knew what his choice would be and brought him a chocolate-iced cake doughnut from one of the grease-stained boxes. Quinn took a sample bite. Terrific. He wasn't sure where Sal and Harold got their doughnuts, or if they paid for them, and figured it wiser not to ask.

He glanced at his watch. Six minutes after nine. Everyone was here except for Jerry Lido, the Q&A tech whiz, who might be too hungover to struggle out of bed.

Nobody was talking right now, so Quinn jumped in:

"All the girls' families have been notified," he said, "at least in time for them not to learn about their daughters' deaths on the news."

"Musta been all kinds of hell," Harold said. He had too much empathy for a cop, and occasionally threw up at crime scenes.

The street door opened, and warm air and exhaust fumes wafted into the office. A car horn honked three times, fast, outside, as if something had drawn the driver's attention. Or as if to announce something with a trumpet. Coincidental, surely.

Officer Nancy Weaver entered. The NYPD liaison Renz had mentioned.

9

Weaver had worked with Q&A before. She would fit right in, as long as she and Pearl didn't actually come to blows.

She was an attractive, compactly built brunette in her forties, with a keen intelligence and an overactive libido. She'd gotten the hell beaten out of her on her last go-round with Q&A, but she still had her slightly crooked grin and the same good-to-go glint in her brown eyes. Quinn heard she'd been working with the vice squad. Typecasting, he thought. Her sleeping with superior officers was legendary. She was known as the officer who had put the "cop" in "copulate." It was all exaggerated and rather unfair, Quinn thought. On the other hand, how could he know?

She was wearing what looked like six-inch heels, a short, tight red skirt, and a form-fitting bowling team shirt lettered DO IT IN THE ALLEY. Dressed for work with the vice squad, Quinn hoped.

Weaver grinned and nodded a hello to all of them. She was carrying a cardboard brown accordion file tied with a brown cord that looked like a shoelace.

"Can you actually bowl in that outfit?" Pearl asked.

"When I do," Weaver said, "it doesn't matter where the ball goes."

Quinn cut in before Pearl could reply. He told Weaver it was good to see her. He did admire her tenacity. As did Pearl, although Pearl was silent while the rest of Q&A welcomed Weaver. Quinn knew that the two women had some time ago come to an understanding with each other, something reminiscent of a Middle East treaty.

"I've got the first on-the-scene officers' written statements here," Weaver said, "along with their brief initial interviews of hotel guests in adjoining rooms, and potential witnesses."

Quinn waved an arm, indicating that Weaver had the floor.

"Enlighten us," he said.

Weaver moved to a spot near the center of the room. She said, "Grace Geyer, Christy Mathewson, Sheryl Stewart, Dawn Kramer, Lucy Mitchell. And their teacher and guide, Andria Bell." Weaver looked up from the paper bearing the names. "The victims," she said. "They seem to have little in common other than that they attend—attended—some academy in Cleveland and were chosen for the trip because of their interest and/or talent in art. Mitchell and Stewart were best friends and shared secrets. Grace Geyer was something of a daredevil and troublemaker. She was on probation—the school's, not the law's—and was on the tour primarily because she was the one with the most artistic talent."

"Figures," Harold said.

No one asked him why.

"The victims-to-be all checked in without anything unusual happening. Andria Bell asked the concierge down in the lobby about directions to the Museum of Modern Art. That was about it. The girls didn't raise any hell or cause any trouble or play music too loud. The only other hotel guest who even recalls seeing them was a woman on the same floor, a writer named Lettie Soho—small *h*—down the hall about four rooms. She happened to take an elevator up from the lobby with them and saw them all go into their room. Everything seemed normal, she said. There were some giggles in the elevator. One of the girls poked another in the ribs. Their teacher tour guide gave them a look. Then they went out, and while Soho was trying to get her card key to work, she watched them all file into their suite. This was on the day of the crime, approximately an hour before they were killed. When Soho went down to the hotel restaurant for dinner, she saw the older woman, Andria Bell, let a man into the room."

The Q&A detectives were silent and leaned slightly toward Weaver.

"Probably he was the killer," Weaver said. "Soho didn't get a good look at him before he went into the suite and the door closed."

"But the uniforms got what Soho had to give. Some kind of description."

"Yeah," Weaver said. "Average size and build, but maybe taller or shorter. Hair brown or black, cut short or medium. Eyes maybe dark, or possibly blue. Wearing gray pants or maybe jeans. White or blue shirt. Possibly a tie, yellow or brown. Age, somewhere between late twenties, mid- or late forties."

"Okay, we get it," Quinn said.

"No distinguishing marks," Weaver said.

"Don't push it," Pearl said.

Weaver smiled. "Might have moved with a slight limp."

Quinn's body gave a start. *The plane crash in Maine!* "Which leg?"

"Nothing on that," Weaver said.

"Did the uniforms find out if Lettie Soho is the woman witness's real name?" Harold asked. "Sounds like a nom de plume."

"Right you are," Weaver said. "Her real name's Marjory Schacht. She uses a pen name and writes chick lit."

"What the hell is that?" Quinn asked.

"Hard to explain," Pearl said. "Think of it as women's light fiction."

"No sign of drugs or alcohol in any of the victims," Weaver continued.

"Now, that's odd," Fedderman said.

"Could be they just didn't have time to get a buzz on before the bastard killed them," Sal said.

"Small amounts of marijuana in the purses of Kramer and Geyer," Weaver said.

"Geyer again," Quinn said. "I wonder if the killer used her to get into the suite. Did Margory Schacht see who let the man in?"

"She isn't sure, but she thinks it was Andria Bell."

"Still," Quinn said. "He might have learned about their presence from Geyer. Seen Geyer as the wild one in the flock and struck up a conversation with her."

"At the museum, maybe," Pearl said. "She was an

artist, and he might have pretended to be one. He could have gotten her chatting about art."

Weaver folded her papers and slid them back in the brown accordion file. Finished with her presentation, she moved from the center of the room and stood near Pearl's desk.

"We need to get back to the hotel," Quinn said. "Talk to whoever was staying near the victims. Talk again with Marjory Schacht—Lettie Soho."

Harold said, "Christy Mathewson."

The name of one of the victims.

Everyone looked at Harold, waiting for more. Harold was used to being looked at that way.

"He was a great ball player. Old time pitcher. Way back when they used little gloves."

"Is the victim's name spelled with an *ie* or a *y*?" Pearl asked Weaver.

Weaver reopened her brown file folder, shuffled some papers, and looked. "Uniform spelled it with a *y*." The male spelling.

"Like the baseball player," Harold said. It got him another look.

"Do you know how the ballplayer spelled his name?" Sal asked.

"No," Harold admitted.

"So you think the victim was a male impersonating a female?" Fedderman asked.

"Naw," Sal said. "The uniformed cop probably just spelled it his way."

"If Christy was actually a male," Quinn said, "Nift would have noticed."

"That's for damned sure," Pearl said.

Quinn's cell phone buzzed and vibrated. He worked it out of his pocket and saw that the caller was Renz. He walked over near the coffee brewer for something like privacy before answering.

Renz filled him in on what the NYPD knew. Pretty much what Weaver had covered minutes ago. Then: "Nift said all the victims were tortured with the knife, some worse than others. But especially Andria Bell. Also, she died last."

"He wanted something from her," Quinn said.

"Looks that way. Like he was trying to get some information from her. I wonder if he did."

"My guess," Renz said, "after looking at the body, is that she told him whatever he wanted to hear. Then he made sure it was the truth."

"The girls . . ."

"The asshole saw them as a bonus. Might not have even known they were all staying in the same suite, until he was inside and they'd all seen him."

"Yeah," Quinn said, "we have to allow for that possibility."

"We do have a security guy at MoMA says he saw Grace Geyer talking with some man, away from the rest of the group. In the fourth floor painting and sculpture section."

"But he doesn't remember what the man looked like," Quinn said.

"Right. We tried to find the guy on the security cameras, but had no luck there. And the guard says he couldn't pick the guy out of a lineup."

"If we get a suspect," Quinn said, "he sure as hell is going to try."

"I'm going on Minnie Miner's show tomorrow," Renz said. "I won't mention the security guard. Guy's liable to leave town like a rocket."

"If he's smart," Quinn said. He didn't think the museum guard would be much of a help as a witness, but the killer wouldn't know that for sure. "If we need him, we can reach out and get him. Whatever you tell or don't tell Minnie Miner, be careful with it."

"She'd really rather talk to you," Renz said, sounding a little miffed.

"That would just impede the investigation," Quinn said, feeding Renz what he wanted to hear. Not that it wasn't the truth. "Maybe someday," he said, "we can use Minnie."

"Weaver see you yet?" Renz asked.

"Yeah. She filled us in on what the uniforms first on the scene had."

"Tell her what you know," Renz said, "so I can know it."

"You bet," Quinn said, and broke the connection.

The detectives were all staring at him, wondering if they had anything new to work with.

"Was that Renz?" Fedderman asked, unnecessarily.

"Yeah. Grace Geyer was seen by a museum security guard talking with a guy in MoMA. They were standing away from the rest of the group."

"Maybe trying to pick her up," Fedderman said.

"Or just talking about brush strokes," Sal said.

"You ask Renz about Christy Mathewson?" Harold asked.

"While you and Sal are on the way to get verification statements from potential witnesses at the hotel," Quinn said, "why don't you call Nift and see about this

Mathewson thing." *Keep us from possibly looking stupid, now that you've brought it up.*

"Good idea," Harold said. "Touch all the bases."

Quinn gave him a look that might have meant he was perplexed or angry.

Sal said, "Let's get out of here, Harold."

They left, Sal thinking you really never knew for sure about Harold.

10

Tucker could see the bombs slung beneath the planes' fuselages as the pilots brought the Stukas in single file, bow to stern above the *Sondra*. He hoped the German pilots would consider the small fishing boat too minor a target to waste bombs on.

He got his wish, but that didn't rule out the machine guns mounted beneath the planes' wings.

The little boat rocked this way and that as the captain attempted to zigzag. That helped some, but not much. A man in a French army uniform stood up near the bow and aimed his rifle at the incoming lead Stuka. He was cut nearly in half by machine gun bullets. Two of the crewmen hacked lines and launched a small dinghy the boat might tow, but no sooner had the dinghy hit the water than the crewmen both spun and dropped overboard beneath the hail of bullets. The boat's grizzled old captain stepped halfway out of the pilothouse to yell some instruction, then fell in a red mist of blood.

Immediately after the first pass, the planes wheeled

to the left, maintaining their single file line, as they maneuvered for another run at the boat. This time, as the first plane approached and the winking muzzle blasts of its guns became visible, men began diving and jumping overboard.

BEF Corporal Henry Tucker, huddled near the stern, decided it was time to abandon ship.

He scooped up his backpack, leaving all other equipment and belongings behind, and jumped off the stern into the roiled water in the boat's wake.

Tucker had forgotten how heavy the backpack was. It began to pull him down into the swirling water. He tried to release it, but one of its straps was tangled around his wrist.

He was actually underwater when a hand gripped the backpack's strap and he felt himself lifted out of the water. He thumped painfully into the bottom of the wooden dinghy and was lying on top of the backpack.

"Easy, mate," a voice growled.

Tucker raised his head to look around. There were two other men in the boat. Both were badly wounded. One in the chest. The other—the one who had rescued Tucker—was a young blond giant with a nasty head wound.

Tucker realized that he himself was bleeding. His blood was turning the water sloshing around the bottom of the dinghy a deepening red. He raised a hand to touch his head, probing for damage.

He was frightened by what he felt.

He heard the persistent drone of aircraft and knew the Stukas were returning. Would they sink the fishing boat? Would they consider the dinghy too small and unimportant to strafe? A waste of ammunition?

Of course it is! Of course! It's nothing but a bleed-ing rowboat!

The drone of the engines grew to a roar. Changed tone as the planes dropped lower and flattened out their trajectory.

Tucker carefully raised his head again and saw an aircraft approaching alarmingly low over the water. Coming straight at the dinghy.

His breath swelled cold in his chest and he prepared to die.

But there was something different about this aircraft. It didn't have the awkward gull-like wings of the Stukas and, unlike the Stukas, its landing gear was retracted.

The plane waggled its wings and Tucker now clearly saw its markings—RAF markings. As it flashed over-head, the craft assumed the familiar silhouette of a British Hurricane fighter plane. Off in the distance, dark specks circled and climbed and dived in the sky. The Hurricanes had engaged the Stukas. The German planes were dive bombers and not fighter planes. Tucker felt some satisfaction in thinking they wouldn't escape the Hurricanes. Not all of them.

One of the other two men in the dinghy began to shout, then stood to cheer. It was the blond giant. Tucker could see the inside of his skull behind his left ear. The other man remained unmoving and silent.

Within a few minutes the sky was clear of all but one Hurricane, which circled protectively over the dinghy.

The water around the tiny dinghy was unbroken. There wasn't even debris floating to show where the *Sondra* had sunk.

The silent man in the dinghy's bow looked dead to Tucker. The blond giant who'd cheered and shouted was still excited. He stared at Tucker with unnaturally bright blue eyes and said, "We gotta row, mate. We row and we'll make it."

"Don't be crazy," Tucker said. "We'll never make it all the way to England. If we just drift, one of the other boats might pick us up. That Hurricane's marking our location."

"It'll run low on fuel and have to leave," the man said.

Tucker hadn't thought of that. It was a possibility.

As if its pilot had overheard their conversation, the Hurricane waggled its wings again, then flew away toward the direction of England.

"Pick up a bloody oar and row!" the blond man in the boat said.

Tucker figured he should do that. The man was twice his size and might throw him overboard if he didn't comply.

He worked his way up to a sitting position, and was behind the big man and couldn't take his eyes off the back of his head. It was a wonder he could even sit up, considering the terrible wound that he seemed not to know about.

Tucker sat facing France and rowed in the direction the Hurricane had gone, toward England, praying his head wound wasn't as bad as the one he was looking at.

Far away, to the north, it was clouding up as if a storm was brewing.

11

Quinn dreamed again of Maine, of a dark and ominous shadow shape that blocked what slanted sunlight lanced between the planks of the rickety dock. Beneath the dock as he was, he could smell the dank scent of the rotted wood at the waterline, the decaying life-and-death cycle of the lake. The almost casual slow footfalls of the dangerous thing above him, plotting his death. Quinn shuddered in his sleep. Death was so near. The long gun the killer carried might as well have been a scythe.

The lake began moving with a private tide. The dock began to creak. Water lapped at wood. One by one the thick cross planks were lifted and flung away, like boxes being opened and their lids tossed aside.

And when the box containing Quinn was opened, the killer would smile down at him. And death would—

Quinn was awake. All the way back in the real world. It seemed a magician's trick. He was no longer about to scream in pain despite his efforts to be silent. Hiding, fearing.

Pearl lay sleeping beside him, covered with a light sheet. The curvature of her form beneath the thin material, the rhythm of her breathing, reassured Quinn that he wasn't at the lake in Maine. He was on the West Side of New York, and no one was stalking him with a rifle.

He glanced at the glowing numerals of the alarm clock beside the bed. Only 3:00 A.M.

Faint recognizable sounds made their way into the bedroom from beyond the tall windows. Some of them were barely loud enough to hear. The city that never slept, resting. Human sounds. Death seemed far away.

Reassured, Quinn rolled over and felt himself drifting again toward sleep.

He dreamed again of Maine.

When Quinn was alone in the office, Helen Iman, the NYPD profiler, came in.

"One fun day after another," she said, observing that he must not have gotten much sleep last night. "Except for the occasional disembowelment."

Quinn wasn't surprised to see her. All six foot plus of her. Helen, with her short cropped red hair, lanky build, and minimal makeup, put Quinn in mind of a women's basketball coach. She seemed always to have a slight sheen of perspiration on her freckled flesh, as if she'd just come from a strenuous workout. In fact, she had more intellectual than athletic ability or desire. And she had that essential that so many profilers lacked—a track record. Helen had provided the psychological insight that had helped Quinn mold his own reputation. She was the only profiler he believed in.

Renz had sent her around, not as a spy, but because he, like Quinn, appreciated her abilities and knew her history.

"I hear you're working on the big one," Helen said. She stood near Pearl's desk and crossed her arms. "Six victims."

"So far."

Each knew the other was sure the killer would try to take more victims. Otherwise, Helen wouldn't be here.

"I don't think he's a mass murderer on purpose," Helen said. "Mass murder wasn't his plan when he entered the hotel."

Quinn leaned back in his desk chair and smiled at her. "Go ahead," he said, "See if we read it the same way."

Helen moved farther into the office and perched with her haunches on the front edge of Pearl's desk. She was wearing blue-and-white running shoes with her jeans. The jeans looked a little baggy on her, and were an inch or so too short for her long legs, so her rolled white exercise socks showed.

"My guess is that he didn't realize the schoolgirls and Andria Bell were all staying in one interconnected suite," she said. "Who wouldn't want to be alone after putting up with a gaggle of young girls most of the day? When he knocked on the door and Andria opened it, he assumed they were alone together. His mental scenario pictured two adults."

Quinn knew what she meant by "mental scenario." Serial killers had two plans to deal with two possibilities: victim cooperating or victim resisting. Those plans weren't the same when more than one victim was involved.

"That's how I see it," Quinn said. He absently reached for the desk drawer where he kept his Cuban cigars, then drew back his hand. Helen would rat him out to Pearl. "Of course we might be wrong. He might have planned on killing six women even before entering the hotel."

"I doubt it."

"Me, too."

"He probably had a gun," Helen continued. "It would be hard to keep all those girls in line with only a knife—not impossible, though. However he was armed, it's easy to talk people into thinking you won't harm them if only they'll do as you say. They've got nothing against you personally that you know of, so it's easiest for them to cooperate. With a knife he could have been in charge. With a gun he would've been king."

"You think he tied down and gagged Andria first?" Quinn asked.

Helen rubbed her long chin. "Maybe. I'm guessing he had a gun and was in complete control, so he could've done anything he wanted. He most likely held all the girls at gunpoint and had one of them—or maybe Andria—tie up and gag the others. It wouldn't have taken long, using their shoelaces and panties." She paused, looking up at the wall clock as if she were being timed. "Using the panties would have humiliated the girls as well as quiet them. Seems like it'd be a male thing to do."

"Agreed," Quinn said.

"So I figure our killer used a captive helper to secure everyone, then he used his knife on the girls that were bound and gagged lying side by side on the bed."

"That must have been hell for all of them," Quinn

said. "Especially for the last few, who had to watch their friends suffer and die."

"It wouldn't have been quick for any of them," Helen said. "The killer had plenty of time, and he used it to enjoy himself."

"What about Andria Bell?" Quinn asked. "Why was she tortured the most and killed last?"

"Because she's the reason the killer was there."

"And that reason is?"

Helen grinned and shrugged her bony shoulders. "Wouldn't we like to know?"

She uncrossed her long arms and straightened up from where she'd been supporting herself on the desk, looking as if she was getting ready to try a free throw. "I dropped by the morgue," she said. "Talked to Nift and saw the photos. Did it look to you as if the killer got whatever he wanted from Andria?"

"You mean did she tell him all her secrets?"

"Yes. Her big secret, anyway."

"And then he stopped torturing her?"

"Sure. He'd have accomplished his purpose. And he wouldn't have wanted to hang around forever in the middle of all that damning evidence."

Quinn thought about Helen's question. "There's no way to be sure," he said. "My guess is Andria died during torture, probably from shock rather than loss of blood. But that doesn't mean the killer didn't get what he wanted. He might have decided to make sure. Or simply to amuse himself by drawing out his victim's death."

"But what's your gut feeling?"

They both knew this was a serious question to put to a cop. Especially at this stage of an investigation.

Quinn said, "I think she told him what he wanted to hear."

Helen leaned back against the desk edge and crossed her arms again. Quinn found himself wondering if she would have a temporary crosswise crease in her ass from the desk.

"You think D.O.A. is still alive and did these killings?" she asked.

"The experts said nobody could have survived that plane crash," Quinn reminded her.

"No human remains were found at the scene of the crash," she said.

"Tracks indicated predators probably dragged the body away," Quinn said. But he recalled Weaver's witness, Lettie Soho, saying the man she saw at the Fairchild Hotel had a slight limp. Slight. Maybe.

"What about a parachute?" Helen asked.

"The plane was too low, and a chute would have been seen. The medical examiner and the court decided D.O.A. died in that plane."

"Yeah."

"He *was* a careful killer," Quinn said. "He thought ahead. Made contingency plans." Quinn watched Helen chew the inside of her cheek. "Maybe we've got a copycat," he added. "Is that what you wanted to hear?"

"Hmm."

"What does 'Hmm' mean, Helen?"

"We'd all like it to be a copycat," she said. "Easier all around."

"Except for the victims," Quinn said. "If our killer's a copycat, he really went to school on the earlier murders. The real and original D.O.A. couldn't have been more vicious and sadistic."

They looked at each other, waiting for what had to be said.

"Of course you're right," Quinn said. "We do *want* it to be a copycat. And it well might be. The more sensational the killer, the more likely some twisted animal will emulate him. That's how these monsters think."

"We forget sometimes they're individuals," Helen said. "They don't all think alike all the time about everything."

"The killings stopped after the plane went down," Quinn pointed out.

"Or paused," Helen said.

"Or paused," he agreed.

As she knew he would.

12

Loose talk at the hotel bar, overheard by Harold, yielded another witness who might have glimpsed the killer entering Andria Bell's suite. He was still registered at the Fairchild Hotel. He'd complained about something he'd seen or heard and the management had moved him up a floor at his request.

Sal had phoned from down in the lobby, so the witness, a middle-aged man with thin brown hair and a thick waist, was standing with the door open so Sal and Harold would notice him waiting a short way down the hall from the elevator.

He was about five foot ten and all soft angles, with his scant hair neatly combed straight across. Pink tie, white shirt, and gray blazer. He didn't fit his name, which was Duke Craig, if Harold had it right.

The man introduced himself as Craig Duke.

"Nice room," Harold commented, though it was nothing special. "Spacious and clean." Starting the interview on a positive note.

"I guess it's okay," Duke said. "I've stayed here before." There was a small gray sofa and a matching armchair in the room. And a desk with a wooden chair. Duke motioned for Harold and Sal to sit in the sofa and armchair. Sal took the uncomfortable desk chair before Duke could get to it. Duke eschewed the armchair and sat on the edge of the bed.

People. Sal thought he'd never get tired of watching them. The older he got, the more predictable they became. Yet now and then there was *somebody . . . something . . .*

Harold got his worn black leather notepad from a pocket, along with a stubby yellow pencil. He'd take copious notes during the interview, but Sal knew Harold often was merely sketching little fish. None of them the same size, but all swimming in the same direction. He had asked Harold about that once, and Harold had given some complex explanation involving salmon that Sal found incomprehensible.

"You said you've stayed here at the Fairchild before," Sal said to Duke in his voice that was more like a growl. Then waited.

"The annual convention's here," Duke said. "Glow View Paint. You've heard of us?"

"No," Sal said.

"I sure have," Harold said. "You guys are nationwide."

"That's right!" Duke seemed buoyed about Harold knowing that. "What we cover stays covered. I'm a sales rep. Reps and other Glow View employees are here from all over the—"

"Where are *you* from?" Sal interrupted.

"St. Louis."

"East?"

"West. Missouri."

"About last night," Sal said. "How did you happen to be looking out your door and see—most likely the killer—enter Andria Bell's suite?"

"I've been reading all about that in the papers," Duke said. He seemed suddenly ill at ease. A paint salesman from Missouri caught up in murder in New York.

"That doesn't exactly answer the question," Harold said.

"Well, I heard this knocking and thought it was on my door." Duke looked off to the right, the way people are supposed to be doing when they're lying. Harold didn't think that common belief was true. *Or is it to their left?*

"And . . . ?" Sal asked, looking straight ahead.

"I mean, I thought . . ."

"You can speak freely, Mr. Craig," Harold said.

"Why shouldn't I be able to?" Duke asked. "And it's not Mr. Craig, it's Mr. Duke."

"Mr. Duke," Sal said, "you're not in any way a suspect in this." But even as he spoke, Sal wondered. Duke was a male in the same age group as D.O.A., and like a lot of other men, he fit D.O.A.'s general description.

Sal told himself he was way off base, but he should keep an open mind. The way you had to do with Harold around.

"Of course I'm not a suspect," Duke said. "I didn't mean that."

Harold flashed him a reassuring smile. He pretended to check his notes. Fishes. "What kind of knocking was it? I mean, hard and loud? Knocks close together? In a pattern? Like somebody had something important to relate to you?"

"Nothing like that. Just knocking. That's why I went to the door and looked out in the hall. But there was nobody at my door."

"You sound as if you were disappointed, Mr. Craig."

"It's Duke. I was, slightly. I was hoping it was one of the Glow View color people. If it wasn't, I was gonna go down to the bar and look for somebody to talk with. Nothing else to do, I guess. I was waiting for the drying competition. You know, how long it takes different brands to set up in various temperatures and humidity."

"Sound's interesting," Sal said, stifling a yawn.

"Like watching paint dry," Harold said, perfectly deadpan.

"So you saw a man and a woman at the door across the hall?" Sal asked, hoping to keep Duke on track.

"Yeah. I got a good look at the woman when she let him in." He swallowed. "I found out later she was one of the victims. Andria Bell. She was the guide or chaperone for those young girls." Duke looked slightly nauseated and absently touched his stomach. Swallowed hard enough that Sal and Harold heard phlegm crack. "Jeez, what a shame!"

"What did the man look like?" Sal asked.

"Well, he was kinda facing away from me. He looked pretty average. I think he had brown hair, but I'm not sure. He had on dark slacks and a gray or pale blue sport coat, I think."

"How tall would you say?" Sal asked.

"Think in terms of the door," Harold said. He drew a fish.

Duke looked at him.

"The door's height is standard," Harold said, "so you can use it as a guide to height."

"Yeah, I guess you can," Duke said. "I'd say he was right around six feet. Maybe a little taller, maybe a little shorter."

Good work, Harold. "What about eye color?" Sal asked.

"Oh, I never got that good a look at him. She—Andria Bell—stepped back right away and let him in."

"Did you see a weapon?"

"No, but he could have had one shielded from view by his body, the way he was standing."

"Close your eyes and look at him going into the room again," Harold said, closing his own eyes. "See it in your imagination. Smell it. Hotels have a certain smell. Breathe it in. *Be* there. Look around again. You might see something you didn't notice before."

Sal wished Harold would shut up. His role in the interview was supposed to be simple. He was supposed to keep the conversation flowing from Duke, and to pretend he was taking notes. Maybe even take some notes.

"Anything?" Harold asked.

"No," Duke said. "Sorry."

"Keep your eyes shut. Go through it again. There's the knocking." Harold rapped a mahogany end table with his knuckles. "Now you walk to the door."

Sal was about to put an end to this nonsense, when Duke said. "Scar."

"Star?" Sal asked.

Harold looked at Sal and silently mouthed *Scar.*

Sal looked bewildered.

"Odd how I'd forgotten that," Duke said. "The look I got of the man, sort of a quarter view from behind, gave me a glance at the side of his face when he stepped across the threshold. Just before the door shut. There was a kind of curved scar on his right cheek."

"Like a knife scar?" Sal asked.

"No, no. Slightly reddened, slick skin. More like a burn."

"Like he was in an accident and got burned?" Harold asked.

Duke shrugged. "I'd assume it was an accident."

"Like a car accident. Or a plane," Harold said.

Duke nodded. "Could be, I guess."

"Did he walk with a limp?" Harold asked.

"Limp?"

"A slight one."

Duke thought. "I couldn't say he didn't."

"After you saw this, when you knew the knocking wasn't on your door, what did you do?" Sal was hoping Duke might also recall that he'd heard screaming, or some other indication of the hell that was going on across the hall.

But the horror was suffered in silence or near silence.

"What did you do?" Sal repeated.

Harold chimed in, "These are routine questions."

"I did like I was thinking about," Duke said. "Went down to the bar. Had a scotch. Ate enough pretzels and nuts that I didn't feel like having supper. I didn't see anybody from Color View, so I talked for a while with Bonnie the Barista. They call her that because she's responsible for coffee as well as booze."

"It's crept into the language," Harold said.

"Then I went to one of the ballrooms where the paint setup contest was going on. Watched that for a while. Met up with some Color View guys from Milwaukee and went back to the bar with them. We drank and talked till about eleven o'clock, I guess. Then I came up to my room and went to bed. I woke up this morning, went down to breakfast, and heard about Andria. Made me sick. I came back upstairs and heard somebody knocking on a door. This time it *was* my door. It was you guys. Not you two personally, but the police."

Sal thought this was a logical place to stop the interview. He thanked Craig Duke, and he and Harold moved toward the door.

Harold turned. "Who won the paint drying contest?"

Duke seemed surprised that he'd be asked, but he answered without hesitation. "Guys from Minnesota. They always win. It's cold there and the paint's blended to set up fast."

"Doesn't seem fair," Harold said.

"Like life," Duke said. He made a head motion toward the door and the suite across the hall. Meaning, that was where it always ended. Sooner or later, in one way or another, death had its way with us, and fair didn't enter into it.

There was a thought to cheer you down.

On the descending elevator, Harold said, "Time not to have a drink."

Knowing Harold code, Sal understood what he meant. It was time to drop in at the hotel bar and talk to Bonnie the Barista.

13

Early as it was, there were only a few people in the Fairchild Hotel's bar. Four solitary male drinkers were spaced about the place as if trying to be as far apart from each other as possible. Two women sat at a small round table. One very attractive woman was perched on a stool at the end of the bar.

Sal and Harold took stools at the opposite end of the bar from where the woman sat nursing some kind of drink that looked like a bloody Mary. Yep, there was a stalk of celery on the napkin where the glass rested. The woman picked up the celery, dipped it in the drink, then took a bite of it that could be heard around the bar. She pursed her lips and chewed. Harold had never thought of eating celery as sexy, but now he did.

A tall woman about fifty, in a white shirt and red vest, came over, and Sal ordered seltzer water, Harold an espresso. Sal flashed his shield, given to Q&A detectives while they worked for hire for the NYPD. The barista looked at it briefly and then went and got their drinks. She set them on cork coasters in front of the two detectives. A small plastic nameplate pinned to her vest identified her as Bonnie. She had one of those round, perpetually almost-smiling faces that made her hard to read. An all-purpose expression.

"You here about what happened upstairs?" she asked.

"Yeah, I heard about it," Harold said.

Bonnie looked confused. "No, I mean—"

"He knows what you mean," Sal said. "He's being a smart ass."

Bonnie smiled all the way. It was like the sun coming out. "Like half the people who come in here," she said.

Sal didn't doubt it. He asked, "You know something, Bonnie?"

"No, I'm listening."

"No," Sal said. "I mean do you know something *we* should know?"

"I know none of those murdered women was in here while I was on duty. The girls were too young, and their chaperone stayed dry to set a good example. They were an up-an'-up bunch. It's tragic, what happened."

"Nobody even came in the bar for a latte?" Harold asked.

"Nope. You gotta remember, they were only here one night." She shrugged, smiling at about half amperage. "Sorry to be a dry fountain of knowledge."

"A fella who kind of interests us did come in, though. Said he did, anyway. One of the paint convention people."

"Plenty of them were in here," Bonnie said.

"How about at guy named Craig Duke. Middle-aged, thinning brown hair, mighta had on a gray blazer, white shirt, pink tie."

Something changed in Bonnie's eyes, and she smiled. "Yeah, I know Mr. Duke. From the Midwest. Some kinda paint salesman. With the Glow View people."

"Was he down here yesterday evening?"

"Sure. About six o'clock on."

"On what?" Harold asked, not surprised that Bonnie's account of last night was going to differ from Craig Duke's. "Does that mean he was here till closing time?"

"No, no. I mean he just stayed here for a while." Bonnie looked uneasy and her gaze shifted to the woman at the other end of the bar. What was going on here? She knew she'd better play straight with these two. And it wasn't like she had something to hide. "He left around six thirty," Bonnie said. "But he came back later."

"Alone?"

Sighing, Bonnie said, "You probably oughta talk to Wanda Woman." She motioned with her eyes, ever so slightly, toward the woman down the bar.

Sal added up the conversation and looked at Bonnie. "You're kidding me? Wonder Woman?"

"*Wanda*. And it's a nickname. She works this lounge on her own."

"Works it, huh." Sal was thinking. *There's a lot of vulnerability here. How best to use it to get to the truth?* "She a barista, too?"

"Not hardly," Bonnie said. "She's not exactly a hotel employee."

"Ah," Harold said.

"Nobody's pimping for her," Bonnie assured them. "She says her real name is Wanda Smith."

Sal sipped some seltzer. Waited. Letting Bonnie

think about that vulnerability. About how she'd better level with the law. This was a homicide investigation. And the homicide was one of the worst this city had ever seen.

Harold was wearing his disinterested look. *Yeah. Sure.*

"You want the real story?" Bonnie asked.

"Yep"

"It won't go no further?"

"We'll do what we can," Sal said. "But remember this is a murder investigation."

"And a newsy one." Bonnie pretended to be thinking it over, weighing options, knowing she'd better not be so vague about the times.

Finally she said, "Wanda came in with Mr. Duke about six o'clock, they had some drinks. He left here a little after six thirty. Then, a few minutes later, Wanda left."

"Left just here, the bar, or the hotel?" Sal asked.

Bonnie shook his head. "I dunno. Couldn't see from here even if I'd tried. Which I didn't particularly wanna do, as I had no reason."

"That you knew of," Harold said.

Bonnie nodded. "That's right."

"Mr. Duke come back here alone?" Sal asked.

"Yeah. Well, not exactly alone. I mean, not with Wanda. He went to the desk, I heard to get a different room. He was spooked by something."

Right after he saw the killer enter Andria Bell's suite, Sal thought. So that part of his story holds.

"About seven forty-five Duke comes back, only not alone. He was with some other paint convention peo-ple. They came and went, hung around a while and got a good buzz on. Duke sort of stayed on the fringes. That's all I know," Bonnie said, "which ain't much."

Harold chewed his mustache. Sipped his espresso. Sal sat staring into his seltzer water.

Sal's cell phone buzzed and danced against his thigh. He pulled it from his pocket, turning away, and glanced at the phone and saw that the caller was Quinn.

He walked half a dozen paces away so he wouldn't be overheard and filled Quinn in on what he and Harold had discovered at the Fairchild.

After a few seconds, Sal broke the connection and turned back to Bonnie and Harold.

"Quinn?" Harold asked.

"Quinn," Sal confirmed. "He's a few blocks from here. Said to go ahead and start talking with Wanda Woman before she's joined by somebody or leaves. He'll be here in five or ten minutes."

"Motion for Wanda Woman to come over here," Sal said to Bonnie.

Then Sal said, under his breath, "Maybe we can find out why somebody's story is a bunch of bullshit."

But he had a pretty good idea why. Craig Duke didn't want to be caught with his pants down with a prostitute, who didn't want to be caught plying her trade, and was friends with or working for Bonnie the Barista, who didn't want their relationship to become known. These people were worried about their reputations and jobs, maybe marriages.

Like this didn't involve six dead women.

People and their secrets.

He watched Harold draw a fish.

14

Wanda looked uneasy when Sal and Harold identified themselves. But then lots of people looked that way when they met cops. For all she knew, they were from the vice squad, and everybody had a vice.

Sal took the bar stool next to her, and Harold stood on her other side, not trying to be openly intimidating with their closeness. Their presence should be sufficient.

Wanda Woman didn't seem intimidated. More like amused. She looked at Sal, then glanced at Harold as if he were a worm. She had strong features framed by dark brown hair, and would have been tall even without her six-inch heels. Narrow-waisted, with a large bust and plenty of hip, there was a kind of force about her. Her unadorned black dress would have looked plain on most women. But then most women didn't have her legs and cleavage.

"I'm minding my own business," she said in a throaty voice that went with the dress and all the rest. Harold thought she was probably great at telephone sex.

"We're not interested in your business," Sal said. "We're not with vice."

"Oh, darn," she said flatly. "I thought you were going to ask me to move on, just so you could see me move."

Harold swallowed. Said, "Mrs. Robinson, are you—"

"Can it, Harold," Sal interrupted.

"Is that straight vodka you're drinking?" the one named Harold asked.

"Water."

"Good for you."

Wanda Woman looked slightly confused. These guys didn't seem interested in her as a woman; they seemed to want to kill time.

"We only want to talk," Sal said.

"Until you change your minds," Wanda said with a wink. "What do you wanna talk about?"

Sal said, "Craig Duke, the paint salesman."

Wanda smiled. "Is that what he does. He told me he worked for the government."

"We all do, in a sense," Harold said.

"This is about what happened to those poor girls," Wanda said.

"And their chaperone," Sal reminded her.

"Yeah. Some chaperone."

"When it happened, you were with Craig Duke, in his room right across the hall."

"Might've been. Truth is, I don't know what happened when. We were about to start—secret agent Duke and me—when he said wait a minute, he thought he heard somebody knocking on the door."

"Start what?" Harold asked.

"A game called find the key. It involves handcuffs and a—"

Quinn had come in. "I thought it was you two when I glanced in here," he said.

"It's us," Harold confirmed. "We were just talking to Wanda—what's your real name, hon?"

"Wanda Tennenger. Sometimes I go by Wanda Smith." She smiled at Quinn. "And I don't have to ask who this handsome gentleman is. I've seen his photo in the paper."

"I wanted to be in on the conversation," Quinn said, sizing up the woman in the tight black dress. A look into her eyes suggested she was a pragmatist.

Wanda didn't seem particularly impressed by Quinn, but she brought him up to speed on the conversation with the other two detectives, to where Duke suddenly lost interest in her. "There was something else," she said. "After the knocking from across the hall—once we knew what it was—me and Duke went on about our business. Though something had gone out of Duke after he looked out the door. I'm not accustomed to that."

She described how Duke went to the door and peeked out, how the knocking was on the door across the hall, and what Duke told her he'd seen.

When she'd run down, she took a sip of her water that smelled like vodka.

"That it?" Quinn asked.

Wanda looked from Sal to Harold and back at Quinn. She knew she'd better not leave anything out or lie to Quinn. "The air kinda went out of us for a while," she said. "I came down here to have a drink. That was about seven thirty. Duke stopped at the desk and made them give him a different room."

Quinn waited silently. He knew Sal and Harold would also remain silent.

"Duke just suddenly stopped," Wanda said.

"Stopped what?" Quinn asked.

"What he was doing. What we were doing up on the room. He just suddenly froze and said he couldn't stop thinking about what he thought he'd heard coming outta that other room. And something else—he looked scared."

"What did Duke say he heard?" Quinn asked.

"*Thought* he heard," Wanda corrected. "He tried to explain it to me, said it sounded like an injured animal wailing, only it was soft like. That's when he told me he'd seen somebody entering the room across the hall. He said maybe the guy had forced his way in. The reason he hadn't said what he'd seen earlier was . . . he had other things on his mind."

"Did *you* hear the sound?" Quinn asked.

"No."

"Could it have been a woman who was gagged and screaming?" Harold asked.

"I suppose. Looking back on it, that's what he mighta heard. Anyway, it gave Duke the creeps, and he didn't want to play anymore." She raised a shoulder in an elegant shrug that made Quinn think of art deco nudes. "Can't say I blame him. Unless you go in for that kinda thing."

"And you didn't see the man who might have forced his way into the room across the hall?"

"That's right. I was on the bed, still tending to my

ankle." She wagged a shoe, making her calf muscle flex. Half smiling. Knowing they were looking. "I'd damn near turned an ankle in these heels when Duke answered my knock and hustled me into his room. I was like, what's *this* all about?"

"He say he was sorry?" Harold asked. One of his seemingly inane questions that sometimes later proved of value. But only sometimes.

"No." Wanda smiled. "They get eager."

Harold just bet they did.

Bonnie the Barista wandered over to see if Quinn wanted a drink. Quinn moved her back out of earshot with a glance whose meaning was unmistakable. *Back off.* Bonnie retreated all the way to the other end of the bar. She managed to look offended and defiant. She, not this cop, ran the place during work hours.

"What did you and Duke do after he heard the first noise?" Quinn asked Wanda.

"The mood had changed."

Quinn could understand that.

"He got dressed and I got out of uniform," Wanda said.

"Uniform?" Harold asked.

Quinn gave him the same look he'd given Bonnie, and Harold scooted back a few inches and was silent.

"Then Duke stuffed his clothes and Dopp kit in a suitcase," Wanda said, "and we went down to the lobby. He went over to the desk and he asked to be moved to another room. More like demanded. Didn't say why, and nobody asked him. The desk clerk just gave him a different key card and room number, and had a bellhop take his suitcase up."

"Then what?" Quinn asked, almost casually. He needed to prime the pump now and then, keep Wanda talking.

"Then I came in here and had some drinks."

"What time was that?"

"I'm not sure. Sometime around seven thirty. I was already here, and had been for a little while, before Duke came back down from moving things into his new room. He was with some convention friends."

So around seven o'clock Duke had heard the torture and multiple murder in progress.

There was a pause in the conversation while everyone sipped his or her drink, maybe thinking about three hotel rooms, one unoccupied, one where murder had happened, and one that had contained a prostitute and her customer, worrying about what people would think and say and do if they were found out.

Something about that infuriated Quinn.

Harold gazed at Wanda and said, "Do you have a business card?"

Wanda looked at him as if he'd grown another head. Then she got a wrinkled scrap of paper from her purse and jotted down her address and phone number. She handed it to Quinn rather than to Harold or Sal. Alpha woman to alpha male. Quinn shot a glance at it and slipped it into his shirt pocket.

"You gonna stay around town?" he asked Wanda.

"Around the hotel, if you guys don't mind."

They didn't.

"None of us heard that," Quinn told her. *Let the wheels of sexual commerce keep going 'round. They will anyway.*

Wanda smiled.

"One thing," she said, "so you don't get confused when you talk to people. I was a redhead last night, not a brunette. I see some of the same clients, pass them in the lobby or halls, and changing my look kinda minimizes men doing double takes."

"You mean triple takes," Harold said. "One take because you look familiar, a second to make sure you're really who they think you are, and a third because there's something different about you."

"You know, that's *right!*"

Quinn mentally shook his head. It was just like Harold to think of that.

Wanda Woman smiled at Sal and Harold and touched Quinn lightly on the cheek as she left.

Quinn had to admit, it had an effect.

As they were leaving the hotel, Harold said, "Hide the key. How do you suppose—"

Sal said, "Forget it, Harold."

PART TWO

I have heard the mermaids singing each
  to each.

—T. S. Eliot, "The Love Song of
    J. Alfred Prufrock"

15

England, 1940

In small ships and large, the evacuees kept arriving from Dunkirk. They staggered or were carried onto shore from ships tied up at docks along the coast, and sometimes where there were no docks.

Some of the evacuees were physically whole, but with hollow features and vacant stares, and memories that would haunt them forever. They were defeated men. Overjoyed to be home, but beaten. Some of them were French, but most were from the British Expeditionary Force, which, according to gossip that Betsy Douglass picked up from the other nurses, had almost ceased to exist on the continent. Where the Germans were.

Many of the men were physically wounded, some in ways fatal that wouldn't claim their lives for weeks, but nonetheless would take them.

Betsy Douglass found herself holding a compress to a head injury to a man in a BEF uniform. He would have been soaked in blood were it not for the work of the Channel waves.

He looked up at her, smiled, and said what some nurses were accustomed to hearing. "Am I in heaven?"

"I'm afraid not," she said, returning the smile.

"Tucker," he said.

"Pardon me?"

"My name is Henry Tucker, and you are my angel of salvation."

"I think you're a little woozy, Henry Tucker."

"I won't be always," he said.

She squeezed his hand with her free one, and watched the blood seep from his head. "That's the spirit!"

He laughed, almost choking to death before regaining control. "The spirit? What that would be, darling, is Churchill and Hitler having at each other in a boxing ring, where nobody would get killed."

"That," she agreed, "would be the proper spirit."

He grew serious and squeezed her hand back. "We'll get the bastards back."

"Yes, we will, Henry Tucker."

He stared up at her. "Says on your name tag you're Betsy."

"Betsy Douglass," she said. "I don't want most people to know my last name so I marked it out on the tag."

"But you told me."

She nodded thoughtfully. "You're different, Henry Tucker." *Let him feel special. He's earned it.*

"Are you married, Betsy?"

"Not hardly. What about you?" She knew she was playing into his hands, being stupid. But there was something about him. Maybe because he might possibly be dead within a few days.

"My wife died three months ago."

"I'm sorry. Truly. In a bombing?"

"Struck by a lorry while she was riding her bicycle. Dead is dead, be it by bomb or lorry. Sometimes I still hear her calling my name. I turn and look, but she isn't there."

"It was probably me you heard earlier, assuring you that you weren't yet in heaven."

He turned away, and she had to adjust the compress. He winced in pain. "Seems like the whole world's turned against us, doesn't it?"

"Seems that way right now, Henry Tucker."

"Douglass! Nurse Douglass!"

The icy hard voice of the head nurse, aptly named Nora Dreadwater, cut through the chatter and clatter of the transportation staging area.

Betsy straightened up, but continued her pressure evenly on the compress.

"Get that gurney into an ambulance!" Nurse Dreadwater commanded.

"Yes, ma'am. Should I ride with the patient?"

"Don't be absurd," Nurse Dreadwater said. She was used to her young nurses falling in and out of love. The new ones, anyway. Before the protective calluses on their hearts had formed.

It was a blow but not a shock when Betsy Douglass went into work at her nurse's station and heard that Henry Tucker had come down with a staph inspection. Worn down to almost a catatonic state, she'd been given two days off. Now, already, she was feeling guilty for those two days. She should have been here, where people needed her desperately. Where people were dying.

She'd sat with Henry Tucker most of the first day off, and was chased away by Nurse Dreadwater, ordered to rest. Dreadwater had even given her pills to take to help her sleep. Betsy hadn't taken them.

She could tell by the other nurses' faces that they understood that in the past two weeks Betsy and Tucker had fallen in love. Love, in fact, was what was supposed to save Henry Tucker. It conquered all, surely it could conquer a head injury, even one serious enough to merit a steel plate inserted in the skull.

Betsy walked swiftly through the ward to Henry Tucker's bed, made semiprivate with an iron frame and pull curtains.

Betsy knew immediately that he was dying. She'd seen so many of them die in the past fortnight, since they'd stopped coming in from Dunkirk, and what should have been the healing had begun.

"I was gone two whole days," Betsy said. "I shouldn't have taken two days off."

"You were here most of the first day," Dreadwater reminded her. "And you needed at least three days to regenerate yourself. You were almost passed out, talking gibberish, a danger to the patients."

"The other nurses do the same."

"Yes," Dreadwater agreed. For a second or two she seemed about to cry. Then her features rearranged themselves in their usual stony expression.

Henry Tucker moaned and said something. Nurse

Dreadwater leaned in close and he repeated it. She looked at Betsy.

"What did he say?" Betsy asked.

"He said to quit wasting his time."

"What does he mean?"

"He wants me to leave you two alone," Dreadwater said. She started to say something else, then cast aside one of the curtains and was gone.

Henry used a forefinger to summon Betsy closer. She moved to be right next to him, then leaned over him and hugged him lightly. His body seemed almost weightless as she embraced him.

He exerted an effort and shifted position until his mouth was near her ear.

Then he seemed to become delirious, hugging her harder and harder with what waning strength he could muster. He began to babble. She couldn't understand much of what he said. Something about his "things." His backpack.

"You'll get everything back when you leave," she told him.

He smiled up at her, humoring her.

Where does he find the strength?

He pulled her closer, and began to whisper to her about what was in the backpack. What she was supposed to do with it.

He became quiet then, with her head resting on his breast.

Too quiet.

The clock by the side of the bed ticked, ticked . . . The only sound in the world.

Betsy was afraid to move. Terrified of the reality. He had died in her arms.

Betsy began to cry, which made her furious. She needed to reestablish her detachment and professionalism, and here she was sobbing for a man who in truth she barely knew.

But they *would have* gotten to know each other better. Much better. If Henry Tucker had survived.

"His head wound seemed to be healing," she said. "He might have survived."

"We thought he had a chance."

Betsy bowed her head and Dreadwater stood hugging her. The curtain was open. People walked past them, staring, then hurried on about their business.

"You have to gain control, dear," Dreadwater said. "These are trying times. We need you. Need you badly."

Betsy stepped away from her and stood up straight. She wiped away her tears with the back of her hand.

She drew a deep breath and nodded. "You're right, of course. It's going to get worse before it gets better."

"I'm afraid so," Dreadwater said. "We will simply have to cope."

Betsy moved to walk away, toward her assigned ward, when Dreadwater's firm grip on her elbow stopped her.

"Henry—Corporal Tucker—had a few hours of consciousness and clear mental function before the infection and medications altered his thinking," Dreadwater said. "No one had told him, but I'm sure, toward the end, he knew he was dying. He left you this." She handed Betsy a sealed white envelope.

Betsy stared at it, then tucked it deep in her uniform pocket. Two patients were rolled past on gurneys.

"I'll read this later," she said. "Work to do now."

"Of course," Dreadwater said, with a thin smile. "I'll let you get to your task." Her shoes' gum soles made a curious squishing sound on the recently mopped floor as she walked away. Betsy would hear that sound in her dreams.

Betsy worked with almost demonic intensity, well into the evening. She tended to an artilleryman who'd lost his right arm to a sniper's bullet. A French officer with a machine gun bullet lodged in his hip. A ship's captain with half his face missing after a bomb blast. An RAF pilot with a head wound not so unlike Henry Tucker's. The pilot asked her if he was going to recover, and she reassured him that he would.

"Gotta get back up top," he said with a smile.

Her sadness, her pity, her emotions threatened to overwhelm her—but she successfully forced them away to the edges of her mind.

She realized that many of the other nurses, and doubtless the doctors, whom she'd thought so dispassionate, had learned emotional detachment before she had. That was the only difference between them and her. The violence and blood and futility was scarring them internally, and had been all along, even though it couldn't be seen. None of them, not the nurses, patients, doctors, none of them would come through this unscathed. If they were lucky enough to survive physically, still they would bear scars.

Betsy couldn't imagine a day when the memories would no longer sting and bring tears to her eyes.

That evening, before nightfall and the blackouts, she sat alone on a park bench and in the dying light read what Henry Tucker had written in his failing hand.

It wasn't exactly what she expected.

It was a thank you and a plea, and a set of instructions.

16

New York, the present

Jeanine Carson had pedaled nine miles and gone exactly nowhere.

She was on her usual stationary bicycle in Sweat it Out, the neighborhood gym where she was a member, and where she spent every other evening. The heavy, stationary bicycle was set at an angle to the large window looking out on the sidewalk. Now and then passersby would glance in at Jeanine. Some of the men would smile.

Not that she was dressed to attract attention, in her baggy knee-length red shorts, oversized black T-shirt, and red elastic headband that kept her blond curled hair away from her perspiring face. Mostly away. Now and then her hair dangled in a curtain down one side of her face. Even so attired, and with her hair in what she considered a mess, Jeanine was still an attractive woman of forty.

Forty! God! How did that happen?

Well, it *had* happened. She decided she should be thankful that in the right light she could pass for thirty. Or so she'd been told.

She pedaled harder, as if trying to outdistance her troubles.

A guy in a gray business suit, lugging an attaché case, bustled past outside the window. He glanced her way and grinned.

Jeanine couldn't help herself. She grinned back. Mostly out of appreciation. He was about her age and still handsome. In the game—maybe. Or maybe he had a wife and six kids out in Teaneck. What would it be like to be married to a man like that, to come home to him and six kids?

Jeanine let her mind roam, keeping her legs pumping on the pedals. Narrowing her focus as well as her waist.

What would it be like to come home to a man in an Upper West Side apartment, with no kids involved? Now that was more in the realm of possibility.

Her thighs were beginning to ache, and she tightened her grip on the handlebars and concentrated on her exercise, forcing the embodiment of her dreams from her thoughts.

Back to the drudgery of a regular exercise regimen. Reality and self-recrimination. If she was overweight, it was simply because she ate too much. She was the one to blame. The one in control of her fork.

Personal responsibility.

That thing about pain and gain.

Those were the sorts of thoughts that ran through Jeanine's mind now, as her body performed its repetitive assault on itself: *My fault. I don't see anyone else around here to blame. Too fat, too fat, too fat . . .* though she was only a hundred and twenty pounds, at five foot six. But it was a *fat* one-twenty.

The stationary bike continued its whirring clacking accompaniment: *Too fat, too fat, too fat . . .*

Such were the musings of an unemployed financial consultant, some of whose problems might be easily solved if she weren't . . . too fat in some places.

She pedaled on, going nowhere, sweat rolling down her face, down her neck, tickling her—

The short clacking sound of a coin tapping on glass made her raise her head and look outside.

There he was, out on the sidewalk, grinning and staring at her through the gym window. Mr. Executive with the gray suit and attaché case. He was back.

I'm the reason why.

He made a motion as if he held a knife and fork, an obvious invitation to dinner. She deliberately looked away from him, allowing herself to smile slightly, as if she couldn't help herself under the onslaught of his charm.

Jeanine knew how to play this game.

Discouragement and encouragement could look pretty much alike. It could be a challenge to figure out which was which. Some men couldn't resist a challenge.

Later that evening, Fedderman and Sal sat at their desks at Q&A and sipped bad coffee. At the far end of the room, Jerry Lido was working at his laptop, unaware for the moment that there was a world not digital. Helen the profiler sat lounging in a turned-around chair near Pearl's desk. Her long, bare arms were crossed, displaying firm biceps and forearm muscles. Fedderman wondered at times about Helen's sexuality, then figured what the hell, it was none of his business. He was befuddled anyway in what seemed a new world of sex roles. What was a bride these days? A groom? Who was what, when, where? It was all confusing to Fedderman. He'd told Penny once he wasn't sure if they were really married, the way the laws kept changing.

"Who should send who chocolates?" Fedderman unconsciously mumbled.

"What was that?" Helen asked.

Fedderman realized he'd spoken his thoughts and had been overheard. Time to back and fill.

"Penny and I had an argument," he said. "Then after we made up, I asked her which of us should send the other chocolates, what with the new marriage laws."

"I'll bet she was amused," Helen said.

"And flattered," Sal said in his growl of a voice. "I'd say her reaction was—"

"Let me guess," Helen interrupted. "She was pissed off."

"Well—"

At the other end of the room, Jerry Lido said, "Craig Duke."

There was an immediate silence.

"What about him?" Fedderman asked. His own voice seemed not to carry.

Lido leaned back away from his computer. "I probed the net and learned more about him than he knows about himself. He's exactly who and what he claims to be. A paint salesman in town for a convention. And his background checks out. He's pretty average, far as out-of-town conventioneers go. Sits in on exciting paint panels, drinks too much. Brags too much. Bounces on some of the hotel slave trade. Then he catches a flight out of town and goes back and plays family man with the wife and kids."

"Sounds like a nice life," Fedderman said.

"Yeah," Sal growled. "House, woman, car."

"Maybe all a man needs," Sal said.

Helen smiled and said, "You guys are so full of crap."

"Whatever," Lido said. "But I think we can cross Craig Duke off our suspect list."

"I concur," Sal said. "He never did seem good for it."

"Not to me, either," Fedderman said.

Helen shrugged.

"So whaddya think?" Sal asked her.

" 'Bout what?"

"The paint salesman," Fedderman said.

"Remember to forget him," Jerry Lido reminded them.

"Remember what?" Helen asked, playing dumb.

"Who we talking about?" Sal asked.

"I dunno," Fedderman said. "I forgot."

Jeanine wasn't surprised when she came out of the gym forty-five minutes later, and there was Mr. gray business suit, waiting for her.

He was taller than he'd appeared through the window. And better looking. Not exactly handsome, yet there was nothing wrong with him. Search and you couldn't find a flaw. It made him kind of anonymous, yet alluring. He smiled, and it was a good one. His teeth were white and even; a movie-star mouth. This guy was ready for his close-up.

"I saw you through the window," he said.

She'd slowed down so they were both walking, but almost in place. "I saw you seeing me."

"Wondering what I was thinking, no doubt."

"I think I know what you were thinking."

"No, no," he said. "It wasn't like that. Well, not exactly not like that. I just . . ." He searched for words, then he shrugged. "Just wanted to get to know you."

"And here we are. You're doing that."

"So what's your name? Where do you work? *Do* you work? Are you—my God, you're not married, are you?"

She had to laugh. "Single," she said.

"In a relationship?"

"Not at the time."

He feigned great relief, mopping his brow. "I didn't think so, but still, it's a relief. My little voice wasn't wrong."

Jeanine stopped walking. "Little voice?"

He read the worry on her face and laughed. "No, no, not that kind of little voice. I'm certifiably sane. It's the kind of little voice almost all men have. It says, 'You've got to get to know this woman.' "

His widened smile fairly screamed *normal!* Everything about this guy was normal. Flawless.

Little voice. That was okay. She sort of had one herself.

He seemed relieved now that they were standing still. "My name's Thomas Gunn. I'm thirty-nine, divorced once, a long time ago, no children. I'm in real estate, and I'm moving to Nevada in three weeks. I'm a member of a partnership that's going to build condominiums."

"Isn't it a bad time to be doing that?" she asked. "With the economy the way it is."

He gave his Wheaties-box smile. "Not if you build them convenient to the casinos. Those are the kinds of buyers who'll take a chance."

Jeanine had to admit to herself that that made perfect sense.

"I'm Jeanine Carson," she said, "unemployed art restorer and sometimes financial consultant."

"I'd have guessed model," he said. "Or actress."

"And I'd have guessed you were an actor or professional athlete."

They simultaneously laughed and shook their heads, acknowledging without saying that each of them knew the other was full of bullshit.

Not lies, but bullshit. For Jeanine there was a critical difference. Bullshit was play. Lies were . . . something else. Lies were what damaged people. Diminished them.

In a way, bullshit was the opposite. If all parties involved knew it was a game, what was the harm?

"What's your little voice saying now?" Jeanine asked.

There was no hesitation. "That I should ask this beautiful woman to have dinner with me tonight."

"That's all?"

He cocked his head to the side, as if listening.

"Just what I thought it would say," he told Jeanine. "It told me anything beyond dinner is totally up to the lady."

Jeanine flipped an errant strand of hair out of her eyes in a way she knew men liked.

Patience. Caution. At least a show of resistance.

More than she'd put up so far, anyway. She knew the rules. The ancient warnings.

It was just that there was, as they say, something about this guy.

She said, "I like your little voice."

17

Dwayne paused in the dark hall outside the bedroom where his father and Maude were sleeping. His heart was like a huge bird beating its wings in an attempt to escape his body.

He knew they'd be sleeping deeply now, exhausted. They'd had sex, and then sent Dwayne downstairs to get the drinks, a whiskey sour for Maude and a Jack Daniel's on the rocks for his father. Then they'd told him to return to his bedroom.

He lay there for over an hour, most of it listening to his father snore. Maude didn't snore, but Dwayne knew she would also be asleep. He knew the sleeping habits of both of them.

And he knew their plans.

In the morning Dwayne's father and soon-to-be stepmother were going to board a flight to Las Vegas. There they were going to be married and spend the weekend drinking and gambling. Dwayne had heard them talking about this as he lay exhausted beside them, keeping their voices low because they thought he was asleep and wouldn't hear.

But this was simply a confirmation. He'd learned to use the big house's air-conditioning vents as listening devices. The afternoon after Dwayne first heard of their marriage plans, Maude told Bill Phoenix about them inside the cabana.

Bill Phoenix and Maude had laid plans of their own. A month after Maude's marriage to all that money, Dwayne's father would die in a boating accident. Maude would be wealthy, and after a few months she would marry Bill Phoenix and he'd be wealthy. They would dole out money to keep Dwayne in a good boarding school, out of the way until he graduated and found employment, and then they could properly ignore him.

Maude suggested that Dwayne might be in that boating accident with his father, but Bill Phoenix said he didn't like killing a kid. Maude had said, "Whatever. We can wait a while."

Dwayne knew he couldn't afford to wait.

So when he went downstairs to the kitchen to get the drinks, he slipped his jeans on and taped a long kitchen knife to his lower leg. And he added one extra ingredient to the drinks—some sleeping pills he'd ground up between two spoons.

Now, in the dark hall outside their bedroom, Dwayne sat cross-legged, listening, his bare back against the wall. He'd removed his jeans and was nude. Fingerprints didn't matter. After all, he still lived here.

Dwayne's father's snoring had evened out, and from Maude there was only silence. Dwayne took a deep breath, holding the long knife in his right hand and staring at it. The knife was going to solve all his problems. He was sure of it.

Gripping the knife loosely against the carpet, he crawled silently into the bedroom.

His father's snoring was louder now, and would cover just about any noise Dwayne made short of a shout. Between the sonorous rasping of his father he could hear Maude's gentle, easy breathing. The booze and pills had done their job.

Dwayne stood up and approached the bed.

His father was lying on his back with one arm up over his head. He slept nude, his hairy chest exposed and vulnerable. Maude had rolled onto her side and was facing away from him. She'd put her thin blue nightgown back on put not her panties. The sheet had slipped down to her knees, and Dwayne stood for a moment transfixed by the curve of her buttocks and hips, thinking she looked so much like some of the medieval paintings he'd seen in museums.

Careful not to disturb Maude, he leaned over his father and swiftly inserted the long blade up beneath his sternum to his heart. Dwayne leaned into the knife, twisting and pushing, feeling warm blood on his hands and wrists.

His father moved his legs around some, and stopped snoring and gave several hoarse gasps. Then he was still.

He hadn't even opened his eyes.

Dwayne was surprised to find himself thinking that his father's death had been too easy.

It wasn't going to be that way with Maude.

Dwayne went to the closet and grabbed a handful of

his father's silk ties. He tied a large knot in the middle of one tie, then laid the others on the bed near Maude.

Maude opened her eyes and stared at Dwayne. Her eyes widened as her brain caught up with what was happening. When she opened her mouth to scream, Dwayne shoved the knotted tie into it. He fastened it with a tightened knot behind her neck. She reached for the tie with splayed fingers, but he slapped her hard and brought her hands back down. He rolled her onto her stomach and bound her wrists behind her with another tie, this one with a striped pattern he'd never liked on his father.

She began to kick, but Dwayne expected that and was ready for it. He held her legs together and waited for her to run out of energy. Then he sat on her legs and tied her ankles, then her legs at the knees.

Her body went into spasms and she emitted a low and frantic moan, over and over. Dwayne knew she had discovered the dead body next to her.

He rolled her so she was again lying on her back, still moaning. She was terrified to look over at Dwayne's dead father now, and kept her wide, wide eyes fixed on the ceiling. She began kicking with both legs together, so he wrapped the sheet tightly around them so she could kick in only a limited way.

Dwayne stood over Maude, knowing she was helpless. The knife was still jutting from his father's chest.

Dwayne removed the knife. It slid out easier than it had gone in. He held it where Maude had to look at it. She screamed into the knotted tie, one of his father's favorites. Dwayne was sure no one could hear her outside the room, much less outside the house. Smiling down at her, he laid the knife gently across her exposed throat. Her horrified eyes were fixed on him. She couldn't look away. Beneath the horror, she was pleading.

Dwayne couldn't get out of mind how easily his father had died. Had passed on, or over. Or descended into hell.

Maude was going to have to suffer for both of them. For what they did. For who they were. For who and what he had become.

At the end, the final moment of her life, the beginning moment of her death, they would both know that he possessed her and would possess her for all time. She'd be like an exquisite piece of art, a thing of beauty forever suspended in amber. Whatever happened to her after that, to her corporeal self, didn't matter.

Leaving the knife where it was, feeling her frantic gaze follow him, he crossed to the bureau and picked up the pack of cigarettes lying next to his father's wallet and keys. There was an expensive gold lighter there, too.

He walked back to the bed and lit a cigarette, though he didn't smoke.

They both knew he didn't smoke.

He watched her watch the cigarette as he moved closer.

18

Quinn knew that Helen the profiler was waiting around the office for the others to leave. When they were gone to their various tasks, she pulled a wooden chair over and sat down in it so she was facing Quinn across his desk.

"Renz has decided to go large with the media," she said.

Quinn absently reached into a desk drawer for a cigar. He drew out one of the Cuban robustos in its brushed-aluminum sleeve.

Helen smiled and said, "Pearl will kill you, if that cigar doesn't."

"How would she know?" Quinn asked.

Helen continued to smile.

He put the cigar back. "I'm assuming Renz instructed you to tell me about the going-public-with-all-guns plan."

"Yeah. He's curious as to your reaction."

"Actually, I agree with him. It's all going to leak out anyway. At least this way, all the cards will be on the table."

"Per Renz's instructions, I've made myself available to be interviewed, instead of him, on the *Minnie Miner ASAP* show."

"Was Minnie agreeable to that?"

"About like a cat getting declawed."

Quinn closed the drawer that housed the Cuban cigar. "Better thee than me."

"Minnie would have preferred you. Or even Renz."

"Not a good idea," Quinn said. "I wouldn't want to have to lie to her, but I might. Renz would love to lie to her."

"So, not all the cards will be on the table."

"Maybe a few up my sleeve."

Helen crossed her arms. She already had her long legs crossed. She seemed to be settling in with more to say. "Wanna know what I think?"

"You're going to ask for my cigar," Quinn said.

"Not hardly."

"Okay. Think about what?"

"Lots of things, all pertinent."

Quinn settled back in his desk chair, in a waiting position. "I can count on you for that, Helen."

"Our killer, whether he's the original D.O.A. or not, is going to take another victim soon."

Quinn had come to the same conclusion, but he remained silent. He wanted to hear Helen's views on this. Maybe they were the same as his.

"The mass murder—six women, for God's sake— was a mistake. Even if the killer might see it as a stroke of good fortune. When he entered Andria Bell's room, he had no idea the connecting door to the next room would be unlocked. Probably didn't suspect he was entering what was in effect a suite. Then suddenly there he was, with a knife and six women."

"Could have been that way," Helen said.

"Okay. When he'd finished making Andria helpless, he herded the women into the adjoining suite and threatened one so that she helped tie and gag the others. He bound and gagged the remaining one—his terrified helper—then he had his idea of fun."

"Not for long, though," Quinn said, recalling the nature of the wounds. Andria Bell had been the one who was tortured over a long period of time.

"It was Andria the killer wanted to get busy with," Helen said. "Andria was the one who had information he wanted. The Richard Speck act with the other five was done partly out of necessity and enjoyment, and partly because the killer wanted to make a splash in the news. Wanted to be somebody right away."

"He got that," Quinn said, "though maybe not as much as he wanted."

"He never will get as much as he wants. The point is, whether he would have killed five, ten, or fifteen women in that hotel suite, the effect on whatever drives him will be the same as if he killed only one."

"Think so?" Quinn asked.

Helen nodded. "Obsessions compel action on a mental timetable, not a body count."

Quinn rested his elbows on the table and knitted his fingers. "You're saying he has no choice other than to feed his obsession."

Helen said, "He's whetted his appetite, and in a big way."

"You gonna bring that up when you're on the *Minnie Miner* show?" Quinn asked.

"Yes. We'll see what she has to say."

"Won't she be the one asking the questions?"

"She'll think so."

Quinn unlaced his fingers and sat back. "Helen, do you have anything even remotely good to tell me?"

Helen smiled. "Soon as I get outta here, you can fire up that cigar."

But Quinn didn't light the cigar. He was going to meet Pearl in a few hours for dinner, and he knew she'd smell tobacco smoke on his clothes. And if Pearl happened to have a cold, her daughter Jody would certainly smell cigar smoke and rat him out. Jody had become Pearl's surrogate snoop. As well as Quinn's.

Quinn tapped a beat on the desk with his fingertips and pondered.

The whole damned family was like that.

For a moment it unnerved Quinn. Renz's view of the world might be right.

19

Jeanine Carson's date, Thomas Gunn, appeared across the street, but didn't see her. When the traffic signal changed, he crossed at the intersection and strode toward her building. He was wearing light tan slacks, a navy blue or black blazer, and carrying a light coat draped over his arm. Jeanine didn't think rain was in the forecast. So why—

He saw her, smiled, and her doubts disappeared in a part of her mind where she didn't want to go.

Limping slightly, he came toward her on the sidewalk, where she was waiting just outside her apartment building. "I didn't think you'd come down and meet me," he said. His smile caused a long but faint scar on the side of his face to crinkle. Somehow sexy. He seemed pleased that she was displaying such eagerness. Flattered. "I brought this for you." He drew from beneath the folded raincoat a bottle of red wine. "It's Australian, and it's great. A friend tipped me off about it."

"Does it go with Vietnamese food?"

"Sure. It goes with anything. If you're thinking about

that Vietnamese restaurant two blocks down, then we're thinking in the same channel."

"So happens I am," she said, telling herself that this might be an omen, the way their minds were synchronized. Feeling better about Thomas Gunn, she added, "We can drink the wine with our food, or bring it back here and have it afterward."

"Afterward?"

"After dinner, I mean." *Yeah, yeah.* They both knew the possibilities.

He smiled and nodded. Knowing when not to press. Half the battle was getting them slightly drunk. Putting them at their ease. *Half the battle was the bottle.*

Dinner went fast. A blur of food and music. The killer couldn't pronounce half the food, but it was good. Jeanine picked at it. Accompanied by some kind of string instrument, a woman was singing in what the killer presumed to be Vietnamese. He thought she sounded as if she had a flute stuck in her throat.

After dinner they had green tea, which was okay. They still hadn't touched the bottle of wine. That was okay, too, the killer thought. Let it age. And if it didn't taste quite right to Jeanine later in her apartment, after he poured, that would be okay, too, as long as she drank it down. It would be the ketamine, one of the many date drugs he employed. He figured that with the dosage he had in mind, she would be very compliant in a very short time. She'd be thinking clearly enough, but her muscles wouldn't respond to her signals from the brain. Her body would be his. And then her mind. And then the truth that would follow.

It was a BYOB restaurant, so nobody raised an eyebrow when they eschewed more tea and decided to enjoy a few glasses of wine before leaving.

"How come," Jeanine asked, not yet beginning to feel the ketamine he'd added to her glass when she was in the restroom, "you aren't on Facebook?"

"I'm a Twitter guy," he said.

"I looked there, too." Her words were just beginning to slur.

"You must have missed me somehow. If you have a computer, I'll show you when we go to your place."

" 'Kay," she said.

He glanced at his watch as if they had to be some specific place at a specific time and were running late.

As for Jeanine, she was beginning to feel kind of odd. As if the restaurant had become much more spacious and she . . .

"I think I'm growing smaller," she said. It was simply an observation.

He smiled. "That's impossible."

What did he mean by that. *What the hell . . .*

She saw him signal for the check. Time seemed to lurch as he paid cash, leaving a large tip, judging by how the waiter thanked him.

And just like that, it seemed, they were out on the sidewalk. He was still carrying the folded raincoat, and he'd brought the bottle of wine. The sidewalk tipped slightly, and she leaned on him for support. He patted her hand that she noticed now was clutching his arm.

They began walking arm in arm. Everything seemed

normal except that she was so damned small all of a sudden. She tried to say something about that to Thomas but couldn't articulate it. Her voice, which had moved off about two or three feet to the side, said something incomprehensible.

A man was standing near them, leaning slightly. He had a raincoat on even though it wasn't raining. His head seemed to be off center on his shoulders. "She okay?" he asked in a concerned voice.

"Fine," Thomas said, rolling his eyes. "She had too much to drink again."

Well, that's not true . . .

There was her apartment building. They were up the steps to the vestibule and inside. Then *wham!* There they were at the elevator. What the hell had happened to time? *Thank God Thomas is here.*

He helped her walk along the hall to her apartment door, or she would never have made it. *Thank God . . .*

"I have the key," she managed to say.

He laughed softly. "I hope so, darling."

Darling . . . That was nice . . .

The soreness in her back was what brought her around. As Jeanine regained consciousness, she was aware of Thomas Gunn looming over her.

"Thomas . . ." is what she started to say, but something—she realized it was silky material, wadded . . . her panties—was crammed into her mouth so she could merely make a humming sound if she tried to speak or scream.

He held up a long-bladed knife with a sharp point. Rotated it nimbly so it danced with reflected light.

Ignoring her muffled screams, he started with her armpits. The pain was incredible, causing her bound body to vibrate and bounce on the table. She felt her bladder release. He was ready for that, and swiped the table around her with a wadded dishtowel.

"Quite a mess," he remarked.

He tossed the dishtowel onto the floor and held up the knife as he had before. This time it had blood on it. Her blood. She began to whimper.

He waited patiently.

When she was quiet, he said, "I'm going to remove your gag, and you're going to be quiet unless spoken to. Is that understood?"

Pain in her neck flared as she nodded.

Smiling at her as if it were an act of love, he little by little removed the wadded panties from her mouth.

Her eyes were wide, unblinking. She did not make a sound.

"There," he said, when he was finished. He held the knife up where she could see it and rotated it again to catch the light.

He placed the very tip of the blade in the hollow just beneath her larynx, exerted light pressure that wasn't quite enough to draw blood. But it stung. Oh, how it stung! He had only to apply the slightest more pressure and . . .

Her entire body began to tremble. He placed the spread fingertips of his free hand lightly on the soft vibrating flesh of her stomach. He saw, felt, knew that the fear had her. It had consumed whatever resistance she might have tried to maintain.

So there could be no misunderstanding, he moved the knife up so its point touched her forehead, where he would soon be carving his initials. The vibrancy of her body tingled through his fingertips at an even higher pitch. It heightened his own anticipation and hastened his heartbeat.

This was a woman who read the papers, who kept up on the news. There could be no doubt that she knew who he was.

Her terror was unbearable. She was ready to do whatever he told her. Small favors were all she might earn.

"Now," he said, "we're going to have a conversation."

He didn't mention that afterward they were going to share, from two different perspectives, a remarkable and transforming experience.

Both of them, for very different reasons, were looking forward to it with keen anticipation.

20

Finally Betsy Douglass's shift was over. Which seemed to her a godsend, as she felt close to the limits of her endurance.

She denied herself the doses of medications some of the other nurses employed to artificially increase their energy. Betsy had seen the eventual results of that, the slurred speech, the permanently haggard features that aged young women before their time. And sometimes the breakdowns. She drank tea. Endless cups of tea. And she chewed chocolates, which contained sugar and caffeine enough to boost her energy level.

But the human body could take only so much, and Betsy knew she was on the verge of trembling and losing her concentration. There was a time for a nurse to push on despite exhaustion, and a time to realize more harm than good can be done by pressing on.

She slipped a light jacket over her nurse's uniform and made her way to the vast basement of the hospital. The part of the building above the basement had been bombed so that much of the rubble remained. The sagging ceiling had been bolstered with heavy wooden supports, and tarpaulins had been set up to divert rain leakage. Still there were a few puddles to be avoided, and a dank, persistent dimness. All over the floor, in some semblance of order, were stacked the patients' personal belongings, with identification cards pinned where it was most convenient, listing the items and their owner.

The smell in the basement sickened Betsy, but she knew she should remove Henry Tucker's effects before the end of the week, when the items belonging to the dead would be removed to make more room.

Tucker's pile of personal effects was typical, except for the tan canvas backpack, which wasn't uniform or BEF issue. But other escapees from Dunkirk's bloody beach had brought non-issue bags, and even a few small suitcases. Dunkirk had been chaos, and the men occupying hospital beds had made it clear that the only rule there was to survive.

Betsy looked at Henry's pitiful collection besides the backpack. A hastily folded bloody uniform. No helmet. Either the Germans or the sea had taken that. Socks and underwear had been disposed of rather than saved. Lying on top of the folded clothing was a pair of worn-down muddy boots. There was a fresh-looking notch in one of the heels, as if a bullet had come close to Tucker's foot and left a reminder.

Betsy used a pencil to line out everything on the ID card except the backpack, and weighted down the card with one of Henry's worn-down boots. For some reason she smiled, realizing she was worn down in the same way—like Henry's boots.

Knowing that fatigue had muddled her mind, she lifted the backpack—heavier than she'd thought—and carried it by one of its straps toward the exit.

As she was leaving the hospital, Betsy was motioned to the duty desk by Nurse Nora. The head nurse had been working hard, too. Her hair was wispy and mussed, and there was a sheen of perspiration on her beefy face.

She pointed and drew Betsy down to the end of the long desk, where they wouldn't be overheard.

"A woman was by earlier about Henry Tucker," Nurse Nora said, her intense dark stare locked on Betsy's face.

Betsy was confused. "You mean she didn't know he was dead?"

"Oh, she knew he died, all right. What she wanted was the body and his possessions."

"Henry's wife died," Betsy said.

Nurse Nora nodded. "I know. In a lorry-bicycle accident. It was listed on entry."

"What did you do?"

"Sent her away. She didn't argue after I showed her this." The older woman handed Betsy an envelope with Betsy's name on it. "I took the liberty of opening and reading it, as that kind of personal relationship between patient and nurse is forbidden."

"But that's—"

"If you read it," Nurse Nora said, "you'll see it's a note from Henry Tucker bequeathing his earthly goods to you."

"A will . . ."

"Same as," Nurse Nora said.

Betsy read the letter quickly. It was simple, and it was signed *With Love.*

"I'm assuming," the head nurse said, "that the letter refers to that backpack and whatever is in it."

"I'm assuming that too," Betsy said.

Nurse Nora smiled wearily. "Have you looked inside?"

"No."

"Wait till you get home to do that, so I don't have to lie if that woman comes back with some kind of authority."

"I will." Betsy hoisted the backpack off the floor. "And thank you."

"I didn't see you, and we didn't have this conversation."

"No, ma'am."

When Betsy was halfway home, a cabdriver pulled over to the curb and invited her to get in with her heavy package. He would drive her to where she was going without charging her. Betsy knew it was because of her nurse's uniform showing beneath her light jacket, but she was no less grateful for the driver's generosity.

It was odd how the war was bringing out the best of the British people. Betsy thought that if Hitler knew that, he would also know the Germans didn't stand a chance.

As she climbed into the back of the cab, she saw that the driver was a man in his sixties, wearing a black eye patch.

"Wasn't for the likes of you in the last war, I wouldn't be able to see out my other eye," he told her with a crooked smile.

"There's plenty of the likes of me," Betsy assured him, pulling the cab's door shut.

He ground the gears and the cab rolled forward.

"You wouldn't know it," he said, "but I'm winking at you."

It was a relief to be rid of the backpack's weight when she got home. She thought about opening it right away, then paused. She was sure it would contain Tucker's change of clothes, possibly tin military-issue eating utensils, maybe a second pair of boots, a few other personal effects.

For now, she slid it beneath the bed.

Then she lay down on the bed, thinking she had never been so tired.

She was admitting also the real reason she wanted to put the backpack out of her mind. It would pierce her heart to open it and have to sort and feel various objects and material that had been so intimately Henry Tucker's.

Briefly as they'd known each other, she had lost something dear when he died, and she didn't want to visit its reminders.

Sleep would help her to escape.

Betsy could ignore Henry Tucker's backpack for only so long. Grief at last gave in to curiosity, and finally she slid the backpack from beneath her bed. She was surprised again by how excessively heavy it was. She hoisted it up onto the bed and then sat beside it at an angle so she could work clasps and buttons.

When she opened the canvas flap, the scent carried her back to the hospital, to charred flesh and antiseptics and stale human sweat. To cries in the night.

But how much of that was in the mind?

There was actually little that was personal in Corporal Henry Tucker's backpack. Nothing that made Betsy think jarringly of him. Things inside were either dry or only slightly damp, still smelling of the Channel water that had tried to claim Tucker. She stared at an address written on a water-stained, folded sheet of paper. It was pinned on top of some object that was wrapped mummy-like in a French newspaper and fastened with yards of tape. Also in the backpack were two sealed envelopes. Each bore a name—one male, one female—that meant nothing to Betsy. The ink had gotten damp and spread slightly, but everything was fairly legible.

There was a third envelope, stapled to the newspaper wrapping where Betsy hadn't seen it before. It was also sealed, and addressed in a neat hand to an M. Gundel-heimer.

Betsy didn't know about the letters, but obviously Henry had intended to deliver the heavy object to the address stapled to its wrappings, to M. Gundelheimer, whoever he was. There was no way to unwrap the thing partially without her snooping being obvious. She somehow understood, anyway, that she wasn't supposed to peek.

It was almost dusk. The bombers, after a lull in the Dunkirk evacuation, came mostly at night, so if she hurried she'd have time to take the backpack to the address, and do a last favor for Henry Tucker. It was a promise she knew she had to keep. Betsy sighed, thinking of Henry. There definitely had been something between them, a relationship beyond patient-nurse. If only Tucker had lived . . .

But it was pointless to dwell on might-have-beens. The war had taught her, and almost every other British citizen, that hard fact.

She looked at her nurse's wristwatch. There was still time. And she had a duty that didn't involve nursing.

She replaced everything in the backpack and hefted it. Heavy, all right. But she could handle it. She decided to use it for what it was, and placed it upright on the edge of the table. She backed up to it and slipped her arms through the straps, then stood up straight.

The straps dug in and hurt her shoulders somewhat, but they were wide enough to disperse the weight. She adjusted the backpack so it was more comfortable, then, as the folded paper inside it directed, started out for Treasure Island Collectibles, a shop on Dalenby off of Clerkenwell. It was an area she knew fairly well. Perhaps at the Dalenby address she would meet M. Gundelheimer.

After locking the door to her modest bedsit behind her, she carefully made her way down the creaking wooden steps to the street door.

Betsy might have taken a taxi, but she didn't have the money to spare. And once she got walking at a fast pace, the backpack really wasn't that much of a burden.

It was only a twenty-minute walk, down streets that were ruined on one block and untouched on the next. German bombs were indiscriminate. Betsy found herself walking faster and faster, like others on the streets. People didn't want to be outside longer than necessary. Usually it was later and darker when the bombers came, but the Hun liked to vary their attacks and try to catch the defenses off guard.

Betsy's heart became a weight when she saw the damage to Clerkenwell. Narrow and winding Dalenby had fared no better in the recent bombing. Betsy stumbled along amid rubble that was blackened by fire. Packed ash piles were still damp from the fire brigades. The smell was terrible. Charred wood. And something else.

Would London ever get used to this? Survive it?

One thing was for sure: There was nothing left of Betsy's destination, Treasure Island Collectibles.

An air-raid siren growled then quickly died, as if clearing its throat, or emitting a terse reminder. Night was fast approaching. That meant another blackout, and almost certainly another rain of bombs.

Betsy hurried back the way she had come. She saw in the gaps between the buildings stubby barrage balloons lifting into the low, lead-colored sky. The city was just beginning to dim when she'd returned to her bedsit, lowered the backpack onto the table, and collapsed into a threadbare armchair.

She wanted to drift off to sleep, but instead forced herself up from the chair and closed the blackout curtains.

She had some veggies and tinned beans, and thought about preparing a meal. But she was more exhausted than hungry. And the Germans might interrupt her supper anyway.

She sat in her armchair and fell asleep trying to decide what to do with Henry Tucker's backpack.

* * *

When she awoke, the narrowest of cracks of light showed around the blackout curtains. Dawn. Betsy rubbed her eyes and squinted at her clock on the mantel. Almost eight o'clock.

She recalled no air warning sirens during the night. Whatever air raids the Germans carried out must have been against military targets farther north. Or maybe the bombers simply hadn't been able to find London. She was sure that had happened before, when the city was properly blacked out on moonless nights. Or when the RAF engaged the bombers when they were still over the channel.

Betsy stretched and yawned. Wouldn't it be nice to pretend the war was over?

Sometime during the night, she'd decided on what to do with what was in Henry Tucker's backpack.

There was no time, though, until tomorrow, when she came home from working at the hospital and had a few hours to spare. And then she might be too tired to carry out her plan.

No matter, she told herself, thinking again about the contents of the backpack. There was no rush about it, other than that it nagged.

21

Minnie Miner, around whom the news-talk program *Minnie Miner ASAP* was created, was a small, African-American woman with the energy of a Consolidated Edison power plant. She sat in a chair angled to face her guest, and dispensed deviousness and venom through the smile that made her a beautiful woman. She moved fast, in unexpected directions, and she talked the same way. News was her addiction, and she yearned to be right in the middle of it.

This afternoon her guest was the NYPD profiler, Helen Iman. She welcomed Helen vociferously and then put on a serious expression that was no more sincere than the smile it replaced. "You are, in a way, Helen, not a stranger to the D.O.A. killer."

Helen leaned forward in her armchair that was part of the set. She sensed one of the several cameras being dollied to a closer position, and tried to ignore it. "That's true," she said, "but remember, we aren't sure this is the same killer, pursuing his sick hobby in his old killing ground."

Minnie squirmed and inched forward in her chair. "Sick hobby? Is it your opinion as a professional profiler that the killer is sick?"

"He wouldn't agree with me," Helen said, "but yes, sick."

"Do you believe in evil, Helen?"

"I do, but—"

"Do you believe in demonic possession?"

"Er, no, I—"

"Might the killer be sick without being evil?"

"Pigs might fly." Helen was feeling irritated. She told herself to calm down; this was Minnie Miner's method, to get her guests to, accidentally or otherwise, say something important—or at least entertaining.

Minnie also cautioned herself. Helen had been on her program more than once, and had a way of using her without it being apparent.

"It's difficult not to think of him as evil," Helen said.

"But what if he really believes he's helping those women leave an evil and unforgiving world, helping them because *they* were too afraid or too unknowing to help themselves? I mean, maybe he's crazy but not, in his own mind, evil."

"He wants to be evil," Helen said. "If he is D.O.A., operating again in the area he so terrorized a few years ago, he's back in New York for a reason."

"He might know what he's doing is wrong, but if it affords his victims an escape, as he might think of it, from a callous and dangerous world, he might see his motivations as pure."

Ah, this was precisely where Helen wanted to go. "The thing is," Helen said, "he tortures them and creates tremendous pain. Some of his victims died in shock, their bodies simply unable to accept what was happening. It was urgent to the victims that they should tell the killer the truth; it was the only way to stop the pain for whole minutes."

Minnie made her eyes round, above the red O of her lips. "God, that sounds so awful."

"One might even say evil."

"Yes, yes, I understand now what you mean."

"And what the killer wanted his victims to know was that *if they lied to him* their futures were indefinite. So they spilled their guts, going back to school days, afraid of what *not* to tell."

"Do we know that for sure?"

"One would assume it after just a glance at the morgue photos."

"You make it all seem so logical—at least in the mind of the killer." Minnie shifted her weight, unable to sit still, and stared intently at Helen. "But why did he come back here, to New York, to resume killing? Isn't that especially dangerous for him?"

"Definitely. He wants it dangerous. He's egomaniacal. He doesn't doubt for a minute that he's the smartest one in this game of grisly chess."

"Egomaniacal," Minnie said. "Grisly chess games. That brings us around to Captain Frank Quinn."

"Yes," Helen said, "it certainly does. The killer sees Quinn as his alter ego, his flip side, his nemesis."

Minnie looked out at the world through the camera lens, wearing a puzzled expression. "But if Quinn is his nemesis, it would be easier for him to take up killing again in a different city."

"The different city wouldn't have Frank Quinn," Helen said. "If you were a chess master, you would want to avenge perhaps the only time you'd been out-witted, embarrassed, made a fool of for all the world to see." Helen shook her head in disgust. "As if the world is interested in this pathetic creature."

"So he sees himself as a loser?"

"God no," Helen said. "He sees himself as the victim of incredibly bad luck. Not for one second does this nutcase think he can be outwitted by the law, especially the law as represented by Frank Quinn."

"So he's convinced he's the better man. Or the better chess player."

"In his mind, they amount to the same thing."

"So he came back here to New York to resume his murders," Minnie said, trying to squeeze some more sensationalism out of Helen. "One of the world's biggest losers, here to kill some more."

"Not exactly," Helen said. "He came here to play chess. The sadism, the things he's done to these women, the sick torture techniques, those are just a bonus."

"Wow!" Minnie said, shaking her head as if she had water in her ears. "For once I'm happy to be my gender."

Helen sat looking at her.

"It's not always good to be king," Minnie said. "Especially in chess."

22

Nift, the obnoxious little ME, was on the job, bent so low that Quinn could see a bald spot on the top of his head. He looked as if he wanted to climb inside the dead woman on the bed.

Quinn, with Pearl at his side, looked beyond Nift to where Harley Renz stood with his fists on his broad hips, watching. He looked pissed off, as if he knew the dead woman, but Quinn figured the real source of Renz's anger was that the D.O.A. killer had taken another victim in his city. With Renz, that was personal, as was everything that posed a threat to his political life.

Quinn stepped closer to the bed and saw the familiar initials carved neatly into the victim's forehead. Nift had removed the wadded gag from her mouth, and her jaws gaped wide. Even with such a grotesque expression, it was obvious that the woman had been attractive.

"Hi, Pearl," Nift said, without seeming to notice Quinn.

Pearl didn't seem to notice Nift.

"Play well with others," Renz said.

All three of them ignored Renz.

Quinn moved forward, giving Nift a look he hoped would be a warning. He looked at the cuts, punctures, and burn marks on the naked corpse, heard in his heart the terrible silent scream of her gaping mouth.

"Same kind of injuries as with the Fairchild Hotel victims," Nift said. "No doubt we've got a D.O.A. victim here."

"Sure it's not the work of a copycat?" Renz asked.

The little ME seemed to swell. "I know my business, Commissioner."

Renz looked as if he might be about to lean into Nift. This wasn't the way an ME talked to a commissioner, especially one who had definite if distant ideas about the office of mayor.

Quinn shook his head slightly when Renz looked at him. There was no point in getting angry with Nift. That's how the little bastard got his jollies, getting under people's skin.

"What's with the catalogs?" Quinn asked, seeing colorful art catalogs spread all over the floor. Some of them had blood on their pages.

"The victim was an art restorer," Renz said. "Worked at museums and galleries. Doing restoration work at the Kadner Gallery down in SoHo. Looks like she was also an art connoisseur."

"Or our killer's the connoisseur. He seems partial to museums and the women who frequent them."

Quinn leaned low and read one of the subscription labels on the magazines. "Jeanine Carson?"

"That's her," Renz said.

"Was, anyway," Pearl said.

"They could have both been," Quinn said.

"What," Renz said.

"Art connoisseurs."

Renz said, "There's a question mark in blood on the bathroom mirror."

"No surprise there," Quinn said. "He's taunting. Saying, 'come on, play harder!' He's pretending to be bored."

In the corner of his vision, he saw Nift's hand run gently over one of the dead woman's breasts, pausing at the nipple. It made Quinn think of all those whispered stories about necrophilia that were considered NYPD myth. Nift didn't look so mythical to Quinn.

"Shame to kill a woman with a rack like this," Nift said, glancing at Pearl.

"Shame not to kill an asshole with a mind like yours," Pearl said.

Quinn sighed. He was relieved to see Renz smiling rather than angry.

"Let's talk out in the hall," he said. "Let the ME do his job."

"If we can trust leaving the victim alone with him," Pearl said.

"Enough of that kinda talk," Renz said. "It's nasty."

"What if it's true?"

"Even nastier." He led the way out of the bedroom, down the hall, through the living room crowded with CSU techs, and out into the hall.

They moved down about fifty feet so the uniform guarding the apartment door wouldn't overhear them.

"Who found the body?" Quinn asked.

"Super, name of Fred Charleston. He had an appointment to repair a dripping shower head. When he knocked and didn't get an answer, he figured the tenant had left for work. He let himself in with his key, found what you saw, and said he backed out of there and called the police. Uniforms got his statement, if you want to see it and talk to him."

"I'll read it and get to him later."

"He's no good for this," Renz said. "Was up arguing with his wife until late into the night, well past when the victim died. Got up early and went to the diner down the street for breakfast, stayed there until after the time of death."

"It happens at that diner," Quinn said.

Renz didn't get the joke. That was okay with Quinn. It bothered him when the commissioner came across as having a sense of humor.

"I'll go talk to Fred the super if you want," Pearl said.

Quinn nodded. "Good idea."

"Keep an eye on Jeanine with Nift," Pearl said.

Renz said, "Jesus, Pearl! The man's an employee of the city, just like I am. Let up on him."

"Nift will soon have her all to himself in the morgue, anyway," Quinn said. "She's beyond caring about anything he can do to her."

That seemed to mollify Pearl, in a smoldering-fuse kind of way.

23

Ｓhe would ship it by sea, to a place Henry Tucker would think suitable.

Betsy Douglass had spent much of the early morning locating a sturdy wooden shipping box that would contain Tucker's backpack. Finally she found one in the basement, where she had stored some blankets. She emptied the wooden crate and placed the backpack snugly inside.

She held the definite impression that the object it contained was real and valuable. Why else would it be the center of so much danger and concern? Whatever it was, it deserved her care. She owed that to Henry, whom she missed more every day.

She had assumed that when someone you loved died—and she realized she *did* love Henry—that the ache of parting would gradually become more dulled. Hers had sharpened by the hour and sometimes felt as if it cleaved her heart.

Inside the box containing the backpack, she laid the addressed instructional letter Henry had left. It was undeliverable, and probably its intended recipient, M. Gundelheimer, was dead. Most of the people on that heavily bombed block had died or were still missing, buried beneath the rubble.

Alongside the letter that had come in the backpack was another letter, this one written by Betsy to her sister, Willa Kingdom, and Willa's husband, Mark.

Mark had lost an arm when the merchant ship he was serving on had been torpedoed by a German submarine and sank in the Atlantic. He'd been one of only a few lucky survivors. Now he and his wife, Willa, were leaving England to settle in Ohio in the USA. Betsy wanted the box shipped to America so it would be waiting for them at their Ohio address when they arrived.

She found hammer and nails in the basement and nailed the box tightly shut so it would make its Atlantic journey without breaking open. Of course, there was always the chance of yet another U-boat attack. Betsy sighed, making a sound like a hushed breeze in the dim, silent basement. Life of late had become dangerous at every corner.

It wouldn't feel so perilous if Henry had lived. If only he and she had . . .

She turned away from that kind of speculation. From torturing herself. She wasn't the only one suffering because of the war. Now and again, like so many others, she had to remind herself of that fact.

Betsy found the two-wheeled wire cart she used to transport groceries, took it up to sidewalk level, then dragged the wooden box up after it.

She was breathing hard from the effort, and her legs

were trembling. Barrage blimps that sagged and looked partly deflated were visible beyond the end of the block, trailing what from this distance looked like slender cables.

The morning was quiet except for the steady, distant hum of traffic. A siren wailed forlornly from the direction of the hospital, where she would soon be helping to tend to the wounded, and comforting the dying.

She managed to lay the rectangular wooden box sideways across the top of the wire basket. Avoiding pits and cracks in the paved sidewalk, she began rolling the cart with surprising ease.

Here was something, at least, that was easier than she'd anticipated.

There was a fine morning mist in the air that smelled vaguely of charred wood, and something Betsy didn't want to dwell on.

She opened her mouth slightly and pulled in deep breaths of the air for whatever clean oxygen it contained. Now and then someone on the street—usually a man—would pause and look and seem to contemplate helping her. She shook her head to refuse them, and they went on about their business. A few of them gave her approving smiles. She continued on her way to ship her wooden box, knowing that Henry Tucker, if he were alive, would appreciate her faith and tenacity.

And love.

Only a few hours later Betsy reported for duty at the hospital. The shipping of the backpack and its contents seemed in a sad way to have severed all of her ties with

Henry Tucker. At the same time, it freed her from some of her grief. If he could rest easy in his grave, then, when the time came, so would she.

How very often she thought about death in this war.

What had being so close to it, day after day, done to her?

It was almost 1:00 A.M. when Betsy stumbled, exhausted, up to her apartment and undressed for bed. She removed her nurse's uniform and put it in the washstand in cold water with soap. Tomorrow morning, before leaving for the hospital, she would hand wring the uniform, then hang it up to dry.

She took off her slip, then her garter belt and white cloth stockings. Her knickers and the stockings she wadded and tossed so they landed near the washstand. She would retrieve them tomorrow and let them soak while she was on duty at the hospital in her second uniform.

Wearing only her nightgown and padded slippers, she ran enough water from the tap to capture in her palm and used it to wash down one of several white pills she'd brought home from the hospital. She didn't so much need the pills to help her get to sleep, but they aided sometimes in preventing the dreams from invading her slumber. Without them, she might experience some of the horrors of the day again, and wake up sweating and shivering. Afraid. So afraid . . .

The physical effort of what she had done today, starting so early in the morning, had taken its toll. As had being with men in various stages of their dying. She had tried desperately to be offhand and make them smile. Sometimes she'd been successful. But all the time she knew they would be leaving her as had Henry Tucker, changing for their survivors the world in which they'd lived.

For too long Betsy had suffered a lonely and miserable existence without Henry. Without understanding. Without love.

England was fighting for its survival, and there was no time for romance, but that's when the most irresistible kind of romance found a way.

To be on the safe side, Betsy swallowed a second pill.

After making sure the blackout curtains were secure, she dropped backward onto the bed as if launching herself sightless into a dark abyss.

She so welcomed the escape of sleep.

Only a few minutes after lying down, she heard air raid sirens. The raids were occurring more and more often, almost becoming routine. Unless you happened to be in the target zone. Then nothing routine might happen ever again.

Fate. That was all it was about. Good luck or bad.

Betsy knew she should wake up all the way. Go to the building's lower level, or to the underground stop a block away. But she didn't want to be in the crowded train tunnel, or alone in the musty basement, or share her terror with old Colonel Tattersilk from upstairs who, when they were sheltered, seemed to be hoping for loud near misses so he had an excuse to hug her close in the night.

She didn't want to get up. She was so, so tired . . . Exhaustion was an antidote for fear. That and the mind-numbing regularity and frequency of the air raids. The waves of German bombers, with smaller fighter planes sometimes flying escort. More and more often they were engaged by RAF fighters, leaving twisting, turning white contrails hanging like indecipherable messages in the sky.

Betsy lay motionless in the darkness, waiting for tonight's crisis to pass. Maybe the Luftwaffe wouldn't visit England tonight. Even Germans had to rest.

After a while the air raid sirens seemed to be fading. Sleep was about to claim her, and she was willing.

Betsy might have been dreaming the throbbing hum of the marauding German aircraft. Dreams and reality were becoming almost interchangeable.

It sounded as if there were a lot of planes, but they were well off in the distance, to the south, perhaps still out over the channel.

Too far away to care about. So spent was Betsy that she decided to ignore the German bombers. Britain was winning the war in the air. Churchill had said so just yesterday. The raids were becoming less frequent, and the odds that bombs would fall where she was were slim.

She slipped back into sleep, and didn't awaken even when aircraft engines pounded directly overhead.

She never woke up.

24

Building super Fred Charleston and his wife, Serri, sat side by side on the sofa, trying not to look frightened. That wasn't easy, with the big cop and the busty beauty with the intense dark eyes sitting in chairs opposite them.

They were in the super's cramped apartment on the first floor. The big cop, Frank Quinn, was slouched in the chair where Serri usually sat, reading her papers or watching TV and bitching about how badly the world was being run. The Middle East, especially, concerned her.

Charleston was a stocky, fidgety man in his forties, with unruly black hair and a face made to look pinched by an oversized nose that left him little upper lip. He wore a gray outfit that was more or less his super's uniform. His wife, Serri, was also in her forties. She had blond hair that was lighter than her eyebrows. She would have been attractive were it not for an air about her, as if she minute by minute detected a different suspicious odor.

"So you figure you and Serri began this big argument about seven thirty?" Quinn said to Fred Charleston. Cops' eyes, neutral yet at the same time unnerving, bore into Charleston.

"I know it was around seven thirty," the super said. "Serri was upset about poison gas in the Middle East, and it got so I couldn't finish my dinner, which we always start to eat at seven on the dot."

"Why is that?" Pearl asked.

"So the tenants know," Serri said. "That way they won't be pestering Fred and me during our dinner. You wouldn't believe some of the shit they pull."

"But last night, *you* pestered him. Or so he says."

"No, I can become a pest, I know. And a loud one. But sometimes you gotta stand up for yourself."

"That's for sure," Pearl said, flashing looks at Quinn and Fred, becoming Serri's friend and ally in the war of the sexes.

"It ain't like you're an expert on the Middle East," Fred Charleston said to his wife. He glanced toward the kitchen. "Now, poison gas, maybe."

"See the crap I gotta put up with?"

"Yes," Pearl said.

Fred gave Pearl a surprised look. The big cop wasn't going to get involved. He looked neutral as the Supreme Court. Fred was being ganged up on here. He said, "We'll be helpful as we can."

"You don't have to be an expert to see what's wrong over there," Serri said, looking at Quinn, then at Pearl. "And I figure what Fred and I say to each other's private anyway. None of the neighbors' business."

"True enough," Quinn said, "but you can count yourself lucky some of those neighbors were eavesdropping last night, and you two were giving them a show at the same time Jeanine Carson was being killed. Of course, the time's not nailed down. Stories change. The investigation is fluid."

"Fluid? You mean just because I found Jeanine's body means I might have murdered the poor woman?" Charleston asked. He seemed astounded. Serri didn't.

"*Might,* sure," Quinn said. "Going into an investigation, we suspect everybody. Starting with the last person to see the victim alive, and the first to see her dead."

"Like on TV."

"We like it when it ends like on TV, too," Quinn said. "All wrapped up tight and tidy for a commercial."

"Seems to me the *first* person to see a victim dead would be the killer," Fred said. He had a nasty, almost invisible little grin. Quinn was beginning to dislike him a lot.

He wasn't the only one. Pearl looked peeved.

"Don't get all smart with us," Pearl said. "Alibis were made to be broken."

"What the hell does that mean?" Serri asked.

Wrong way to go, Pearl thought, remembering how, in domestic cases, the partners often wound up siding with each other against the investigating officer.

"It's just something we say."

"Fact is," Quinn said, "most of the tenants don't recall hearing the fracas between you and your wife." He didn't mention that the tenants on either side of the super's apartment *did* hear it. Quinn fishing.

Fred rose like a gullible guppy to the bait. His features reddened—a man with a temper. "These old walls are about two feet thick. That's one of the reasons folks rent here. Neighbors don't tend to overhear each other's conversations in this building."

"There's always the vents to carry sound," Serri said. Nipping at her husband. She leaned slightly forward when she spoke, and projected a tireless tenacity.

Quinn was beginning to side with Fred, even though he disliked the man. Maybe because he disliked the wife more. Pearl was secretly grinning at him.

"Wouldn't know about vents," Fred said, in control of himself now, if not his wife. "I work mostly on the plumbing."

"Which is how you discovered the body," Pearl said.

"Roy Culver, who lives in the apartment above Jeanine Carson's, had a leaky toilet where the bowl went into the stack and needed it looked at. He knew I was gonna go into his apartment this morning—you can ask him."

"Did," Pearl said.

"Looked like water from the bowl was gonna run down into Jeanine's bathroom, right underneath, and it had to be stopped right away or there'd have been a lotta damage."

"Culver called you last night, but you waited till this morning to tend to the plumbing."

"Had no idea as to the seriousness of it until I actually looked at it and learned the stack was involved. That's when I knew I had to talk to Jeanine, and fast. Get her permission to do some work in her apartment. Ordinarily, I wouldn't let myself into her place on my own, nor anybody else's, but you know how much destruction water can do."

"We do," Quinn said. "And the neighbors *did* hear you arguing almost nonstop till about midnight."

"That's when the wife got tired," Fred said.

Pearl glanced at the seething energy that was the wife. It was hard to believe she was ever tired.

"Is it possible," Quinn said, "that the neighbors heard the victim and killer arguing and assumed it was you and your wife?"

The super was silent for a long time. "I guess it is," he finally said. "But truthfully, it ain't in the least likely."

"Hmph," Quinn said, nodding thoughtfully.

All of a sudden nobody had anything to say.

"I've gotta agree that the Middle East is a bitch," Pearl put in, looking at Serri. It was odd how, even with her blond hair and blue eyes, Serri Charleston possessed a vaguely Middle Eastern countenance. Or maybe Mayan. Strange . . . Like two components that didn't mix. "Your maiden name—" Pearl began to ask.

"O'Reilly," Serri said.

"She might be half Irish, but she's knowledgeable on the Middle East," Fred said. "Television, newspapers and all. Serri thinks all those explosives used on innocent people is a crime."

"I guess she's right," Quinn said.

"Acts of war," Serri said. "All that military hardware being used over there."

"You're not an expert on munitions," her husband told her.

"I know a war when I see one. And don't tell me I don't know munitions."

Quinn was beginning to get weary of the problem with the Charlestons' marriage. It was a dogfight not to join. He and Pearl didn't want to get embroiled in a politically charged discussion.

"I guess war is war," Pearl added. Nothing like a little overarching, meaningless philosophy to throw a blanket on things.

"It's what happened in Jeanine Carson's apartment last night that interests us," Quinn said.

"The neighbors would recognize our voices," Fred said, having given the overheard argument scenario more thought. "We both have real distinctive voices."

Which was true.

Serri Charleston said, "We're alibied up,"

"Hmph," Quinn said. "You do watch a lot of television."

"Including the military channel." Serri, not letting up.

"That might be what the neighbors were hearing coming from your apartment last night."

"They were hearing the real thing," Serri said. "And it don't look like me or Fred shot at each other. And I never noticed any tank tread marks on the carpet."

"But then you weren't looking for them," Quinn said.

"Actually," Pearl said to both Fred and Serri, "we're more curious about what you might have seen or heard than about whether you have alibis."

"We told the cops in uniform about where we were and what we done and how it came to pass that I found poor Jeanine Carson's dead body," Fred said. He swallowed hard and seemed suddenly in danger of vomiting. Then he appeared to have fought back the impulse. "All that blood and . . . the rest of it. That ain't a sight I'll soon forget."

"We know how it is," Quinn said softly.

"I don't see how the two of you stand it," Fred said. "The business you're in."

Quinn ignored the comment. "There's a lot of art on the victim's apartment walls," Quinn said. "She ever talk to you about it?"

"No. She was into art. Some kind of art repairer for the museums is what I gathered."

"An artsy type," Serri said. "Liked to think so, anyway. Had a thing about French painters. At least that was my impression."

Quinn stared steadily at her. Her expression was blank. Being with Serri was something like being with Harold.

Fred Charleston had turned pale and was making a visible effort to breathe evenly. Concentrating. Trying to get his memory out of that bloody apartment, away from the dead woman. Not paying the slightest attention to what his wife was saying. He'd pay for his lack of attention later.

Quinn decided the super couldn't be faking it. Vomiting would certainly add to his credibility, but Quinn had learned how to read people like Fred, and figured the henpecked super had never killed anyone. Quinn didn't need to see any real regurgitation to be convinced.

The queasy super's story seemed simple and honest enough. Quinn thanked him and his wife and stood up, letting them know the interview was over. Pearl left a card on the coffee table, snapping it down as if it were a high card out of a deck, and said, "Call us anytime."

Fred stayed seated, still obviously upset by walking in on a butchered woman who had been a tenant and at least something of a friend. An artsy friend at that.

"Thanks both of you for your help," Quinn said. He meant it; he had seen a lot of what it was like when someone's life intersected suddenly and bloodily with the dead.

Serri stood, tucked the card in a pocket, and escorted them to the door.

"It's jarring to discover a dead body," Pearl said. "Especially when it's a murder victim. Sometimes a session with a professional counselor can help. Jeanine Carson's death seems to have hit your husband hard."

"Like a rocket-propelled grenade," Serri Charleston said. Still in the Middle East.

"Those things make a lot of noise, cover up a lot of other noises," Quinn said.

Leaving her to wonder.

25

Quinn wished the mayor smoked cigars. Then he, Quinn, wouldn't have to wonder so much, be so uneasy. He could never remember when and where cigar smoking was legal in New York. Or what the penalty was if you were caught puffing illegally. Death, probably. If not by lethal injection, then from the cigar.

So here Quinn was, walking to the office from a subway stop that disgorged its passengers in a neighborhood just now being gentrified. Amid the paint fumes, the rancid scent of ages-old plaster dust, the stench of trash and garbage still curbside for pickup, the odorous assault of exhaust fumes, strolled Quinn with his offending cigar.

The horrified and angry glances of a cluster of passersby indicated to Quinn that he was probably breaking the law. He puffed on.

Quinn's cell phone rang. Nothing tricky about it—just the regular, well-worn repetitive ring that had presaged so many meaningful conversations since Alexander Graham Bell had turned the device loose on society.

It took Quinn a few seconds to wrestle the thing out of his pants pocket.

He squinted down at the tiny illuminated screen. Renz was calling.

"What've we got, Harley?" Quinn asked, veering toward a low brick wall in front of a vacant-looking stone building.

"A break," Renz said.

Quinn sat down on the wall and exhaled cigar smoke.

"Are you smoking one of your Cubans?" Renz asked. Casually, as if an admission of guilt might slip smoothly out of Quinn.

"Cuban what?" Quinn asked, with an inner smile.

"Never mind."

"So what's the break?"

"We found Jeanine Carson's cell phone tucked down between the cushions of her sofa. The sofa was the kind that opened and became a bed, so the phone slid down out of sight in the mechanism."

Quinn felt his interest quicken. "Anything helpful on it?"

"Maybe. There were a lot of calls to the phone from Andria Bell's number."

"Any recorded messages?"

" 'Fraid not. The last such call was made from La-Guardia airport the morning of Andria's death and the mass murders at the Fairchild Hotel. Another call that day, from Jeanine Carson's phone, went to a Winston Castle."

A new player?

"Is that a person or a place?" Quinn asked.

"Both, in a way. A guy named Winston Castle owns a restaurant called the Far Castle, on the Upper West

Side. He runs the establishment, along with his wife Maria."

"I don't know the place," Quinn said.

"It hasn't been open all that long. One of those trendy theme restaurants. It's been renovated to resemble a medieval castle, with towers, narrow vertical archers' windows, concrete cornices, gargoyles, and a serene English garden where customers can dine among statuary and topiary. The garden was put in when the neighboring building, a closed lamp and fixture shop and showroom, collapsed and created an empty lot. Castle extended his long lease on both lots. Did it in such a way that the leaser receives a cut of restaurant profits."

"You're telling me this Winston Castle is a kinky businessman type."

"Weaver went to the restaurant to size him up. She said phony stands out all over him."

Quinn didn't like the idea of Weaver running around without his supervision, but he knew there wasn't much he could do about it. And he trusted her judgment.

"Anyway," Renz continued, "there was enough space and rich enough soil to extend the garden. There's even a miniature but baffling English hedge maze."

Quinn was surprised. "A valuable piece of Manhattan real estate used for a garden and maze?"

"Yep. New York for you. When Castle is asked about selling it, he laughs and tells prospective buyers he's planning on putting in a moat and alligators."

Quinn looked across the street, where a Con Ed crew had arrived and had put up cones and sawhorses to divert traffic. Four husky guys wearing hard hats, swaggering around and striking poses as if they were on camera. And maybe they were. One of them was wrestling a jackhammer from the back of their dusty van.

"And Jeanine Carson talked to this guy on her phone the day Andria Bell died?"

"Talked to him or his wife."

"Maybe she called to order takeout," Quinn said. He took a silent pull on his cigar and exhaled carefully, turning his face away from the phone.

"You think I would have called you before checking that out?" Renz asked. He sounded genuinely injured. Weren't they both pros here? *He* must be a pro—he was the goddamned commissioner.

"Sorry, Harley," Quinn said, halfway meaning it. "I'll get on this."

"Whatever you come up with, let's keep it under our hats for now."

"By 'our' you mean only Q&A Investigations and you."

"Correct, Quinn."

"And Nancy Weaver?"

"Of course. She's a great snoop. Got the balls of a cat burglar."

"I don't know that much about her anatomy," Quinn said.

"You *don't?*"

Quinn understood the incomprehension in Renz's voice.

"That's her reputation, Harley, not her anatomy."

"Whatever works for you," Renz said. He paused. "You absolutely sure you're not smoking one of those Cubans?"

"Sure as sure can be," Quinn lied.

"I know that tone, even over the phone. You could be lying to me about cigars and Weaver. Probably you're batting at least five hundred."

"You got an address on the Far Castle restaurant?" Quinn asked, steering the conversation away from cigars and Nancy Weaver and batting averages. There was already enough rumor and innuendo about the woman. It all seemed to overlook the fact that she was a damned good cop.

Renz gave Quinn the address, a block off Amsterdam.

"Your part of town," Renz said. "Moats and alligators would fit right in."

"My cigar smoke keeps alligators away," Quinn said. "And for some women it's an aphrodisiac."

"You bastard! I knew it. You're smoking a Cuban! You know damned well there's a law against—"

Quinn broke the connection. He wondered if there were alligators in Cuba.

There must be, he decided.

26

After talking with Renz, Quinn walked back toward the office, unobtrusively smoking his Cuban cigar until it was a mere stub. He dropped it on the sidewalk, stepped on it with a crushing turn of sole, and deftly kicked it into the gutter.

A heavily perspiring woman in blue Lycra and walking a bicycle glared at him as if he'd just killed a puppy.

"Biodegradable," Quinn said.

She seemed not to hear.

He didn't enter the office. Instead he passed it by half a block and got into his old Lincoln, parked in the shade of one of the larger trees lining the sidewalk. The trees sprouted from five-foot squares of bare soil. Some of them had flowers planted around them to create miniature gardens.

It was too hot to walk, so Quinn drove the Lincoln to the Far Castle and found an illegal parking space near a fire hydrant. He placed his NYPD placard, which he'd taken with him when he retired, on the dashboard and strolled back to the restaurant on the corner. It oc-

curred to him that he was becoming something of a
scofflaw. Which made him smile.

Harley hadn't been kidding about the English garden. There was all sorts of greenery near the restaurant
itself, which did indeed resemble a small medieval castle, complete with gargoyles and turrets and a crenel-
lated roofline. There was room for half a dozen or so
tables near the garden, protected by a fringed green
awning.

The garden was deliberately slightly shaggy, in the
way of English gardens, with geraniums and hibiscus
plants, and various flowers and tall grasses Quinn
couldn't identify. A large concrete birdbath was almost
completely overgrown with vines. There were a number of rosebushes here and there, some of them with
obvious thorns.

The only part of the garden that didn't seem to have
taken root by chance was the hedge maze. It was about
seven feet tall and in the slanted light presented a
somewhat ominous entry point. The maze didn't cover
a lot of ground, but it made a lot of right-angle turns.
Quinn saw a woman's languid bare arm extend and
wave near the center of the maze. He heard her laughing. She was having fun and not calling for help. He
figured it would be hard to stay lost in the maze for
long.

He watched a young server come outside and set up
a large tray so she could deliver lunches to some of the
tables. Glad he wasn't wearing armor, Quinn went inside where it was cooler.

Despite it being the slow time for restaurants, between the lunch and dinner crowds, the Far Castle was fairly busy. It was softly lit, with dark paneling beneath thick wainscoting. Some of the lighting was from the narrow archers' windows high above the tables. Between wainscoting and windows were mounted large posters featuring European films. Quinn recognized some of the better known ones: *La Dolce Vita, The Man Who Loved Women,* the Italian versions—or originals—of Sergio Leone/Clint Eastwood spaghetti westerns. There was a small bar where a few people enjoyed drinks while waiting for tables. Food servers in simple black-and-white, vested outfits bustled among the white-and-red checked tables, balancing large round trays of food. A door between dining area and kitchen seemed perpetually swinging. Soft opera music—Puccini, Quinn thought—wafted throughout the restaurant.

A maître d' in a black tuxedo appeared with an amiable smile and Quinn unobtrusively showed him the NYPD shield Renz supplied Q&A during these work-for-hire cases. He asked to speak with Mr. Castle. Quinn felt foolish the instant he pronounced the name, wondering if there really was such a person.

Well, why not? There was a Ben. There was a Jerry.

The maître d' didn't change expression. He led Quinn to the swinging door. Quinn was made suddenly hungry by the spicy scents that engulfed them as, timing it just right, the maître d' escorted him through the opened door to the kitchen. Some kind of pasta dish on a tray flashed past Quinn almost near enough for him to take a bite.

He'd expected to see Winston Castle in his office. Instead the maître d' motioned for Quinn to wait just inside the kitchen door, out of the way of the controlled madness, and went to speak to an overweight man in his forties in a white shirt and black-and-white tie. A white apron was tied around his bulging stomach. He had broad shoulders, a broad face. A stout, rather than sloppily fat, body. He gave the impression he might be extraordinarily strong and tireless.

There were two other chefs, thin, wiry types, who looked as if they were trying hard to keep up with human dynamo Castle.

The maître d' motioned for Quinn to come forward, which Quinn did, making sure he avoided the hot sauces and flashing knives, cleavers, and spatulas. Something sizzling and being deep-fried in a tall pot flecked hot grease with a slight sting on the back of Quinn's hand as if trying to draw his attention as he passed.

As he advanced through the warm and busy kitchen, and the assault of hot oil and spice scents, Quinn saw that Winston Castle's black mustache turned up at the edges in a way that made him appear to be always smiling, as if the surrounding havoc somehow pleased him. The kind of guy who always saw things as being under control, and so, for him, they were.

He led Quinn through a door at the rear of the kitchen that opened out into a section of the garden that was semiprivate, about twenty feet from the tables outside that were placed along the sidewalk. There was a single round metal table there, uncovered by a cloth. Castle motioned with a sweeping arc of his arm for Quinn to sit in one of the wrought iron chairs.

Quinn settled into a chair and looked around appreciatively. You usually didn't see a garden like this in Manhattan unless it was on a roof.

* * *

A waiter appeared with two tumblers of ice water on a tray. When he was gone, Castle lowered his bulk into a chair near Quinn's. It was cooler at this table, the view mostly limited to green shrubbery, some of it trimmed as topiary: a bird with plumage, a small horse, a large rabbit. This part of the garden was well tended and symmetrical, and the traffic sounds from beyond the shrubbery seemed out of place and time. Where was the stomping and blowing of horses? The bark of dueling pistols? The clashing of swords and lances?

Castle was wearing black boots that looked as if they belonged in a pirate movie. A watch on a gold chain peeked out of a small pocket in his vest. Despite the heat of the weather and the kitchen, he wore a puffy blue-and-white ascot. Quinn felt as if he were talking to someone from the nineteenth century. Or was it the eighteenth?

It made him feel odd when he said, "Messages to your cell phone suggest you know someone named Jeanine Carson."

Castle seemed to think over his answer, which seemed odd. He either knew or he didn't know the late Jeanine.

"I knew her, but not as a friend." He affected a slight English accent. "She did call me several times."

"What was the purpose of those calls?"

"I'm not sure. I had to leave our conversations rather abruptly because of pressing business. You might have noticed we're understaffed here."

"No," Quinn said. "It looked to me as if you had so many employees they were getting in each other's way. How about Andria Bell? Know her?"

Castle gave his broad smile, but it seemed slightly forced. "Busy as I am, I keep up on the news. I know Andria Bell as one of the victims in that horrible mass murder at a hotel. I'm assuming that's why you're here." His smile grew even broader, revealing impossibly perfect, very white teeth, perfect for clenching a knife blade as he swung aboard another ship. "Am I a suspect?"

"You and over ten million others."

"It sounds as if you have long and tedious job."

"It works out that way sometimes."

"You'll need extra help from time to time, as I do here at the restaurant."

The jovial smile remained the same on Castle's flesh-padded features, but Quinn understood that this wasn't a stupid man; Castle was more than ready to play conversational darts. "Did Jeanine mention anything that might have suggested she felt she was in danger?"

"Not that I could surmise. But when I saw her name in the paper, and what had happened, I determined to phone you."

"But you didn't."

"That's because I had another, more curious phone call, and I wondered if the calls might be connected."

"Why is that?"

"I said I didn't know Jeanine Carson as a friend, and that's true. I also know that Andria Bell and Jeanine were . . . quite close. They were both involved in the art world. So was a woman named Ida Tucker, who called me."

Quinn was wondering where this conversation was

going—if anywhere. He was trying to keep it straight even as he wondered about Winston Castle's sanity. This guy was too much of a character to be genuine.

"That would be after Andria's death," Quinn said.

"Yes. This Ida Tucker tried to negotiate by phone to buy a piece of art that I don't possess." Something, along with a wider smile, an added sheen to his complexion and sparkle in his dark eyes, transformed Castle's face. "She claimed it was a lost Michelangelo sculpture titled *Bellezza.*" He leaned closer to Quinn and dropped his voice even lower. "That means—"

"It means *beauty* in Italian," Quinn interrupted.

"Very good! The Tucker woman described a small white marble bust of a beautiful woman that was said to have been modeled after a *very* influential courtesan of the church. Legend has it that she was murdered to ensure her silence."

A courtesan of the church.

Quinn met Castle's glance, trying to determine what the game was. *What the hell am I getting into here?*

Castle seemed dead serious.

"So what did this marble bust look like?" Quinn asked. "Other than it was white?"

"She didn't describe the bust in detail, but said she inherited some letters her brother-in-law, Henry Tucker, wrote on his deathbed that do describe it. She said she was afraid to mail such information or discuss it over the phone. So she gave the letters to a trusted friend, who was traveling to New York with some students anyway. She was to show the letters to me."

"Andria Bell," Quinn said.

Castle nodded. "Exactly. She phoned but didn't

make a connection. When she did reach me and we talked, she seemed to be feeling me out. She did say she had some letters, but she was hesitant to show them to me."

"Why would she be hesitant?"

Castle shrugged his beefy shoulders. "I suppose she wanted to make sure I was the right man. I would think this bust is worth a great deal of money."

Quinn smiled. "Money enters into almost everything."

"Yes," Castle said, "but this seemed to be about something other than money. Something more was making her cautious."

"What would that be?"

The thick black mustache across from Quinn perked up in a grin. "That's what I want to hire you to discover." Castle's twinkling dark eyes looked beyond Quinn.

"Ah, Maria!"

Quinn looked where Castle was staring and saw that a dark-haired woman, attractive but built somewhat too short and heavy to be fashionable, had come outside to join them.

"My wife, Maria," Castle said, with a sweeping motion of his right arm, as if introducing a celebrity. "Detective Quinn is about to agree to help find *Bellezza*."

The fleshy, dark-haired woman smiled warmly. Flesh crinkled around her dark eyes, but not in a way that made her look older. "That's wonderful."

"I haven't exactly—"

"We're paying him fifty thousand dollars if he's successful," Castle said.

Maria seemed unmoved by the number.

"You have to understand," Quinn said. "I'm leading the efforts to find and stop a serial killer."

"The one who killed Andria Bell and those other poor women."

Maria appeared distressed. Quinn thought she'd surely cross herself, but she didn't.

"This is something of a bonus for you, Detective Quinn," Castle said.

Quinn wasn't thinking of the money. Well, the money came second in his musings. The city of New York was compensating Q&A generously, but Castle had a point in suggesting that this wouldn't be a conflict of interest. The missing bust and the mass murders at the Fairchild Hotel had become intertwined—find *Bellezza* and find the killer. That seemed to be how Winston Castle saw it. He was probably right.

This was, Quinn decided, one investigation. Why had D.O.A. become not only a serial killer but a mass murderer? The likely answer to that was something in his conversation at MoMA with Grace Geyer. As he was stalking Geyer, she had unknowingly tipped him to even bigger game. D.O.A. had simply seized opportunity.

Quinn saw the possibilities here. If the killer had stumbled into something that enticed him, and that had unexpectedly developed into mass murder, maybe it would be one of his rare mistakes. The one that might lead to his death or apprehension.

"You will accept our payment for your services?" Castle asked.

"Let's see how the investigation goes," Quinn said. "See just what the connections are. Then we can talk about the return of the bust."

Castle suddenly seemed to get taller, paunchier, distressed and insulted. Quite a gamut of emotions played over his wide features. "I can assure you the bust is not stolen property from some museum."

"We'll check the museums as a matter of routine," Quinn said. He was somewhat surprised by Castle's concern for his honor and reputation.

"We shall shake on it," Castle said, extending his hand. Another abrupt change of mood. He moved in on Quinn and pumped his hand with a crushing grip. No limp-handed English handshake here. This shake had sealed the deal.

"This is wonderful!" Maria said, beaming at Quinn. "We were so distressed by the deaths of both girls."

Quinn was confused. "There have been seven victims."

"Yes, of course. I didn't mean to slight anyone." Now she actually did cross herself, absently and so quickly that Quinn barely saw it. "It's the two who most concern us, but the others are held just as close and dear to the breast of—"

"Which two are those?" Quinn asked.

Maria clasped her hands, and her Renaissance peasant features became solemn. "Andria Bell and Jeanine Carson."

Quinn felt as if he were lost in the nearby hedge maze. D.O.A. had slain Jeanine Carson to keep his hand in, to divert, to taunt Quinn. Other than what might have been a coincidental involvement with art, that was the two women's only connection—they were tortured and killed by the same sadistic, cunning animal. Used as pieces in the game he played.

"Sisters," Maria Castle said. "They were—God help them—sisters."

27

"Sisters, all right," Jerry Lido said.

He had spent much of the night doing ancestry research online. He'd informed Quinn that he hadn't had a drink since the day before, so Quinn wasn't positive of Lido's findings. The Q&A tech whiz did his best work while fueled by alcohol. While skunked, actually.

He was slumped in an uncomfortable wooden chair angled toward Quinn's desk. His shirt was half tucked in and his tie was loosened and askew. Quinn noticed that Lido's hairline had receded what seemed like another inch or so, leaving a sharp widow's peak.

"Andria Bell and Jeanine Carson are daughters of Ida Tucker and Robert Kingdom. Jeanine was briefly married to a Brady Carson, who died three years ago in a boating accident on Lake Erie."

"What kind of accident?"

"Explosion. Fumes from the boat's engine compartment built up and went boom." Lido shrugged his bony shoulders. "It happens with some frequency.

Nothing suspicious about it, and nothing to suggest there was an investigation."

"Was he alone on the boat?"

"No, he was with a fishing guide. That's whose boat it was. The guide lived long enough to tell his rescuers what happened. Carson had ducked below deck to get some tackle, and he lit a cigar. It was unlit in his mouth when he lowered himself down through the hatch, and he had a book of matches in his hand. That was all the guide remembered. He'd yelled for Carson to be careful, but it was too late." Lido gave a weary, wicked grin. "Bad things can happen when you light a forbidden cigar."

Quinn pondered that.

"Learn anything useful about the sisters?" he asked.

Lido gave his weary shrug again. His inebriated mannerisms had invaded his sober world. "Both dead," he said.

"Don't give me a lotta crap, Jerry. I get enough of that with the menagerie I have to contend with here."

"Every one a Sherlock," Lido said. "Speaking of which—Weaver."

Quinn rested his elbows on his desk and leaned toward Lido. "Nancy Weaver?"

"The same. While I was doing my research, I came across her tech footprints."

"Meaning?"

"She'd recently visited several of the sites I explored."

"Doing her own exploring?"

"Looked that way. No surprise. She belongs to Renz." Lido raised his eyebrows. "She has to be pretty good on a computer, judging by what I saw."

"Weaver has multiple talents."

"That's what I hear, but who really knows?"

Quinn's land line desk phone rang. He nodded to Lido, dismissing him, and snatched up the receiver. The phone's caller ID said the call originated at the Far Castle.

Quinn identified Q&A and himself, watching Lido drift out the door. On his way to catch up on either his drinking or his sleep. Quinn knew how he would bet.

"This is Winston Castle," said the voice on the phone. It was well enunciated and deep. Castle's BBC voice. "There's been a development that might be of interest to you."

"Try me," Quinn said. He couldn't get over the feeling that he was being played by Castle. He reminded himself, not the first time, that the business he was in might create that kind of suspicion. Everyone he met while on a case didn't necessarily have some sort of angle or ulterior motive. It only seemed that way.

"That woman called me again, about ten o'clock last night," Castle said. "Identified herself as Ida Tucker again and said she was a distant relative of my wife."

"Is she?"

"Maria isn't sure."

Quinn bet Jerry Lido could be sure. He wished now that Lido hadn't left. On the other hand, even Lido might not be able to straighten out this mess. "So why did Ida Tucker call?"

"She wanted to negotiate some more on that Michelangelo bust, *Bellezza*."

Quinn was beginning to really like this case. "Negotiate what?"

"Not just the missing art, but the letters she claimed are with it, the ones Henry Tucker wrote on his deathbed, just before he succumbed to wounds he'd suffered at Dunkirk. She wanted me to come to someplace called Green Forest, Ohio, and examine and purchase the letters. I asked her to simply mail me copies, but of course she wouldn't do that. What's valuable—in her mind, anyway—is what the letters contain, as well as their authenticity."

That made sense to Quinn. So did something else. "Why didn't you simply tell her no thank you and hang up?"

"Because I'm curious. And so are you, eh, my friend?"

Quinn smiled. Castle had him there.

"We're both afflicted with that dread disease, curiosity," Castle said. "The one that killed the cat. And there's something else. This time when we talked, Ida Tucker seemed especially interested in whether the police had found any letters among the contents of Andria Bell's luggage, or in the hotel suite where the murders took place."

"And what did you tell her?" Quinn asked.

He could almost see Castle's devilish dark smile over the phone. "I told her nothing, of course. She was so curious, I thought I'd leave her that way. Knowing you'd understand."

"Oh, I do," Quinn said.

* * *

Quinn caught up with Jerry Lido at the Dropp Inn lounge, a few blocks from the office. It was a bar with a step-down entrance that caused first-timers to stumble. Regular customers amused themselves by silently watching newbies for interesting falls and reactions. Dim and cool inside, the Dropp Inn at this time of day was almost deserted.

Quinn knew about the tricky threshold, but nevertheless had to take a quick double step to maintain his balance when he entered.

There was one other drinker besides Lido in the lounge, an absolutely ravished looking gray-haired woman in her sixties. She had an expensive-looking choppy hairdo, and without the wrinkles in her clothes she would have been stylishly and crisply dressed, as if for finance and business. There was a sadness about her bearing that was almost tangible. She made Quinn wonder if the stock market had tanked.

Lido was slouched in a cramped wooden booth near the opposite end of the bar. At least he'd had sense enough to stay away from the woman. Though he was glancing in her direction.

"That's how you're going to wind up," Quinn said, motioning toward the life-worn woman as he slid into the seat across from Lido.

Lido squinted at the woman and brought her into focus. "Oh, her. I happen to know she's eighty-seven."

"Like we are," Quinn said.

"She's a gin drinker," Lido said.

"I've seen you drink gin."

"I've seen you try to keep up."

"Not one right after the other in slow-motion suicide."

"She was probably beautiful once," Lido said, still staring at the woman. "I can perceive that in her still."

"You're beginning to sound like Winston Castle."

The bartender came out from behind the bar and stood over the booth. These weren't free, these seats on the sidelines while the world slid past outside.

Quinn ordered the same kind of beer Lido had—a microbrewery brand he'd never heard of—and a fresh one for Lido. Quinn figured Lido had had time to consume about three or four beers, so he might be at his perceptive best.

"I need to ask you something more," Quinn said.

Lido gave him a mushy grin. "I didn't think you followed me here to assess the female presence and possibilities."

"Not that female," Quinn said, with a nod toward the woman at the bar. "A woman named Ida Tucker. Do you recall where she fits into the family tree whose roots and various branches you researched?"

A certain gleam appeared in Lido's bloodshot eyes. A sharpness that Quinn recognized. In its strange way, alcohol acted as some kind of cerebral lubricant that allowed Lido's thoughts to follow appropriate tributaries to surprising headwaters.

In a voice not at all slurred, he said, "Let me tell you about Ida Tucker."

"And the rest of her family. The whole mess of a maze of them."

Lido smiled. Sipped. "I took it back to Henry Tucker, a British soldier who died in an English hospital after escaping the German advance at Dunkirk." Lido fixed a bleary eye on Quinn. "We're talking World War Two here."

"I figured," Quinn said.

"Henry had a brother, Edward. Edward had a wife, Ida. Okay?"

"Sure."

"Henry, at the time of his death, was having a hot affair with an English nurse named Betsy Douglass. Betsy had a sister, Willa, living in Ohio and married to a Mark Kingdom."

"Okay," Quinn said. "Mark and Willa Kingdom. Should I be writing this down?"

"I'll give you a printout later," Lido said. He continued. "For medical reasons, Willa and Mark couldn't have children—he'd been injured in the merchant marines—and they adopted two wards of the state: Robert and Winston. That's where the two families intersect, in the breeding grounds of Ohio. Winston died in childhood."

"Wait a minute," Quinn said. "Winston Kingdom? Winston Castle?"

"Not yet," Lido said. "He's actually Robert Kingdom, Jr. He's something of an Anglophile."

"I'll say."

"Still, he's married to Mariella Lopez, a Mexican immigrant."

"Maria? Are you kidding me? I assumed she was Italian."

"She is Italian. Her last name was Righetti until she married a Mexican mathematician named Lopez. He died five years ago."

"Don't tell me his boat blew up."

"No, he was struck by lightning. A year later, Mariella migrated to the U.S. and married Winston Castle. Whose name was Kingdom, Jr. then."

Quinn took a long pull of his beer. "Isn't anything the way it appears with this family?"

"No. And they seem to take some delight—or at least satisfaction—in that. That sort of thing is genetic, don't you think?"

"Yes," Quinn said. The older he got, the more madness he had seen, and the more he thought people were, at least to some extent, slaves of their DNA. But with this family, blood relationship didn't seem essential to share the lunacy.

Lido continued: "After Willa Douglass and Mark Kingdom died in a tornado, Ida Tucker divorced Edward, and married Robert Kingdom, Sr. She continued using her former name, Tucker. They adopted sisters, Andria Bell and Jeanine Bell. Also they adopted a son, Robert Kingdom, Jr., who now, for reasons of his own, calls himself Winston Castle."

"Ah! Anybody else in the family using an alias?"

Lido shrugged.

"Why was this family so eager to adopt?"

"Money accompanied children who were wards of the state. That's one reason. Another might simply be that they were big-hearted people."

"Those kinds of people do exist," Quinn admitted.

"It's not just you and me," Lido said.

"Or maybe they do things simply because they are mad."

"But with purpose," Lido said.

"Robert Kingdom, Sr. and Ida Tucker," Quinn said. "Despite the *Senior,* wasn't she robbing the cradle?"

"Ida was considerably older. But judging by photos I saw on the net, she was a hot potootie. Maybe still is."

Lido took a swallow of beer, licked his lips, and continued:

"Willa must have hunted down Edward Tucker after the war. The two families intersected and merged into the bunch we have now. Many of them were adoptees, or the sons or daughters of adoptees. Orphaned or farmed out. Dependent on each other. Maybe more so than in other families. The more I learned about them, that's what came out. The entire zoo struck me as . . . needy. And I don't mean just for material things." Lido lifted his shoulders and dropped them as if they were suddenly burdened by great weight. "I dunno, Quinn. I guess plenty of people are needy. I'm no expert on family life, but it seems to me there are lots of families like this one, the way marriages and parenthood have gone all to hell."

He looked as if he expected Quinn to agree or disagree.

Quinn had no feel for the subject. He did consider that his ex-wife and daughter lived in California, and he lived with Pearl and the young woman he considered to be like his own daughter, who was by blood Pearl's daughter.

Was any or all of this bad? Or inevitable? Who knew? The Tuckers and the Kingdoms and their offspring, natural or adopted, did constitute a support system. Perhaps one that filled a greater need than if they'd been blood relatives and belonged to something whether they liked it or not.

Quinn said, "So Ida is making arrangements to claim the bodies of her daughters."

"Looks that way," Lido said. He drank some beer

and then wiped his foamy upper lip with the back of a knuckle. "Will she be coming to New York?"

"I don't know." Quinn finished his beer and placed the bottle precisely in the center of its round coaster. He had to admit he was curious about this "hot po-tootie." "Talking about her dead daughters isn't something I look forward to." He had discussed the grisly deaths of relatives too often in his life.

"Don't worry," Lido said. "That's why you have me."

"To worry?"

"To do things like this," Lido said, and unfolded a sheet of paper and laid it in front of Quinn. "I worked up a sort of family tree."

Quinn examined the neatly handwritten document

Henry Tucker/Betsy Douglass

Edward Tucker (brother)/Ida Tucker (Divorced)
Willa Douglass & Mark Kingdom
Adopted: Robert (Sr.) Kingdom &
Winston Kingdom (died as infant.)
Ida Tucker/Robert Kingdom (Sr.)
Adopted: Robert Kingdom, Jr. (AKA Winston
*   Castle; takes Winston's name as family name.)*
Andria Bell
Jeanine Carson
Winston Castle/Maria Castle

"What are they," Quinn asked, "a family of traveling gypsies?"

"Maybe something like that," Lido said, "but they don't do that much traveling."

"They aren't really that much family. A lot of them aren't even blood relatives."

"Maybe they're even closer than blood relatives," Lido said.

"How could that be?"

"Need."

Quinn thought back. "Maybe."

"They tend to lie a lot. Play roles." Lido grinned. "You want I should find out more about this family?"

"It would take a load off my mind," Quinn said.

Wondering why Winston Castle had pretended Ida Tucker, his adoptive mother, was a stranger.

Also wondering how much of Lido's information was accurate. In various families, for various reasons, subterfuge was deeply ingrained. Sometimes it was for reasons long forgotten, and left behind like a curse.

28

The killer watched from deep shadow as Nancy Weaver emerged to ground level from her subway stop near her apartment. She looked right and left like a good girl and crossed the street. This part of the Village consisted mostly of walkup apartments slightly larger than shoeboxes. And Weaver's block featured old-fashioned streetlights that, scenic and period New York as they were, cast very little light.

They suited the killer's purpose.

He crossed the street farther down the block and was directly behind Weaver again. Keeping close to buildings and taking advantage of shadows, he observed her moving from pool of light to pool of light. One psychologically safer island, then another.

Not that she was afraid. Uneasy, maybe. Which wasn't the same thing. The killer had to grin as he watched Weaver making her way home. Unaware. Unafraid. She exuded confidence. Who did she think she was? Badass cop with a gun in her handbag.

There was a warm fog tonight in the Village, and

few people were out walking in it. Those who were would probably have a difficult time identifying other walkers. Vehicle traffic had slacked off, too. Now and then a truck rumbled along the narrow streets. Or a cab, its tires hissing on the damp pavement, not slowing down for pedestrians. It seemed that all the cabs were occupied. A mist and a spritzle of rain could do that in New York. It was as if the cabs had pop-up passengers that were activated by a mere drop of rain.

Weaver was easy enough to follow without being seen. Her buxom narrow-waisted figure was simple to identify in the dim light, and the few men who passed her walking in the opposite direction usually reacted by glancing back at her.

The killer understood how she'd gotten her spotty reputation. A woman like that would always be thought about first in sexual terms. He wondered if she'd decided, since she was going to have such a reputation anyway, that she might as well do the deeds and enjoy life with the proceeds. Let the heads shake and the tongues wag. The killer could understand why a woman would think that way. He fancied he knew a lot about women.

This one, Weaver, for sure. She had quite a reputation in the NYPD and was easy enough to research. Once he'd seen her with Quinn, and coming and going at the offices of Q&A, he had plenty of information to build on.

He was glad she was in the game.

He walked on through light and shadow, his soft-soled shoes making only the slightest scrunching noises on the hard damp concrete. He thought it was time to prod Quinn again. Not by going after Pearl. Or Quinn's adopted (if she was) daughter Jody, or his daughter Lauri, in California (off the game board).

Nancy Weaver.

Yes, Weaver was the best choice, a woman who for years had been a part of Quinn's life.

They were closer to each other than they knew.

The killer understood that there was nothing of a personal or sexual nature between them, but their friendship, being a lasting one, would be the loss of something held dear. Weaver might be an informer for the idiot commissioner, Renz, but she was also protective of Quinn, and he of her.

How would Quinn feel if his faithful friend arrived contained in several boxes shipped to him on consecutive days?

How the killer wanted him to feel, that's how. And such shipments could certainly be arranged. They would, in fact, be great fun.

The killer had familiarized himself with Weaver's building. It was one of a row of narrow brick structures whose architecture suggested they were built in the nineteenth or early twentieth century. Its big, heavy street door opened to a small foyer. There was no elevator. Another heavy, paneled door led to a narrow stairwell. That door required a key.

The killer's plan was to close the distance between him and Weaver as soon as she'd entered the foyer, but before the street door had closed behind her. He would press all the way inside quickly, perhaps as she was keying the stairwell door, and have a gun digging into the side of her neck before she realized what was happening. He would slide the gun lower, raking her back with it so that it was at waist level. That way he could shield it from view with his body, in case they encountered anyone coming down the stairs. The gun would stay there tight to her body while they slowly climbed the stairs, and Weaver unlocked her door and they entered her apartment.

With the door closed behind them, he would strike her head hard with the heavy butt of the gun, enough to daze her if not knock her completely unconscious. It was a tactic he'd practiced long and diligently, and he knew exactly where and how hard to hit. Weaver would be down and dazed before she knew what happened.

Then the fun would begin.

It was all choreographed in the killer's mind, every move, every reaction, every counter move. Like a simple dance that, if the dominant partner led quickly and forcefully, would always end the same way, with a woman stunned and helpless before the killer.

If she happened to remain semiconscious, Weaver would still be vaguely wondering what was going on.

She was a cop. So what? A cop knew what a nine-millimeter bullet would do to her if she disobeyed. Weaver would have her choice of obedience, or having bloody chunks of her bone, muscle, and internal organs blasted all over her apartment wall.

Weaver slowed and was fishing around in her purse for her key to the stairs. She came to a complete stop at the three concrete steps leading up to the small stoop and door to her apartment building.

Then she found the elusive key, withdrew it from her purse, and placed her right foot on the first step.

The killer's heart began to race, not from fear but from anticipation. The scenario he'd mapped out was firm in his mind. Weaver had no choice but to follow the script.

God, he loved this!

When she was on the stoop, with her back toward him, she reached forward to open the door to the foyer.

That was when the killer tensed to move.

Then froze in position, leaning forward but luckily still in shadow.

A figure had approached from the opposite direction, tall, darkly dressed. With a cap the killer recognized even through the mist.

This was a uniformed cop.

As the killer watched, the cop entered the pool of light from the electrified nineteenth-century gas street lamp near Weaver's building. He was in his thirties, broad shouldered and with the paraphernalia of his trade dangling from his thick black leather belt. Including a holstered gun.

Weaver had turned and was coming back down the steps to the sidewalk. She and the cop came together in a tight embrace, then kissed each other on the mouth. The cop bent her slightly backward and she lifted one leg like the star of an old movie, as if her calf was a lever that released some of the pressure of her passion. The big cop probably saw it at the lower edge of his vision and was proud that he was responsible.

Finally they came apart, each stepping back, holding each other's hands, gazing into each other's eyes, and grinning stupidly.

They finally broke physical contact with each other and entered the apartment building together.

The killer moved farther back into the shadows and watched a light come on in the window that he was pretty sure would be Weaver's. As if to confirm the fact for him, Weaver appeared at the window. Then the cop loomed behind her, cupping her ample breasts in his hands as she reached for a cord and closed the drapes.

The two lovers remained somewhat visible, but only as moving shadows on the drapes, distorted by folds of fabric. The killer leaned his back against the unyielding support of a brick wall and continued watching the window.

Shadows merged, separated.

Merged. Separated.

The light went out.

Half an hour passed.

The bedroom light came back on, but the uniformed cop didn't leave.

It disturbed the killer, the way fate had intervened in the form of another cop and saved Weaver's life. He couldn't help but suspect that it might be an omen. Or a reminder. Fate was on his side, but he mustn't count on it too heavily. He must continue to plan carefully, to be bold yet detail-minded.

The formless shadows were back, wavering and dancing behind the closed drapes, sometimes pulling apart, sometimes merging. The killer knew Weaver's reputation, her sliding scale of ethics, and there she was enjoying her base instincts, saved by her crassness and immorality.

Rewarded for her bad behavior.

It hardly seemed fair.

The light behind the drapes went out again. The killer stood in the mist, looking up at Weaver's blank window for a long time.

Angry, determined, patient.

And, he had to admit, lonely.

The dark window stared back at him like a disinterested eye. He could only imagine what was going on behind it. He tried not to think about it. He and the cop wanted the woman for entirely different reasons.

Or did they? Both of them wanted, in their own ways, to totally possess her, if only temporarily.

There's the difference. The temporary part.

There was nothing temporary about death.

That dark knowledge didn't make the killer any less lonely. The ache was still there, living and squirming in the pit of his stomach.

How could certain women do this to him? Even the doomed ones?

Especially the doomed ones.

He knew the cop might not leave until dawn. Maybe he and Weaver would even go someplace together and have breakfast. Bending toward each other over second cups of coffee. Sharing their conversation after sharing their passion.

The killer wondered what they'd say to each other. What secrets would they trade like cards that might be played later?

Annoying complications, the police.

Eventually he walked a few blocks to a corner and hailed a cab.

The driver spoke a language he didn't understand.

PART THREE

A life is beautiful and ideal, or the reverse, only when we have taken into our consideration the social as well as the family relationship.

—HAVELOCK ELLIS, *Little Essays of Love and Virtue*

29

Quinn had called for an appointment.

He sat in a comfortable wing chair in the director's office at the Kadner Gallery on Fifth Avenue. It was a small gallery that also acted as a brokerage, directing art sellers to Sotheby's and Christie's, as well as to smaller, specialty auctions or private sales. Occasionally the gallery featured an exhibit by a hopeful artist, and even had discovered a few who became famous.

Relatively famous.

Someone who had worked with Jeanine Carson had made the appointment for Quinn with the Kadner Gallery director, a large-headed, narrow-shouldered man in a well-cut blue suit. His name was Burton Doyle. He'd lost most of his graying hair up top, and compensated by wearing it long on the sides, where it curled wildly over his ears and at the nape of his neck.

When Quinn was settled in the wing chair, Doyle sat down behind a wide desk that had what Quinn thought were Queen Anne legs. Papers were piled on the desk, including a tented bright Christie's catalog. A cup of tea or coffee sat steaming on a folded paper napkin serving as a saucer. Three wire baskets laden with papers were stacked vertically and crookedly. They were labeled IN, OUT, and LIMBO. Next to them was a ceramic mug stuffed with pens and pencils. It was the desk of a busy man.

"*Bellezza,*" he said, smiling at Quinn. "I suppose you want to know where it is."

"If it is," Quinn said.

Doyle seemed to assess Quinn, as if he might have some value in the art market, then smiled. "Oh, it exists, all right," he said. "Or at least it's thought to exist. No one with a true appreciation of art or beauty could destroy it, and no one with even a hint of its monetary worth would consider devaluing it in any way."

"Even if it were stolen and unsalable on the open market?"

"Especially then."

"I can understand," Quinn said, "why some people would find great satisfaction in simply owning it, looking at it from time to time by themselves."

Or owning in a different way, like our killer, who might own and cherish the memories of beauty's violent end at his hands. Not for nothing did the French describe orgasms as "the little death."

"Fanatical collectors," Doyle said. "The art world is full of them. Always has been."

Quinn thought it likely that the killer he sought was one of those fanatical collectors, hoarding precious recollections of dead women instead of art.

Or might he collect both?

It seemed likely.

Serial killers often had a horrible or confused relationships with their mothers, or sometimes their sisters. A woman of true beauty, of marble perfection, might provoke extreme possessiveness. Or murder.

Doyle leaned back at a dangerous angle, causing his desk chair to squeal the way Quinn's chair did at Q&A. "If you really understand such people," Doyle said, "and you think *Bellezza* is in the hands of some obsessive connoisseur who probably won't so much as hint that he or she has the bust, why are you wasting your time trying to find it?"

"I'm not sure the kind of collector we're talking about has the bust."

A gray, arched eyebrow raised. "Oh? Why not?"

"There isn't a story," Quinn said.

"Story?"

"About what happened to *Bellezza*. People who are willing and able to sit on valuable stolen merchandise usually provide some sort of explanation as to what happened to it—a fire, maybe. Or destruction by vandals. Or another art thief or a gang steals it to resell. Or they don't know its value and destroy it. Or it's in somebody's attic, or was painted over and made into a lawn ornament."

"I understand. It's easier if you have an explanation, even if it isn't terribly plausible."

"But they're *all* plausible? Given the context."

Doyle absently ran his manicured thumb back and forth over a sharp pencil point. "All those things are possible," he admitted.

"At least on *Antiques Roadshow*." Quinn crossed one leg over the other and cupped his knee with laced fingers. "My guess is that the bust doesn't exist, or that whoever has it doesn't realize its value."

"Then what do you want?"

"To know more about it."

Doyle raised his gaze so he was looking up at a point somewhere above Quinn's right shoulder. The expression on his face changed to one of . . . what? Reverence?

"It's said that the bust was sculpted from marble by the hand of Michelangelo himself in the early sixteenth century," Doyle said. "It was commissioned by the church. As you probably know, the subject and model for the sculpture was a woman who was of questionable moral fiber, especially for those days. Still, she was a favorite of many high in the priesthood."

"How high?"

"Think big, Detective Quinn."

"Ah."

"The bust had its place in the nave of the great cathedral, but a new pope didn't like its connotations, or its political implications, so he had it removed. Some said it was battered to dust and scattered in the hills."

"But you don't think so."

"I don't know. It seems to have turned up in the hands of a wealthy merchant in Venice around sixteen hundred. A man who dealt mostly in spices, but was also a collector."

"What about Bellezza? The flesh-and-blood one?"

"Congratulations," Doyle said. "Most people forget to ask that. She disappeared at the same time the bust was removed from the cathedral."

"What did Michelangelo have to say about all this?"

"Nothing, as far as we know."

"And the wealthy Italian Merchant?"

"After his death, his premises were searched and, supposedly, *Bellezza* wasn't found."

"Untimely death?"

Doyle shrugged.

"What did the church do?"

"It provided solace. As it is now, it was then in the business of saving souls, not solving crimes. In the nineteenth century, *Bellezza* turned up in the collection of an Egyptian art aficionado who died a violent death. Though no one I know of actually claims to have seen it. It is said that the man's brother claimed the bust, and took it with him to Morocco. A wealthy Moroccan bought it for an unknown price, and the sale was contested. The French government declared it theirs, as the French were wont to do, and it was shipped to Paris and installed in the Louvre."

"Then it's real. There's a record of it being in the Louvre."

Doyle smiled. "Yes and no. The records of the Louvre became more than slightly altered during and immediately after the Second World War and German occupation." Doyle made a face as if there was a bad taste on his tongue. "Shortly after the occupation of Paris, the Nazis confiscated much of the city's great art. Among the pieces they . . . stole, was *Bellezza*."

"Or so it's said."

Doyle again shrugged his almost nonexistent padded shoulders. "Lots of people tell lots of lies about things that are beautiful. The truth is, we don't know what happened to *Bellezza*. Rumor had it the bust became part of Hermann Goering's personal collection, but that seems not to be true. There's no record of it ever reaching

Berlin. But that was true of a lot of art. It doesn't mean *Bellezza* didn't get there. For that matter, maybe Goering *did* obtain it. If so, who knows what happened to it. Goering was a madman."

Doyle took a sip of coffee or tea. Both eyebrows raised. "I've been remiss. Would you like a cup of tea? Coffee?"

"Thanks, no," Quinn said.

Doyle blew on the cup, as if the tea were scalding. "And now you are attempting to find our missing beauty." He sipped cautiously. Didn't say ouch. "Forgive me if I'm cynical, but I have reason. You aren't the first to search for *Bellezza*. For a while it was the great daydream accomplishment of hundreds of art students. That's all changed now." Another sip. "I'll be glad to talk to you anytime. To help you any way I can. But I can't pretend I don't think your quest is hopeless. You might as well have dropped in to ask for help in finding the Holy Grail. The possibilities are about the same. Virtually nonexistent. Everyone has conceded that *Bellezza* isn't going to be found."

"Not everyone," Quinn said. He stood up, stretched, and thanked Doyle for his time.

Doyle didn't stand up immediately. He still had his enigmatic smile pasted to his face. Kept it while he stood and offered his hand. "Good luck, Detective Quinn."

"Do you think the bust was ever real?" Quinn asked. "Existed at one time? Still exists somewhere, somehow?"

"I thought I made that unclear," Doyle said.

"What if I talk to other people in the art world?" Quinn asked.

"That's where I got my information." Doyle shifted his weight, deepening the soft squeaking of his swivel chair. "If you don't mind my asking, why are you so interested in finding *Bellezza?*"

"I'm not," Quinn said. "I'm interested in finding a serial killer."

"The dead women at the Fairchild Hotel," Doyle said. "What do they have to do with a sixteenth-century bust?"

Maybe everything.

Quinn moved to the door. "Maybe *Bellezza* can tell me."

"If she does," Doyle said, "I want to introduce you to Mona Lisa."

30

Barefoot, wearing only a pair of shorts, Dwayne looked in on his dead parents before going down to the garage. He flipped the opener light switch to Off so the garage stayed dark when the heavy overhead door rose. The roll and rumble of the door seemed unusually loud in the still night.

Leaving off the lights of both cars, Dwayne moved his father's big Mercedes out of the driveway. Then he backed Maude's Chrysler convertible from the garage and out of the way. He had some trouble with that one, as it was a stick shift and Dwayne had practiced only on cars with automatic transmissions.

But he got the job done. Then he moved his father's car into the garage, and replaced it in the driveway with Maude's. The third car in the garage, his father's Porsche, he didn't touch.

Now it would appear as if his father had driven to his office as usual in his Mercedes. When Bill Phoenix came by later this morning, as Dwayne knew he would, he would see only the Chrysler convertible parked in the driveway—his signal that Dwayne's father wasn't home and it was safe for Phoenix to "clean the pool." Maude should be waiting, probably sprawled in her lounger with a catalogue.

After flipping the toggle switch to its usual position, so the light would come on when the garage door was raised or lowered, Dwayne went back upstairs.

He looked in on Maude and his father, like a dutiful son.

Neither had moved. Everything in the room was the same.

Remaining only in his shorts, Dwayne went to his bedroom and set his alarm clock. He knew Bill Phoenix would be at the house at ten o'clock, and seeing Maude's car, he would pull in behind it with his service van. It was where he usually parked; in the driveway, sheltered by the palms and bougainvillea, the van couldn't be seen from the street.

Then Phoenix would walk around the house to the pool, where Maude should be waiting. After a little while, they would stroll together to the cabana, where they were safe from being seen by any part of the outside world.

Since it was summer, and there was no school, they would assume that Dwayne, a late riser, was still asleep in his bed. Dwayne didn't much care for swimming, so even when he happened to be awake, he always stayed in the house. So Maude and Phoenix thought.

Dwayne switched the ceiling fan on low and got back in the bed. He lay curled on his side, his cheek resting on his upper arm, and almost immediately fell asleep.

He didn't dream.

* * *

At 9:45 A.M. Dwayne's clock radio played the recorded-and-saved Cyndi Lauper number about girls and fun.

Dwayne's eyes opened but he didn't move right away. His throat was dry, so he swallowed several times and then yawned. Memory of last night came to him in pieces, and he smiled.

People underestimated him because he was young. He didn't mind that. It was an advantage, and even at his age he'd learned how to use it to the fullest. He had a handle on things.

Dwayne relieved himself in the bathroom off his bedroom, adjusted his shorts, then flushed the toilet. He rinsed and dried his hands, then got half a dozen tissues from the dispenser on the granite vanity.

He carried the tissues to his Father and Maude's bedroom and removed the knife from the bed.

He had plans for the knife.

31

At 10:01 A.M., here came Bill Phoenix.

From where Dwayne crouched concealed by the oleander bushes near the garage, he watched Phoenix's white pool service van hesitate at the bend in the driveway, then continue and park where Phoenix and Maude had determined the vehicle couldn't be seen from the street.

Phoenix climbed down out of the van, walked around it, and got a long-handled pool skimmer out of the back. A breeze ruffled his swept-back dark hair as he swiveled his handsome head to look in all directions. His gaze slid right over Dwayne.

Dwayne knew the skimmer was a prop. In the off chance somebody dropped by and caught Phoenix and Maude together, Phoenix could stop whatever else he was doing and begin skimming leaves and debris out of the pool. Just like that, he would become the proper and preoccupied hired help, engrossed in his job rather than in his employer.

With the skimmer propped on his shoulder, he strode across the lawn toward the back of the house and the pool, where he assumed Maude would be waiting as planned.

As soon as Phoenix was out of sight, Dwayne went to the van and opened the door on the passenger side. He gave the knife that he'd used on Maude and his father a final wipe with the tissues so it would be free of any fingerprints that weren't smeared. Then he slid the knife beneath the passenger seat, closed the door softly so Phoenix wouldn't hear, and hurried out of sight, concealing himself near the bushes by a big date palm.

Less than another minute passed before Phoenix reappeared, carrying the pool skimmer at waist level now. After leaning the skimmer against the van, he walked up to the front porch. He wore a slight frown, and seemed aggravated and vaguely puzzled.

Dwayne knew what Phoenix was thinking. Maude was probably still in bed. Her husband was gone, and even if he wasn't and came to the door, Phoenix could go into his pool cleaner routine. The worst that could happen is that Phoenix would actually have to clean the pool. If Dwayne's father wasn't around, Dwayne himself might come to the door and would tell him where Maude was.

Assuming an attitude of boldness, Phoenix leaned on the doorbell.

When he got no response, he knocked.

Knocked again. Harder. This was turning out not to be a good morning.

His hands propped on his hips, he left the porch and strode back toward the van. Then he changed his mind, kicked a small rock off the driveway, and went back up on the porch. He knocked again.

This time when he got no response he tried the door-knob.

It turned. The house was unlocked.

Phoenix eased the door open, stuck his head in, and yelled hello. Shouted, "Pool man!"

Dwayne had never heard Phoenix refer to himself as "pool man." It sounded like some kind of superhero who rescued people who bumped their heads on their diving boards.

After the third hello, Phoenix called for Maude. When he got no response he called Dwayne's name.

Phoenix stood for a while, pondering, then seemed to gather resolve. He went inside, leaving the door open about a foot.

Time passed. The jagged shadows of palms trees dancing in the breeze moved this way and that on the porch.

Dwayne waited.

When Bill Phoenix emerged from the house, he was white. Dwayne was surprised. He didn't think a person—especially one with such a great tan as Phoenix's—could suddenly turn so pale. Phoenix was stumbling as he walked toward his van. Something that had to be vomit glimmered on the chest of his sleeveless T-shirt and down one leg.

Dwayne stepped out onto sunny the driveway and walked toward him, grinning. He raised a hand in greeting. "Hi, Bill. You seen Maude?"

Phoenix staggered past him and didn't seem to have seen him.

"Hey, Bill . . ."

"Don't go in there!" he heard Phoenix call, as he

clambered into his van. "For God's sake, don't go in there!"

Dwayne watched as the van roared and shot backward. It swerved back and forth, once even going off the driveway and onto the grass. Leaving tire marks. Good. Dwayne couldn't see the van when it reached the street, but he heard its tires squeal as it sped away.

Dwayne would have liked it if the van had slammed into one of the palm trees, but this was okay.

He walked back to the house to phone the police. He wanted to call them before Bill Phoenix did. If Phoenix ever would.

Not that it mattered. The police would contact Phoenix.

32

"The police have released the bodies of my girls," Ida Tucker said.

Sitting primly across from Quinn and regarding him over his desk, she looked much younger than she had to be, which was somewhere in her eighties, perhaps nineties. Her back was straight, her chin outthrust and confident. Her blue eyes were steady. From years ago, a beautiful woman looked out from the ruins. "I've come to take them home, where they can rest with their family."

"I can't tell you, dear, how sorry I am for your loss." Quinn meant it, and his sincerity came across in his voice.

Ida Tucker swiped at an eye with the knuckle of her right forefinger. Quinn pulled a tissue from a box on his desk, then stood up and leaned over the desk so Ida could accept it. She folded the tissue in halves, then in quarters, and used it to dab.

"It's a hard thing," Quinn said. "Time might not cure, but it can help."

"Time is my best friend and worst enemy," Ida Tucker said.

"So it is with us all." *Thinking deep thoughts.*

"I suppose." She took a final dab at her eye and slipped the tissue into a pocket of the blue cotton tunic she was wearing.

"May I make an observation?" Quinn asked.

"That's part of your job, Detective Quinn."

"Andria was rather young to be your daughter."

"My husband Robert and I took her in as a ward of the state when she was quite young. We later adopted her."

"She was an orphan?"

"Let's just say she was unwanted."

"I see." Quinn wondered if there was any kind of police record, juvenile or otherwise, on Andria. He doubted it. Jerry Lido wouldn't have missed that kind of information. But then, why would he even look in that direction? This family seemed to have been pieced together with disparate parts, yet there was a curious glue that held them together. Before Quinn sat a woman who seemed too frail to be thought of as their guiding matriarch, but age and experience could harden a soul and give it the gift of guile.

Ida Tucker clasped her hands in her lap. "I was glad when I got the message at my hotel that you wanted to see me, Detective Quinn. I also wanted to see you. Have there been any meaningful developments in the murder investigation?"

"We're always working to develop new leads."

Her blue-eyed assessment suggested that Ida Tucker knew bullshit when she heard it.

"I take it you haven't learned anything new," she

said. "It's my understanding that if they're going to be solved, most murder investigations are successfully concluded within the first forty-eight hours."

"If that's true," Quinn said, "it's because in most homicides it's obvious who is the killer. Quite often it's the spouse standing over the body with a gun."

She gave that some thought. "Yes, I can see where that would be true beyond the make-believe world of entertainment."

"But very often it's evidence we discover during the first forty-eight hours that turns out to be important."

"I see. So you still have hope?"

"Absolutely."

"Our family hasn't fared too well when it comes to the timely solving of crimes," Ida Tucker said.

"Tell me about this unsolved crime," he said.

"During the war—the big war—an English woman shipped something to Willa Kingdom in a large wooden crate." Ida held her steady gaze on Quinn, making sure he understood. "From England to Ohio, where Willa lived with her husband, Mark. They'd just moved to Ohio. Mark was in the Merchant Marines and was badly wounded when his ship was sunk by a German submarine."

"That's too bad," Quinn said, thinking about how her information dovetailed with Lido's.

Ida shrugged. "War." She carefully adjusted her skirt, which had worked to within a few inches of one of her wrinkled knees. "When Willa pried the box open, it contained some bricks, and under the bricks were handwritten letters explaining what had been in the box, and why."

"Were the letters from the English woman?"

"Yes. Betsy Douglass was her name. The letters related what a British soldier named Henry Tucker had told her. It all made sense, except for the bricks, which obviously replaced what Betsy Douglass had shipped from England."

Quinn considered asking Ida if what Betsy might have shipped was *Bellezza,* but he decided to play that card close instead. There was no reason to tell Ida Tucker more than she needed to know. And there was reason to see how much she'd tell him.

"Why did this Betsy Douglass ship something to Willa?"

Ida leveled her gaze at Quinn. "Betsy Douglass was Willa's sister. Willa was born in England."

Quinn was interested in where this was all going. At sea on the waves of lies.

"Where are the letters that accompanied the box of bricks?"

Ida shrugged a bony, somehow still elegant shoulder. "They went missing."

"Stolen, you mean?"

"Possibly. They were available, then they were gone." She gave a sad grin that was almost a grimace. It made her suddenly look her age. "Part of the unknown original contents of the wooden crate."

"Willa must have read them."

"No. She simply glanced at their headings and signature, then replaced them in the box to examine them later. She was going to read them, then something interrupted her. I think she received a phone call. When she went to retrieve them, they were gone."

"So none of you knows what was in the box?"

"It appears that way.'

You sly old fox. You know what the box contained.

"So who was the phone call from?"

"That I don't know. People were calling Willa all the time. She volunteered a lot at church."

Quinn just bet she did.

Ida took a deep breath. "But that's not what we're talking about. And I'm here to claim the bodies of my daughters."

"Andria and Jeanine?"

"Of course."

"I'm just trying to keep things straight," Quinn said. "But they aren't really sisters. I mean blood relatives."

"Andria and Jeanine, as it happens, had the same biological father. He was a man they were well away from."

Hmmm.

Quinn's desk phone jangled like an alarm. He held up a hand, raising a forefinger to signal Ida Tucker that they weren't finished talking. As he picked up the receiver, Ida settled back in her chair. She was dug in, prepared to accept the worst of whatever Quinn might dish out.

The caller identified himself, before Quinn could get a word out. "Renz."

"I'm busy right now," Quinn said.

"Okay, but there's something you oughta know."

"I keep running across that," Quinn said.

"Something new on the DNA findings. Somebody at the lab doing a standard reevaluation of the blood samples noticed it. Two of the killer's victims have very similar—"

"Sisters," Quinn said. "Or maybe cousins."

"Choose one or the other," Renz said.

"Cousins for now. But I wouldn't want to make my guess permanent. It's complicated."

"That's a good word for it," Renz said.

"You know that hedgerow maze at the Far Castle?"

"Yeah," Renz said. "It looks confusing."

"Well, that's how this is."

Quinn looked across the desk at Ida Tucker.

She was smiling.

33

The killer wanted to see if Weaver went someplace unexpected. Someplace where there would be privacy if he arranged for them to be alone.

It wasn't unexpected that she headed directly toward work at the offices of Q&A. Maybe she had paperwork to catch up on. Runaways to find, burglars to apprehend, killers to kill.

All in a busy day.

Weaver paused near a doughnut shop, and stood as if contemplating. It was still morning. Not so late that she shouldn't enjoy a breakfast doughnut. Or maybe she'd already had breakfast and was going to buy doughnuts for the other cops. They'd owe her something in return. Unless she was repaying a doughnut debt of her own. That was how cops thought; somebody always owed somebody. Doughnuts were the coin of their realm. They took that crap seriously.

As Weaver crossed the street toward the doughnut shop, the killer found a place where he could lean on a black painted bannister and pretend to study a map. He looked like a tourist today, even carrying a cloth bag advertising a Broadway show. A long-running revival of a revival starring a burned-out cast. Something a tourist would savor.

Through the doughnut shop's steamed window, he saw Weaver slide into a booth while balancing a mug of coffee and a plate containing several doughnuts.

All for herself. *Selfish bitch.*

Or maybe not. She had to watch what she ate, with a body like that. A beauty for sure, but she'd have to control her diet in middle age.

If she reached middle age.

The killer settled in, knowing he'd be here awhile. Within a few minutes, he found himself getting hungry for a doughnut.

Quinn hung up the phone after his conversation with Renz. He hadn't told Renz about the box of bricks and straw that had been shipped from England, and he didn't mention the letters. They seemed to have disappeared, anyway.

Ida Tucker was still sitting patiently in her chair, her hands folded in her lap.

"Who do you think took the letters that were in the box?" Quinn asked her.

"Whoever took what else was in the box. Unless you think someone actually sent Willa a box containing nothing but bricks and straw all the way from England."

Quinn thought it was possible that the box's original contents were stolen in England, before the box was shipped, but he didn't mention the possibility.

"What do you think happened to whatever was taken from the box?" he asked.

Ida gave her frail shrug. "It's a mystery."

"Here's another one," Quinn said. "Why did Andria Bell call Jeanine Carson several times from LaGuardia airport the day she died?"

"I wasn't aware that she had. Maybe Andria simply wanted to let Jeanine know she was in town. They *were* sisters."

"That's true. DNA samples indicate that Andria and Jeanine were actually related by blood."

Ida fixed icy eyes on Quinn, as if her lies were a match for his facts any day. "It isn't a pretty picture. It involves degradation and rape."

Quinn tapped the sharp point of a pencil over and over on his desk and regarded Ida Tucker. She must have such ugly memories, know so much that she dreaded reliving even in her mind. Quinn decided not to make her paint that picture once again. Or the original picture, painted over.

Ida visibly swallowed. "Some of the foster homes the children were placed in were nightmares. When Robert and I decided to adopt, we met Jeanine. She was only ten years old. We had to have her. Then, when we learned she had a younger sister, we felt the kindest and best solution was to adopt both girls, raise them the rest of the way like the sisters they were."

"Did it work out okay?"

"Yes. Until they encountered the madman in your city."

"I apologize for my city," Quinn said. He leaned forward and gently patted the back of her hand. "I mean that, dear."

"I'm sure you do."

"It's odd though, wouldn't you say, that both sisters would happen to encounter the same madman?"

"A giant statue of a woman with a torch, standing on a tiny island out in the ocean, is odd. Riding in trains under the ground is odd. A seriously undressed cowboy playing a guitar at a busy intersection is odd. A giant ape climbing a skyscraper is odd."

"That last is just in the movies," Quinn said.

"And the other three?"

"Well . . . I get your point."

Ida stood up and smoothed her skirt. "If we're finished here, I'll go about the process of claiming my girls' remains."

"One thing more," Quinn said. "You never mentioned your adopted son, Winston Castle."

For a moment Ida seemed to draw a blank. "Oh! Is that what he's calling himself now?"

"Yes. He owns a restaurant here in town."

She waved a hand and smiled. "Good for him. He can be . . . rather aimless at times." Her smile broadened. "Like the rest of us. Anything more?"

"No," Quinn said, marveling. "You might drop by and see Winston."

"I might. Thank you for bringing him to my attention."

Quinn was finished talking to her anyway, so he let her call time. He had a feeling they'd have more conversations.

At the door, she paused and turned. "Will I have to identify the bodies?"

"They'll probably request that you do. It won't be as bad as you might imagine. They try to make it as easy as possible. Would you like me to send someone with you?"

"No," she said, after giving it a few seconds' thought. "I've seen worse, though I can't remember when. I can manage this."

"If *you* have any questions . . ." Quinn said. "Remember you have my number."

"I do have questions," Ida said. "Some I want answered, and some I don't."

He watched her go out into the sauna the city could become after a summer rain.

One of the questions Quinn wanted answered was who were the other people on Jeanine's cell phone? Most of them, he was sure, were simply friends, business associates, neighbors, businesses she frequented. Checking each number might be a waste of time, but it had to be done. And who could know if a real clue might present itself?

And if this family was so close, why had Winston Castle pretended that Ida Tucker wasn't his mother? And why would Winston Castle's mother not mention their relationship? Or seem not to think much of it when Quinn brought it up?

The logical answer, it seemed to Quinn, was that she wanted to protect her son.

Mothers were like that.

34

When Weaver left the doughnut shop, the killer counted to twenty and then fell in behind her.

All the doughnuts. She'd eaten all of them on her plate, and then gone to the counter and ordered more doughnuts to go. The killer was amazed again that she could eat so prodigiously and still have such an impressive figure.

The doughnut boxes left no doubt where she was going, so he cut over a block and picked up his pace. There was no way she could somehow spot him following her if he was ahead of her.

By the time Weaver, balancing the two flimsy white boxes of doughnuts, crossed the street toward the converted building that housed the offices of Q&A Investigations, the killer had found a suitable observation post. He watched from where he was shielded by a van some workers were loading with cut-rate furniture.

It was starting to rain. Just a drizzle, but some of it was running inside his collar and down the back of his neck.

Before Weaver entered the building, an elderly woman

exited. She tried holding the door open for Weaver, but Weaver won that contest, even with the boxes. The woman walked slightly bent by age, taking small, careful steps. Her head was bowed, as if she were thinking or depressed.

Weaver was almost certainly going to be at Q&A for a while. The killer fingered the cigarettes and lighter in his pocket. Thought about the knife taped to his leg.

Weaver could wait. This other woman, gray haired and obviously quite old, interested him. He was sure he'd seen her before, but the moving cloud shadows, the gray drizzle, hampered his view.

As the old woman left Q&A she turned to her left, away from the killer. He yanked his collar up higher, but it didn't help much.

He decided to give Weaver another day to live, so he might satisfy his curiosity about the old woman.

Where had he seen her before?

Then he had it.

The way she tilted her head to the side when she walked, as if she were a bird using her near eye to search for worms. The way she held her arms in tight to her body. A defensive stance.

Something about her reminded the killer of one of his victims at the Fairchild Hotel. Which one, though? He trudged after the woman, fastening the top button of his light raincoat.

It would come to him.

Wait! There was Weaver. She'd come out of Q&A's offices and turned left. It took the killer only a few seconds to realize Weaver was following the old woman who'd just exited Q&A.

Then he realized that an extraordinary piece of luck

had come his way. Weaver, saved once by her illicit coupling with a cop, was now being practically handed to him. Two victims would serve his purpose nicely, especially if one was an old woman related to one of the Fairchild Hotel victims. That would further confound Quinn.

If it weren't for the drizzle that had become a mist, Weaver would surely have seen or sensed him approaching from behind.

But he was sure she hadn't.

He fell back, plotted, anticipated, enjoyed.

At Broadway, the old woman stopped and stood in a shop doorway.

Then Weaver surprised the killer. As he watched, she approached the woman and the two of them stood talking for a few minutes beneath the shop's awning, where it was relatively dry.

So she wasn't simply tailing the old woman; she was protecting her. A mission Quinn had no doubt assigned to her.

Weaver stepped out into the mist and waved both arms as if attempting to fly, trying to hail a cab. The killer smiled. On a rainy day in New York, cabs seemed to morph into objects unlike vehicles.

As soon as the two women gave up, they would take a subway. Crowded as the subways would be, he could easily follow them without being observed.

Then, miraculously, the laws of probability turned upside down, and the unthinkable occurred before the killer's eyes. A cab veered from the flow of traffic toward the curb and braked to a halt directly in front of Weaver. Weaver held the door open for the old woman, then scooted into the back of the car with her.

Watching the cab drive away, the killer ran out into the street, waving for another cab. One honked its horn at him and then almost ran him down. He jumped back onto the sidewalk, dragging one foot. Water sloshed into his shoe.

The killer simply wouldn't accept this. *He wouldn't!*

He trudged over and stood beneath the shop awning where the two women had stood. The mist still reached him. He bitterly jammed his fists deep into his pockets. This was so like when he was a child, and nothing he did was right. He was an abomination. An unexpected and unwanted kind of horrible growth that had to be cut out of his mother's stomach.

Then he'd done something right.

Playing the dumbstruck, grieving child had been easy. The police had picked up Bill Phoenix and found the knife in his car, stained with the blood of Dwayne's father and Maude. Dwayne didn't have to make up much to describe details of Maude and Bill's secret affair.

Bill Phoenix knew he didn't have a chance, and Florida was a state that executed killers. He tried to evade the police in his white pool-service van, but didn't get far. He was apprehended in a motel parking lot.

Dwayne had inherited a multimillion-dollar trust that became his at the age of twenty-five. He'd established accounts under different identities and invested wisely, most often in art that he obtained surreptitiously through straw parties and then kept to and for himself. Much of the rest of his wealth was with various money management firms that he drew on from time to time. There was no reason anyone else should know his true wealth.

For years after his father's and Maude's deaths, he would dream about them writhing in the flames of hell. They would be aflame themselves, perhaps even clutching each other in their hopeless desperation. Screaming and dancing in their wild and terrible knowledge. Paying for each and every sin.

These were not nightmares.

Possibly all that money had spoiled the killer. That and his previous success and notoriety as D.O.A. By now, he was used to obtaining whatever he wanted. And he wanted Nancy Weaver.

The mist continued to send persistent trickles beneath his upturned collar and down the back of his neck. He ignored it. Head bowed, he made his way toward a subway stop, where it would be crowded but dry. Where he was sure luck would swing his way.

Nancy Weaver. He knew where she lived.

No matter how long he had to wait for her, he would wait. If she brought the uniformed cop home with her again, or another sexual partner, he would wait. He smiled his tight smile.

That Weaver didn't know he was waiting was immaterial. Soon she would belong to him.

So would the perfect woman who had no way of knowing his intention. She would someday become his most prized possession.

Women like Nancy Weaver were steps to the ultimate.

35

Nancy Weaver was tired of being wet. After dropping Ida Tucker at the morgue, and offering to go in with her and lend support, Weaver had stayed in the cab and given the driver her address and the nearest cross street. Until the cab pulled away from the curb, she watched Ida Tucker, moving like a much younger woman in her high heels, pick her way through pedestrians and umbrellas. Then Weaver slumped with the side of her head against the window, and through half-closed eyes watched traffic joust with traffic.

It took Weaver's cab almost half an hour to reach the intersection near her apartment. Close enough. The short walk to her building she made in almost a dash.

So relieved was she to be almost home and dry, that she didn't notice the nearby figure step silently from the shadows. His timing was exquisite. As Weaver pulled the heavy door open and moved inside to the foyer, he matched her step for step, all the time raising his long-bladed knife to her throat.

He was up against her before she knew it. She felt the knife point jab at the side of her neck, near the carotid artery, and smelled and felt the warmth of his breath, the fetid wetness of his long raincoat. The coat was black, and held the odors of the street: exhaust fumes, and the cloying garbage scents of whatever was in the pavement and set free by the rain. He had brought the night in with him.

The knife blade never wavering, he guided her up the stairs and along the hall. No one came around a corner, or happened to open their door and see them.

As they entered her apartment she heard him kick the door shut behind them.

The lights were off, and her assailant wanted to keep them that way. With the blinds open as they were, inside light would create quite a show for anyone down in the street who happened to look up, or for someone in one of the buildings across the street.

"We're walking to your bedroom," he said, pressing harder with the knife. The length of his body was tight against hers. She had no choice but to move forward. To lead the way. She knew that once he got her in the bedroom and down, she was lost.

As he propelled her forward, she pulled her purse open. Its clasp was magnetic and made no noise. At the same time, she veered slightly, toward where she knew the hassock sat near the corner of the sofa. It was low, and almost the color of the carpet, difficult to see in the dimness.

"I hope you're not dumb enough to—" the killer began, then tripped over the hassock that she'd barely brushed against.

Weaver spun while pushing free of the arm and hand

wielding the knife, throwing herself forward. As she fell, she dumped the contents of her purse out in front of her on the floor. This had to be fast. She wouldn't have time to root through the purse.

The killer was still frozen with surprise, but that would last only another few seconds.

She fell with an "Oomph!" onto the array of items that had spilled out of her purse onto the carpet. One of the largest objects was pressing against her rib cage, just beneath her right breast. It was either her wallet or her small .22-caliber Smith & Wesson handgun.

She rolled to the side, fumbling for whatever it was, and was dismayed to see that it was her wallet.

But lying right next to it was the small nickel-plated semiautomatic. Her hand darted toward the gun.

The killer tried to stamp on her hand, but just missed and merely thumped his foot on the carpet.

He'd figured the odds even before Weaver had considered them. He made the errant stamp serve as his first step toward the door.

He was opening the door as she was snatching up the gun.

He was through it as she aimed.

She knew the door was closing behind him but fired anyway. The shot was like a loud slap with an immediate double echo as the bullet penetrated the slammed door.

Weaver, trembling, was sitting up now, gripping the small gun with both hands, still aimed at the door. But she knew she couldn't fire a second shot. Not blind, through a closed door. The area outside the door had been momentarily blocked when the killer had closed it behind him. Now that space might be filled by a curious neighbor.

Or by Weaver's assailant, crumpled on the hall floor, dead or wounded.

She got shakily to her feet and plodded toward the door, keeping the gun raised and ready. When she got close she saw the neat round bullet hole in the door, about four feet above the floor. With the gun in her right hand, she used her left to rotate the knob and pull the door open slowly.

The bullet had chipped out a long vertical splinter as it passed through the door on the other side. Weaver opened the door another six inches and peered out into the hall.

Nothing. No one was lying on the floor. There was no sign of blood. Not enough noise had been made by her small-caliber gun to rouse any of the neighbors. They might have heard a door slamming, making a funny kind of sound, but so what? Maybe a family argument or lovers' quarrel. Maybe something even more serious. Nothing they'd want to be involved in.

Weaver walked to the stairwell and back, and saw no blood on the hall's tiled floor. Apparently her shot had missed the killer entirely.

She had little doubt that her assailant had been D.O.A. For the past several days she'd been well aware that she was being watched, followed. Not all the time, but sometimes almost every day.

Helen the profiler had warned them that D.O.A. might try to get to Quinn through Pearl or Weaver— maybe even Pearl's daughter Jody. All three women were supposed to be taking special care.

But was special care enough to stop a special killer?

* * *

Her heart still hammering, Weaver trudged back to her apartment to phone Quinn. She wished she'd gotten a better look at the killer's face, but in the dim light all she'd seen was a shadowed figure. Dark hair, but she didn't know how dark. Average height, maybe slightly on the tall side. Strong. She remembered the strength almost humming like electricity through his body as he'd held her fast to him and near death at the point of a knife.

He was strong beneath his damp raincoat, and he knew what he was doing.

As she got closer to her apartment door she looked again at the vertical splintered exit hole made by the bullet she'd fired. The building's doors were staggered. When she looked to the opposite side of the hall, she couldn't see anyplace where the bullet might have entered and embedded itself in the wall. Which suggested that the shot she'd gotten off might be lodged in her assailant.

Weaver turned again toward her apartment. She would need a new door, but not immediately. This one would still prove a barrier when locked.

She wouldn't have to change her locks. Obviously, the killer hadn't had a key, or he wouldn't have had to force his way in behind her. He would have been waiting for her inside her apartment.

But Weaver was curious. She went to one of the dimly glowing ornate sconces on the hall wall and reached for where she kept a spare door key on top of the ancient brass. The key she would use if she lost her purse, along with her entire set of keys. Or if, for some inexplicable reason, the key she usually used simply didn't work.

The key wasn't there.

She stood on tiptoe and felt around again for it, this time more carefully.

Plenty of dust. No key.

So he might well have had her spare key but still chose to wait for her outside her apartment and force his way inside with her. Frighten her all the more.

And leave me with the impression that he doesn't have a key. No need to change the locks.

This was part of his game! He was going to torture me but not kill me. He isn't finished with me!

But she knew that was probably wild imagination. It was unlikely the killer planned so intricately and trusted so much to what *might* occur.

She locked the door, using the same key on knob lock and dead bolt, even though the killer might well possess her spare door key, then shoved the heavy sofa in front of it. She placed some dishes on the sofa arm so they'd fall and break, and awaken her if someone tried to visit her during the night.

Someone with a key.

Weaver would wait until tomorrow morning, when the shops were open, to call a locksmith.

She wouldn't wait to call Quinn.

After talking to Quinn, she would call Renz.

It struck her as odd that she wanted to tell Quinn first. She was NYPD and first of all worked for Renz.

Didn't she?

She decided she'd better call Renz first.

36

They were in the living room of the West Side brownstone. The sun was about to set. It sent slanted lances of golden light through the tall windows, illuminating lazily swirling dust motes. Quinn had just finished telling Pearl about his conversation with Ida Tucker, when his cell phone buzzed. He dug the phone out of his pocket and saw the call was from Nancy Weaver.

Quinn walked into the dining room so neither Pearl nor Jody, who was directly upstairs in her bedroom above the living room, would overhear.

When he returned, the expression on his face made Pearl worry. It was probably a case call on his cell, and judging by his expression, it didn't figure to be good news.

"The bastard tried to get Weaver," Quinn said. His jaw was set, his eyes were narrowed, and a vein in his temple pulsated. Just then, he looked more like a determined thug than a former NYPD captain. He scared Pearl when he looked that way. Lots of things might happen.

Pearl was sitting half sideways on the sofa, so her legs were resting on the cushions, as she listened to Quinn. She looked concerned but not surprised.

"I hope Nancy fed him pieces of himself," she said.

"No," Quinn said. "But almost." He related what Weaver had told him about D.O.A.'s attempt on her life. The near miss with the purse gun she carried when she was out of uniform and went without her Glock.

"She might have nicked him," Pearl said.

"Weaver searched personally. There was no blood. Renz is there now. Got CSU and a bunch of uniforms."

"Bunch of press, too, I'd imagine," Pearl said. "Where's this leave Weaver?"

"If I know her," Quinn said, "she'll want to continue what she's been doing. She probably wants the killer to try again."

"She's seen what he did to those other women," Pearl said.

"She's seen worse." Quinn doubted it, but it sounded good. And he knew Weaver wouldn't quit the case. If she was going to be bait, she'd be bait that bit.

But Quinn figured the killer might move on to another victim, somebody Quinn held dearer than Weaver.

"You better call Renz," Pearl said. "Have him put some guardian angels on Jody."

"And on you," Quinn said.

"Don't be silly," Pearl said. "I'm an ex-cop. He's more apt to go after you again, the way he did in Maine. You're unfinished business."

"I'll know when he's going to do that," Quinn said. "I know how he plays the game."

Game! This was exactly the kind of conversation that infuriated Pearl. "Okay, I wouldn't think of intruding on your macho idiocy. I'll save my worry for Weaver. She's unfinished business, too. Out there with her life on the line."

"Weaver's an active cop. You can bet people are gonna be assigned to look after her. Ask me, I think you, Jody, and then Weaver need special protection."

"Didn't ask you," Pearl said. "And Jody's gonna resist."

Pearl's daughter Jody—who was no less a daughter to Quinn—was an attorney with a small firm specializing in what she called social justice cases. Right now, she was defending two men and a woman who were under arrest for urinating in a public place to protest the lack of available public restrooms in New York City. According to Jody, the city was losing millions in tourist money because of the bad experiences tourists had when unable to find public restrooms. They talked about the situation in NYC when they went home to Anywhere, USA, where there were plenty of public toilets. Not to mention, Jody maintained, the considerable income the city could be collecting from pay toilets.

After talking with Renz, Quinn called Jody down and she sat next to Pearl on the sofa. Pearl laid her legs across Jody's lap and crossed her ankles. Jody didn't seem to mind. These two were close. Sometimes they ganged up on Quinn.

Quinn explained the situation to Jody, who said, predictably, "I want to help."

"You're already helping thousands of tourists walking around town double time in desperation."

"It's not a joke."

"You're telling me," Quinn said.

"I can take some time off the public urination case."

"Are your clients in jail?"

"Yes. They resisted arrest."

"You've got to think of their best interest, get them out at least until their court date."

"They resisted arrest. One of them urinated on a cop."

"Damn it, Jody!"

"He had no idea it was a cop. The guy was in plainclothes. So one of my clients . . ."

"Well?"

"The cop got wet, then he got mad, then he got wetter."

Quinn waited.

"Then a fight broke out." She looked mad enough to spit. "I've got witnesses say he just lost his composure. Went berserk."

"The cop?"

"My client. He started swinging with both fists, kicking with both feet. Some kind of martial art that turned him into a fighting machine."

"The urinater."

"Turned out the cop was an undercover narc, working a big case, and my client got his name and photo in the *Post* next day."

"Your client's name and photo?"

"No, the cop's."

"Jody! . . ."

"All my client did was—"

"Jody!" Pearl said. "Accept that you're going to have protection—if the NYPD is still talking to you. It's obvious that your client needs you."

"Clients, plural. I'm representing PRR."

"I thought they found homes for stray cats."

"No, this one's Public Restroom Relief."

Quinn walked to the window looking out on West 75th Street. An NYPD radio car was parked at the curb, directly in front of the brownstone. Quinn turned and looked at the two main women in his life, along with his daughter Lauri, who lived in California.

Quinn felt a sudden chill. Did D.O.A. know about Lauri?

He carried his cell phone outside, exchanged nods with the uniform behind the cruiser's steering wheel, then walked half a block down and pecked out Lauri's phone number in California. He talked to her, then to her mother and his former wife, May. They both took him seriously and said they'd take precautions. Quinn then called an old friend in the LAPD, who said the budget was small and the city needed more police, but he'd do what he could.

And that was all Quinn could do, what he could.

He went back into the brownstone. Pearl knew whom he'd been talking to and didn't ask him anything about the call. Though they were on the sofa, where and how he'd left them, both women were now drinking diet Coke out of cans.

He knew they'd be reasonably safe, but that there couldn't always be a cop on duty simply to stand guard. Sal and Harold would do most of the guarding. Which would take them off the rest of the case.

Was that part of the killer's strategy? The real reason for the attack on Nancy Weaver? A diversion?

Not likely, considering the risk, and the fact that he'd almost been shot. The killer had tried to torture and kill a cop. He must have known what that entailed.

Was this another stratagem? If Weaver wasn't safe, was Pearl any safer?

Was Quinn himself safe?

"I'm going to see Weaver, maybe Renz," Quinn said.

Pearl said, "I'll stay here with Jody."

Quinn thought that was a good idea.

37

The killer had walked, then ran, away from Nancy Weaver's apartment building. He hadn't wasted any time leaving, his back muscles bunched as he waited for another shot to be fired. For all he knew, he'd been hit by the first shot and didn't feel it yet. He knew bullet wounds could be like that. Bullets could be numbing, their effect not realized until whomever had been shot examined himself or herself later.

But if he could run—and he could—he probably hadn't been shot.

He was reasonably sure he hadn't been seen, though he did think he heard a few doors opening and closing behind him.

Out on the street now, back in the mist, he felt safe. A close call. A prospective victim with more resources than he'd imagined. He realized his mistake, thinking of Weaver as vulnerable because she was a woman, making light of the fact that she was also, and primarily, a well-trained, tough cop.

His heartbeat had slowed, and he was no longer breathing hard.

As he strode along Eighth Avenue, he unobtrusively passed his hand here and there over his body, probing for injuries. He knew he was lucky to have avoided a bullet. Luck was something he appreciated, but not something he could depend on. Not like fate. Luck could be fickle; fate was a long-term friend.

He tried to look on the bright side. He hadn't achieved his objective entirely, but surely he'd rattled not only Weaver but the rest of his pursuers. He did feel a certain satisfaction in that.

In fact, as he walked, with every step regaining his ego and perspective, he felt a great deal of satisfaction. The near miss with Weaver would surely be on TV news, in tomorrow's papers, above the fold. People would be impressed.

He'd wanted to question Weaver before letting her die, not just for his pleasure, but to find out if Q&A and the NYPD knew what Jeanine Carson had told him. Not that he suspected Carson might have lied to him. He was an expert in administering agony and using it to extract the truth. With every painful fiber of her body, for every extra second of life she could buy, with any currency she could think of, she'd told him the truth.

Still, he'd wanted confirmation that the narratives matched.

It would have been wise to hear the truth from Weaver, whispered through lips distorted by pain. The pure truth.

He glanced at his wristwatch. The daily television news/entertainment show *Minnie Miner ASAP* would soon be on New York One. It was a program he enjoyed, especially when Minnie or her guests were talk-

ing about him. She had contacts throughout government and the law in New York City, and knew things
sometimes minutes after they happened. (Her detrac-
tors said sometimes before.) Maybe she'd have something to say about the daring attempt on Weaver's life.
About him.

When the killer was safely home in his apartment,
he leaned with his back against the closed door and
took in the warm and slightly mildewed scent of the
place. It made him feel much better, safer, like the cozy
and well-concealed nest of an animal. But this nest had
cream-colored walls on which classic art was carefully
arranged, from chromolithographs to charcoal sketches;
candle-glow Vermeers to sun-dappled Rembrandts; sun-
flowers by Van Gogh to trees by Klimt.

Near a low tan leather sofa in an alcove was a silver
art deco nude woman on a pedestal, stretching lan-
guidly with both arms raised high, fingertips lightly
touching, as is she were about to dive from a high place
into deep water. There was a similar pedestal, unused,
near the opposite end of the sofa.

What all of this art had in common was that it was
part of a display of skillfully produced copies. Quality
stuff—just not the real stuff.

The real art, the great art, was elsewhere, much of it
in Mexico, and some in Europe. Locked away safe and
tight even if it happened by chance to be discovered.

Feeling *much* better, the killer started to take off his
dark raincoat and paused.

There was a hole—large enough to fit his little finger through—in the coat's waterproofed material. He
stared at it, knowing it was a bullet hole. It was actually
in the coat's right hand pocket. His hand darted inside

the pocket and found the bulk of the semi-automatic he carried. He felt the coat's material beneath and beside the gun. No pain. No apparent injury. He explored with his fingers the bottom of the pocket, the inner seam. No bullet.

Think about this.

The bullet must have penetrated Weaver's apartment door and been deflected when it hit the coat, found its way into the fabric.

It must be here.

But it wasn't.

When he removed his gun to make his search easier, he felt and then saw the small caliber bullet lodged in the checked wooden handgrip. If it had continued its course, it would have struck him in the hip. Would probably be lodged in bone the way it was stuck in the gun's grip.

The bullet wasn't so deformed that a ballistics test wouldn't have revealed it was fired from Weaver's gun.

Proof positive that he'd been the man in her apartment.

Enough evidence to hold him while they connected him to other crimes. He knew how it worked. Like dominoes. That was why he'd vowed never to be taken alive. He would die true to himself, in his own fashion, in his own time.

He didn't feel so much like watching the news now. Instead he went into the European-style kitchen and poured three fingers of scotch into a crystal tumbler. Added a cascade of cubes from the stainless steel refrigerator's growling ice maker.

Holding his drink level, he returned to the living room and stood among the almost real works of the real greats, knowing with a glow of pride that this was only a shadow and reminder of what was his and his alone. Like a woman's drawer of paste jewelry that em- ulated what she had that was genuine and valuable.

But like a dog with a rag, his mind kept returning to his recent close call. And to Quinn.

He sat on the sofa and tried not to conclude that he was shaken, running afraid now, and making mistakes.

He knew that Quinn feasted on those kinds of mis- takes.

38

Quinn was seated in a plush chair facing Renz's desk. Renz was slouched in his chair behind the desk, in full and glorious uniform. He was dressed to attend the funeral of a cop who'd been killed earlier that week in a drug-arrest shoot-out on Broadway near Times Square.

The office was stuffy and smelled as if someone had recently snuffed out a cigar. Quinn wondered if someone had.

"The trouble is," Renz said, "we can't control how the media will interpret the killer's try for Weaver."

"That won't matter if they don't find out about it. Nobody actually saw D.O.A. in Weaver's building, and the bullet hole in the door can be patched before anyone takes a close look at it and figures out what it is."

"That's already been done," Renz said. "We're lucky." He held up both hands, palms out. "No, I'll start over. We're lucky—but only in a way, for God's sake—for all the fuss in the media about Wallace."

Wallace was the young cop who'd been shot and killed on Broadway.

"I know what you mean, Harley. I'm not going to quote you."

"The Wallace shooting is a tragedy. A gallant officer leaves behind him a wife and two young children."

"I'm not going to quote you," Quinn repeated, wishing Renz would stop talking like a distraught TV anchorman.

"Yeah," Renz said. He shook his head. "Poor bastard. And the truth is, he *was* a good cop."

"It's better the media's singing his praises and squawking about the dangers of Times Square than concentrating on D.O.A."

"You said it, not me," Renz said. "It's a cruel friggin' world."

"How's Weaver holding up?"

"The lady has balls." Renz patted his breast pocket, as if absently reaching for a cigarette. Or a cigar. "We didn't make too big a fuss after the attempt on her life. Just a couple of radio cars. The CSU van. Far as we know, the press isn't in on the deal, doesn't even know it happened."

"It should seem that way to the killer," Quinn said, "as if nothing newsworthy has happened."

"And that'll drive him nuts. At least according to you and Helen." Renz did his reaching thing again, this time only brushing a fingertip over his breast pocket. "You really think D.O.A. is starting to crumble?"

"He's showing signs," Quinn said. "He might even be carrying a bullet."

"The hospitals would tip us to that one."

"Not if he knows an agreeable doctor. Or if it's a minor wound and he can treat it himself. A twenty-two slug doesn't hit like a broadaxe. But it made it through the door and we didn't find it, so maybe it's inside the killer." Quinn stretched his legs and crossed them at the ankles.

Renz held up two crossed fingers.

There were three soft, evenly spaced knocks on his door, more like a signal than a request to enter. Renz said, "Showtime." He stood up and buttoned his uniform jacket. Smoothed the material with both hands. "These two dead sisters, or cousins, or whatever the hell they are. This family from Ohio. How do you read all that?"

"Not sure," Quinn said.

"Maybe they're not family at all. Maybe it's all bullshit. Like some kind of cult thing. You know, like the Manson Family."

"It seems that way sometimes."

Quinn got up out of his chair so he could leave the office with Renz. "According to Helen, that they're not all related by blood makes them all the needier and tighter with each other."

"Hmph. Helen. You believe that psychobabble malarkey?"

"Sometimes," Quinn said. "I'll see that you're kept up on it."

Renz held the door open for him.

"Bagpipes," Renz said. "I've heard them so many times at funerals. I can't listen to them and not think of death."

"They strike a sad note."

"Can I drop you someplace in the limo?"

"Wouldn't seem right," Quinn said.

"Guess not," Renz agreed. He shook his head. "Lord Jesus, I hate bagpipes!"

*   *   *

Larry Fedderman stood where the killer had stood and observed Weaver leave her apartment building. Fedderman was a tall man, skinny but with a potbelly. One of those guys who look like he'd be in good shape if he hadn't swallowed a basketball. His wife Penny had bought the blue Armani suit he wore, but it still seemed not to fit him. One shoulder was higher than the other, and his right shirt cuff extended unbuttoned like a white surrender flag. If he happened to be carrying a cup, Fedderman might become the only panhandler in an Armani suit to collect a handout.

A black traffic-control car pulled to the curb in front of the apartment building. It didn't sound its horn. Two men sat in it. Both looked as if they were wearing eight-point NYPD caps.

They must have called upstairs with a cell phone, because a minute or so after the car had parked, Weaver, wearing her own eight-point cap, emerged from the building in full uniform.

She looked right and left. Her gaze seemed to hesitate on Fedderman and then moved on.

Fedderman observed that, in uniform, even wearing dark sunglasses—maybe especially with the glasses—Weaver was an attractive woman. He'd been around her enough to have no doubt the uniformed cop was Weaver. How she was built, curvy and sturdy, born to make different kinds of trouble.

Few of her neighbors who hadn't realized she was a cop would recognize her with the uniform and glasses.

The right rear door of the traffic control car opened and she slid smoothly inside. The whole thing hadn't taken half a minute.

Fedderman knew where they were going—to that kid Wallace's funeral. Okay, there was probably no place where Weaver would be safer, surrounded by grieving cops.

This gave Fedderman the opportunity he needed.

He decided to let himself into Weaver's apartment. He had the briefcase containing the equipment Quinn had given him.

Fedderman was pretty good at bugging apartments, so he'd only be inside Weaver's for about ten minutes. Besides, he was a cop and had a right to be there. Sort of. It could be argued.

Weaver, being Weaver, was too stubborn to move out of her apartment. She would continue with her life, perhaps even adding to her dubious reputation. Fedderman had heard so many stories about her that some of them had to be true. No doubt her conversations would be interesting, even if the killer didn't try for her again.

The thing was, there might be phone conversations with the killer, if he did what a lot of these sickos did. They liked to call their once and future victims to let them know they were still on the hook. There might be conversations with Minnie Miner, *when* she called. Or with the NYPD, if Weaver called someone there.

For this to work, of course, Weaver would have to be unaware that her apartment was wired. (Not *wired,* actually. Fedderman had been given a wireless setup by Jerry Lido.)

Fedderman was in the apartment less than a minute when he detected a problem. The most unlikely, and therefore best, place to plant a bug was where someone suspicious was least likely to look. He chose a plastic wall plate with a lamp plugged into one of its sockets.

The plate itself conducted sound well, and the free socket was still live. It was where it wouldn't be used unless Weaver chose to plug in a vacuum cleaner or some such thing. The bug would be interfered with then, but it would regain its effectiveness as soon as the vacuum or any other device was unplugged or turned off.

The plan presented only one problem to Fedderman. The plug already contained a listening device behind its plate.

Fedderman knew where to look for any additional bugs.

It didn't take him long to determine that the entire apartment was already bugged. It wasn't as sophisticated a system as the one Fedderman had brought, but it was effective.

Who would have—could have—done such a thing?

A few names immediately leaped to mind. *Renz! Minnie Miner!*

The killer?

Would D.O.A. have had the time and opportunity? The balls?

Fedderman decided to let Quinn wrestle with those questions. But before he left the apartment, he did a simple splice into the listening system.

That kind of amused Fedderman. New technology partnering with the old.

Now it was a party line.

39

Sarasota, 1993

The courts building's air-conditioning system was operating, but not very effectively. It couldn't keep up with the heat. Florida Power and Light would get around to finding the problem and setting it right as soon as possible. Meanwhile, the courtroom in downtown Sarasota was almost too warm to use.

The judge was a balding, cantankerous man well into his sixties, with a weight problem and what appeared to be a drinker's nose, bright pink with ruptured capillaries. He wanted this trial to progress at full speed. The jurors looked either aggravated or bored. The foreman's obviously dyed black hair was plastered flat to his forehead and dripping perspiration onto his face, and then onto the front of his white shirt. The judge was in shirt sleeves, and had given everyone in the courtroom permission to be the same. The only three people wearing jacket and tie were the prosecutor, the defending attorney, and the defendant, Bill Phoenix.

The witness, Dwayne Aikin, was wearing faded

jeans and a green T-shirt. The shirt's chest and back advertised a surfers' supply store and bore the image of a slim, graceful man riding a wave. The prosecutor had requested that Dwayne look and seem young to the jury, thus the shirt. As if the word of anyone youthful who surfed could not be impugned. A surfer was an innocent; not like Bill Phoenix the amorous pool cleaner. The judge knew what was going on and didn't like it, but he wasn't surprised. This prosecutor, Elliott Murray, not much older than the defendant, was a smartass.

But Murray, a tall, blond man who himself looked like a surfer, was a smartass with a solid case. The jurors had seen photos of the victim's dead body, and of the pool service van parked in the driveway of a house whose pool didn't need cleaning, and wasn't scheduled to be cleaned the day of the murder. There was a close-up photo of the murder knife, taken where it was found hidden beneath a front seat of the defendant's van. The victim's blood was on the knife blade.

Smartass Murray was the only one in the court room who didn't seem to be in a hurry to reach judgment and go to some cooler place and get something cold to drink. He was also the only one in the room who wasn't drenched in sweat, despite the coat and tie.

"Did the defendant visit the victim, Maude Evans, only on days the pool was to be serviced?" Murray asked in a calm voice.

Dwayne Aikin said, "No."

Murray shot a knowing look at the jury, whose members he had charmed from the first day of the trial. "Did these visits last longer than it takes to clean and service a swimming pool?" he asked the witness.

"Sometimes. Uh, yes."

"Was the pool serviced on a regular basis?"

"Yes."

"Did the defendant visit to work on the pool *between* these regular visits?"

"Yes. Sometimes."

"Fifty percent of the time?"

"No."

"Higher or lower?"

"Higher."

The jury stirred despite their impending heat prostration.

"Did the pool actually *require* servicing on all of the defendant's visits?"

"I'm not sure what you mean."

"Was the pool maintenance man there because something was broken?"

"No."

"Or because the pool needed regular maintenance?"

"No."

Murray had begun a confined little pacing, three steps each way, with the rhythm of his questions. "Did the pool usually need cleaning when he came to the house and spent time with Maude Evans?"

"No."

"Did the defendant spend some of his time with the victim out by the pool?"

"Yes."

"*Most* of his time?"

"Yes."

"Did you ever hear them discuss the victim's husband's will?"

"Yes."

"Did they discuss how the proceeds of that will could be obtained?"

"Yes."

Three steps this way, three steps back.

"Did this process involve the premature death of the victim's—"

"Objection!" yelped the defendant's lawyer. He had his jacket buttoned and his tie knotted at his throat, like Murray's, but he was gleaming with perspiration. Weary to begin with, he had suddenly realized his own body was moving to the rhythm of Murray and the witness's little verbal dance.

"Goes to motive," Murray said calmly.

"Overruled," said the judge.

"Did they sometimes leave the pool and go into the house together?" Murray asked.

"Yes."

"Would you say the defendant made himself at home?"

"Objection! Calls for—"

"Sustained." The judge, who himself had been swaying with the testimony, now wanted to hurry this process along.

Murray obviously knew that and was now happy to oblige. "Mr. Aikin, did you ever see the defendant, Bill Phoenix, engage in sexual activity with—"

"Objection! Objection! Objection!"

"Overruled," said the judge. "Witness may answer the quest—"

"Yes."

"But not yet." The judge sighed and held up a hand palm out to signal for silence. A bead of perspiration ran to the tip of his florid nose, clung for a few seconds, then dropped onto some papers before him with a faint but audible *splat.* "Mr. Murray, you may now complete your question—*without* interruption."

"Of course, your honor. . . . Sexual activity with the victim?"

"Yes."

"Did they ever, before, after, or during sex, discuss what they would do with the inheritance money if your father were to die?"

"Obje—"

"Overruled." The judge used an already damp handkerchief to dab perspiration from his forehead. He wiped his face, smacked his lips, growled, and said, "On with it."

After the jury found the defendant, William Alan Phoenix, guilty of first-degree murder, the jurors were released and filed out. There was no doubt in their bearing or on their faces that at his sentencing appearance, Phoenix would learn he was to die at the hands of the state.

Dwayne Aikin was sitting in the back of the courtroom. He watched without expression as Bill Phoenix was led away in handcuffs, to be transferred to a holdover cell. Phoenix caught sight of Dwayne, locked gazes with him, and didn't look away, craning his neck to see him until it was impossible.

The fear and wonder in Phoenix's eyes was something Dwayne would never forget. He enjoyed calling it to memory from time to time when he needed something to think about in order to fall asleep.

40

They were in the Q&A offices on West 79th Street. Quinn was seated behind his desk, leaning back in his swivel chair with his fingers laced behind his head as if he were a POW. He was leaning dangerously far back in the chair, but Helen the profiler, who was half sitting, half standing, with her haunches propped on Pearl's desk, wasn't worried about him falling. Quinn habitually sat that way, and never had fallen. At least not when anyone was around to see him. Helen wondered.

Quinn was wondering, too. His gaze took in the entire six feet plus of the lanky, athletic woman. Like many redheads, she had a sprinkling of freckles along the bridge of her nose and on her upper chest. The freckles on her chest were visible because her baggy T-shirt sagged enough at the neck almost to reveal whatever cleavage there was. Quinn was musing that he'd not heard of Helen dating or getting involved with a man—or another woman, for that matter. Well, it was none of his—

"It's none of my business," Helen said, "but what are you thinking?"

As she so often did, Helen had picked up something in his demeanor. "About the case," he lied.

"Which case? D.O.A. or the missing Michelangelo piece?"

"They're the same," Quinn said.

"Really? You think D.O.A. killed Andria Bell and Jeanine Carson because of *Bellezza?*"

"There's not much question about it."

"But some question?"

Quinn shifted forward in his chair, looking much larger behind the desk. He was a man who could loom even when seated. "There's almost always some question."

"What about the killer trying for Nancy Weaver?" Helen asked. "That wouldn't have anything to do with *Bellezza.*"

"Which means it successfully diverts and lessens our resources. Feds is on that job now, playing unseen guardian angel for Weaver. Sal, and then Harold, will relieve him."

"They're angelic, all right, all three of them."

"Less sinful, anyway," Quinn said with a smile.

"By a long shot."

"What do *you* think?" Quinn asked.

"I think D.O.A. went after Weaver to turn up the heat on you," Helen said. "Not because he's searching for some Renaissance marble bust. It's part of his sick game." Helen crossed her arms, muscular as a man's against her baggy shirt, beneath where breasts must be. Her triceps rippled. "On the other hand," she said, "it doesn't have to be either/or."

"If *Bellezza* is involved," Quinn said, "it *can't* be either/or. It has to be both."

As he often did when frustrated, Quinn wished he could light a cigar. He played with the idea of depending on Helen not to rat on him, and then decided he shouldn't compel her to keep something like cigar smoking secret from Pearl. Or from Jody.

He would play it safe and go cigarless.

"You said you were thinking about the case," Helen reminded him.

"About that oddball family," Quinn said.

"Oddball in what way?"

"They're thick in the way few families are, and it's hard to keep straight who's a blood relative. Most of this family isn't actually part of it. They were adopted, or somehow fell in together."

"Give me a for instance."

"Ida Tucker. She says she's the dead girls' mother, but looks too old for the part."

"Not if they were adopted," Helen pointed out.

"Yeah. Maybe. And what about this package of bricks and straw shipped from England during World War Two?"

"It strongly suggests that something about the size and weight of a small marble bust was stolen in transit, and replaced with bricks and straw. That kind of petty crime was probably a common occurrence in wartime."

"Not so petty if Michelangelo really sculpted it."

"Big *if*." Helen said.

"Also, it was sent by somebody else who apparently wasn't a blood relation. A nurse who for God's sake died in the blitz. That was a long time ago."

"Those people lived and breathed and made mistakes," Helen said.

"And most were actually related. Not like this bunch. The lack of DNA in common seems to have bonded this family with an extra strength."

"Oh, it has," Helen said. "The reason why is they *need* each other more than ordinary families. They feel grafted to the family tree, even though they aren't actually descendents of the original green shoot."

Quinn laced his fingers back behind his head. "Yeah, I guess I can see that." But he couldn't. Not really. On the other hand, he knew how he felt about Jody.

"Family is thicker than blood," Helen said.

"That's not exactly how the old saying goes, but I hear you. So where does *Bellezza* figure in? Is Michelangelo a distant relative?"

"In a way. *Bellezza* is their raison d'être. That's French for 'reason for being.' "

"And what would that be for this family?"

"Michelangelo created it."

"You're saying the missing marble bust is what makes their lives meaningful."

"No, *the search for it does*. It's what makes them a real family, with a common cause, common branches if not roots, and a common dream. It's the glue that holds them tight to each other in a shifting world, and I wouldn't underestimate its strength."

"So it doesn't really matter who's actually related and who's pretending. Or who changed their name how many times. Or if Robert Kingdom became Winston Castle so he could open a New York restaurant for Anglophiles."

Helen nodded. A strand of red hair fell over one

green eye. "Not as long as the other family members pretend along with the pretender. If virtually everyone is an imposter, then nobody is. Not in the common adventure they're living out together."

"Life is just a dream," Quinn said.

"Yeah. Not just a song title. For these people, apparently. And maybe for the rest of us, too, only we don't know it."

"Helen, Helen . . ."

She smiled, stood up straight, and stretched. If she wore six-inch heels, could she touch the ceiling?

"Sounds like a cult," Quinn said.

"Like the Manson family."

"Or the Flintstones, or Simpsons."

"See," Helen said. "they're not real families, either, and look how close they are."

Quinn did understand what she was saying. It was what drew criminals back together when they were released after serving long terms in prison. They were willing to risk everything simply by associating with each other while out on parole. They trusted each other as they trusted no one else.

There were families and then there were families. Most people knew about the biggest crime family, but there were also plenty of smaller ones. Gang members who went where the other members went, did what they did, ate what they ate. They sometimes referred to themselves as "family."

"One thing, though," Quinn said.

Helen flexed her long fingers as if preparing to play a piano. "What's that?"

"Everything we just agreed on wouldn't mean diddly to the courts if it came to inheritance law." Quinn's gaze went to the drawer holding his cigars and he forced himself to look away. "Or if it came to splitting the fortune that some obsessive collector is going to pay for a stolen Michelangelo bust."

"They'd never sell *Bellezza*," Helen said. "Because then the search would be ended."

"Couldn't they start a search for something else?"

She smiled. "Dreams don't work that way."

"There's another way dreams don't work," Quinn said. "This family has acquired a member they definitely should regard as a black sheep. He's killing them one by one because he *does* want the search to end."

Helen thought about that.

Said, "Don't kid yourself."

41

When Helen had left Q&A, Quinn thought about what she'd said. Thought about the letters Ida Tucker had mentioned.

He phoned the Ohio number she'd given him, not knowing if there had been time for her to return home and deliver her daughters to a local mortuary.

The phone in Ohio rang five times, then Ida did pick up.

"Nice to hear from you, Detective Quinn. I hope the air conditioner in your office is working better today. And that you don't lean so far back in your desk chair that you actually fall."

Quinn thought she sounded much younger over the phone. And was something of a smart mouth for a mature and dignified woman.

"Caller ID," he said.

"So everything up to date isn't in Kansas City," she said. "Have you learned anything more about the murders?"

"That's why I called. You mentioned some envelopes that were in the crate that came from England.

Are these letters that might have been taken from Jeanine's safe?"

"I suppose it's possible. I don't know how much they might help you. They might be letters I wrote."

"*You* wrote them?"

"Yes. I don't mean the original letters. The ones that were found with the bricks and straw in the box. They seem to have disappeared years ago. The letters we're talking about now are my letters, describing what was in the originals. How Henry Tucker and Betsy Douglass met, how love bloomed in the hospital, and then poor Henry's death from his wounds. Then they tell how a German bomb killed Betsy, but not before she'd shipped the crate to her sister Willa, all the way across the ocean to the United States." Ida Tucker paused as if to catch her breath. "It must have been horrible, that war."

"Horrible," Quinn agreed. *Letters describing what was in letters. How would that kind of evidence hold up in court?*

But he knew how.

The information Ida's letters contained might reveal something that could lead somewhere interesting. If it was true. Or maybe what was in the letters would simply be a rehash about what was already known: that Henry Tucker was given a marble bust that he passed on to Nurse Betsy Douglass, and that she shipped it from England to her sister, and then was killed in an air raid. Somewhere along the way, the bust, if it ever existed, disappeared.

And how could Quinn find out how, with the truth concealed among layers and layers of lies? It might be impossible to find because there was no truth.

No, he told himself. *There's always a truth. Don't doubt that.*

"Detective Quinn," Ida said. "I do hate to cut this conversation short, but there are preparations still to be made for a double funeral." Serious now. This woman could playact.

"Of course," Quinn said. "I shouldn't have called so soon." He added, "Where might we send flowers?"

"Oh, that really isn't necessary. The girls will be buried in the cemetery behind a church they attended. It will be brief. A simple family ceremony."

"Of course. Family."

"So if you'll excuse me . . ."

"Of course. I'm sorry for your loss, dear."

Ida Tucker thanked him and hung up.

Quinn sat thinking about a cemetery behind a small church, a family standing before two open graves and mourning its loss. There would be sobs and quiet tears and bowed heads. A somber minister clad in black, like the mourners. Rows of aged and crooked tombstones. Like a somber but picturesque Norman Rockwell painting.

But Quinn knew this was all his imagination. It might not look like a Norman Rockwell painting at all. Things were seldom as they seemed, or as we wanted to see them.

He reminded himself never to forget that.

Still, the rows of crooked tombstones, the trembling lips and reddened eyes, the lugubrious minister gripping his Bible tight to his breast.

The two open graves.

It was a scene firmly lodged in Quinn's memory, though he had never seen it and never would.

Life is just a dream . . .

42

Sarasota, 1993

Snowbirds. That's what native Floridians called the swarms of people who headed to Florida to escape winter up north. They were from everywhere. New York, Minnesota, Canada . . . all frigid places on the continent. And more than a few snowbirds were European.

Sarasota, because of its charms and beautiful white beach, became more crowded every year. Dwayne Aikin didn't hate the snowbirds, like some Floridians. On the other hand, he didn't like them.

Except for the women. So many women. Lounging on the beach, picking at salads in restaurants, laughing in bars and other night spots. The women, talking, shopping. Tempting, many of them.

There was a higher class of woman at Pike's, on the beach, just off Highway 41, the Tamiami Trail. Pike's had a driftwood look about it, as if it had weathered the worst of the hurricanes. It was also an art gallery, sometimes showing work by some of Sarasota's more well known artists, who regarded Sarasota as an art mecca. The paintings here weren't priced, but deals were made, and for considerable amounts of money.

Canapés and wine were served inside. A smaller version of the inside bar, and several tables, were outside, beneath a roof fashioned to look as if it was thatched with palm fronds. When the weather was good, which was almost always, there were more people outside than inside at Pike's. Wine and mixed dinks were served there, and art was discussed.

And Dwayne listened. He was fascinated by art and the art world. And he'd learned enough about art to recognize that he had little talent, but a powerful yearning to possess.

Dwayne was still too young to drink there legally, but Peter Pike, the owner and curator of Pike's, would secretly serve him wine inside, and limited amounts of alcohol outside. And why shouldn't he? Dwayne's father had helped to make Pike rich. Now Pike was aware that when Dwayne turned twenty-five, Dwayne would be wealthy. It might be said that Pike was nurturing a future wealthy patron of the arts. Whispered, anyway.

Dwayne wasn't hurting financially now. That was thanks to his father, not his slut of a mother.

Dwayne liked to sit at one of the small tables near the end of the outside bar, which was very near to where the beach began. Close enough, anyway, to get sand between your bare toes. At night soft breezes wafted in off the Gulf. If the breeze turned cool, large kerosene heaters would provide warmth, and transparent plastic and mesh curtains would be lowered to contain it. The heaters and curtains were seldom needed.

Women would come to Pike's to watch the colorful sunsets, and Dwayne would observe them while he sipped his Coca-Cola spiked with Maker's Mark bourbon.

The women were considerably older than Dwayne, and many of them knew about art. Not the spring breakers. They not only tended to be college age, but also were gibbering fools. That was how Dwayne saw them, anyway. The older women, some of them widows on the hunt, were not only smarter and more discerning, but seemed quieter. Their conversations had a softer, more confiding tone. Sometimes urgent. All women, it seemed to Dwayne, talked too much about too little. Though there were notable exceptions.

Like the quiet blond woman with a model's cheekbones who drank alone, and sat on the peripheries like Dwayne and observed. She was probably into her twenties, and had a lean, taut body that was tan from the sun so that when she wore a skimpy blouse the lighter marks from the straps of her swimming suit were visible. Maude used to have vertical strap lines like that on her back and above her breasts.

Occasionally men would approach the blond woman, but she seemed to have a way of rebuffing them without making them angry or embarrassing them. Wayne liked that about her. It was what some people called class.

Sometimes, when she was sending away a sad suitor, she'd glance over at Dwayne. Was she wondering why he hadn't approached her? Did she think, as he did, that they might be kindred spirits?

Dwayne wasn't long on friends, especially since the trial. At first he'd been something of a celebrity, but that had worn away fast. Then he realized some of the friends he had left were in his orbit simply because he was a rich kid—or was soon to be rich. He didn't tell them he was living on a stipend until he came of age. At least it was a stipend compared to what he was worth. He made sure that they knew he wasn't going to throw money around, and they, too, fell away as friends. That was okay. In fact, Dwayne used his temporary not-yet-rich status to drive away his most annoying hangers-on. Especially the girls.

He would obtain what he wanted from them, and then he was finished with them and would let them know it. They were used goods. He always made sure that they understood that. That they *felt* it. They were like his mother. Only she'd been smart. And evil. Using her wiles to be a user of others.

Maybe that was in the genes, being a user of people. Or maybe she'd learned it from those who'd used her. We embrace what we can't escape. What was the alternative, but winding up on the scrap heap with ninety-nine percent of the rest of humanity? Most people didn't have what it took to be users. Dwayne knew he did. Ask Bill Phoenix. Ask Maude. He smiled. No, it was no good asking Maude.

Or his mother.

As he sat at his outside table at Pike's, listening to the rush of the surf and watching the blond woman, he admired the way she lifted and lowered her glass. There was a special grace to it, little finger extended, her movements measured. It was the grace of tigers.

Sometimes she would go into the gallery alone and move slowly from painting to painting, as if she were judging them in a contest.

More and more Dwayne saw in her something he'd observed in Maude, and in his mother. A worldly, dangerous exterior that was no act, yet still didn't quite conceal a vulnerability. They were both users, like most women, but they understood their power and knew its limits. They could also be used.

And they deserved to be used.

The night air was warm. The moon was almost full. You could stare at its pocked surface and make of it what you would. A cloudless sky glowed sequined with stars, and Dwayne had gone heavy on the illegal booze component of his drink that Pike allowed.

Maybe it was the alcohol, or maybe it was the moon. Something caused him to decide that this was the night he should approach the blond woman. She hadn't changed her attitude. Dwayne knew that. He was the one who had become more entranced, the one who needed to know the other's soul.

Drink in hand, he stood up unsteadily and walked the fifty feet or so to where she sat alone at her outside table. She was gazing out to sea, and seemed not to notice him.

After standing for a few seconds at her table, he said, "I've been watching you."

She didn't bother turning her head to look at him. "And I've been watching you."

He could see by the curve of her cheek that she was smiling slightly. He amused her. Her thinking he was funny—that would change.

"Want to talk?" he asked, thinking immediately that he sounded like what he was, an inexperienced kid struck almost dumb by graceful shoulders, generous tanned breasts, upswept blond hair only slightly ruffled by the breeze. That same breeze brought to him the faint scent of her lotion, and of the ocean.

"That's what we're doing," she said. "They call it talking."

He wasn't sure what to say.

She turned around in her chair and looked straight at him with those blue-green eyes. A lump formed in his throat.

"Sit down," she said. Her voice was soft but there was command in it as well as invitation. She wasn't someone to be disobeyed, even slightly.

He thought about his mother as he sat down. He wondered if the blond woman somehow knew that. And for the first time, he wondered if they had met before. Had she been a friend of his mother or father? Or of Maude?

No. Not possible. I'd remember this one.

"You're here . . . often," he said, simply for words to speak.

"So are you."

"I'm Dwayne." He offered his hand to shake.

She ignored it and said. "Linda." She lifted her glass in a brief toast to him, or to both of them. "Why have you been watching me, Dwayne?"

He was gaining his equilibrium now. "For the same reason other men watch you."

"Which men are those?"

"The ones who come to your table and get sent away."

"I didn't send you away."

He felt himself blush. "I didn't think you would."

"And why not?"

"You'll laugh."

She simply stared at him, unblinking.

"I think we're kindred spirits," he said.

She smiled with just her lips, then opened her mouth wide and laughed.

"Gee," she said, "I don't think I've ever heard that one."

Dwayne felt small enough to climb down out of his sandals.

Linda quit laughing and gazed at him with something like contempt. He couldn't help it; he began to squirm.

Linda said, "Let's walk." She stood up, but not before leaning over and giving him a good look at her cleavage. He glimpsed where tan flesh turned pink in a place mysterious. He was surprised by how tall she was. As he stood up from his chair, he glimpsed down to see if she was wearing heels. She wasn't, but the rubber soles of her sandals were thick. He thought that if they were both barefoot she and he would be almost the same height, which made her tall for a woman.

They left the island of light that was Pike's and walked side by side south along the shore. Neither spoke, but the waves applauded again and again. When the beach narrowed, Dwayne leaned down and rolled up the cuffs of his pants. Linda removed her sandals so that her legs were bare below her shorts. They walked in the packed wet sand, among tiny broken shells, where every once in a while the surf would reach them and swirl about their feet.

"Tell me you're not an artist," she said.

"I can honestly say that. What about you?"

"I dabble."

"I bet you dabble great."

"I've seen enough paintings of sunsets, leaping marlins, and squinting old men with faces marked by the sea."

"Me too," he lied.

"There," she said suddenly, and pointed.

To their right, beyond the curved beach and a stretch of sandy soil, were the lights from a string of condos and rented beach cottages. Linda was pointing at a rectangle of yellow light that was a large window or sliding-glass door in a two-story hotel, kept low by building ordinance and the slightly taller hotel across the street from it.

"That's the Tipton Hotel," he said.

They'd stopped walking. His back was to the ocean. Because of the moon he could see her glowing face as she smiled. "How do you know that?" she asked.

"I'm from around here. I've driven back and forth on the beach road."

She widened her eyes in a way he knew was an act. "You're old enough to have a driver's license?"

"You know I am," he lied. She was making fun of him and he couldn't keep the anger from his voice. A rage she didn't yet know.

Or knew all too well.

She surprised him by taking his hand. Her own hand was dry and surprisingly strong. She took a few steps, pulling him along until he began to walk.

"I'll show you," she said.

"Show me what?" His heart was banging away.

"Where I'm staying," she said. "Ever been inside the Tipton?"

"Couple of times," he said. *Once. In the lobby.*

She was smiling again, amused by him again.

He realized he was smiling on the inside.

She didn't know that.

43

There was a wooden deck outside the back of the Tipton Hotel, with a scattering of empty lounge chairs several rooms down. Also farther down were the lights of the hotel swimming pool. A few shrill children's voices reached Linda and Dwayne. No one seemed to be seated outside in the warm Gulf breeze, watching the kids. Or maybe everyone, including the parents, was in the pool.

Smiles and splashes. Family life. Dwayne didn't think a lot about it.

Still holding his hand, Linda guided him up the wooden steps and across the narrow deck to the rectangle of light she'd pointed out when they were down on the beach. He saw that it was much larger than a window. Two floor-to-ceiling sliding-glass panels.

Linda reached out with her free hand and slid one of the panels aside. It moved smoothly in its track, making barely a whisper.

"Don't you lock your room when you leave?" Dwayne heard himself ask.

"Nobody would dare steal from me," she said. Kidding him again. Making fun. Lies large and small would flow from her, and then, finally, the truth would be revealed.

The room was small and neat, with furniture that was sparse and obviously expensive. The Tipton was definitely one of the better hotels in a string of hotels and condos along the beach road.

The bed was made, with its gray-and-green duvet drawn taut. A single large suitcase sat closed on a folding luggage rack near what must be the door to the bathroom. The suitcase looked like real alligator dyed red, but Dwayne knew it probably wasn't.

Just like the woman looks real.

A pair of red high-heeled shoes with pointed toes stood precisely side by side before a louvered closet door. Above a small desk, a TV was mounted on the wall. Its large screen was gray. The brass bullet lamp on the desk provided the only light.

Linda finally released Dwayne's perspiring hand and went to the sliding-glass doors. He couldn't look away from the smooth play of her hips as she walked.

She pulled a cord, and gray-and-green drapes that matched the bedspread made a ratcheting sound and rushed to meet each other. The room, small to begin with, suddenly seemed half the size it had been when the dark sea and beach were exposed.

The moon no longer contributed any light. In the intimate dimness, Linda unbuttoned and pulled her shirt over her head, leaving her blond hair a tangled mess that Dwayne couldn't help staring at. Until she bent forward, elbows out, in that curious birdlike motion women have, and deftly removed her bra.

She draped blouse and bra over the back of the desk

chair and stood looking at Dwayne. Her eyes went to his erection and immediately it seemed twice as large to him.

"Better take those pants off while you can," she said.

Neither of them said anything until they were both completely undressed, then they fell together onto the bed. They rolled back and forth, hugging, kissing, wrestling for dominance. She wound up on top, kissing him with her mouth open, using her tongue.

When they drew apart in order to breathe, he said, "Wait a minute! Just a few seconds." His mind was whirling.

"You okay?" she asked.

"Yeah." The clothes he'd practically ripped from his body were wadded on the floor beside the bed. "I've got a rubber in my wallet."

She smiled broadly, then laughed. "Really? How long's it been in there?"

"I replaced it this morning," he said.

More laughter. "That's wonderful!"

He rolled onto his side, still half on the mattress, and his groping hand found the rough material of his pants. He felt for the pockets.

Found his knife.

It was past 2:00 A.M. when Linda finally died. Dwayne had been careful not to leave fingerprints.

But after showering and dressing again in his shirt, shorts, and sandals, he stood before the closed drapes and found that he didn't want to leave.

Not yet.

Careful where he was stepping, he made his way to

the bed, where what remained of Linda lay, bound with electrical cord and gagged with one of her bikini bottoms, knotted in her mouth, then knotted again at the nape of her neck. Her wide eyes were fixed and staring at the slowly revolving ceiling fan. Dwayne thought her stare was as empty as her thoughts. He had everything of her now.

Dwayne knew that blood would no longer gush. He drew his knife, leaned over the bed, and deftly carved his initials in Linda's smooth pale forehead.

Now she was marked. Branded.

Forever.

His.

PART FOUR

The place where optimism most flourishes is
the lunatic asylum.

—HAVELOCK ELLIS, *The Task
of Social Hygiene*

44

Quinn's desk phone jangled. He liked the sound. Cell phones imitated it but couldn't get it quite right.

He rolled his chair closer to his desk and picked up on the fourth ring, said who and where he was.

"Detective Quinn, this is Ida Tucker."

He scooted even closer to the desk so he could see the remote caller ID. Yep, Ida Tucker. Ohio number.

"Is everything okay?" Quinn asked. He'd picked up the stress in her voice. *How can everything be okay when you've just yesterday buried two of your children?* "I mean, considering."

"I'm afraid not," she said, a catch in her throat. "My ex-husband, Edward, had a heart attack."

Christ!

"I'm sorry, dear. Is he—?"

"He's dead. The doctor said it might have been brought on by the girls' funerals. All that stress, all in one day."

"Is there anything I can do for you, Ida. Anything you need?"

"No, no. But I thought you should know."

"I'm glad you called me. I wish I could ease your grief."

"Well," she said, "it isn't only my grief. That evening, after Edward was . . . gone, his old friend and longtime attorney, Joel Price, came by the house to talk to me. He told me that years ago Edward had given him the letters."

"Your letters explaining what Henry Tucker wrote before he died in England?"

"No. Henry's letters themselves. The *original* originals."

Quinn sat for a few seconds trying to process that. "Why would Edward do that and keep it secret from everyone?"

"I don't know." The catch was back in her voice.

"Have you—"

"I haven't gone to the bank to open the box where the letters are. Joel Price suggested he be there with me, in case of any legal ramifications. He still has the key and would be witness to what's in the box. He thought, since the letters and the girls' deaths are part of a police investigation, you might want to be there too when the box is opened."

"Joel Price is a smart lawyer," Quinn said. "As soon as we hang up, I'm going to book a flight to Columbus and then drive to see you. That is, if you're ready to do this, Ida."

"I'm not just ready, Detective Quinn. I'm eager."

* * *

They landed at the Columbus airport in Ohio, where they rented a Hertz black Jeep. Quinn drove, and Pearl sat beside him. When they hit open highway and greater speeds, the squared-off little vehicle rocked in the wind but remained easy to control.

They got into Green Forest before dusk and settled into the room they'd reserved at the Flower Bed Hotel, a place recommended by Ida Tucker. It was a four-story frame building painted a soft green with brown shutters. The walkway from the parking area to the entrance was lined with pink- and blue-flowered foliage in full bloom, punctuated by bright red geraniums.

Quinn and Pearl checked in and rode the single elevator to the third floor. There they were met by a bellhop who'd gotten a head start on them while they were getting conversation and instructions from a girl who looked like a teenager at the front desk. A good place for supper, they were advised, was the Crazy Fish, just down the block.

After placing their luggage where they directed, and needlessly pointing out where the bathroom and TV remote were, the bellhop, a lean, older man with bushy gray hair, introduced himself as Leonard and asked if there might be anything else they'd need.

Quinn told him not at the moment and tipped him twenty dollars, creating an instant friend.

Leonard looked as if he might click his heels and bow, but didn't, and thanked Quinn profusely.

"Anything you need," he said, " just let me know."

Quinn said that he would.

On the way out, Leonard said, "Word to the wise: I wouldn't do supper at the Crazy Fish."

When they were alone in the heavy silence, Pearl said, "Now what?"

Quinn said, "Get a third opinion, I guess."

After supper at the Crazy Fish, which was surprisingly good, Quinn called Ida Tucker, and he and Pearl drove to the Tucker home.

They found Ida waiting, dressed in black and leaving a scent of lavender as she ushered them inside the white frame house. It was a brick-and-frame two-story with a porch that ran across the front and around one corner. Ivy grew densely up one of the brick walls. There were three Adirondack chairs and a wooden glider with a fat cushion on the porch. It looked like the kind of place where Harry Truman might have grown up if he'd been from Ohio.

Ida looked as if she'd been crying but seemed to have it under control. Quinn looked closely at her eyes. She didn't seem medicated.

A tall, slender man with a long face that looked as if it had never once displayed an expression stood by a sofa and coffee table. Ida introduced him as Joel Price, longtime friend and attorney of Edward. He was wearing a black pin-striped suit, white shirt, and black tie. Quinn knew that Ida must be in her eighties or nineties, Price in his nineties, but both looked . . . not so much younger, but well preserved.

At Ida's direction, they settled into chair and sofa, Pearl and Quinn in matching brown leather armchairs, Ida and Price on the sofa.

"Would anyone care for refreshments?" Ida asked, as if suddenly she remembered her manners.

Everyone said no, that they were fine.

"I was surprised that the funeral was so soon after Edward passed," Quinn said.

Ida was clutching a wadded white handkerchief and raised it as if to dab at her eyes, but instead lowered it back onto her lap. "Edward was cremated," she said. "That was what he requested."

"Had he been ill?" Pearl asked.

"He'd been old," Ida said.

Joel Price smiled grimly. "Something that at least isn't contagious," he said.

Ida appeared shocked. "Oh, I'm sorry, Joel. I forgot you and Edward were about the same age."

"Actually," Price said, "I'm four years younger." Again the grim smile. "But you didn't come here to listen to us reminisce."

"Didn't they?" Ida said. "The thing to remember is that, despite the matrimonial wars, despite the divorce, Edward and I never really fell out of love."

"Your subsequent husband—"

"*Maybe* we didn't come here to reminisce," Ida said.

"The letters written by Henry Tucker . . ." Quinn said, glad they were dealing with an attorney who knew how to get to the point. He didn't want to get lost in the Tucker/Douglass/Kingdom family-tree maze. "Have you seen them yet?"

"Oh, no," Price said. "Neither of us has. Edward was adamant about that. I recall that quite vividly."

"So the letters are in your safe?" Pearl asked.

"No, no." Price's right arm trembled slightly. The only sign of advanced age he'd shown since they arrived. "They're in a safety-deposit box at the bank, in both my name and Edward's. The key was kept in a file at my office. I have it with me now, but of course at this hour the bank is closed. I requested your presence here so we can lay down some ground rules for when the box is opened in the morning."

"That's kind of difficult to do when we don't know what's in the letters," Quinn said.

Price nodded, as if he'd expected that response. "That's the point. We don't have the slightest idea what the letters contain. I thought it would be a good idea to have police presence when the box was open, primarily so it will be established that the contents weren't trifled with." He leaned forward on the sofa, seemingly so light he didn't dent the cushion. "You must understand that Edward Tucker is my client, and I owe my allegiance to him even though he's passed."

Quinn didn't think so, but the last thing he wanted was a legal problem. He waited to see what Price had in mind.

"We'll go to the bank together tomorrow," Price said. "I'll unlock and open the box in plain sight of all. I would like to be able to examine the letters first, to make sure there is nothing of potential damage to Edward's reputation or his family. Then I will give the letters to you to read. If they constitute some kind of evidence in an active homicide investigation, they will pass to your possession if you request them." He placed bony hands on his kneecaps and smiled widely with straight but yellowed teeth. "Is that acceptable?"

Quinn returned the smile. "So far. We'll take it a step at a time."

"Fair enough," Price said.

"Edward would approve," Ida Tucker said.

Quinn and Price exchanged glances. Both knew that, being dead, Edward Tucker didn't have much in the way of legal standing. He couldn't voice his legal opinions now.

At the same time, being dead, he couldn't be harmed by the law.

45

Prentis, Florida, 1995

"Let me out of the damned car, Dwayne!"

Honey Carter was twenty and blond and beautiful. Dwayne was well aware that she resembled both his mother and Maude, reflecting his father's taste in women.

Honey had something else in common with those two women. She didn't love Dwayne, and never had.

She'd gone out with him a few times and then rebuffed him, called him a rich freak.

Well, she might as well have called him that. She'd made him *feel* that way.

What did she want? He was young and reasonably good looking. Rich, but how could she count that against him? And he carried a 3.9 grade point average at the University of South Florida. Higher education was a snap for him. Read the book (on or off his computer) in a single sitting, then relax and ace the course.

Not that he was going back. College bored the hell out of him. And some people began giving him odd looks, fearful looks, and avoided him. Rumors bloomed even if they couldn't take root. Others on campus had found out who he was, and about the murder of his father and stepmother-to-be.

This last part actually attracted a certain kind of woman to him—as long as there were other people in the room. Rumors, rumors, rumors about him. Some of them must be true. And if he was rich, he was probably guilty. Wasn't that the way it always worked?

This final attempt to save his and Honey's relationship (at least as Dwayne saw it) wasn't working out very well. They were in his car on dark and isolated Lagoon Road. It had seemed romantic to Dwayne, a perfect setting for reviving a love affair showing signs of strain.

Until the sun went down.

Now they were surrounded by darkness. He was amused. Honey was faced with the classic dilemma: stay and screw, or get out of the car and be in grave danger. He wanted to see how she'd deal with the problem.

She was pretending now, he was sure. Showing him she didn't take that kind of treatment from anyone, male or female. But it was all a show.

He used the car's lighter to fire up a cigarette, took a deep drag, and leaned his head back so he was staring up at the headliner, thinking about what he might do with the cigarette's glowing ember.

"Do you *really* want to get out of the car here?" Dwayne asked.

Honey lost her focus on him, and suddenly realized how dark it had become.

"There are gators out there," Dwayne said. "And python snakes."

People in the area had kept pythons as pets until they got too big and dangerous. Then they set them loose in the swamp, where they thrived and multiplied. There had been state sponsored hunting seasons on the pythons. Many of the snakes were over twenty feet long. They were still out there. Now and then there were stories in the Florida papers. Along with photographs.

Honey, a journalism major, read the papers.

"Drive me goddamned home!" Honey demanded. There was a catch of fear in her throat.

Home was where she lived off campus, in an apartment with two other young women.

Dwayne had seen Honey walking off campus, near a coffee shop where he was going to search for her. Instead, there she was, striding along the sidewalk, alone. He'd pulled to the curb in front of her and opened the door on her side of the car. Honey didn't like scenes. Dwayne made it clear to her that if she didn't get in the car so they could go somewhere and talk reasonably, he would make a hell of a scene.

He wanted her to hurry because no one they knew was around to see her get in his car.

Not knowing better, she hurried.

Now no one knew Honey was here with Dwayne, on godforsaken Lagoon Road, in the deep, deep swamp. She suddenly understood the meaning of their aloneness. The realization of her vulnerability passed between them like electricity.

Something was going to happen here, tonight.

He moved toward her to hug her to him, as if to reassure her of her safety.

Her eyes widened and she slid away from his grasp. The door handle clicked and the dome light flashed on.

"The classic dilemma," Dwayne said.

"You really want to give me that choice?" she asked, her door already open six inches.

The fear in her eyes made something tighten in the core of Dwayne. A coil of pure pleasure. How terrified she was!

But she was bluffing. He was sure of it.

He decided to call her bluff, and in a fashion she wouldn't like. It was time for the stuck-up bitch to learn a lesson.

"I'm not giving you a choice," he said. "I want you to go."

She pushed the car door open wider, as if about to leave.

He had to hand it to her. She was going to take it to the wire.

He stared straight ahead, smiling. She was going to break, beg, give in completely to her terror.

But she didn't.

The door opened wider, swung shut. And Honey was gone.

Dwayne sat stunned.

More balls than I thought.

He shut the passenger's side door so there was no interior light. The car already was well off the road where it wouldn't be noticed, and hardly anyone drove this road at night.

Nothing to do but go after the bitch.

She'd be a manageable bundle when he found her. He might hide and watch her awhile before rescuing her. Let fear dissolve what was left of her willpower. Then it would be her turn for a fate worse than death.

He got a flashlight out of the glove compartment, opened the driver's side door, and slipped out of the car and into the black and fetid swamp.

Honey's heart was fluttering irregularly, like something wild trying to escape the prison of her rib cage. She'd never been so frightened. She was breathing hard, making soft whimpering sounds, running, simply running through the night, splashing through shallow water, flailing away at branches scratching at her face. There were creatures around her, terrible creatures, that she could sense and sometimes hear.

She knew there must be another road running parallel to Lagoon, but she couldn't think of one.

Then it came to her.

Yes, last summer, when she was helping Helga Ditweiler learn to drive.

What's the name of that road? Cypress? South Road? Or is it just a number? Maybe—

She splashed through ankle-deep water and slammed head-on into a thick tree trunk.

And became part of the darkness of the swamp.

Dwayne took two steps into the swamp and his flashlight went dead.

Batteries. Damn it! I haven't replaced the batteries in months.

He stopped and stood still, listening.

There were only the sounds of the swamp at night.

Insects thrumming, larger things stirring, what might be the distant grunt of a gator.

"Honey!"

His call was unanswered.

Again.

Carefully, so he wouldn't lose his bearings in the night, he back-stepped toward the road. He held the dead flashlight as if it was a club. He hated it when things got out of control like this, and it was no fault of his own.

Flashlight batteries aren't made for this kind of climate. They go bad practically overnight.

Why did the damned bitch have to run into the swamp?

His heel found hard pavement. *Civilization!* Grateful for firm footing, he turned and strode toward his car.

And stopped.

He didn't have a flashlight that worked, but he had matches. And cigarettes.

And he was sure he could find his way to Honey. She couldn't have gone far in the thick foliage and mud that dragged at every step. And he couldn't hear her splashing around. She wasn't moving, he was sure. She probably thought she was hiding.

He glanced left and right into darkness. Surrounded by swamp country, no one would hear her screams. And if anyone did hear them, they'd assume the noise was being made by some animal, probably in the jaws of a gator.

If Honey did make it back to civilization, she wouldn't get all that much sympathy. If he applied the cigarettes to the folds of her body, where they were barely visible, her scars wouldn't look nearly as painful as they were. And there was no way she could prove he'd done anything to her.

He told himself that Honey would eventually be okay. She'd have a hard night, then she'd turn up somewhere, hysterical and cursing, and yammering a story that no one would believe. Not coming from such an "adventurous" girl.

A hard night in the swamp. He wondered what that would be like.

Well, it wasn't *his* fault. He wasn't the one who got stubborn and ran blindly away in the night. And he'd searched for her, hadn't he? It wasn't his fault that the flashlight went dead. Was he supposed to keep fresh batteries in the damned thing just in case some stupid cow did a dash into the swamp at night?

The swamp at night.

Now look what she was going to get for being such a nose-in-the-air bitch.

He shivered. Then he made sure there was nothing to indicate that Honey Carter had been in his car tonight. If she tried to implicate him in her panic and dumb dash, he'd simply deny it all, say she was lying. She'd gotten herself lost in the swamp and run into the wrong kind of people. Probably teased them, the way she liked to do. So they attacked her, had their fun with cigarettes and who knew what else. Now she was using *him* for a convenient scapegoat so she wouldn't seem like such a boob. Maybe there'd be no real, serious harm done, anyway. Just another he said/she said thing. People would soon forget. And pretty soon there'd be more and different rumors about Honey, tease that she was.

*   *   *

Dwayne found her within half an hour, unconscious at the base of a tree. He used the sash of her dress to tie her arms behind her, then bound her ankles.

Then he began with the cigarettes, and she came awake fast, squirming and screaming. He didn't bother to gag her, simply slapped her hard enough, often enough, and she suffered in silence. Well, she whimpered, actually.

Until she passed out.

He studied her for a while, knowing she was still alive. Then he removed the sash belt, and his own belt that he'd used on her ankles.

He walked away from her, wondering, if she lived through the night, what kind of story she would tell.

46

Pain dragged Honey up from sleep. Her eyes, her face, her lips, everything had been burned and stung like a thousand needles. She remembered last night, Dwayne bending over her with a glowing cigarette.

Through her pain, Honey became aware that there was a great weight on her. She attempted to lift whatever it was that was weighing her down, but she couldn't. She squinted straight up through cypress branches at a bright morning sky and felt better, more confident. Last night was like a terrible dream. But the dream was over.

A bird gave something like a shrill warning cry, but she ignored it. After all, she'd made it through the night.

She attempted again to lift the weight from her chest, then woke all the way and felt its surprising heft and roundness, was aware of the difficulty she was having breathing. The thing was dry and smooth.

And moved!

She realized what it was, but not that this was actually happening to *her*.

Honey screamed, so terrified now that she lost awareness of even her painfully burned face.

Nothing happened. Her desperate shrill cry was lost in the swamp.

She screamed until she was out of breath, felt the python shift slightly and tighten its grip around her entire body. She thought about getting up and running, but it was only a thought. Her legs were pressed together with such force that her knees ached.

The huge snake tightened its grip again, and Honey heard a sound like steam escaping a valve under pressure. Her right arm was smashed tight against her ribs. She flailed with her left. Every move she made seemed to prompt a countermove and a slight increase of vise-like pressure. She screamed again. Inhaled to follow with another scream, and found that she couldn't draw in enough air to muster any sound. Her waving loose left arm—the only part of her that was free—found the damp mud of the swamp floor and she pressed her palm against it, futilely attempting to rise.

More pressure. There was a muffled cracking sound, and an agonizing pain in her right side. *A rib breaking? I'm going to die here! I'm going to die!*

She was struggling mightily for precious oxygen now, making a series of gentle little puffs of exhalation. No more inhalations.

She managed to raise her head an inch. Two inches. And stared with wide eyes into eyes that were not human and held no hint of mercy.

She realized with horror that the head of the snake

that returned her stare with its own implacable gaze was larger than her own head.

Her wail of utter horror emerged only as a faint puff of breath, and was another signal for the thing to tighten its grip.

47

Unemployed oil rig worker Bailey Conners, driving on Lagoon Road later that day, braked reflexively when he saw something glowing dully in the sunlight among the weeds. It was about a hundred feet off the side of the road, near some cypress trees, and he had no idea what the damned thing was.

Well, he didn't have anything else to do other than to satisfy his curiosity.

Bailey steered his Dodge pickup onto the soggy shoulder, wondering if the truck's oversized but worn tires would have the traction to get it going again in the mud. It was a risk he had to take. He understood that he had to find out for sure what he'd seen, and that his mind on some level had rejected.

He climbed down from the truck's cab and rolled up the sleeves of his blue work shirt, knowing he was stalling to keep from approaching whatever was ahead of him in the tall grass. Nothing was visible now, without the advantage of seeing it from the truck's raised cab.

The sun beat down on him, and he picked up the

scent of his underarm odor from a shirt worn a day too long. There were crescents of perspiration beneath both arms of the shirt. He'd begun to sweat heavily.

He was considering returning to the truck when the grass stirred. His heartbeat picked up. He was aware of the copper taste of fear.

Grow some balls, Bailey!

He didn't have any more sleeves to roll up, so he took a deep breath and moved forward.

Bailey didn't see it at first, because it was almost the color of the swamp. Then there it was in recognizable form, like a trick of the light. Once he realized what it was, its configuration was obvious. How had he missed it at first? The coiled body of the snake was immense, thicker than a fire hose, colored a mottled tan and green that made it nearly invisible.

There had been a state-sponsored python hunting season recently, to try to keep the python population in check. Obviously, the hunt in this area hadn't been successful.

Why do people turn these things from hell loose so they can grow and grow?

As solid ground gave way to mud, Bailey's boots began making slurping noises with each step.

He was within twenty feet of the snake, but the tall saw grass was blocking some of his view.

The snake moved slightly.

So the damned thing is alive.

Not that he'd thought otherwise—merely hoped.

Bailey slowed his approach, altering direction slightly to stay on relatively solid ground.

Then he saw something that turned his fear to horror.

A patch of blue cloth had emerged from between the python's coils. Surely part of an article of clothing. He saw that one side of it was edged with lace.

A dress.

My God, he was looking at a dress!

A rage he didn't understand helped to overcome his fear, and he moved forward to slightly higher ground. He saw what he dreaded. Pink flesh. An ankle and foot. Unmoving.

He inched closer and saw the horror in its entirety.

The python paid no attention to him. Perhaps because it was feeding. As snakes do, it had unhinged its jaws to consume larger prey headfirst. The girl's blond head had almost disappeared inside the snake. Little of her slender body was visible among the tightly wrapped coils that had slowly and by degrees crushed the life from her.

A trembling Bailey found himself wondering if she'd been dead before the snake—

He refused to finish his thought.

The snake paused in its feeding and was perfectly still, staring at Bailey with calculating eyes.

Sweet Jesus!

On unsteady legs, Bailey took three cautious backward steps. Then he turned and hurried back to the truck to get his shotgun.

Everyone who knew Honey Carter was shocked by her death. Dwayne was inconsolable. And like everyone else, he had no idea what Honey had been doing that night in the swamp.

Mrs. Collingsworth, Honey's former biology teacher,

said that Honey had possessed a growing interest in nature and all its inhabitants. Creatures of the swamp, in particular, had fascinated her.

Dwayne knew that Honey had snowed Mrs. Collingsworth to raise her grade point average. He made no mention of it.

Four days after Bailey found Honey in the coils of the giant python, a man with a twelve-gauge shotgun entered a biker bar in nearby Plainville and blasted three of the regular customers off their stools. When the police arrived, the killer burst from the diner barefoot and shot one of them, then leaned over his shotgun and used a toe to trip the trigger and blow himself almost in half.

Dead at home from shotgun blasts were the man's wife and two children. The media quickly discovered that one of the casualties in the biker bar had been involved in a secret affair with the killer's wife.

That was pretty much the end of Honey in the news.

There were a few suspicions and aspersions cast Dwayne's way, but he ignored them and they gained no substance or credibility. As far as the sheriff's office was concerned, Honey had met with a terrible accident, and that was that.

Like the rest of her friends, Dwayne professed to be crushed by her death.

48

Green Forest, Ohio, the present

Quinn parked the rental car in front of Ida Tucker's frame house, in the shade of a big mimosa tree. When they opened the car's doors and climbed out, the sweet scent of the tree's pink blossoms was like perfume.

All in all it was a nice morning, still not overheated by the summer sun. Ida suggested that they walk.

A plain black Ford SUV pulled into the Tucker driveway, and Joel Price climbed down from it, moving with the stiffness of old age. They invited Price to walk with them, but he declined, got back in the truck, and drove the few blocks to the Tradesman First National Bank.

He was standing in the shade of a large oak tree, in the center of a paved roundabout in front of the bank, when they arrived. Those on foot were feeling too warm and wished they'd heeded the advice of the attorney, looking dry and comfortable despite his dark suit. His tie had a small checked design on it today. Not a black tie like yesterday, but certainly not festive. Price had been around long enough to hit the right notes.

He smiled in greeting, then led them solemnly into the bank.

The air-conditioning was keeping up in there, and it was quiet in the way of banks with lots of carpeting and wood paneling.

There were two tellers' windows open, and half a dozen employees at desks or wandering about with papers in their hands. Quinn counted only three other customers. One at each window, and one at a long oak table near the bank's lettered window. Behind the tellers' cages was a large, polished steel safe with its door open.

"Hi, Maggie," Price said, to the youngest of the two tellers. Not that either of them was a spring chicken. Maggie looked about forty, the other teller fifty. Maggie had chopped-off looking dark hair. The other teller was a woman with gray hair worn in a long braid down her back. She was looking up something for a stout Hispanic woman holding a handful of what looked like deposit slips.

Maggie gave her customer some sort of form to fill out regarding a new mortgage. When the refinancing customer was gone, Maggie smiled at the small group near her teller's cage. Said, "Hi, Mr. Price."

Price said, "We need to get into a box, Maggie."

She bent down and got some keys and what looked like a black leather ledger, then came out from behind the marble counter.

When they'd reached a small table near the gaping entrance to the vault, Maggie placed the leather book on the table and opened it.

"Not my usual box, Maggie," the lawyer said. "Number one-fifty."

Maggie turned some pages and seemed to study the

book for several seconds. "Long time between visits, Mr. Price."

"Part of my job," Price said. He signed and dated the book.

Carrying a jingling ring of keys, Maggie led him into the vault.

A few minutes later, they emerged. Price was carrying a long, gray metal box with a locked door on one end. Maggie moved ahead of him and held open a door to a carpeted ten-by-ten room with a single oak table and two oak chairs. There was a tablet of paper on the table, along with a lamp.

Maggie laid the long metal box on the table, unfastened one of the locks with her master key, then nodded to them, and left the room. Joel Price had the second key needed to open the box.

Quinn went to the door Maggie had left by and worked the lock on the knob.

He nodded to Price, who withdrew the box's key from a small, sturdy envelope with the box number written on it.

Ida Tucker moved closer, which seemed to cause Pearl to edge toward her. Quinn moved directly toward the box as Price worked his key and then lifted the hinged lid that was about half the length of the box itself. Everyone in the room leaned toward the box, staring.

It was empty.

Price seemed flabbergasted. "I don't understand this any more than you do," he said.

"Were you and Edward Tucker the only ones with keys?" Quinn asked.

Price nodded. "Yes. I had mine, always, in my desk

drawer or in my pocket. I don't know where Edward Tucker kept his key. I do know it would take the person with the activating key and the person with the other legitimate key to open the safe before nine a.m., when the bank opened and the timer would kick in within the safe."

Price explained that at precisely 9:00 A.M. the safe's brass handle could be moved to the left 180 degrees and the heavy steel door, balanced on its bearings, could be swung open with very little effort. It was usually left that way until the bank closed. Then the safe door would be shut and would automatically lock tight on its timer. It couldn't be opened except with explosives until nine the next morning.

No one, even if they'd wanted to, could have entered the vault and removed and unlocked Joel Price and Edward Tucker's safe deposit box. Joel Price had a key. Edward Tucker had an identical key. The bank had the second key, necessary to get into any of the boxes.

Joel Price asked everyone to remain, then left the room for a few minutes and returned with Maggie the teller and Mr. Earl Tanenger, the bank manager. Tanenger was a corpulent, bald man in his sixties and took up a lot of space. They were all crowded into the little room where the boxes could be opened in private by customers. Maggie had the leather record book. She was wearing too much of her new perfume, Heaven's Gate, that made a few people—Pearl among them—sniff and sneeze.

In front of everyone, Earl Tanenger opened the leather-bound book, stared at it, and proclaimed that no one had entered the vault and removed box 150 since October 12, 1998, when the box was rented and the register was signed by both Joel Price and Edward Tucker. Mr. Tanenger had been bank manager for almost twenty years and remembered that day well.

Said he did, anyway.

Quinn had his doubts. He said, "I want to talk to all the employees." He was aware that he had no jurisdiction here. Also aware that Earl Tanenger didn't want the county sheriff involved and for this thing to get out of hand.

"Certainly," Tanenger said.

They all left the room and moved toward the lobby, where Tanenger motioned them toward the conference room while he went to temporarily close the bank and summon the employees.

No one spoke. A few sniffled, still under the spell of Heaven's Gate.

Pearl said, "I hope we can get this cleared up fast."

Quinn thought her swollen nasal passages made her sound like Porky Pig, but he said not a word.

Earl Tanenger returned only a few minutes later, with the teller who'd been working with Maggie behind the counter. She was a whippet-thin gray-haired woman in her fifties, who would have been perfectly cast as a severe librarian or teacher who would abide no breaking of the rules.

"This is Miss Luella Morst," Tanenger said. "And she can explain." He took a step to the side and motioned with his right arm. "Luella, the floor is yours."

"Four days ago, Monday it was, Maggie was home sick with the swine flu."

God! Pearl thought.

Luella pressed on. "Mr. Edward Tucker and another man came into the bank, and Mr. Tucker asked for his safety deposit box. I gave it to him, and he and the other man went into one of the privacy rooms. They were only in there a few minutes, then came out. I went back with Mr. Tucker, and we returned his box to the proper place, locked it, and I escorted him out, then watched both men leave. They were both very polite and businesslike." Miss Morst flushed and for the first time seemed defensive. "I'm not used to working the deposit boxes. I did everything right, except I forgot to have Mr. Tucker sign and date the register."

"Mistakes happen," Earl Tanenger said, and rested a hand lightly on Luella Morst's shoulder.

"Do you know Edward Tucker by sight?" Quinn asked Luella Morst.

"Yes. I've seen him around town for years."

"The other man?"

"Never saw him before."

"Do you recall what he looked like?"

"Didn't pay much attention, tell you the truth. Average size, maybe too fat."

"Hair?"

"Yes. Dark, I think."

"Scars? Facial hair? Tattoos? Glasses?"

"Not glasses, I don't think. The rest of it I don't know. I do recall that he had a Band-Aid on his face, like he'd cut himself or got cut."

Quinn almost moaned. It was an old technique for a crook to wear a Band-Aid on his or her face. It would probably be all any witnesses would remember about how they looked.

"Did Mr. Tucker seem as if he was at ease?" Quinn asked. "Did the other man seem to be controlling him in any way?"

"Not at all. They acted perfectly normal."

Quinn thanked her. Earl Tanenger instructed her and everyone else to return to work. Then he looked at Quinn and shrugged.

"Human error," he said.

"He probably wouldn't have signed his name anyway," Quinn said. "Just be glad you've got an employee with the guts to come forward."

"I should give her a bonus for her forgetfulness?" Tanenger said.

"Yes," Pearl said.

"What could Edward have been doing?" Ida Tucker asked the world in general.

"Whatever it was, he might have been doing it under duress, despite what Luella Morst said."

"He'd never do anything illegal."

"Whatever was in that box, it belonged to him."

"It belonged to the family," Ida Tucker said, with more than a touch of bitterness.

They went back out on the sidewalk and crossed to the paved roundabout in front of the bank. It had gotten hotter outside. Uncomfortable.

They all said their good-byes. Quinn and Pearl repeated their condolences. Joel Price assured them he would call if there were any developments.

There were just the two of them now on the hot and dusty street, Quinn and Pearl.

"This is what a dead end looks like," Pearl said.

"Maybe," Quinn said.

"What happens now?" Pearl asked.

"Whatever it is, it'll happen in New York."

Only it didn't.

* * *

Before they could get in the car, Ida Tucker came huffing up to them, forcing a grin.

"I don't know what I was thinking," she said, "not inviting you to come to the house afterward and have some lemonade."

"Really," Pearl said, "that's very kind of you but it isn't necessary."

The grin widened. She'd been pushing herself, Quinn thought, especially considering her age. He wondered about her. Was she simply what she seemed—a gentle and artful mother? What role, if any, had she played in making Henry Tucker's letters disappear? People who were experts in conning others often thought themselves more clever than they were. If Ida Tucker had been in on whatever had happened that made their trip from New York futile, was it possible that she *couldn't* simply allow the con to end? Were she and some of the others secretly enjoying themselves too much, and had to extend the advantage they'd already exercised? Was that what he was seeing here? Did Ida Tucker, on a subliminal level, want to rub it in?

"I'm thirsty," Quinn said. He smiled at Ida Tucker. "Lemonade sounds perfect, dear. But let's drive back to your house in our car."

"There's an offer I'll accept," Ida said, "since you so graciously accepted mine."

Gracious. Yes, that was the game they were playing.

49

Everything in the Tucker house hit the correct note—the flowers, the cards and letters of condolences. Everything but a black wreathe on the front door. Or had he missed it?

Quinn was more interested in the permanent objects in the house, rather than those that would be discarded after a period of grieving. The books in the matching white bookcases, for instance. Many of them were on travel. Some were fiction. Eric Ambler, John le Carré, Ruth Rendell, Jonathon Kellerman, Len Deighton . . . clever writers, all of them. No romance, or supernatural, or street-level cop novels here. Psychological mysteries. Suspense. Kellerman was even himself a psychologist. Quinn figured the readers of such books got their enjoyment out of trying to outwit the writers.

Would Ida or her late husband be the sort to write critical Amazon reviews or send taunting e-mails to the writers?

They didn't seem the type, but mightn't that be camouflage?

Pearl must have had some idea of what he was thinking, and disagreed. She gave him a look and a shake of her head. Her meaning was unmistakable: *Let's get out of here.*

But Quinn had gone from examining books to looking over the family photos on top of the bookcase. Lots of outdoor shots of happy people, their images frozen by the click of a camera. There was Andria, standing close beside Jeanine. Their arms were draped over each other's shoulders. Neither seemed to have an inkling of what lay in store for them.

There was an interesting man in the background of one of the photographs, wearing an apron and wielding what looked like a large spatula.

"That fella," he said, to Ida Tucker, who had just entered the living room with glasses of lemonade on a tray. "He looks familiar."

"That handsome man in the background by the lake? That's my nephew on my mother's side, Rubin Hasabedo. He was one of the most famous bullfighters in Spain."

And my nephew on my father's side invented the thing that is better than sliced bread. "Not him," Quinn said. "The man by the grill, playing chef."

"Oh, him." A glass rattled faintly against the metal tray, and Ida Tucker seemed to miss a beat. Like a tightrope walker shifting weight slightly the wrong way, then immediately regaining balance and resuming the seemingly casual stroll along the wire.

She began to circulate with the tray, passing out the frosted glasses. "That's Robert Kingdom, Jr.," she said, knowing he'd already identified the man.

"You mean Winston Castle," Quinn said.

"That's what he's calling himself now, I suppose. He loves medieval things. Mostly anything British." She helped herself to the remaining glass, sipped from it, and laid the tray aside on a folded newspaper on the coffee table. "In fact, anything British. Heaven knows why."

"He has a mustache now. And he's put on a little weight."

"He was always robust."

"You say he's a family member?"

"Oh, I think we both know the answer to that one. It's yes and no. Winston was taken in as a ward of the state. He didn't stay long. He was a restless boy, living in a make-believe world of his own. Kingdom was a good name for him. Castle is, too, I suppose. Doesn't his restaurant in New York resemble a medieval castle?"

"Very much so."

"So vedy, vedy British."

"I'm surprised you didn't drop in and see him while you were in town."

"Well, I wasn't exactly there for a happy occasion," Ida said. "I didn't have time for social calls."

"Too bad you didn't have a fortnight."

"We were never all that close, really. Not bad blood, though. Just distance. People do grow apart for no reason other than geographical distance."

"It can make the heart grow fonder, too," Quinn said.

"I suppose. But I often suspect those noxious little homilies. May I offer you more lemonade?"

Quinn glanced down and was surprised to see that his glass was half empty. "I'd like to," he said, "but we have a plane to board in Columbus."

"If anything of interest occurs, we'll keep you apprised," Joel Price said, struggling to his feet with an old man's hesitancy and obviously sore lower back.

Quinn believed him. He also believed Price still regarded Edward Tucker as his client, however dead Tucker might be.

Quinn shook hands with Price, and everybody said their good-byes. Price was the only one who didn't seem to have noticed that the ground had shifted. But Price knew.

On the drive back to Columbus, Quinn and Pearl sat silently for a long time, listening to the tires thump rhythmically on the pavement seams. They were both pretty sure of the same thing, that Winston Castle had been the man accompanying Edward Tucker to his safety-deposit box. The average this, average that man with the Band-Aid on his face.

The Band-Aid disguise. Where did he learn that?

Winston Castle and Ida Tucker were playing in a dream game that had become deadly. A game that had been joined by a serial killer who murdered for more than mere profit.

Not that the killer wouldn't pursue potential profit if it passed before his eyes. It was valuable to him in the way of monopoly money. A prize and a leg up in the game. But nothing more.

Quinn knew he didn't have to voice any of these thoughts. He and Pearl were mostly of the same mind on this.

"I hope yon Far Castle knight's face has healed," she said as they took the cutoff to the airport.

"Not me," Quinn said. "Not yet."

Jerry Lido had some information for Quinn that he texted shortly after the plane had landed.

There had never been a Spanish bullfighter named Rubin Hasabedo, famous or otherwise.

Possibly, Quinn thought, Ida Tucker had invented the name on the spot.

Along with a lot of other inventions. Handsome Rubin Hasabedo probably had never been within ten feet of a bull. He might have been Photoshopped from an old menswear catalog into the group photo. Nicely done. Until you thought about it, very convincing.

Olé! Quinn thought.

50

Dwayne waited for a proper time, then he determined to get out of town when few people noticed him leaving. It was spring break. Honey wasn't mentioned much in the news these days. Especially with the college kids rolling in and partying all over Florida. Already, an Illinois sophomore in Clearwater had fallen to his death from a third-floor balcony while drunk and convinced he could leap to the next balcony. He had boldly announced his intention so there would be plenty of photographs and YouTube videos. A record of his feat.

Nobody had seemed able or willing to talk him out of it. As the photos showed, he only missed by a few feet, which made for even more public interest and tons of news coverage for a subject other than Honey.

For someone so financially secure, Dwayne didn't have a lot of worldly goods that weren't in real estate or in trust. So it was easy to pack some large suitcases, a few cardboard boxes, and drive to the opposite coast, and then north.

It occurred to him one sunny morning that maybe he should continue driving north, all the way to New York. The city teemed with the activity of people on the make, on the way up, down, sideways, drowning. Probably Honey's death hadn't even been covered in the news there. Or if it had, it would have been in a simple sidebar.

Under the fold, as they say in newspaper biz. Dwayne's women wouldn't give him any trouble once they were under the fold.

Just outside St. Augustine, he stayed in a motel with a red tile roof. It was designed to look old but was actually built only a few years ago. Its king-sized bed was amazingly comfortable and conducive to dreams. He thought he heard the sea whispering to him that night, but couldn't be sure. In the morning, he drove into town and located the main library.

It was easy to research New York City, and easy to understand how people could lose themselves in such a place.

Or find themselves.

He took the next several days driving to the City, skirting the East Coast and taking his time. For an hour in the Carolinas the killer drove through heavy rain, and occasional hail the size of peas. During a break in the downpour, he stopped for gas and was told there were hurricane warnings beyond Cape Fear. He ignored the warnings. He was from Florida and gave not a damn for hurricanes.

During the next half hour, trees bent with the wind and shed some of their leaves and small branches, but there was no hurricane. A man's voice on the car radio said the weather on that part of the coast had been downgraded to a tropical storm. He sounded disappointed.

When the killer arrived, he was amazed. Every direction he looked was sensory overload. Was that a celebrity he'd just walked past on the sidewalk, or was he simply someone who resembled a person Dwayne had met along the road? Faces seemed to glide past him. There were celebrities on signs, billboards, and almost certainly in the throngs of people on the wide sidewalks. Odd that in the city of anonymity, a person could become famous overnight.

There was media of every kind here, all over the place. It struck Dwayne that this was the ideal city in which to practice and perfect his craft. There was an endless supply of potential victims.

Not just any woman would do. They would be blond, preferably with blue eyes, and on the fleshy side. Such women would be in the most danger. But there would be other potential victims. He'd know them when he saw them. Innate victims. Prey for the predators. He knew them already. They recognized in him something perilous that drew more forcibly than it repelled.

The city had a police force numbering in the tens of thousands, but as far as Dwayne was concerned, that was simply lots of cops to get in the way of other cops. They were no match for him. Now and then they screwed up and did something right, but not so often that it did more than amuse him.

Which was why Dwayne was glad to find in his research a police lieutenant named Francis Quinn, who had made his reputation tracking and apprehending (or destroying) serial killers. Dwayne would strain forward and read more closely whenever he came across information about Quinn.

The guy was a throwback. He played straight, but he was more interested in justice than in legalities. He was tough, smart, and could be mean as hell. Sometimes he heeded red tape; sometimes he ripped it to shreds. Purportedly, he loved the theater and had even been spotted at the ballet. Odd, that. He looked more like a thug than a cop—a definite advantage in his world.

The only way to win a great war was to choose a great adversary. Quinn, who was practically worshipped by the New York media and, it seemed, by the NYPD, provided the ideal pursuer to match someone like Dwayne.

Did the man have experience and street creds? Dwayne read three times a piece about Frank Quinn in the *New York Post*. The journalist who interviewed and wrote about Quinn could hardly have drawn a meatier assignment. Some of the most gruesome homicides in the city's history had been solved by Quinn. The photographs alone gave Dwayne an erection.

The *Times* saw Quinn as a human thinking machine, who was always two steps or more ahead of his adversary, and whose toughness and relentlessness never failed.

This man would be Dwayne's principal opponent. His opposite number on the game board of New York.

Dwayne would kill in such a way that it quenched— at least for a while—his desire to kill certain women. The women he needed to kill, and those he knew when he saw them the first time. Women like Maude. Like Honey. It had come to him in a nighttime revelation that from the beginning he'd known he would kill the women.

He'd been their fate. And he would be the fate of more women.

New York would be his killing field, and he'd devise a calling card so the police would attribute each murder to him. He *wanted* them to know who was commandeering these women's lives, putting them in hell, and flirting—only flirting—with the concept of dying with them.

He would, from time to time, feed the press information. That might seem to be a help to the police, until further thought would remind them that most if not all early initial information could be used to foul up an investigation.

Dwayne smiled at the idea of his "calling card," the letters *D.O.A.* Those hunting him would assume the initials stood for Dead on Arrival, and not Dwayne Oren Aikens. Probably they would never become aware that there was a Dwayne Oren Aikens.

He would kill with increasing frequency and viciousness, this D.O.A. killer. Quinn and his minions would never find or stop him.

The police—Quinn—would come to respect him. Eventually they would envy him. He knew the police by now. He knew how they thought. And he knew the inevitable realization that would creep into their minds.

Secretly at first, even to themselves, they'd understand that they envied him. That they wished they could do what he did. That they were who he was.

They'd sample only an inkling, mostly at night in dreams, but that would be enough to inform them of what they were missing.

But of course they wouldn't have the courage to expand, to experience. They would not act out what played in the theaters of their minds.

They could only guess how it was. Could be. Would never be. For them.

Dwayne paused to sit for a while on the steps of the Metropolitan Museum and watch the women walk past. Women of every sort and dressed in any fashion. There went the casual sophisticate in slouchy disdain and denim; the prim and businesslike in the costume of commerce (except for shoes made for walking); the twentyish undergrad type with unkempt hair and minimal makeup; the fashion model striding with crossover steps as if on a runway; the intellectual charmer, perhaps a researcher or book editor; the counterculture teenager new to drugs and sex, afraid and on the make.

They thought they were beautiful, these women, but they were not nearly as close to perfection as the women on canvas and in marble inside the museum. In timeless repose, displayed for the admiration of all who passed, *their* beauty was forever.

There, at an ascending angle to the steps, went a small blond girl with a pert way about her. What used to be called a vest-pocket beauty.

Dwayne realized he was smiling. He had *so* enjoyed his role in Honey Carter's death. The manner of her death intrigued him. She had died slowly, inch by inch, breath by breath.

His only regret was that he hadn't been there to observe her.

51

"So that's where we are," Helen the profiler said to Quinn.

Sal and Harold had just left to take over the watch on Weaver. Jody was with Pearl. Helen and Quinn were alone in the office. Fedderman was off someplace with Penny, trying to preserve his marriage.

Quinn poured himself half a cup of atrocious but hot coffee from the gurgling brewer and walked over to stand near Helen.

"Where is *that?*" he asked. "The *that* where we are, I mean."

"A family—or what passes for one these days—finds purpose in its existence by searching for a missing piece of art."

"*Bellezza,*" Quinn said. "Maybe it's of great enough value that it's worth the search." He shrugged. "On the other hand, it's not the Holy Grail."

"It is to them," Helen said.

"Most of them aren't even blood relatives."

"Are you sure of that?"

"No. And I'm afraid to start counting."

"Maybe not being blood relatives makes them need a cause all the more," Helen said.

Quinn thought there was a kind of twisted logic to that. But then "twisted" was his game.

"One thing's for sure," he said, " when they're talking, as often as not they're lying. We can't believe anything we hear unless it's been substantiated."

"They simply have a different slant on what's factual," Helen said.

"Those are the kind of distinctions that tend to disappear in courtrooms."

"Has it been firmly established that Michelangelo sculpted *Bellezza?*" Helen asked.

"The church would say no, that *Bellezza* never existed in flesh or stone. But we know she exists. Rumor had it that a collector named Samuel Gundelheimer had her in his private collection when the Germans occupied France in World War Two."

"He was also a very successful banker in Paris."

"You know this how?"

"I've looked into the Gundelheimer family," Helen said.

"Seems out of your bailiwick," Quinn said.

Helen shrugged. "I'm Jewish."

She said it in a way that Quinn knew meant something. He waited. Helen crossed her long arms, fought a mental conflict that showed on her face, and decided to share.

"Samuel Gundelheimer and his wife, Rebecca, were sent to Bergen Belsen in 1944," she said, "and there is no firm record of them or of any of the Gundelheimer family after that. There was a daughter, Elna, thirteen;

and twin sons, Jacob and Isador, eight years old. The girl was of no use to the Nazis, and the boys were too young for forced labor. There is some indication, but no firm knowledge, of Samuel and Rebecca Gundelheimer dying of typhus in 1945. The children seem to have been transported to other camps, where they simply became part of the missing dead. They might have been gassed, or used for medical experimentation—especially the twins—then possibly incinerated. They might have become part of a mass grave near the camp that contained several thousand."

"Good God!"

"He was nowhere to be found at the time," Helen said.

Quinn was surprised to see she that she'd teared up. "You see this shit on the Internet and it becomes real again if you let it. My great grandmother . . . my . . ." She could no longer force the words out.

Quinn snatched up a tissue and moved out from behind his desk. He gave the tissue to Helen, who folded it into quarters and dabbed at her eyes.

Quinn patted her shoulder. "It's okay, dear."

She shook her head. "Men into monsters. How does it happen?"

We're supposed to know.

He gave her another tissue, then sat on the desk corner. "You're not assuming this case has something to do with the Holocaust . . ."

"Nothing and everything," Helen said. She dabbed twice at each eye and then slipped the wadded tissue into a pocket. "Samuel and Rebecca Gundelheimer didn't want to surrender any of the world's beauty to the enemy."

"The enemy got a lot of it," Quinn said, "though plenty of it was recovered, too."

"The Nazis didn't get our girl," Helen said, "thanks to the Gundelheimers and some others."

Quinn almost smiled at her, then realized she might not understand. "We're thinking the same thing, I'll bet."

Helen nodded. "A serial killer talks with Grace Geyer, setting her up to be a victim, and out of the blue she says something that piques his interest. After pumping her for more information, he realizes he might have stumbled onto something big. He decides to cut himself in on what might be a valuable missing piece of art."

"But he needs to know more," Quinn says.

"Right. He follows Grace and the others to the Fairchild Hotel, intending to torture and question Andria Bell, being alone with her, taking his time. After all, she's the expert in the group. Then he discovers Andria's suite adjoins another, where five art students are staying, including Grace Geyer. Mass murder ensues, as well as skillful and agonizing torture, and the passing of information. That's when the killer and our overactive family intersect."

And what began as a vendetta chess game between the killer and Quinn develops into a treasure hunt and murder spree.

"Grace wouldn't have known much," Quinn said. "And Andria would have resisted talking."

Helen said, "Under certain kinds of torture, *everybody* talks." Her voice was sad. "No exceptions."

Quinn had seen enough of the tortured and dead not to differ with her.

Helen waited, eyes dry now. Her face was still flushed, making her freckles less obvious.

"Are we still thinking the same thing?" she asked.

"Henry Tucker's backpack," Quinn said.

Helen managed a ragged smile. "You'll find whatever was inside it. You'll find the letters."

"How can you be so certain?" Quinn asked.

"I'm certain of you."

52

Honor Tripp looked at the man across the table and counted herself among the lucky.

So far.

They'd had only three dates, eaten three dinners together, and attended two off-Broadway shows. Neither show had been very good, but they didn't much mind. That was because they did get along. This man, unlike so many others, seemed truly interested in her. What she was, who she was, what she thought. And he seemed to like her.

Well, more than *like* her.

The one thing about James Bolton that gave Honor pause was that he seemed somewhat secretive. He was skilled at deflecting questions.

So he was wary, she told herself. Like most men. Like most people in the singles society. A person gets hurt so many times and then puts up defensive walls.

Honor understood that and was patient.

Still, she wondered. She probed. It was in her nature.

"You're not a native New Yorker, are you?" she

asked, sitting across from Bolton in Beaux Arts Espresso in the Village.

Bolton gave her the slow smile that had first attracted her to him, the way it crinkled the faint scar on the side of his face. That and the way he was dressed—casually, with dark slacks, a gray shirt with its long sleeves hiked up almost to his elbows. And there was something about his hands, so strong yet sensitive. He was always unconsciously caressing things, his coffee cup, the small table's centerpiece vase, the backs of her hands and fingers. . . . That was why she was drawn to him, she realized. He was so very tactile.

Bolton hadn't answered. Honor cocked her head in what she fancied was her puzzled but pleased look. "So where are you from?"

"Around. Right now I'm living over on the East Side, near First Avenue and 57th Street."

"That's a nice neighborhood, but I wouldn't say it's nearby. What are you doing here in the Village?"

He sipped his coffee, smiling at her with his eyes through the steam wafting up from the cup. She thought it made him look kind of mystical.

"I followed you when I saw you the other day," he said.

Honor was flattered but puzzled. She wasn't ugly, and did have a trim figure, but she wasn't the kind of femme fatale who drew men along behind her as if they were attached by a string.

Or am I?

"Why follow me?" she asked, and sipped her own coffee. "Didn't you have better things to do?"

"There are no better things to do."

"But why *me?*"

"One reason is I liked your looks when I saw you coming out of the Marlborough Book Shop. You paused at the curb and waited for traffic, standing almost as if you were posed. You would have made a perfect photo. That image rang some inner bell in me. I had to walk across the street and try to get to know you better. To see what you thought."

"Thought about what?"

"Oh, you know. Did Shakespeare write all his plays?"

"You need to know what I think about that?"

"Desperately."

"So what *do* you think?"

"I have no idea," he said.

She mock clapped her hands. "Finally! Do you realize how rare you are?"

"I'm not sure."

"You're a man who understands he doesn't have all the answers."

He smiled. "There are more and more of us gaining that insight."

She cocked her head at him and looked inquisitive. Was he serious? Or was he painting a picture of himself he knew she'd like?

Why not come right out and ask him?

"Are you playing the feminist card?" she asked.

"To what end?"

"To get what you want from me."

"To be honest with you, I'll play all the cards in my hand, if it means I get more acquainted with you."

"But you wouldn't lie?"

"I don't think I'd have to lie to you. Soul mates don't harbor secrets. Not from each other. They can't."

She studied him even more closely, as if looking for some telltale sign somewhere on his clothes. Some giveaway stain. They hadn't talked too much before.

"Okay," she said, "I'll tell you the truth."

"I wouldn't expect any less from you."

"I wasn't in that bookstore to buy books. I went there to see if they had any of mine on the shelf."

He didn't understand at first, and then he beamed. "You're a writer?"

"Indeed." She immediately felt like a numbskull. "I mean, yeah. Yes, I'm a writer."

"How many—"

"This is my first novel."

"Where do you—"

"I get my ideas from life. Experiences like this one."

"What's the—"

"Title?" they said in unison.

"*Strange on the Range,*" she said. "It's an occult western cooking mystery."

"I heard women were writing more and more mystery novels," he said.

"Have you read any?"

"I will now."

"You really should. There are some great female mystery writers—Sara Paretsky, Sue Grafton, Linda Barnes, Nancy Pickard . . ."

"You *know* these people?"

"I've met them at conventions."

He sat back and grinned. "Neat! I know a real writer."

Her smile was tentative. "I'm not sure it will change your life all that much."

"Nonsense. You've changed it already." He reached across the table and lightly touched the backs of both her hands. His fingers seemed to emit low-voltage electricity. "I've often thought of writing a book myself."

She drew her hands back, cocked her head again the way she did. "Tell me something. You didn't plan all this as a way to get to meet me so I could help you get published, did you?"

He looked flabbergasted. Actually stuck out a forefinger and crossed his heart. "Not a chance. Do people really *do* that?"

"More often than you'd think."

"All I've done is *thought* about writing a book. I'd never attempt one."

She appeared curious. "Why not?"

"Well, I guess because I'm not a writer. I mean, when did you know you were a writer?"

"I've always known."

"Well, I've never known and don't know now."

"But you'd like to write."

"Well, somewhat."

"Maybe you won't know till you try."

He laughed. "I wouldn't even know how to try."

She said, "I have an apartment full of books that teach people how to write." The words had come from her mouth automatically. She was embarrassed now, wishing desperately that she could snatch them back.

His hands were touching her again. He said, "The least I can do is look at them." He shrugged. "Who knows, I might be another Nancy Paretsky."

"Anything's possible," Honor said. "Maybe we'll even solve that mystery you asked about."

"Mystery?"

"Was Shakespeare a phony?"

"You probably could tell me more than your books about that."

"If you asked the right questions, maybe." She felt the blood rush to her face and hoped he didn't notice. She sipped some more coffee as a diversion.

"You could show me what questions to ask," he said.

"I'm no expert on the bard," she said.

"I wouldn't know the difference."

Honor flipped a mental coin, knowing even as she did so that it was the same on both sides.

"I'm only a few blocks from here," she said.

The killer knew where she lived but decided not to mention that. No reason for her to know he'd followed her home one evening. He'd even thought, momentarily, of paying her a visit. But he'd known the time wasn't right.

He left a tip and they walked from the coffee shop. She noticed he had a black leather case, almost like a purse, slung by its strap over a shoulder. It must have been out of sight beneath the table.

"What's that?" she asked.

"It's sometimes called a European wallet." In truth he'd seen such cases called that only in an advertisement. "Or a man purse." He grinned over at her. "I prefer 'European wallet.' "

"I kind of like man purse," she said. And she did. She liked a man who dared to be different. "What do you keep in it?"

"Oh, just things that I use."

"For what?" she asked coyly.

"This and that."

"Like maybe staying the night someplace and still being able to have a fresh shirt and shave?"

"That, too," he said, and felt to make sure the black leather flap was locked.

PART FIVE

Cookery is become an art.

—ROBERT BURTON, *The Anatomy of Melancholy*

53

"She wrote a cooking mystery," Fedderman said.

They were in Honor Tripp's apartment. She was lying dead on her bed, on her back, wrists and ankles bound so that her legs would never again straighten in response to what she wanted, because she was past wanting anything. The expression on her face suggested she had died in pain. The knife and cigarette burn injuries on her nude body indicated how intense that pain must have been.

Quinn and Pearl were there with Fedderman, along with Captain Harley Renz, who'd come right over from his office when he heard about the homicide call, and that the letters *D.O.A.* had been carved in the victim's forehead.

Nift the nasty little ME was there, hands on hips, staring down at what was left of Honor Tripp.

"Straighten her out," Nift said, "and she would have been a good looking piece of trim."

The others ignored him, as well as the CSU techs bustling around the apartment. Except for Pearl. Quinn heard her slight intake of breath and sensed her body tightening. Nift could get under skin, and had sensed that shortly after they'd met. There was nothing she could do about it but endure.

"A cooking mystery," Renz said. "No doubt she shared her knowledge about her special dishes with her killer."

"He would have asked her about them," Quinn said.

"Tenderized meat dishes especially." Nift said.

"Just make yourself useful," Quinn told him, sensing Pearl was coming to a boil.

"Okeydoke," Nift said, seemingly unconcerned. He used a stainless steel probe for a pointer. "The carving in her forehead occurred after death. But don't assume the killer showed her any mercy; he simply wanted there to be less bleeding than if her heart was still pumping. Less mess that way, and his carving would be legible."

"D.O.A. I guess that means the obvious," Pearl said. "Dead on Arrival."

"Who called it in?" Quinn asked Fedderman.

"Neighbor in the apartment upstairs. Said he heard a lot of moaning and sobbing around midnight. It went on for over an hour. A short while after that, he heard somebody leave."

"He do anything about it?"

"Said he considered it and decided not to. Figured it might be his neighbors making love."

"With the sobbing?" Pearl said.

Nift smiled and said, "*Strange on the Range.*"

"The neighbor still over there?" Quinn asked Fedderman, before Pearl could launch a zinger at Nift.

It was Renz who answered. "Yeah. I talked to him after Fedderman did."

Renz wasn't wearing his uniform. The neighbor had probably assumed he was an ordinary detective in a sharp suit.

"His name's Justin Beck. Laid-off engineer."

"Midnight's a good approximate time of death," Nift said. "I can make it more precise later." He resisted looking at Pearl's breasts, or making a smart remark. Quinn didn't figure he was reforming. Nift smiled. "Honor Tripp and I will get together later at the morgue, and she'll reveal all her silent secrets."

"So screwed up . . ." Pearl said, under her breath.

"You and Quinn have got this one," Renz said.

"So we figured," Quinn said. He remembered that Jeanine Carson had been killed around midnight. It was a popular time for murder. Also alibis.

Renz gave an exaggerated sigh and glanced around the bloody bedroom, like an animal seeking an exit. "I'll be in my office at the precinct," he said, finding the way out.

Quinn looked at Pearl. "Let's go next door and talk to Mr. Beck."

"You kids needn't be concerned with me," Nift said, motioning deftly with his probe. "I'll be here for a while, having fun."

Pearl said, "We won't give you another thought. People say you're a jerk-off, and they're right. It's lucky you don't have any real authority."

Nift's features remained impassive. Quinn had to admire his coolness. Pearl could be a tough in-fighter.

"I'll stay here and keep Nift company," Fedderman said, helping to keep Pearl cool.

"Just stay away from the corpse," Nift said. "I

wouldn't want anything to fly out of your suit and contaminate the scene."

Ignoring Nift, Quinn said to Fedderman, "If he says anything you dislike, shoot him."

"Come get me first," Pearl said, "so I can help."

"Just make sure you get him in a crossfire," Quinn said.

"I might only be a bit player in these little dramas," Nift said, "but I always get the girl."

54

New York, earlier that morning

The killer sat at an outdoor table of a restaurant almost a block away from the building where Honor Tripp had lived and died. His bare forearm was in bright sunlight and resting on the warm metal table. The rest of him was in the deep shade of a large green umbrella sprouting from the table's center.

What was going on down the street, and the cold beer the waiter had just brought, made for good entertainment. All the more so because he was the cause of it. The script was written and was being followed. And it was his script.

The black leather man purse he'd carried rested on the pavement beneath the table. Its contents would have been of extreme interest to the police presence down the street.

He sipped his beer and watched the police milling about in practiced consultation, trying to fit together whatever small and confounding pieces of the crime they possessed. Or thought they possessed. There were emergency vehicles, radio cars from several precincts, plainclothes detectives moving about and deferred to like royalty. Flashing lights of various hues defied the brightening morning and faintly painted the surroundings. A TV van with large station letters on its sides and a satellite antenna came on the scene. A TV crew spilled out of it and worked to set up for one of the local stations. Everything seemed to center around a newscaster wearing a tight skirt and low-cut blouse. The wind mussed her hair, and an assistant ran forward and rearranged it, then shot it with aerosol spray to keep it in place.

Ah, the aftermath of murder. If there could be such a thing as a delicious sight, this would be it.

There was the body, not so long ago a beautiful woman within his hands, now being wheeled to a waiting ambulance with its doors standing open. The paramedics were moving with precision but not with any sense of urgency. "*Action! Action!*" he felt like shouting, as if he were a silent movie director spurring on his cast. Few arranged dramas could be more invigorating. More deeply arousing. This must be what it felt like to be an arsonist observing a fire he'd started. Or to be God.

Action! Let's have her die trying to claw her way out of the ambulance! One last burst of life.

But he knew that had been impossible for hours. His plan had taken it into consideration.

He saw the rotund cop in the tailored blue suit leave, driven away in an unmarked black Ford with a uniformed cop at the wheel. So the higher-ups in the NYPD were visiting the crime scene—a measure of the impact the murders were having on the city.

The killer gave silent thanks to the media. He really

should call in to *Minnie Miner ASAP* and thank the woman who cracked the whip at that circus.

Another car, unmarked but obviously a police vehicle, even down to a stubby aerial on its trunk, remained where Quinn and the other plainclothes cop, Pearl Kasner, had left it, angled in at the curb. Next to it was another anonymous black Ford, this one badly dented. Two uniformed cops, belonging to a patrol car parked nearby, were stationed at the apartment entrance.

A little barrel-chested guy in a dark suit got out of the dented black Ford. He was toting a large black bag. Obviously, he was the ME. Running a little late, the killer thought.

Perhaps a letter of complaint would set him right for the next murder.

A dusty van that the CSU working drones had arrived in was almost squared away with the building's glassy entrance. A woman in a white outfit, including white gloves, got something from the van, then hurried back inside the building. In front of the van was a second ambulance, this one with its back doors closed, waiting but not in any rush to leave. If there was another victim inside the building, probably he or she wouldn't require haste.

This was a lot of excitement for the quiet East Village neighborhood. On the sidewalk opposite the apartment, knots of people stood about watching. Other people at the round metal outdoor restaurant tables were obviously distracted by whatever was going on down the street, but weren't so interested that they were going to stop eating or drinking and walk to get a closer look. This was New York. Like the bumper stickers said, *Shit Happens.*

The killer sat and watched it all unfold, like fate that he'd decreed. Honor Tripp hadn't made a grand exit, being in a body bag. That was a little disappointing, what with her face being covered.

With the star of the show gone, things began to wind down. The crowd of onlookers had lost its center and was beginning to thin. One by one, the police and emergency vehicles departed.

Soon only Quinn and Pearl's car remained.

There was little going on inside the apartment now other than predictable routine. Neighbors would be interviewed. Statements would be taken. Honor Tripp's apartment, already minutely examined by the Crime Scene Unit, might be given another cursory examination.

Toiling and toiling over a crime scene—that was a large part of police work. Until, gradually, they'd find something interesting. Though not necessarily immediately helpful.

The killer had been careful about what he'd touched before donning his latex gloves. He was certain he hadn't left fingerprints, or any bodily fluids. He'd even worn a condom, just in case. *Sorry, NYPD, no DNA.*

The apartment building down the street seemed almost back to normal. A sloppily parked car remained at the curb. Another, a patrol car, was parked half a block down. Some yellow-orange Crime Scene ribbon surrounded the scene.

Things were pretty quiet on the outside of the area the tape encompassed. And they were quiet on the inside. Everyone had left, other than a stoical uniformed cop standing watch, and detectives Quinn and Pearl.

Everything was as it should be. As the killer had planned and wrought.

Not the first time, it occurred to him that what he was doing was almost biblical. "Playing God," as Minnie Miner had described it on her nightly newscast.

Tilting back his head, he finished his beer. God allowed him a belch.

He left, satisfied.

55

New York, three years ago

While he was eating breakfast, Quinn's cell phone beeped. He glanced at it and saw by the number that the caller was Renz. Quinn didn't want to talk to him just now, but he knew he'd better, or the busy and ambitious Renz might make himself difficult to contact. Though Renz had the capacity to ruin a good breakfast, even over the phone, Quinn pressed the proper button and said good morning.

"You won't think so after talking with me," Renz said.

"Big surprise."

"What was that?"

"How are you going to ruin my appetite, Harley?"

"If I'd known you were at breakfast, I wouldn't have called."

"Go ahead, Harley, ruin my eggs Benedict."

"In 1993 a murdered woman name of Linda Bracken was found tortured and murdered in a Sarasota, Florida, hotel. There was some carving on her forehead that might have been the letters *D* and *O*, then something indecipherable. She'd also been tortured with a knife and a lighted cigarette. In December 1995, outside a fly-speck town called Prentis, also in Florida but north of Sarasota, a woman named Honey Carter was found killed by a giant python—"

Quinn lowered his fork full of eggs Benedict. "A what?"

"Python, as in snake. People down in Florida keep them as pets, then turn them loose in the swamp when they get too big to feed or handle. Damned things grow to over twenty-five feet. They can even kill and eat an eight-foot gator. So they thrive there, and one of them somehow got wrapped around this Honey Carter. Squeezed her to death. Had a start on trying to swallow her. Those things can displace their jaws and expand, swallow whole animals."

Quinn dropped his fork on his plate. "Jesus! You saying the snake killed her?"

"Looks that way, but unless the snake smoked cigarettes, somebody else participated. There were cigarette burns on her body, applied in an effective, familiar manner. Touched to her closed eyelids and the corners of her lips, behind her ears."

"So it seems to be the same killer that did in Linda Bracken," Quinn said, "minus the snake, in Linda's case."

"Looks like Honey was tortured by the killer and left for dead in the swamp, then along came the snake," Renz said." The ME says it was the snake that did her in. Crushed her to death. I guess you could say the snake was an accomplice. It's not talking, though. The guy who found her shot it."

Quinn found himself thinking it was too bad somebody hadn't come along and shot Honey Carter before she had to die in the tightening grip of a twenty-five-foot snake.

"Linda Bracken, Honey Carter . . ." Renz said. "Put it all together it means Dead on Arrival. Seems we got ourselves a traveler serial killer."

"And one who's in town," Quinn said. "And maybe claimed more victims than the four we know about. He's been here awhile and may have hidden some of them where they haven't been found."

"Is that likely?"

"According to Helen, not likely, but possible. Like an artist who doesn't want to lose his touch. They'd simply be listed as missing persons."

"Maybe he'll keep traveling north, toward Toronto. That'd put the crazy bastard in another country so we wouldn't have to screw around with him."

"Predators go where there's the most prey," Quinn said. "He's ours." He sipped his coffee, but it didn't taste very good. "Media wolves know this cigarette torture thing?"

"Minnie Miner probably does. She finds out everything even before it happens. She'll be trying to get hold of you for an interview."

"I'll refer her to you."

"Seems like somebody's already referred her to you."

"I wonder who."

"Enjoy your eggs Benedict."

Quinn broke the connection and shoved his plate away.

Hugged to death by a snake.

God Almighty!

56

New York, the present

Fedderman hadn't slept much last night, but this morning, over breakfast, he and Penny had talked like adults. At least that was how she'd described it. That shaky gyroscopic balance that unkillable marriages somehow achieved had been regained.

All in all, it was a reason for Fedderman to feel pretty good.

The morning's conversation had even prompted him to dress neatly before leaving the apartment, knowing Penny would notice. He was wearing yesterday's baggy dark pants, but a clean white shirt, and the jacket of the Armani suit she'd advised him to buy. He had his usual mismatched look about him, but still, who could complain? It was his style.

He was on his way to interview a neighbor of the late Honor Tripp.

There was no sign that the building had recently housed a crime scene. The tape was gone from downstairs, as well as the cop on duty. Honor Tripp's apartment was still sealed, but that seemed to be the only visible irregularity in the hall.

Fedderman knocked on the door of the apartment adjacent to the one where Honor Tripp had died and waited for her neighbor, Justin Beck, to answer.

Beck responded to Fedderman's knock almost immediately. As if he'd been waiting at the window and seen Fedderman approach the building.

Beck was average height and weight, about forty, and handsome if you were a woman who liked squared-up guys with buzz cuts who appeared to have just been mustered out of the military. He was spiffed up in a gray business suit and looked ready to leave for some gray business. He made a nice contrast to Fedderman. However, as he stepped back to let Fedderman in, he did a double take on the Armani jacket. Fedderman smiled inwardly.

Beck's apartment was identical to that of Tripp's. Small entry hall, midsized living room, short hall to bathroom and bedroom. Gallery kitchen off to one side, bathroom to the other. It was a prewar building, as someone selling New York real estate would have been quick to point out. Meaning you couldn't hear through the walls.

Which, to Fedderman, cast a faint shadow of doubt on Beck's account of why he'd called 911.

Beck seemed loose and amiable enough, despite the fact that he looked like part of a toy soldier set. Fedderman declined an offer of coffee—it would have been his fourth of the morning—and sat down on a sofa that creaked like vinyl rather than leather and was cold even through the seat of Fedderman's out-of-season wooly pants.

While Beck was in the kitchen getting coffee for himself, Fedderman looked around. The wood floor was highly polished. There was a square rug in the center of the room. Furniture that looked like luxury Ikea was placed as if by the giant hand of a decorator.

Beck returned with coffee in a plain white mug and sat down in an angular wood-armed chair across from Fedderman.

"Sure you don't want a cup?" he asked with a smile. Precise white teeth. "It's exquisite and comes from a country in South America nobody has heard of."

"It all tastes pretty much the same to me," Fedderman said.

Beck nodded. "You've got a point."

"You off work today?"

"I took a day off," Beck said. "I guess I'm still shook up about the murder. Right next door. I about had a cow."

"You told the uniformed officer who talked to you that you were an engineer of some sort."

"Yeah. Structural engineer. I subcontract out to various developments."

Fedderman didn't know quite what that meant but let it pass. The scent of the coffee was stronger and started to make Fedderman hungry.

"I'm sure you get tired of going over your account of Honor Tripp's murder," he said, "but—"

"Not at all," Beck interrupted. "Sharing the experience kind of eases my mind."

This presented a problem for Fedderman. He had a copy of Beck's statement and sure didn't want to sit through hearing it read out loud.

"Read this," he said, taking the three folded sheets

of paper out of one of the Armani jacket's inside pockets. "I want to make sure it's accurate, then we can talk about it."

Beck plunked wire-framed reading glasses on the bridge of his nose and read studiously, as if seeing the material for the first time. Fedderman watched his concentration, how Beck's pupils danced line to line over the three sheets of paper.

Finally Beck placed his coffee mug on the floor, on a *Home Progress* magazine where it wouldn't leave a ring. He took two steps up out of the chair and leaned halfway across the living room, passing the rolled-up statement toward Fedderman as if it were the baton in a relay race. Fedderman leaned forward, accepted it, and fell back into the sofa.

"Summarize," he said.

"I'd fallen asleep about ten o'clock," Beck said, "reading a book about how the Panama Canal was built."

Was this guy serious? "Is that anyplace near where your coffee came from?" Fedderman asked.

"Probably," Beck said with a straight face, and that was when Fedderman knew Beck was messing with him. Making sport of him.

That made Fedderman mad, but he wasn't going to let Beck see that side of him. He'd play right along. It interested Fedderman that a murder next door and a statement to the police, and now a police interview, didn't seem to cow Beck. It seemed instead to give him a welcome chance to play games. Overconfident killers—which most of them were—thought that way. They were the smartest guy in the room, even if it was full of Nobel Prize members.

Fedderman got his black leather notepad out of his pocket. Dug deeper and found a chewed-up pencil. He settled back and pretended to take notes.

"You'd fallen asleep about ten o'clock . . ." he reminded Beck.

"Yes, and around midnight I was awakened by what sounded like screaming, only . . . kind of muffled. Then, in between screams, what sounded like whimpering."

"No one else heard any screams," Fedderman said.

"I'm not surprised. These screams wouldn't carry very far. I told you, they were muffled by something, and I'm—I was—her closest neighbor."

"Your bedrooms are precisely side by side, I believe," Fedderman said.

"I suppose they are."

"You share a wall. And a heating and air-conditioning duct."

"I guess we do. What's that supposed to mean?" Beck seemed more annoyed than afraid of where Fedderman might be taking the conversation. And slightly embarrassed. Yes, his bold warrior's features were definitely flushed. Fedderman knew why. Honor Tripp's sex life was part of Justin Beck's, too.

Make sport of me now, you voyeuristic toy soldier bastard.

Fedderman smiled and shrugged. "Means you do what thousands of other New Yorkers do when they happen to find themselves side by side with an attractive neighbor, separated by only a vent. If that neighbor has any kind of sex life . . . well, it's inevitable that you're going to hear things. Sometimes it must seem almost like being a participant."

Beck took a deep breath. He seemed to think about that.

"Okay," he said at last. "The night of the murder, Honor was with a man in bed. I thought what I was hearing were sounds of sexual thrall. Instead . . ." He swallowed.

"You overheard the murder," Fedderman said.

Beck nodded. "I didn't know it at the time. Not at first, anyway."

"Of course not." Fedderman didn't want this guy to go dry. "Listen, Justin, you could be a help to us. You must have been able to hear just about everything through that vent. Did you hear either one of them say anything?"

"No. Like I told you, she was gagged."

"And it never occurred to you that this was something more than sex?"

"There are all kinds of sex practiced by all kinds of people."

True enough, Fedderman thought. "What about him? Did you hear a man's voice at all?"

"Now and then. He told her . . ."

"What?"

"That he was going to do this or do that. With the knife and the cigarette. I couldn't make out the words through the wall. That's when the muffled screaming would start."

"Was he interrogating her?"

"I don't think so. It was difficult to be sure. He seemed more into issuing orders. Now and then he'd give a cold kind of laugh. The bastard was enjoying himself. I thought they both were. I never imagined what he was doing, how far he was taking it."

"So that's why you didn't call the police, or try to stop what was going on."

"Right. I figured what was going on might be perfectly normal for them. The usual S&M behavior. Sexual games. Far as I knew, he wasn't doing anything Honor didn't like."

"What about the screams?"

"I told you, they were muffled. All part of kinky sex, far as I could tell."

"But eventually you *did* call."

"I got to thinking about it. How she sounded. I decided . . ."

"What?"

"It didn't *really* sound like kinky sex. It sounded more like somebody might really be hurting her. Still, I didn't know enough to go pounding on her door, or go barging in there to save her. And I knew the cops would be here fast once I called." He let out a long breath and sat back. "Which is how it happened." He bowed his head. "Not fast enough."

"You couldn't have broken in and saved her," Fedderman said, staying on Beck's side. "Probably you would have just hastened her death, then maybe caused your own. This guy doesn't play gently, and you would have been between him and freedom."

"So he's the D.O.A. guy? Back with us?"

"Not much doubt about it." Fedderman snapped his leather notebook shut. "We'll need you to go down to the precinct house and add to and sign a statement."

"Assault can sound like sex," Beck said, feeling guilty and fishing for Fedderman's agreement. He needed atonement.

"Sometimes they aren't that different," Fedderman

said. "Then there are those times when one partner turns up dead."

"Then it's time to do my duty as a citizen. And I will." Beck chewed his lower lip for a few seconds. "Listen, if me making a statement gets in the papers or on TV, this killer's not likely to come after me, is he?"

"That's not his game," Fedderman said. "He's probably already stalking his next female victim. But if you're worried about that, the sooner you put your signature on a statement, the sooner you'll be safe. You can't be prevented from doing what you've already done."

Beck visibly brightened. "That makes sense."

Fedderman guessed it did. Would it make sense to a sadistic killer? He wasn't so sure.

57

The hot spell hadn't subsided, but rain was added to the mix. It fell in large drops straight down, bouncing like stones off window ledges, air conditioner covers, metal trash containers, and crawling traffic. If you were indoors, it was a good place to stay.

Some of the detectives were thrashing things out in the office at Q&A. It was a sauna, even though the air conditioner was vibrating and humming along.

Quinn and Pearl listened to Fedderman's account of his interview with Justin Beck. Helen's lanky body was slouched asymmetrically in a chair. It was between their desks, but nearer to Quinn's. Fedderman was in one of the clients' chairs, facing them all.

"Not really of much help," Pearl said, when Fedderman was finished talking.

Quinn agreed. "I didn't hear much of what we didn't already know."

"That's kind of the point," Helen said.

"The killer didn't say anything about the earlier murders," Quinn said, "or any plans he has for future victims."

Fedderman absently straightened a nonexistent crease in his pants. "I got the impression that Beck didn't happen to eavesdrop on Honor Tripp's bedroom *only* the night of her murder. And the killer must have noticed that vent in the wall, right next to her bed."

"He knew someone was listening," Helen said.

Fedderman said, "I kind of got that same creepy feeling. Mess around next to that big vent and someone almost has to overhear."

"But why would the killer want that?" Pearl asked.

"Maybe he gets his kicks that way," Fedderman said, "being watched. Or in this case, heard."

"I didn't read anything important in his statement," Pearl said. "So I'm guessing he didn't overhear anything important in his vent."

"That's the notable thing about what Beck says he overheard," Helen said. "There was nothing about art. And Honor Tripp was a genre writer. A mystery novelist. Mysteries are thought by some naïve souls to be the opposite of art."

"So that's the message?" Quinn asked. "The killer is parading the fact that this murder had nothing to do with art in general, and so not with *Bellezza* specifically?"

"That could be it," Helen said.

Fedderman looked at her.

"Wouldn't a simpler way to put it be that he's trying to throw us off the scent?"

"You know this guy better than that, Feds."

"He's going to up the ante," Pearl said. "That's the sicko's message."

"Exactly," Helen said. "And the pool of his potential victims has widened. From now on they won't have to know anything about art, or be aware of missing Michelangelo pieces. This killer is no longer playing games. The treasure hunt is over."

"Which makes our work harder," Quinn said.

They all sat in silence for several seconds, considering. Trying to get into the killer's mind, knowing it wasn't a nice place to visit.

"He's going to force a showdown," Quinn said.

"Something like that," Helen said. "He doesn't like balancing on the head of a pin."

"All of them eventually come to that place," Fedderman said. "They need for it to go one way or the other. To be over."

Helen said, "You can count on it. The killer wants to press what he sees as his advantage. He regards himself as invulnerable at this point. Godlike. He feels a need to demonstrate that."

"Or?" Pearl said.

"He simply wants us to know he's no longer an art aficionado," Quinn said.

Helen said, "There's a possibility." And smiled.

Quinn knew that smile and didn't like it.

The killer had followed them home from their morning jog, watching them slow to a walk that demanded an occasional little skip, and enter their apartment building on Central Park West. It didn't take him long to narrow down their unit's number on the third floor of the brick and marble building.

Or to learn other things about them. Details were so important.

The man was of least interest. He was in his thirties

and apparently in good shape except for a roll of fat around his midsection. He invariably ran in khaki shorts, a sleeveless white T-shirt, and white jogging shoes. Ben Swift was his name, but he didn't look so swift jogging alongside his wife, Beth. Ben had a lot of side-to-side motion that slowed him down. Beth was built for speed, with a slim body, muscular legs, and a stride that wasted no motion. It was obvious that Ben was struggling to keep up with her. He was forever a yard or two behind, staring at his wife's blond ponytail swinging with the regularity of a metronome. Her jogging shoes were red, her T-shirt white like her husband's, her shorts blue. That amused the killer, who saw himself as something of a patriot.

He put on speed and pulled ahead of them, then slouched on a bench with his head thrown back, as if winded and resting. They huffed and puffed past him and continued jogging as the path fell away. From where he sat on the bench in the sun, he watched them with binoculars, usually focusing on Beth's slim hips, the rhythmic motion of her body.

A perfect running machine, he thought, wondering if she competed in the New York Marathon. She and Ben were an active, healthy couple. Apparently with plenty of spare time. Nothing else to do. So maybe she was in training. He would ask her about that.

But then, what would be the point?

He'd watched the building for several days, and now knew the security setup, and the hours kept by the doorman, Carl.

Carl worked short hours in the morning, then was replaced by another man, Arthur, who worked into the late afternoon. Carl would then show up to provide a doorman presence until midnight. Both men were in their forties and looked fit, except for a slight paunch on Carl. It was a shame they had to wear those hideous brown uniforms with the striped trousers.

However they were dressed, the killer mused, it would be simple for him to deal with whichever man was on duty. The building actually had pretty good security, especially when the street doors were locked after midnight, no doorman was present, and no one could enter without a resident's card key and a five-number code.

The fact was, for someone like the killer, it was easier to get into the building unseen with the doors *un*-locked and a doorman on duty.

No problem at all, for someone willing to go to extremes. Who knew the wisdom of acting promptly and boldly when an opponent was reeling and back on his heels.

The killer cautioned himself against being overconfident. Quinn and his detectives weren't exactly reeling.

The killer smiled.

But they will be.

He checked his wristwatch, then left the park and walked to a diner on Amsterdam, where he knew there'd be a TV tuned to *Minnie Miner ASAP.* It was time for a burger and a cup of coffee. And some quiet contemplation.

Maybe even some information.

People leaked things to Minnie. Sometimes anonymously. When it came to the media, she was one of his favorite people.

And occasionally useful.

58

"I see the same creep watching us whenever we go jogging," Beth Swift said to her husband, Ben.

They were in their apartment kitchen. It was painted pale yellow and had a single window that looked out on an air shaft. The kitchen was the only thing about the apartment that wasn't ultramodern and expensive. Rehabbing it was the next thing on their budget, starting with granite countertops.

Ben stood at a Formica counter next to the refrigerator and continued building sandwiches of cold cuts and vegetables. He was taking his time, obviously deriving some pleasure from his task.

"Most likely you're the one he's watching," he said, laying on blood sausage, lettuce, pickle loaf. He didn't have to be careful about ingredients; Beth enjoyed his monstrous health-and-energy sandwiches as much as he did.

"Am I supposed to feel complimented?"

"In a yucky kind of way."

"Either way, I don't like it. I'm thinking about jogging over to him and asking if we know each other. Just to see what he says."

"You'll probably fluster him and scare him away." Ben added layers of cheese, and then topped off the sandwich with perhaps the most important ingredient. The second slice of Asiago bread, with cheese-flavored, toasted crust. "You can have that effect on people."

"Only those who need scaring," she said.

He added tomato slices and spread some mayonnaise. It took a certain touch, making a sandwich like this. A certain harmony of taste and texture. This was to be their supper. Along with a good white wine. Some of their friends thought they were crazy; doing all that exercising, then shoveling in all those calories. Beth and Ben, who kept almost hourly counts of calories in, calories out, figured they knew what they were doing. Like so many things, it was a balancing act.

It was also, in a way, economical. Because one of Ben's custom sandwiches provided at least two meals.

Beth and Ben had what many people would consider blah jobs. She copyedited advertising, and he was an accountant at a car-rental agency. So they figured a little eccentricity in their lives was a good thing.

They talked no more about the man who might be watching one, the other, or both of them on their daily runs. Ben figured Beth had forgotten about confronting him, but if she hadn't that was okay, too. It might be interesting to see how the man would react. Beth's unabashed directness was a quality Ben liked in her. Adored, actually.

After eating, they put the remaining portions of their

sandwiches, and what was left of the wine—half the bottle—in the yellowed refrigerator Beth so looked forward to replacing. She knew where to put the wine on the top shelf so its temperature would be just right after it sat out for fifteen minutes.

Ben settled into *his* chair and watched the news on TV—more about the nutcase torturing and killing women. Wasn't there always some sicko like that operating in New York? Why couldn't they spot those characters ahead of time and do something about them before they went around killing people?

After the news the couple walked to an art theater in the neighborhood that showed indie movies. There was a Woody Allen film playing there, about three beautiful women in Spain. After the movie, maybe they'd kill the rest of the wine, then go to bed and make love.

Sometimes Beth thought Woody Allen should make a movie about their lives. She'd mentioned that to Ben. He'd thought maybe Quentin Tarantino.

In another part of town, business was brisk at the Far Castle. When he wasn't in the kitchen spurring on the cooks, Winston Castle, looking like a chef in a PBS special, smiled fiercely as he dashed from table to table, reassuring some diners that their food would arrive soon, making sure others were enjoying their meals. This also gave Castle a chance to get outside, since the evening was pleasantly cool and the outside tables were fully occupied. Still, he was sweating from his effort.

He'd assured a well-dressed man, accompanied by a woman who looked like a tramp, that their lamb chop dinners were minutes from being ready, when he glanced across the street.

The man in the gray car was still parked directly opposite the restaurant. He was staring at the Far Castle, watching what was happening. He seemed to be watching Winston Castle in particular.

Castle veered away and stood beneath an arbor of grape wines, where the diners wouldn't notice him. He got out his iPhone, went to contacts, and pressed *Quinn*.

Quinn picked up almost immediately. "What's up, Winston?"

"You said to call you if I noticed anything unusual," Castle said.

"So what's unusual?"

"Maybe it's nothing, but this man in a gray car is parked right across the street and staring over at me."

"Has he been there long?"

"Yes and no. He seems to come and go."

"You sure he's looking at you?"

"Reasonably so, yes. Although I can't see his features, I feel his eyes on me."

Quinn couldn't imagine that, but let it pass. "Has this happened before?"

"Yes. Too often for it to be my natural paranoia. And I have no idea how many times he was there before I noticed him."

"What about Maria? Might he be observing her?"

"She's in the office, not visible."

"What kind of car is it?"

"I'm not sure. It's gray. Looks like it might be a . . . well, anything. Not new but not old. A midsized, four-door sedan."

Average, average. "Unmarked police car?"

"Not impossible, but it doesn't smell that way."

Quinn decided not to ask Winston what that meant. "Is the man alone?"

"Excellent question." Castle moved over and peered around the arbor vines, across the street where traffic was running heavy now.

The car was gone.

"He left."

"You don't sound relieved, Winston."

"When you live as I do, you learn to smell danger. That was danger."

"Isn't that from a Humphrey Bogart movie?" *Isn't your entire family from a Humphrey Bogart movie?*

"You're the one who wanted to know about anything unusual," Castle said "And we hired you for security."

"You hired me to help locate a marble bust. A man looking at your restaurant then driving away doesn't seem relevant."

"It was the *way* he was looking."

"I thought you couldn't make out his features?"

Castle sighed. "You needed to be here."

"If he returns, call me again."

"Then what?"

"Then I'll come there."

Castle made a *humph!* sound, stuffed his phone into his pocket, and looked across the street again.

The gray car was still gone.

The danger lingered.

Castle wasn't reassured. He knew that Quinn considered him and his entire family dramatic posers. So what if they were? Plenty of people acted out their own dramatic lives. There was—and Winston Castle firmly believed this—an art to it. It was *life!*

Humphrey Bogart!

He adjusted his towering chef's cap.

Almost always, people die in Bogart movies.

After breaking the connection with Winston Castle, Quinn used his cell to call Sal Vitali.

Seated at an outdoor table at the Far Castle, Sal answered his phone quickly, before it could disturb any of the other diners.

Quinn spoke first. "See anything of a guy in a gray car parked across the street and scoping out somebody in the restaurant?"

"I'm at an outside table and did notice a car parked across the street for a while, with the driver in it. Next time I checked, he was gone. There was a group of three over there for a while, too, looking over the place, maybe searching for somebody, then they moved on."

"What about that group?" Quinn asked.

"Nothing about them. That's my point. People stare across the street at this restaurant all the time. Maybe they're looking for somebody, or maybe they're trying to make out the specials on the board in front."

"So the guy in the gray car didn't seem suspicious?"

"Not particularly, but maybe you should talk to Harold. If the same guy in the same car was surveying the place during Harold's watch, too, it could be we've got something."

"Winston Castle says he smells danger."

Sal laughed. "What he smells are spices from his own kitchen. The danger is from calories."

"Nevertheless," Quinn said.

"Calories can kill," Sal said, in his hoarse smoker's voice.

After talking to Sal, Quinn called Harold Mishkin and woke him up.

"Sorry to pull you out of a deep well," Quinn said, "but Winston Castle called and said he's worried some guy in a gray car is watching the restaurant. Or somebody at the restaurant. Sal's seen the car, too. I'm wondering if you saw it on your watch."

"I saw it," Harold said. "It caught my attention 'cause the driver never got out. I couldn't make out what make the car was, or the plate numbers. It wasn't new, though. I could tell that by its styling. Maybe five or six years old."

"Anything unusual about it?"

"Maybe," Harold said. "It sort of smelled like danger."

When Quinn was finished talking with Harold, he used his cell phone to call Nancy Weaver.

"You know anything about being a food server?" Quinn asked.

"You mean waitress?"

"If you do."

"I waited tables at a Smokey Torrito long, long ago. Earning my way through school."

"What the hell is a Smokey Torrito?"

"They went out of business a long time ago," Weaver said. "I wasn't responsible."

Quinn said, "Brush up on your skills."

59

Beth Swift closed the drapes all the way so no light from the street below could filter into the bedroom.

The drapes were heavy. She and Ben liked complete darkness when they slept. And they enjoyed almost complete silence. Only a few muffled sounds from the street made their way into the bedroom.

It was well past midnight, and almost always by this time Beth was in what she figured was REM sleep. The most valuable kind. On an ordinary night, she'd be lying untroubled next to Ben, as good as unconscious. Beth had no idea why she couldn't sleep tonight.

Ben was certainly experiencing REM sleep. His breathing was deep and regular. So much so that she was afraid he might begin to snore.

Beth had set in her mind a final imprint of her path back to the bed. She gave the heavy drapes a final adjustment, then in total darkness and by memory returned to her side of the bed.

She lay down carefully, making sure she didn't disturb Ben. The bed springs squeaked, but softly. It was a king-sized bed, so there was enough space between them that her weight didn't shift the mattress beneath him.

His breathing became slightly irregular, but within a few seconds returned to its previous steady bellows sound.

Beth lay on her back and stared up toward a ceiling she couldn't see. Complete blackness. Her husband warm beside her. A heaven with everything in place. She felt drowsier now. Easy in body and mind. She felt sleep approach like a hesitant suitor, taking its time.

That was okay. She was relaxed and comfortable and in no hurry.

It was reassuring and in its way delightful to lie staring into the unbroken darkness and listen to Ben's breathing and her own. As if they were one being, taking turns within itself.

Gradually the muffled sounds of the city faded away. The faint, rhythmic hissing of Ben's breathing and her own was comforting and conducive to sleep.

Idly, half asleep, Beth amused herself by attempting to fix her breathing in exactly the same rhythm as her husband's, but she found it impossible.

She couldn't quite make the adjustment. Ben's inhalations and exhalations were deeper and of longer duration. The hissing of her breathing didn't quite match his, so that—

Something was wrong. *She knew it.*

Her heart was ice. Terror had come before knowledge. She was completely awake and hyperalert. Listening. Dreading. Staring wide-eyed into total blackness. Knowing now without doubt what she was hearing.

There was a third sound of someone breathing in the dark.

60

"They didn't show up for their tai chi exercises in the park," Renz said. "Then they didn't answer their cell phones."

"That was enough to send the super to investigate?" Quinn asked.

Renz nodded, his chin sinking into the smooth pink flesh of his neck. "With these two, yes. They took their tai chi seriously. Took everything yuppie and healthy seriously. They might have lived to a hundred and ten."

A CSU unit was on the way, along with an ME and transport for the bodies. The uniform who'd caught the call was standing outside in the hall, to greet and guide the oncoming rush of specialists that sometimes reached murder crime scenes faster than flies.

Not this time, though, Quinn noticed. He leaned over and waved his hand to shoo a fly from the open eye of the woman. It returned to light on her forehead, and he gave up.

"I checked his wallet on the dresser, and her purse," Renz said. "He's Ben Swift. She's his wife, Beth."

Quinn moved closer to the two dead bodies on the

bed. The man's throat had been neatly sliced, both carotid arteries. There was a lot of blood around the bodies, but a towel had been laid over the man's throat to keep blood from spurting. The expression on his face was puzzled but peaceful.

Next to Ben Swift, Mrs. Swift looked horrified. There were minor cuts and cigarette burns all over her body. Her wrists were fastened with thick silver duct tape to her bare thighs. Quinn could see a residue of adhesive where tape had been over her mouth. She had screamed into the tape but wasn't heard except faintly by the killer.

Both victims had the letters *D.O.A.* neatly carved into their foreheads. Post mortem, so the carving didn't leave much of a mess.

Renz pointed to a head wound near Ben Swift's temple. "Looks like the killer took them both by surprise when they were asleep. Bashed the husband unconscious with a hard, blunt object, then gagged and taped the wife."

"Then he sliced the husband's throat, to get him out of the way, and turned all his attention to the wife," Quinn said.

"It was the woman he wanted," Renz said.

"Probably." Quinn agreed with Renz but didn't like jumping to conclusions at this point in the investigation.

He walked into the bathroom. There was blood on the plastic shower curtain and two of the white towels.

"It'll be his blood," Renz said.

Quinn nodded. "He did the murders nude and then cleaned up in here. All we'll find are smudged rubber glove prints. He always washes most of the blood from the gloves, then peels them off so they're inside out and puts them in a pocket."

"Sounds right," Renz said. "Fits the pattern, anyway. I wonder if he watches too much television, thinks we might be able to get his fingerprints off the insides of the gloves."

"You never know about the lab guys," Quinn said, thinking about the killer years ago who always cut out his victims' eyes so his image wouldn't be fixed like a photo on their retinas. "And when we're dealing with somebody who'd do something like this, he might believe anything."

There was shuffling around and voices coming from out in the hall. Quinn and Renz returned to the living room.

The first one in was the nasty little ME, Nift. He was followed by gloved up CSU techs and a detective Quinn knew slightly, who used to be on vice. Young guy on the make, Quinn figured, who might have something on Renz. He and Quinn exchanged nods.

"Where's Pearl?" Nift asked, making a show of looking around.

"Not here," Quinn said. "She knew you were coming."

"Tell her I missed her."

"You been shooting at her?"

"Pearl and I just joke," Nift said, seeming to realize suddenly that he didn't want to get Quinn mad. He motioned with his head toward the hall. "The bedroom?"

"The bedroom," Renz said. "Make sure you don't touch anything but the bodies."

"I always work that way," Nift said. He brooded as if his feelings were hurt, but Quinn knew better. Any emotion showing on Nift's face was part of his act.

Nift hefted his big black leather bag and made his way with short, rapid steps toward the bedroom.

When he was gone, Renz said, "Necrophiliac little prick."

"Probably," Quinn said.

61

Minnie Miner tried from time to time to entice that horrible little ME Dr. Nift to come on her program. There was something about that guy that made people's skin crawl, but they could no more look away from him than they could ignore a train wreck. Nift always declined, feigning professionalism. Minnie figured he was probably wanted somewhere and didn't care to have his picture flashed around.

She put Nift out of her mind and continued idly watching a DVD of the B-roll for tomorrow's piece on the D.O.A. murders. She was in her apartment near the studio, reclining on the sofa and sipping a vodka martini. The sun was at the windows on the wall near where the big TV sat, and from time to time, in synchronization with puffy cumulus clouds blowing past, she had to squint to see the screen clearly.

There was an establishment shot of the Far Castle across the street, the colorful umbrellas over the round white metal tables, the castle-like stone and tile building itself, then the low fence and the garden next to it, the precisely trimmed hedge maze. The sunlight seemed to cleanse while it brightened the place; everything looked picturesque and colorful, like a damned souvenir postcard. Fox hunters in red livery might stream across the scene any second, accompanied by frisky yapping hounds. Stonehenge might be nearby, instead of Bank of America.

Manhattan traffic rather than hounds running to the hunt streamed past, and lunchtime customers lounged and ate at the sidewalk tables.

The camera brought the long shot in, so it seemed the viewer was crossing the street, then it moved into the restaurant.

Minnie was idly wondering if the place served mead, when something on the screen made her sit straighter and lean toward the TV. Servers were circulating among the tables, clearing them or delivering food. Some were men wearing medieval-looking white shirts with overly bloused sleeves. Others were nubile young (reasonably young) serving wenches, with tight skirts and blouses that matched those of the male servers only cut lower in front to allow for glimpses of cleavage.

At first Minnie didn't realize what had jogged her memory, and she had to stare hard at the TV. She had to run the DVD forward and back twice before she was sure.

One of the serving wenches was familiar. Minnie wasn't one to forget a face, or all that cleavage. This wench looked particularly ready for a roll in the hay. Minnie smiled. It was the dyed blond hair that had fooled her for a while, the carefully mussed Olde World hairdo.

There was no doubt, though, after running the scene back a few times, then freezing it as the wench leaned farther forward to serve some frosted mugs to two businessman types. More than any of the others, this serving wench seemed to enjoy her work.

Minnie smiled, certain now. She had even, some time back, interviewed the now-blond woman for an *ASAP* segment on socially transmitted diseases.

Though the name tag pinned to her blouse said her name was Eileen, yon wench was Officer Nancy Weaver.

Minnie sat back and thought about that. No doubt Weaver was working undercover and wouldn't be in a mood to talk about it.

On the other hand, a word going back beyond the Middle Ages came to mind: *Bait.*

Surely that word had crossed Weaver's mind. With her hair dyed blond and the sexy serving-wench outfit, Weaver had to realize that she might be dangling as a potential conquest of the D.O.A. killer. Good cop that she was, Weaver might not be inclined to discuss this matter with Minnie, until Minnie worked on her a bit. Or leaned on her politically ambitious and vulnerable boss.

Blowing Weaver's cover might put Weaver in danger, Minnie thought, or it might save her life.

Of course, that should be, at least to some extent, Weaver's decision. Or Renz's. Or Quinn's.

But really, it all depended on Minnie, and that B-roll that would be best placed topping the news.

"So here's how it is," Renz said. They were in his precinct house office with the door shut. Sounds from the squad room beyond the door filtered in: a man rapidly explaining how he'd gotten to the wrong place at the wrong time; a woman who wailed as if in agony every few minutes; the calm voices of the detectives dealing with incoming calls. Now and then, laughter, some of it cruel.

"Place needs thicker walls," Renz said.

Quinn sat down on the other side of the desk, facing Renz. The desk was not so much cluttered as carefully arranged so that it seemed cluttered. "You were saying . . ."

"How it is," Renz said. "The unfortunate Beth and Ben Swift were sleeping after sex."

"How do you know about the sex?"

"Lab people know. They ran a rape kit on Beth Swift even though she was dead. No semen, though. And no sign of a condom, though they can't be sure about that. It isn't like on TV."

"Sometimes I wonder. Birth control pills?"

"We'll find out about that," Renz said. "As of now, it doesn't appear that the killer raped her. Except in his own special way with the knife and cigarette." He propped his elbows on the desk and tented his fingers. His hands looked pink and extremely clean, nails professionally manicured. "The hypothesis is that they were both asleep. The killer got in with a lock pick or key. Made his way to their bedroom, where they were sleeping deeply."

"After sex," Quinn said.

"After sex. The killer sliced Ben's throat. Poor guy didn't even have a chance to wake up. Whatever fuss he made was mitigated by the killer, who was at this point nude. Probably slipped out of his clothes in the bedroom, keeping an eye on his soon-to-be victims, listening to their breathing to make sure they both stayed in REM sleep. When Ben was dead, D.O.A. stayed quiet but worked fast. Got out his duct tape and bound and gagged Beth, who probably went into paralyzing shock when she looked across her pillow and saw her husband's tongue hanging out, but not from his mouth."

"Poor Beth," Quinn said, and meant it. He could feel a smoldering rage starting to build in his gut. Or had it been there all along?

"It was just beginning for her," Renz said. "Looks like the killer straddled her, then went to work with the knife and cigarette. Taking his time now."

"Anyone find butts?"

"No. He took the butts with him," Renz said. "Filters, too, if that's what he was smoking. A very meticulous asshole, this one."

"How'd he get past whatever security the building has?"

"There's one doorman or another there till midnight. After that, with a five-number code on a punch pad, anyone can let themselves into the lobby. Carpeted stairs instead of an elevator, so there's no noise at all involved. Carpeted halls, too, which is where Beth and Ben kept their spare door key hidden—tucked neatly under the carpet near their door. That's the second place every burglar looks, after under the welcome mat. Once the killer knew where the couple lived, it would only take a little observation to gain whatever knowledge he needed to get at them. This sicko knows his business."

"What else the techs have to say?"

"Not much, but they're still learning. Nift said it took the woman over an hour to die."

Quinn said nothing, thinking, feeling the anger grow.

How disappointed he must have been when she escaped into death.

"Everything points to the D.O.A. killer and not a copycat," Renz said. "But the techs are still learning. There'll be more info from them."

"Two victims," Quinn said. "A family. Helen said this sicko would up the ante."

"He's trying to pressure you," Renz said.

Not *us*. *You*. Renz covering his ass.

"He's feeling some pressure himself," Quinn said.

Renz's desk phone jangled and he picked up. "I said hold my calls." He stood for a moment with the receiver pressed to his ear. Then: "Go ahead and put her on." He held his hand over the mouthpiece and said almost silently, "Minnie Miner. Something about Weaver." He nodded toward the door, signifying that the call was private. Time for Quinn to leave.

Quinn stayed.

PART SIX

Where beauty has no ebb, decay no flood.

—WILLIAM BUTLER YEATS, *The Land
of Heart's Desire*

62

The way Jerry Lido and Pearl saw it, too many people already knew about the search for *Bellezza,* and eventually knowledge—and rumor and irrational behavior—would begin spreading exponentially.

It wouldn't be that way for a short while. If someone *really* knew about *Bellezza,* they might well know about everything else. So it would be good to find them before they were supplanted by the crazies.

Lido knew his was an important job, searching the Internet for the lost bust or related material. To save time, he used Pearl to explore promising but secondary leads, while he homed in on the ones most likely to bear fruit. Lido was the undisputed tech genius of Q&A, but Pearl was no slouch and kept learning.

It was Pearl who came up with something. An ad in the classifieds of a local New Jersey weekly, the *Teaneck Tattler.* A woman had a marble bust for sale said to have been created by Michelangelo. It had been in her family for years, said the ad, and now she needed money and was forced to sell. There was a number to call.

Pearl called it.

A woman identifying herself as Jesse answered the phone. Pearl said she was trying to get in touch with the person who'd placed the ad.

"She's my aunt," the woman said, "Lucille Denner. And I've been trying since yesterday to get in touch with her myself."

"Is the number in the ad her phone number?" Pearl asked.

"It is. I tried it but got no answer. Left a message. No reply. I went by her house and it's locked up tight."

"Don't go inside," Pearl said, getting a queasy feeling.

"It's not a crime or anything, is it? I mean, something might've happened to her. I just got here, in fact. I've been thinking about calling the police." She gave a nervous little chirping laugh that Pearl didn't like. "And now they've called me."

"Have you looked around?"

"No, but I called Lucille's name and got no answer. She isn't here, I'm sure."

"Give me the address."

Jesse did. A house on Garritson in Teaneck.

"Don't touch anything else, and get away from the house," Pearl said.

"What? Why?"

"No time to discuss it now," Pearl said. "Just do it. Stay outside and wait. Someone will be along faster than you imagine."

Jesse was silent, obviously thinking over this instruction from a woman she'd never met.

"Remember not to touch anything," Pearl said. "Where are you now? Exactly."

"On the front porch."

"Leave it, then stand outside the front of the house, out on the sidewalk, and wait. Please hurry so I can make another call."

"Is my aunt Lucille in trouble?" Her voice was tremulous.

"I think so," Pearl said. "Please do as I instructed."

Jesse promised she would, and seemed eager to meet some authority at the house.

After Pearl hung up, she told Lido about Lucille Denner and her classified ad.

"Doesn't sound like much," Lido said.

"But better than you know what."

Pearl called Quinn's cell.

Quinn walked over to a corner of Renz's office so he could barely hear Renz's conversation on his desk phone with Minnie Miner. He figured Renz couldn't overhear his cell phone call from Pearl.

Pearl stayed on point and kept the conversation brief.

Quinn said, "I'll pick you up on my way."

Renz hung up the landline phone at almost the same time Quinn finished his conversation with Pearl.

"Minnie Miner," Renz said, though he'd already let Quinn know that by using Minnie's name. He was fishing to see if Quinn would reveal his caller.

"Pearl," Quinn said, satisfying Renz's curiosity. "Probably about nothing."

Renz crossed his arms, waiting, so Quinn told him about his conversation with Pearl.

"You're right," Renz said. "Probably some crackpot

with a worthless family heirloom. You'll probably find a bust of Carrie Nation."

"I might not recognize her," Quinn said. "Your call?"

"Weaver."

"You referred to her as Minnie."

Renz put on his innocent face. "No, I didn't. Just mentioned Minnie's name, I'm sure."

Quinn knew Renz was lying, but arguing would get them nowhere. Renz. You had to watch that bastard every second.

"What did Weaver want?" Quinn asked.

"She said people have told her Minnie Miner mentioned her—though not by name—on Minnie's *ASAP* show. " 'A new food server at that delicious new restaurant has a secret in her pretty little head,' I believe were the exact words."

"You gonna pull Weaver?" Quinn asked.

"She mighta just gotten more valuable right where she is," Renz said. Knowing Quinn would understand. Weaver was being classified as expendable, though she'd have all the protection the law could muster while she was being dangled as bait before the killer. Would Quinn go for it?

"Make sure she's covered every second," Quinn said.

Renz gave him a look. "You know we will. She's one of ours."

Quinn knew Renz was sincere. There was no need to mention that leaving Weaver exposed waiting tables while Minnie Miner blabbed away on her TV show might be downright dangerous.

"I'll give Weaver the word," Renz said. "Make sure she knows what's going on."

And reassure her it's safe, so she won't back out.

Quinn left the precinct house and climbed in the Lincoln to pick up Pearl for the drive to New Jersey. When he was tooling along on the FDR Drive, he lit a cigar and used his cell phone to call Weaver. No doubt Renz had already talked to her.

Weaver answered on the third ring, and acknowledged that she and Renz had discussed the Minnie Miner problem.

"You okay with this, Nancy?" Quinn asked, gaining ground on a big stake truck hauling a load of gigantic polyvinyl pipes. For a moment the truck's exhaust fumes smelled stronger than his cigar.

"I've been bait before," Weaver said. "Even did a stint with Vice for a while. And we know this killer already has me in his sights. I wouldn't mind a chance to get back at him. This might be fun."

Quinn doubted that. He was sure Weaver did, too.

He told Weaver about the ad in the *Teaneck Tattler* in New Jersey, and how he and Pearl were going to drive there and check it out. He thought it would be a good idea to keep Weaver clued in from this point on. They owed her that for the odds she was about to accept.

"Could be nothing," Quinn said.

"Good leads or bad leads, they teach us something even if we don't always know it," Weaver said.

Must be scared, if she's philosophizing.

"I'll let you know if anything unusual goes on here at the castle," Weaver said. "Or anything other than the usual unusual."

"Be careful at that place, Nancy. The play acting could become serious."

"Surely you joust," she said. "And don't forget I've got my knights in shining armor."

Quinn drew on his cigar and jacked the car's speed up over the limit, all while passing the truck with the PVC pipes on the right. Though he was on the phone, his eyes were more or less fixed on the road. He was thinking of a dozen things other than driving.

"Don't take any chances," he reminded Weaver.

The phone pressed to his ear, he listened to nothing. The connection with Weaver was broken.

63

Quinn drove hard. He and Pearl made good time out of Manhattan to New Jersey. They were soon in Teaneck, and found Lucille Denner's address on Garritson easily, using the GPS plugged into the Lincoln's cigarette lighter.

Most of the houses on the block were small, built in the flurry of construction not long after the Second World War. Additions had increased the size of some of them as the families within them had grown. Denner's house was one of the smaller ones and well kept, painted a pale beige that was almost cream colored, with dark brown shutters and door. There was a white trellis on one side of the house, in what might have been an effort to make it appear wider. Scarlet roses blossomed wildly on vines that had made it halfway up the trellis. On the opposite side of the house was an attached single-car garage. The grass was thick and green and almost to the point where it needed to be trimmed.

Quinn parked the Lincoln blocking the narrow concrete driveway leading from the closed overhead garage door, just in case.

He and Pearl got out of the car and walked up onto the low wooden porch that was painted the same brown as the shutters. Quinn thought he could smell the nearby roses, but that might have been the power of suggestion.

He knocked on the front door several times, and wasn't surprised when he got no response. Pearl moved over on the porch and tried to peer behind almost-closed drapes but could see nothing inside but darkness. She stayed on the porch while Quinn walked around to the back door and knocked.

Again no response.

He returned through thick grass to the front yard.

"I'm here," a woman's voice said.

They turned to see a middle-aged woman, obviously once shapely but now with a thickened waist and neck. She had long graying hair combed to hang straight down, like shutters she was peering between. Quinn thought a middle-aged woman had to be beautiful to wear her hair that way. It made this woman look as if gravity had a special hold on her features. She had an outthrust chin and worried gray eyes.

"Jesse?" Pearl asked.

"Yes. I decided to stand down the street behind a tree and see who arrived at my aunt's house." She gave an embarrassed smile that showed crooked teeth. "You two passed inspection."

"Did you get away from the house immediately when I told you?" Pearl asked.

"Yes. As soon as we got off the phone."

"Very good," Quinn said. He tried the front door and found it locked.

Jesse said she had a key and fitted it to the knob lock. It worked with a low and hesitant clatter, as if it might be as old as the house and hadn't been used often. If there was any other kind of lock on the door, it wasn't fastened.

Quinn used his large body to block her so he could enter first.

He found himself in a small but well-furnished living room.

Pearl gave Jesse a slight, reassuring smile and said, "You better wait here and we'll call you."

Jesse looked dubious but nodded her assent. Now that there were two more people here, people with authority who would know how to handle things, she wasn't so frightened.

Pearl smelled something all too familiar. Faint, but definitely there.

"Watch where you step and what you touch," Quinn said.

Pearl could see beyond him a huddled form on a dining room floor.

"Lucille Denner," Quinn said.

"No doubt," Pearl said.

"Somebody must have answered her ad."

"A dissatisfied customer."

Quinn led the way as he and Pearl entered the dining room. It was dim, but neither of them wanted to open drapes or turn on lights and disturb a crime scene. Besides, there was more than enough light to see the dead woman on the hardwood dining room floor.

"Careful not to step in any blood," Quinn cautioned.

Pearl moved closer to the body so she could see the dead woman's forehead. The letters *D.O.A.* were there.

They looked like the letters found carved on the earlier victims.

Quinn nodded toward the other side of the dining room, beyond a wooden table and chairs that were centered beneath a wrought iron chandelier.

Pearl moved carefully around the perimeter of the room, past a dark mahogany china cabinet, and saw half a dozen jagged pieces of ceramic on the floor. She fitted them together in her mind and came up with what looked like the head and torso of a bare-breasted woman who might have been *Bellezza*.

If the bust had been marble instead of ceramic.

Or had ever been touched by Michelangelo.

The classified ad in the Teaneck newspaper had obviously sent someone on a futile mission. Quinn could imagine the killer taking one look at the pathetically obvious imitation and hurling it to shatter on the floor before taking out his ire on the unfortunate Lucille Denner. His knife and lit cigarette had been wielded with particular viciousness.

"Do you think she really figured she might sell that thing to some naïf?" Pearl asked.

"Maybe to one out of twenty," Quinn said. "And to somebody who thought they might be putting one over on *her* by getting a great work of art cheap."

Pearl could only shake her head.

"What's the percentage of hardcore addicts who get sick or die because of poison they thought was coke or heroin?" Quinn asked.

"Could be one out of twenty," Pearl said.

"And the one out of twenty here might have been the first caller," Quinn said.

Which made Pearl glance around uneasily, as if fate were creeping up on her.

"I checked," Quinn said. "Her phone's a land line. But we still might be able to get a caller log." Even as he said it, he knew the killer would be too smart to leave a record of his call about the classified ad.

"What strikes me," Pearl said, "is that he'd be too wily even to inquire about that obviously imitation piece of junk."

"It served its purpose," Quinn said.

"Which is?"

"To get us wasting time standing here talking and thinking about Lucille Denner's murder instead of closing in on him."

"Not motive enough."

"Spooking us into thinking he could be going interstate again."

"Still not enough."

"And to demonstrate how powerful he is."

"Motive enough," Pearl said.

Quinn got out his cell phone and called a sergeant he knew in the Teaneck Police Department.

Then he called Minnie Miner. She might as well waste the time they might have wasted.

Quinn saw Pearl raise an eyebrow at the mention of Minnie's name.

"Might slow her down" Quinn said. "Then she can talk about all those ads for *Bellezza* busts being withdrawn from eBay."

"Pearl? Detective Quinn? Anyone?"

Jesse's voice. It sounded as if she had her head stuck inside the open front door.

"Better stay where you are, dear," Quinn said.

But she didn't. Curiosity and concern for her aunt Lucille prompted her to enter the house. Pearl heard her coming and tried to head her off but failed. Jesse saw what was on the dining room floor.

And would have nightmares the rest of her life.

64

The killer parked behind a black SUV, diagonally across the street from the Far Castle. He was driving his old gray BMW. The car was a plain four-door model, and because it was a luxury car, so often had its styling been mimicked that it was a vehicle that drew little attention. It looked at a glance like a million other cars in Manhattan. At the same time, it was very fast. The killer valued anonymity and speed. Who knew when one or both would be needed?

He lowered the windows and switched off the engine and air conditioner. The radio was tuned softly to classical music, Holst's "Jupiter." One of the killer's favorites.

Where he'd parked put him in a perfect position to observe diners at the restaurant's crowded outside tables. He could also see people come and go.

He'd done this kind of surveillance before, but now he knew who he was looking for. The server Minnie Miner had mentioned—though not by name—on her daily TV news show.

The killer was by now familiar with all the food

servers, and he was interested in the most recently hired, a blond woman in her forties. Quite attractive. His trained eye had become suspicious the first time he'd seen her. She looked her part as a Medieval serving wench and seemed to play it with gusto. More gusto, in fact, than skill at her job. Serving food wasn't quite her thing, the first couple of times he'd observed her. Then she became more adept, less often accidentally knocking over water glasses, or stepping on diners' toes, a quick study adjusting to her role. *An adjustable wench.*

The killer had to smile at his own cleverness. Perhaps he'd share the pun with his victim, at the proper time.

Then there was the evening when he was watching and the blond waitress had spoken briefly with Quinn when he passed her on the way to enter the restaurant. It wasn't much, but it was more than an uninterested hello. They'd moved apart quickly, like magnets with opposite polarity. Too fast and too late. These two people knew each other, and had taken care not to display the body language of even a casual encounter.

So the woman was obviously a plant. The killer didn't jump to that conclusion, but it took only a few more days to erase most of his doubts. The restaurant's owner and wannabe famous chef, the unctuous Winston Castle, treated the blond one differently from the other food servers. He was almost deferential when speaking with her. The suggestion by Minnie Miner that there might be a food server who was some kind of spy cinched it—Blondie was an undercover cop.

With a little more investigation and a pair of binoculars he recognized her. Nancy Weaver. The one who almost got him.

What was she doing at the restaurant? Had she made the connection between Castle and the nutcase family searching for the Unholy Grail? She must be trying to solve the killer's perfect murders. What—if anything— had she found out? Had Quinn, Pearl, and the rest of them made the connection between some of his victims and the search for *Bellezza?* Surely they had by now. That was part of the killer's game. He had chosen Quinn as his adversary because the man was no fool.

At first the killer hadn't been interested in anything but playing out his deadly game with Quinn. But after coming across the search for the missing (if it ever existed) art treasure, he'd become more and more interested because of the pure truths told by his dying victims.

The talkative Grace Geyer had piqued his interest at the museum. Grace had led him to question Andria Bell in the Fairchild Hotel at knifepoint and with fire. Andria couldn't have lied to him. Not deliberately. But how much of what she'd told him was fact, he couldn't be sure. He *could* be sure that *she* believed everything she'd told him.

And he'd be sure Weaver would speak the truth. She would tell him what she knew, what the NYPD knew, what Quinn knew. About the D.O.A. killer, and about *Bellezza.*

He could feel the familiar stirring in the very core of his being when he thought about Weaver. Questioning her would be such a pleasure! He simply had to learn a little more about her, so he'd know when she was most vulnerable. Then he'd do what he was best at, and she'd respond as they all did. She'd know who he was, what he was, and resistance would run out of her. They all came to a certain point—and early in the process—when they understood that they were already dead. This time he'd be the victor. Fate couldn't be resisted, so why try? Fate was the trickster and the sly ally of their inquisitor.

That was what Quinn didn't understand, that fate was the killer's coconspirator. Fate had brought the killer, his pursuer Quinn, the family that was on its possibly quixotic search, and *Bellezza,* together. Fate and the killer, who were as one.

The killer had signaled to Quinn more than once that since Grace Geyer's death, the missing art treasure and the murders were intertwined. The killer had seen to that. He'd even taken two victims, a married couple, to make his point. A subtle but unmistakable message as increasing pressure was applied to Quinn; even as Quinn would sense the intensifying needs of his quarry.

There was little doubt that Helen Iman, the profiler working for Q&A, would be telling Quinn that he, Quinn, was winning, that the killer was becoming more and more desperate and irrational. But what did the big, gawky profiler know about what was rational?

What did she know about fate?

As the killer mused about the events that had led him to where he sat in his parked car, observing his next victim, he marveled again at fate. Fate was responsible for everything that had happened since his return to New York. Fate was the architect of it all.

Maybe Helen the profiler would figure that out using the process of elimination.

If not fate, it had to have been Michelangelo.

Yes! Michelangelo!

Surely he was on the cops' suspect list!

The killer laughed so hard he began pounding the steering wheel.

Then he stopped and glanced about. He didn't want people to notice and wonder.

Not that they'd believe the truths that he'd been told.

65

If there was anyone on this earth Helen the profiler felt contempt for, it was the actively curious, self-serving, double-crossing, viciously ambitious, aggressively charming Minnie Miner. So Helen wasn't crazy about Quinn and Renz suggesting that she should be a guest on *Minnie Miner ASAP* and discuss the D.O.A. murders.

But here she was.

Not only that, but a certain part of her had actually warmed to the task.

They'd consulted with Helen on what she should say that would increase the pressure on the killer. And they listened closely to her opinions and suggestions. Both men, to their credit, deferred to her expertise.

Helen was sure the killer felt that he was near the precipice. If she could contribute pushing him over into the void, she'd be glad to do so. Even if it meant dealing again with Minnie Miner.

So Helen found herself seated in one of the two comfortable chairs that were angled toward a small table and microphone. The chairs were much more worn and stained than they appeared on TV. Some of it was wear. Some of it was perspiration created when Minnie put her guests on the spot. Minnie was a clever and insistent verbal predator.

A camera moved smoothly closer to Helen, its bulging eye aimed at her face. Another camera glided in for a three-quarter shot of Minnie. Figures moved in the background. The light became brighter, warmer, as Minnie was introduced. The applause from the audience was mildly enthusiastic rather than deafening. It was mostly comprised of people Minnie's minions had managed to drag in from the street. They fell silent while the applause sign was still held high by a Levi's-clad girl who appeared to be in her teens.

Minnie, smiling broadly, quickly held up her hands as if she had signaled for quiet.

When the studio was silent, she said, "My guest today is a famous profiler. When I say that, I don't mean she's a painter or photographer. For those of you left on this planet who don't know what a police profiler does, it's very interesting and necessary work. She's more interested in what goes on in a criminal's mind than in what he looks like. She's a psychological profiler for law enforcement agencies, and she, maybe more than anybody other than his mother—if she's still alive—knows how the D.O.A. killer thinks. She's trained to know what goes on in his sick mind, how to walk with him along the corridors of his madness. What he feels. *Why* he does what he does. What he might do in the future." Minnie smiled widely and motioned toward

Helen. "This is Helen Iman, and she's here to tell us all about the D.O.A. killer."

The applause was loud, and genuinely enthusiastic this time. Helen had to admit that it made her feel good. Though she'd thought she was immune to the disease of celebrity, so many hands clapping for her brought a smile to her face. She wondered now if she should have worn something more formal than her blue sweats and joggers.

Helen waited for Minnie to open the conversation. Minnie had a reputation for ambushing her guests.

But Minnie also knew how to keep her viewers in suspense.

That was okay. Helen knew how to wait.

"So if Quinn failed to apprehend this killer the first time around," Minnie finally said, "why was he chosen by the commissioner to head the investigation into these latest murders?" *That one oughta knock the profiler off balance.*

"He wasn't chosen by the commissioner. He was chosen by the killer."

Uh-oh! This one is dangerous. Instead of being knocked off balance by the opening question, she had counterpunched.

Minnie decided to ask something safe. "So tell me why you're a police profiler, Helen."

Small talk. "Corny as it sounds," Helen said, "I want to fight crime. The way I can best contribute is to bring my knowledge of psychology and irredeemable criminal behavior to bear."

Minnie put on a wide smile. "You catch killers."

"Among other sorts of criminals, yes."

Minnie raised an eyebrow and wore a look of puzzlement. "You said 'irredeemable.' So you don't think a killer like D.O.A. can find God and be rehabilitated?"

Helen almost choked. "I think such a killer is evil, and cannot be brought back from the hell where he's put himself and his victims."

"Surely this isn't true of all killers," Minnie said.

"Not much is true of all of anything."

Minnie thought about that. Brightened her all-purpose perky smile. "But you think D.O.A. is evil."

"Of course I do. He might well have another side that he shows people, but the killer in him is always just below the surface."

"Satan?" Just a hint of a smile at the corners of her lips.

"If you like," Helen said. *Let the sick creep think he might be Beelzebub.* She leaned closer to her microphone, not taking over the conversation, but nudging it the way she wanted it to go. "I also think there's something about those killers who *are* genuinely evil. The pressure of what they've done builds and builds in them. Every one of them eventually breaks."

"So you think this killer is feeling the pressure?"

"Yes. And he's about to break."

"Break?"

"Come unglued."

"You sound certain."

"I am. I've seen this kind of killer before. He's in the powerful grip of a mental illness, and he's wrestling with himself."

"But hasn't he been from the beginning? What

makes you think the killer is about to break now?" Minnie asked.

"Because now he *wants* to break," Helen said. "He *needs* to be stopped. He knows that, and in an odd kind of way, he'll cooperate in his downfall."

"And he would do that because . . . ?"

"He knows he's evil. If D.O.A. is who we think he is, he's thirty-five years old, and his parents were murdered when he was fourteen. Every year that passes becomes more of a burden. Denial has become impossible."

Minnie clasped her hands as if fascinated. And maybe she really was. "What are some of the signs you see pointing to that?"

"Before I answer that question, you should know some things about D.O.A. Things in general that might not be precise but make up the standard profile of such a killer. He's a male, between eighteen and forty-five years of age . . ." Helen went on to give Minnie and her fans the usual profile of a TV-show serial killer. As she spoke, she could see by Minnie's frozen smile that she wanted Helen to get on to something her audience hadn't already heard dozens of times.

That was okay with Helen; she was talking specifically to the killer, not the audience.

Finally Minnie interrupted, to keep the show rolling. "But what makes you think this particular killer is about to break at this particular time? What are the signs?"

"He's getting sloppy. And he's killing more often and with increasing violence, the way serial killers do when they sense they're nearing the end. They become desperate. They begin making small mistakes. They unconsciously attempt to move closer to whatever kind of death awaits them."

"Can you give our audience an example of the D.O.A. killer's mistakes?"

"Not in the way of clues. That information is closely held by the police."

"But otherwise?"

"Sure," Helen said. "Our D.O.A. killer is obviously becoming desperate. He's raised the ante by torturing and murdering a married couple. He's unconsciously signaling that he's ready to surrender to his fate. His mind has become a jungle of conflicts."

"You make him sound like a hopeless whacko."

"He is. But one who understands his weakness, and that he's nearing the end."

"And his weakness is?"

"Himself, of course."

As she said that, something cold moved in Helen's mind. Somehow—she wasn't sure how—she knew the killer was watching. On his own TV, or on one in a bar or restaurant, somewhere, he was watching.

Mental case? Nearing the end? His weakness is himself? The D.O.A. killer felt like throwing his glass through the TV screen.

He put down the glass and sat back in his sofa, his hands flexing, flexing. He glanced down and noticed them. Knew what he wanted to do with them.

Mental case.

He glanced around at the art on his walls, the artists

whose work he favored. Bosch, with his visions of horror; Van Gough, who spread madness with his brushes; Manet, who was sexually addicted and died of syphilis. As if anchoring these prints of terror were several large Picassos, nude women observed from different, severed angles simultaneously, as if they'd been butchered by a madman with surgical skills, then reassembled like mismatched puzzles pieces and placed on display. Prints of madness.

Possessed and cherished by a mental case?

A vulnerable mental case?

Then he realized that this was precisely how they wanted him to feel. To act. Out of weakness and vulnerability.

They'd find out how weak he was.

He understood his nemesis, Quinn, and what the strategy here was. He, the killer, was supposed to "up the ante" by going after somebody close to Quinn. Like Pearl or her daughter Jody.

Or he might go after Helen the profiler. Seeking revenge for what she'd said. A temptation, for sure.

But that kind of revenge wasn't in his plans. Helen wasn't his type at all. And she might put up the kind of a struggle that could get out of hand.

No, he had a better idea.

And it was the same idea.

Weaver.

Weaver would be next.

Weaver, who was also Eileen the food server and undercover cop at the Far Castle. Weaver, who had drawn attention to herself through her clumsiness at table, who held supposedly clandestine brief conversations with Quinn. Weaver, who knew both sides of the story. Weaver, who had eluded him before.

Who knew what Quinn *and* the police knew. Who was the nexus of the D.O.A. killer investigation and the *Bellezza* search.

The killer sipped his cold beer and licked foam from his upper lip.

Weaver.

Who would tell him everything.

66

After the dinner rush, only about half the tables in the Far Castle were occupied, and some of their occupants were already enjoying dessert. Nancy Weaver, aka Eileen, had reached the end of her shift. She said good night to another waitress and to the cashier, then left the Far Castle, and walked toward her subway stop.

Fedderman fell in behind her, half a block back. When she reached home and was tucked away, radio cars would do frequent drive-bys, and two NYPD undercover cops would alternate keeping watch on Weaver's building. Once Fedderman delivered her to her apartment, he could rest knowing she was safe. And so could she.

Not that Weaver was particularly frightened now, as she crossed the street and continued on her way. She didn't look back, but she knew Fedderman was there. Even if he wasn't, Weaver herself knew how to ward off or capture an attacker, and on dark streets she walked with her right hand in her purse, resting on her nine-millimeter Glock handgun.

Between Weaver herself and her guardian angels, she might be the safest woman in New York.

Though that wasn't exactly the plan.

On dark stretches, like the one they were approaching, Fedderman, too, walked with his hand resting on his gun. He was vigilant but unworried. D.O.A. was heavily into torture, and for that he needed solitude. His victim's were tortured, raped, and killed in their apartments, usually in their beds. What better place for lovers and murderers to suffer their private agonies?

It was in her apartment when Weaver was at her most vulnerable.

If she was vulnerable at all.

Fedderman slowed his pace. He could make out the dark, shadowed form of Weaver up ahead, hear the staccato clacking of her high heels on the sidewalk. Fedderman keyed on that repetitious clacking. As long as there was no change in its rhythm or volume, everything up ahead was all right.

He found himself thinking about Penny. When they'd met earlier for lunch they'd again renewed their determination to make their marriage work. What it took, Fedderman had decided, was his understanding and concern. Penny had to be reassured that he empathized with her feeling that their lives were always on edge. His was a dangerous profession, and they had to work together on living with grim possibilities. Plans for the future were always tentative. That didn't mean they shouldn't enjoy the present.

Or that they shouldn't plan.

Fedderman tripped and almost fell as he snagged a heel stepping off a curb. That had been close to being a turned ankle. Not something he could afford.

Concentrate on what you're doing.

He gazed ahead. There was Weaver, half a block up, slightly farther away than Fedderman liked. She was striding out in those high heels, the way women do if they wear them frequently. It occurred to Fedderman that high heels lengthening women's strides might be why they were sometimes harder to tail than men. Also, it seemed that women wearing high heels were always going someplace in a hurry. Maybe they—

Pain exploded behind his right ear.

He was on the ground, the heel of his right hand burning from where he scraped the skin while breaking his fall.

He was still trying to figure out what happened when something glanced painfully off his right ear and struck his shoulder.

He decided to lie still and think, *think* . . .

He'd been struck in the head long ago by his brother, accidentally, when they were trying to make shore after fishing in darkness that was falling over the lake. His brother had been alive then, and strong; it had been before the cancer. The shadows of the trees leaning out from the bank were lengthening. Overhead, stars were becoming visible. His brother was sitting in front of him in the canoe, straining his muscles and dipping deep with his paddle, when it broke from the water and Fedderman was leaning forward with his own paddle . . .

Darkness gathered over the lake.

67

Weaver awoke in a totally dark place, and it took her only a few seconds to realize she was tightly bound. Her back ached. That was because she was laid out on something hard. On her knees, breasts, and stomach, and the side of her face. Her elbows were pulled back and painfully bound to each other or to something immovable. Her thighs were spread and her legs bent at the knee. Her ankles were tied to something that felt as if it was several feet across. A rope or collar was fastened around her neck and attached to the hard surface she was on, so that she could only barely raise her head.

She attempted to moan. Something, a knotted rag, was stuffed into her mouth, muffling the sound. There was a strong odor of gasoline, and of something else . . .

It came to her like lightning, how she had come to be here. She knew who had her, and she knew why.

Where the hell were my angels?

Fedderman. He was supposed to be shadowing me when I left the Far Castle.

Where's Fedderman?

Maybe she didn't really want to know.

Bright fluorescent lights blinked, buzzed, and then glared steadily.

He walked to where she could see him, an average-sized man in his thirties, well muscled, expensively coiffed brown hair, shockingly kind, even pitying eyes. He did seem to pity her. As if everything was out of his hands now, and it didn't look good for her, poor baby.

She realized she wasn't at all shocked or surprised that both she and D.O.A. were nude, except that he was wearing skin-tight white rubber gloves. Like a surgeon's gloves.

He smiled, gently removed the rag from her mouth, and said, "Hello, Eileen. Or would you prefer Nancy?"

She chose to say nothing, and took a limited glance around her. They were in what seemed like a spacious garage of some kind. Maybe a basement. The ceiling was unfinished, and there was an exposed jungle of ductwork and wiring above. She saw what must be the killer's car, a dusty gray BMW sedan, parked about twenty feet away near a closed overhead door and a sloppily tuck-pointed brick wall.

His smile widened and became ugly. "Officer Weaver?" Gently, as if trying to waken her from pleasant dreams without shocking her delicate system.

She kept her silence.

"We're alone. If you scream, no one will hear. You might try to scream louder, but it won't be loud. Won't even *be,* except for the two of us. Still, I'll have to tighten your choke collar."

He came closer, and fear washed over her like a cold wave.

Terror choked off any sound she might have made. Weaver raised her head, craning her neck. She saw that she was positioned on some kind of crude wooden workbench, wrists and ankles tied to something fastened to the slab of splintered wood top, or to its legs.

"I suppose you're wondering about what happened to your friend Fedderman," the killer said.

She *was* wondering. She couldn't help it. She broke her silence. "Where is he?"

"Feds is fine. Or will be if he wakes up. My guess is he's got a fifty-fifty chance."

"You don't know him. Don't call him Feds. He's Detective Fedderman to you."

He didn't answer her. Instead he moved closer, and yanked the collar so hard that it dug into her throat and she could feel and hear cartilage crack as she made a feeble squeaking noise.

He moved down along the bench, and she was terrified to see that he had an erection. Apparently there were objects laid out on the bench, between her spread thighs. He picked them up and displayed them to her one by one. A roll of duct tape, a large knife with a very sharp point, a pack of cigarettes, a book of matches, something that looked like a wood-handled ice pick, a dark corked bottle containing barely visible liquid.

"Chloroform," he explained to her about the bottle. "That's what I used to get you into the trunk of my car, after I walked you to it. You could hardly walk a straight line. Anybody watching would have assumed you were drunk. I acted a little drunk, myself. Not that it mattered. I'm good at this. I mean, I could have been a great actor. But I could tell no one was watching. I sense it when I'm playing to an audience, however small. No member of any audience can find you and help you."

He leaned in and she felt him touching her. Involuntarily, her body vibrated. His hands closed on the backs of her bare thighs and they immediately cramped, causing her body to slam over and over on the hard bench.

She finally stopped trembling and lay still, but the cramps didn't go away completely. She was afraid to move any part of herself out of fear that they might return.

Calmly, he looked over whatever items were on the workbench, as if debating with himself over which object to choose.

He picked up the knife again, holding it out where she couldn't help but look at it. The fluorescent light above the workbench cast a wavering reflection in the bright steel.

"We both know I'm good at this," he said. "And if someone is good at it, someone else is going to talk. You're going to tell me everything. You won't leave out a thing." Again the smile. "Am I right?"

She knew that he was and tried to nod. It wasn't like in books or movies. A skilled torturer could get a stone to spill secrets.

"Sorry," he said. "I didn't realize the collar was too tight for you to nod." He touched her with the knife point and the vibrations throughout her body began again. Her bare thighs threatened another bout of major cramping.

"We're going to have fun," he said. "One of us, anyway."

She felt the knife blade moving feather-light across her navel. "I love an outy," he said. He withdrew the knife and came closer to her. "Do you want to tell me what I want to know? Or should we get right to the fun part?"

He loosened the collar slightly.

"Officer Weaver?"

"What do you want to know?" Her voice was a hoarse whisper.

"About the other woman, of course."

"Eileen?"

He slapped the back of her head. Hard. She heard herself whimper. Felt the anger. The rage. The terror.

And the helplessness.

He calmly struck a match, stared briefly at its flame, then lit a cigarette and tucked it in the corner of his mouth.

"*Bellezza,*" he said.

She clenched her eyes shut. Felt the skillful touch of his bare hands on the backs of her thighs. The leg cramps were returning.

She made it through the knife and three cigarettes before she told him: "It's in the Far Castle garden, incorporated into the fancy concrete birdbath."

"Incorporated?"

"Inside it."

He leaned back, giving that some thought.

"That fat clown who owns the restaurant has it?" He sounded dubious.

"His family," Weaver said. "They think they own it."

"What are their plans for it? To donate it to a museum?"

"They want to sell it," Weaver said. "Or they wouldn't be keeping it hidden from people like you."

"I know that birdbath," he said. "It looks like ordinary garden statuary to me. It looks nothing like what we're discussing."

"Isn't that the idea?" Weaver croaked.

He walked away from her, holding the knife low in his right hand, hefting it over and over so it bounced lightly against the cupped backs of his fingers. A lit cigarette dangled from the corner of his mouth. The smell of the burning tobacco, along with the constant pain, nauseated Weaver.

The killer suddenly wheeled to face her, as if having made a decision.

"I'm going to give you something I never gave the others," he said. "A chance."

She said nothing, trying not to vomit.

"In exchange for that, I want a guarantee."

"How can I give you a guarantee?" she asked, swallowing the bitterness at the back of her throat.

"We're going to play a game," he said. "I'm going to tie you tight and gag you, and put you in the trunk of my car. Then I'm going to drive it to a place where it can remained parked and unnoticed for days. If you've told me the truth about chipping away concrete and finding *Bellezza,* you'll win, I'll reveal to the police where you are. If I discover you lied to me, you'll stay in the car's trunk and die a slow and painful death." He touched the bloody tip of the knife to her nose. "Do we have an arrangement?"

Anything was better than nothing. "Yes."

* * *

He laid Weaver on her side in the trunk, her wrists bound behind her, her ankles bound together. A large rectangle of duct tape was slapped across her face and he worked it tightly with his thumbs so there was a good seal. She was breathing through her nose. He used the point of the knife to make a small incision in the tape so she could also breath through her mouth if she had to. At least for a while. What she couldn't do was make a noise louder than a soft moan. She wouldn't be heard outside the tightly sealed and locked trunk.

Before closing the trunk, he gazed down at her. He seemed calm and vaguely amused, as if they were discussing something other than her agonizing death.

"If you told me the truth," he said, looking her in the eye, "you'll see the light again. If not, it's darkness the rest of the way. Understood?"

She managed to nod.

"You're lucky I like playing games," he said.

He closed the trunk lid, and she was in darkness.

This was exactly the sort of game the killer loved to play. He and Nancy both knew he wouldn't keep his word and return after he'd secured *Bellezza*. But in her mind was a stubborn element of doubt. It *had* to be there. As the final minutes of her life ticked away, she would cling harder to his words. He'd promised to return and free her. Hadn't he?

If he'd said so, *mightn't* he?

Mustn't he?

Not the slightest sound made its way into the dark and locked trunk. Not the slightest glimmer of light.

With each passing second her terror and hope increased in proportion to each other, and eventually it would be impossible for them to coexist.

Hadn't he promised?

She was sure she'd heard him promise.

68

With Weaver tucked away, the killer checked to make sure that what he might need was in place. He would return briefly and pick it up later tonight. There was an old shovel, and a rusty pickax that had broken halfway up its wood handle but would still be useful. A folded tarpaulin. More duct tape, just in case.

There was other, heavier equipment. A compressor with a muffled engine, a small jackhammer, a set of steel wedges. And there was clothing—a disguise.

It occurred to the killer that he could make a good television commercial about the duct tape, what a useful product it was. A testimonial.

Had any of the infamous serial killers done celebrity television commercials?

Hi, I'm Charles Manson (or the Zodiac killer, or Son of Sam). I'm not a sheep of the herd, but I've played one in the real world, and I wouldn't set out on a kill without my duct tape.

Why not? It was all lies, anyway. Fun and lies.

He began cleaning up, taking his time. He didn't

simply wipe to eliminate fingerprints—he rubbed, sometimes leaning his weight into it. This had to be perfect one time around. There wouldn't be a chance even for a quick cleanup later.

The last thing he did before leaving the building was to wipe the car down carefully, inside and out, still wearing his rubber gloves, so there would be no fingerprints. He had already wiped down the interior of the vehicle's trunk, knowing it would soon contain Weaver.

A less careful man would say this overabundance of caution didn't matter.

But a stray, neglected print might matter someday. A print that might match his own.

He would do as he told Weaver, parking the car, with her in it, at a desolate spot near the East River. There the vehicle would sit for quite a while before someone called the police about it, and it would be towed.

The first surprise for the police would be that the old car had stolen New Jersey plates and was a chop shop vehicle impossible to trace.

The second surprise would be the corpse of Officer Weaver.

Either way she played it, this would be the end for Weaver. If the killer could remove the birdbath and uncover *Bellezza,* why should he complicate measures by telling anyone about an untraceable parked car with a body in it?

The killer hoped she was telling the truth about *Bellezza* being contained in the concrete birdbath at the Far Castle, but one way or the other, Weaver would die of dehydration or suffocation in the car's locked trunk. She hadn't really believed he'd see that she was rescued. But he knew she'd convinced herself that she believed him. It was a shame he couldn't be there to see it. Would she run out of hope before she ran out of air? Or would it be a tie?

He mentally removed her from the game board.

There was no sound.

No light.

And Weaver had no illusions. BMW trunks, even on older models like this one, were tightly sealed. She was sure now that the killer had lied to her. It was a simple horrendous fact. She knew she would soon be dead.

D.O.A. would return and dispose of her body. Or put it on grisly display, complete with carved forehead.

He'll be one up on Quinn. On us.

Men! Damn them!

Men played their asinine games.

Men killed.

She tried moving her arms and legs and found them tightly bound with industrial duct tape. She could move her head slightly. Shift her legs if she moved them pressed together ankle to knee. There was only slight play in the tape. She could work it looser, but never loose enough to work her way free. And even if she were free of her bonds, would she be able to find a way to open the trunk?

She lay nude and sweating in the fetal position. Frustrated. Fuming. Fretting.

That's it. Tape that will stretch only so far.

That's what I've got to work with, if I'm ever going to leave here alive.

69

"Damned paddle!" Fedderman said.

He had somehow been knocked clear out of the canoe, all the way up onto the lake's mud bank.

His brother. He had something to do with this.

Lights were flashing, red, blue, white. Fedderman's clothes were stuck to him, soaking wet, and he could feel something, rain drops, tickling his bare ankles where his pants legs had worked their way up as he . . . what?

Fell?

He blinked, trying to remember. Above him, Batman hovered black and silent against the background flashes of light and darkness. Barely moving like a breeze-borne kite, this way, then that . . .

Not Batman—raining—a black umbrella keeping the light cool drops off his face. Fedderman moved slightly and a wedge of pain slammed into the side of his head, and he remembered.

Some of it, anyway.

"Feds?"

Quinn's voice. Deeply concerned. What a pussy.

"Feds? You hear me?"

"Cold cocked me," Fedderman heard himself say. "Wham! Wow!"

"Who?"

"My brother."

"What?"

"Canoe."

"You're scaring me, Feds."

"How do you think I feel?"

Another voice. Authoritative: "Move that car so the ambulance can get close."

Ambulance?

Somebody must be hurt. Fedderman raised his head to see what was going on.

Wham! The headache. That's what was going on.

But the pain had not only cleaved his mind, it cleared it.

"Weaver," he said.

"We're looking for her," Quinn said

"*Looking* for her? Jesus! I don't know what happened, Quinn. I was tailing her and I got hit by the sidewalk. Gotta find her . . ."

"We'll find Weaver. Worry about yourself now."

Strong but gentle hands slid in tight beneath Fedderman. He rolled an eye and saw a collapsible gurney. There was another, weaker, blast of pain; in his head and down the back of his neck.

He moved higher. Levitating. A patch of night sky and tall buildings were rotating.

Lifting me. Carrying . . .

He knew they were going to put him on the gurney, transport him.

There was Quinn's face, looming over him, revolving with the nighttime view. *Good man, Quinn.*

"I was tailing her and he cold—"

"I know," Quinn said. "We can talk later, Feds."

Fedderman felt the gurney moving smoothly. Did the damn thing have wheels? Or were the paramedics carrying him?

"We'll take care of things on this end," Quinn assured him, as the lighted and cluttered back of the ambulance appeared beyond Fedderman's feet.

"Don't scare Penny with this. Let her know, but don't scare her."

"Not to worry, Feds."

Fedderman was inside the ambulance. "Let me know about Weaver. All my fault. You can't trust anybody in this world."

"Nothing is your fault. Nothing at all."

The ambulance doors slammed shut, and the vehicle was suddenly close and crowded. Voices spoke incomprehensibly. White forms huddled around Fedderman. The siren growled and revved up.

"Don't ever go out on the lake with the bastard," Fedderman said, just before they clamped an oxygen mask over his face.

Five blocks from where Weaver was bound and locked in the trunk of the parked BMW, the killer hailed a cab and took it to an intersection several blocks from his apartment.

He didn't walk toward his apartment, though. Instead he walked east, toward the river, where there were some industrial buildings and a small gray van he'd obtained from a rental firm. He'd used false ID and a hokey story about moving his possessions before his ex-wife claimed everything in divorce proceedings. His first inclination had been to hot-wire and steal a vehicle. He had the skills to do that. But he knew the vehicle might be reported stolen and hit the NYPD hot sheet before morning. That could lead nowhere good. Besides, the semi-legally rented van, with its darkly tinted windows, was exactly what the task required.

He drove to the building where he'd broken Weaver—the fabled criminal returning to the scene of the crime—and loaded the back of the van with a five-gallon can of gasoline that he'd filled two days ago at a BP station in New Jersey. Alongside the gas can he placed the rusty pickax and shovel, and a folded tarpaulin.

All part of his plan. And his plans, once put in motion, ran smoothly.

Halfway to the Far Castle, which had closed and darkened hours ago, the killer steered the van around a corner and pulled to the curb of a shadowed street lined with closed shops.

After a few minutes, motor idling, he drove forward slowly until he saw a space between buildings. He parked near it and turned off the engine. Keeping in mind that there might be concealed security cameras here—because there might be concealed security cameras anywhere—he put on a baseball cap and pulled its bill low, then turned up his collar.

He got down out of the van, making as little noise as possible, and unloaded the five-gallon can of gas from the back. Keeping his head down, he carried the can to the dark passageway and unscrewed the cap. He went deeper into the darkness, then began walking backward, toward where he'd just come from. He was leaning forward and pouring gasoline in a side-to-side motion as he went. Leaving a long trail that, when lighted, would act as an unstoppable fuse.

A voice said, "Wha' the fu—"

The killer stopped, listened, and heard a scraping sound. He looked in the direction of the noise and saw a dark figure attempting to stand up. A man who had been almost invisible slumped against the brick wall.

A drunk. Or maybe it was drugs. The killer didn't know and didn't care. He was grateful that the man was disoriented and continued to scrape the leather heels of his shoes against the bricks in an effort to slither up to a standing position with his back against the wall.

If he did manage to stand, it looked doubtful that he could stay on his feet.

All right. This was unexpected but could be handled. The killer's plans made allowances for contingencies. He screwed the cap tight on the gas can and carried it to where the man had almost straightened up. He was rough looking from living on the streets, wearing torn dress pants and a black T-shirt with the arms cut off to reveal complicated tattoos that involved snakes and nude women. He smelled of stale vomit, even over the stench of the gas.

The killer said, "Let me help you," and raised the half-full gas can high.

"Wha's 'at smell?" the tattooed man asked, just before an edge of the metal can came down hard on his head.

He put out a trembling hand to support himself

against something that wasn't there, then crumpled to
the pavement.

Working faster but wasting no motion, the killer
poured gasoline over the unconscious man, then back-
stepped quickly out of the passageway, bending low
and continuing the trail of gas until the can was empty.

He put the can back in the van, then returned to the
mouth of the passageway and the beginning of the trail
of gasoline. He struck a match and flipped it into the
glistening gas.

Surprised by the ferocity of the sudden blaze, he
hurriedly climbed in behind the wheel of the van and
got out of there.

He watched his rearview mirror as he approached
the corner. An orange glow flickered from the mouth
of the passageway.

It grew suddenly brighter as he turned the corner.
The sound the igniting gas made was a low *Whump!*
that probably didn't alarm or awaken anyone.

Five blocks away, he pulled the van to the curb and
got out a disposable cell phone he'd bought at a drug-
store uptown. He punched out 911, and in a voice that
he made sound excited gave the address of the fire.

"I saw a cop run between the buildings!" he added.
"I don't think he came out. And there mighta' been a
shot. Oh, God! I dunno! The flames are so high!"

"Please try to remain calm, sir. I'm going to—"

He cut the connection, powered the van's driver's
side window all the way down, and tossed the phone so
it skipped once on the concrete and went down into a
storm sewer. His rubber gloves he left on.

It seemed a long time before there was a reaction to
his phone call.

Faraway sirens began a frantic howling, cries that were soon joined by others. The NYPD sirens were accompanied by FDNY wailing. Soon the distant din sounded like wolves calling loud laments to others in the pack.

Satisfied that he'd created an effective diversion, the killer drove the stolen white van away from the maelstrom of flames and sirens, toward the Far Castle.

70

Penny Fedderman lay alone in a king-size bed and stared at a fly walking on the ceiling, seeing things upside down. Or did the kind of eyes flies have automatically flip things right side up in their vision, the way cell phone screens and pads did? *Was* there an upside down, when it came to flies?

The question was like life, Penny decided. On the surface simple, but on a more thoughtful level, amazingly complicated.

She looked away from the lackadaisical fly, toward the dark window. She could see through the rain-distorted pane to the lights of the taller buildings in the next block. Now and then the tires of vehicles swished past on the wet pavement outside.

Here she lay in bed, angry with her husband, because he insisted on working a job that threatened the premature end of his life. Of their life together. But was she unreasonable to feel that way? She'd known he was a cop when they married. She simply hadn't know all that that involved.

So here she was, warm and alone in bed, while he

was away somewhere in a dangerous city, possibly in a place where it wasn't safe, where he was wet and cold.

What were the odds on him coming home at the end of each shift? She'd looked them up and forgotten them, but she knew that only a small percentage of cops actually were wounded or killed on duty. A small percentage unless you were a cop. Or a cop's wife.

Penny switched on the bedside lamp. She was going to read—a detective novel, no less. It would help her to get to sleep, because she knew that the odds were on the side of the detective in the novel, in this case a female PI. She would somehow not only survive any odds, but she would solve the case.

Penny had decided that she owed a certain fidelity to detective novels. They provided a different, safer world. Safer for the fictional detective, anyway.

She knew how life often imitated art, and found that reassuring.

Feds, where are you? Are you dry? Are you safe?

Weaver had managed to work her way onto her side, which gave her leverage as she kicked at the back of the BMW's trunk, which was also the back of the back-seat. She could manage to get only so much strength into her kicks, and the car, a 1995 model, was built solid as a damned brick.

Goddamned German engineering!

She'd known someone with this kind of car, and she knew that in this model the battery wasn't beneath the hood; it was beneath the backseat and extended slightly into the trunk. She gave up kicking at the back of the seat, and instead began kicking at the carpeted floor up near the nose of the trunk's interior. Over and over. In the same spot.

The tape over her mouth remained firm, and she couldn't manipulate her bound body so that she could kick loud enough for it to be heard. She prayed that she could kick in the bottom of the seat back enough so that she might be able to move one of the battery cables. Kick it loose and perhaps bring about some condition that could be used to create noise. Maybe even set off a theft alarm.

But a part of her recognized that the rest of her was being foolish. She was bound head to toe with duct tape. Her possibilities had been reduced, if any had been genuine in the first place. Her battering bare heels could do only so much damage.

Her efforts were causing her nude body to twist around on the carpeted trunk floor so that she was no longer kicking the rear of the backseat. She was kicking with her bare feet the upholstered part of the trunk that housed the power source for the interior lights.

The trouble was that the lights drew current from circuitry that was no doubt connected by a thick wiring harness.

If I could just kick one of the damned battery cables loose!

Her heels ached. Her kicks were softer now, becoming feeble. She realized she was losing strength fast.

What she didn't realize was that her kicks had finally dented the carpeted fitting, and done slight damage to the wiring.

Electrical current arced. She could smell its acrid scent.

But nothing seemed to have changed. No earsplitting

horn blasting, no loud outside signals of theft or van-
dalism.

She couldn't know that outside the trunk, the car's
taillights and one of the reverse lights were silently
blinking regularly and out of sequence. Somewhere in
the rear of the car, she had done enough damage to the
wiring to create a repetitive spark.

But was that good? The car was no doubt parked in
a desolate spot. Maybe even indoors. For all she knew,
it was in the basement parking garage—or whatever it
was—where they'd started from. There was no one
around to notice the spark she had fought so hard for
and finally attained. No one to see, hear or smell it.

Until that spark might ignite the gasoline fumes.

71

The killer had rented a small office in a building across the street from the Far Castle, telling the landlord he was going to set up a mail-order business. The landlord couldn't care less, after the killer paid him six months' rent and a generous security deposit.

From the office's single window, the killer could see not only the outside dining area of the restaurant; he could see the hedge maze in the garden, and near it, the birdbath.

The concrete structure had a floral motif and was bulky enough to contain a smaller, more elegant statue. He found himself sitting and staring at it, imagining what might be concealed inside its rough surface. There was nothing about the birdbath that suggested grace or the magic of true art. It was exactly the opposite, overdone and rather awkward. Lacking an artful symmetry. Surely, the killer thought, the monstrosity couldn't have been created to be itself. It must have some other purpose.

The other thing that particularly demanded the killer's attention was the garden's hedge maze. He sat for hours at the window, memorizing its every turn and angle. It became like a map in his mind.

And now the time to peel the concrete onion had arrived, layer after layer, until the beauty inside held sway, and the ugliness fell away forever.

The last thing on his mind was Nancy Weaver.

The killer knew the best way to do this was out in the open, clearly visible to anyone who would notice him. Not that anyone would pay particular attention to him. He had made himself into a common sight, even at night, in New York City.

His van was white, with "Consolidated Edison" stenciled on magnetic signs on each side. He had on workman's clothes, including boots and a dented and dirty yellow hard hat. Noise was something he didn't want. It might allow someone to approach him unseen. So he eschewed the air-driven jackhammer and stuck to his rusty pick and shovel. He gave himself plenty of light, running a thick wire from the truck's small generator set up next to the rear bumper. It was very directed light, centered on the concrete birdbath, so it didn't disturb his vision if anyone came at him from any direction. The compressor chugged away steadily; he could hear it and smell its exhaust fumes.

Keeping his attention narrowly focused on the birdbath, his senses tuned to his surroundings, he worked steadily with the air hammer and then, for finer work, with the pickax, chipping away concrete to reveal harder marble beneath. The more concrete he removed before trying to transfer the birdbath, the lighter it would be, and the less likely that it would be damaged.

Concrete and marble weren't the lightest and most manageable substances on earth. If he didn't remove one while preserving the other, his task would be herculean as well as futile.

Even over the soft sound of the generator and compressor, he heard now and then the wail of a distant siren. The police were diverted, along with the FDNY. The public, as well as news wolves like Minnie Miner, would be occupied by a major fire, and maybe a dead cop. And the woman who knew too much to stay alive, Nancy Weaver, was most likely dead in the trunk of an old and untraceable BMW sedan.

Engines, sirens, death, flames—that was all somewhere else so he could accomplish his purpose here.

And it was happening! His quest would be satisfied. He couldn't help stopping work now and then to look down to see the cumulative effects of his steady effort with the pickax.

He felt a wild exhilaration. An awe. He was like a shadow Michelangelo, giving marble birth to something rare and beautiful. Doing what sculptors always did—chipping away everything that didn't look like some part of whatever it was they were creating.

The toil of his hands was revealing great beauty that would soon be his.

He would, of course, continue to kill. And he would win his war with Quinn.

Nancy Weaver was in almost complete silence in the darkness of the BMW's trunk. Sweat streamed down her face, into her eyes. Her tears were like acid, burning wherever they touched.

She continued to fight. Her bonds were slightly looser now, the tape twisted. But not nearly enough to suggest she might slip free, even though her flesh was coated with perspiration. Her futile kicks were becoming weaker. Her bare feet were bloody and battered. She tried to kick harder, repeating the single, desperate word in her mind with each effort. *Kick! Kick! Kick!*

None of it seemed to make a difference, but it was all she had.

Outside the car, a reverse light and one of the brake lights continued their repetitive blinking.

At least the result of the electrical arcs she'd created weren't as drastic as Weaver had feared. There was no fire, no gasoline explosion.

But the blinking taillight and reverse light were dimmer. The battery was running down.

72

In the Far Castle's garden, the killer continued to work with pickax and shovel and Consolidated Edison equipment. Enough concrete had been knocked loose from the birdbath's outer structure to reveal *Bellezza*—certainly *Bellezza!* What was left of the concrete clung firmly to the marble, and there was still plenty of mud on what had been revealed.

The killer put down the pickax, backed up a step, and swiped the back of his wrist across his forehead. He felt almost tired enough to consider sitting cross-legged on the ground for a while. But he couldn't entertain that thought for long. His plan didn't allow for staying still in the same place for any unnecessary length of time.

He made a mental note to step up his dieting and exercise regimens, then began using his thick gardener's gloves to brush off what he could of the mud where it caked what used to resemble a birdbath.

When he thought enough mud and concrete chips had been brushed away, he attempted to lift the statuette. He didn't really expect to be able to move it by hand, but he wanted to get some idea as to its weight.

It weighed more than he could lift. He leaned his weight into it and rocked it back and forth until it broke loose from the depression where it had long sat in the garden.

Movement out near the street caught his eye, and he stood still and watched a man and woman stroll past on the sidewalk. They were holding hands, and the woman playfully hopped over the electrical cable leading from the van. To them, this was just another late-night Con Ed job. The utility company making sure the city would awaken to full power. They walked on.

The killer was reassured. He counted to twenty, slowly, then walked out of the garden to get a two-wheeled dolly from his parked van.

Much of the concrete had been chipped away from the birdbath. It should be light enough now that it wouldn't simply damage the dolly.

With the dolly, it should take him no more than ten or fifteen minutes to load the birdbath, generator, and cables into the van.

The rest of the tools he would leave for the losers.

Lucky Amber and his buddy Bill Jefferson, who liked to be called Jamal, were walking through the hot, humid night toward where there might be some traffic and they could flag down a cab. They were both sixteen, but Jamal could pass for twenty-one, which tended to get the two friends in trouble. They'd drunk beer while playing cards, but both boys were sober.

"Sounds like a major thing on the other side of town," Lucky said. "Sirens and shit."

"Maybe somebody with worse luck than me," Jamal said. He was a tall black youth who was prone to taking a short hop when he contributed to a conversation, as if footwork were necessary to make his point. The two were on their way home from a seven-card stud poker game, where Jamal had lost over twenty-two dollars. No small amount in their neighborhood.

"Some of them sirens are FDNY," said Lucky. He was shorter than Jamal, and broader. "My guess'd be a major fire."

"I wouldn't bet against you, man. Not tonight."

"Not *any* night on any*thing,*" Lucky said.

Jamal gave a little hop and said nothing. Right was right.

"That an emergency vehicle or something there?" Lucky said, pointing.

"Maybe a cab," Jamal said.

"A *gray* cab?"

"Guess not. And it's got the wrong kind of lights, and the red one's blinking. Wrong kinda car to be where it is, too. Looks like a Bimmer."

"Might be worth a look."

"So let's go take a look," Jamal said, with his habitual hop. Maybe the car was temporarily abandoned and would contain something worth stealing. Like drugs, cash, or an iPhone. Luck could change, couldn't it?

"Could be somebody wants us to walk over there so they can bash in our brains an' steal our wallets and watches," Lucky suggested. He wasn't called Lucky for nothing; he always considered the downside and seldom took chances.

"Or could be two hot MILFs looking for action." Hop, hop.

Faced with these polar-opposite choices, Jamal's suggestion prevailed. The two men crossed the street and started toward the parked car with the flickering reverse light and what looked like a blinking red turn signal.

But as they approached the car, Lucky saw that the blinking light wasn't a turn signal, or the front signal would probably be blinking white or yellow. And the back-up light should be steady, if the car was in reverse.

"Something's stuck," Lucky said when they were about twenty feet from the car. It was, as Jamal had thought, a BMW, but an old one. With some rust on it, and beat all to hell if you looked closely at it.

Jamal peered inside. The car was unoccupied. Just sitting parked, blinking. "Ghost car," he said

Lucky was beginning to get a bad feeling. "Let's haul our asses outta here."

"It's a BMW, bro. Things shouldn't go wrong with it."

"It's also about twenty years old," Lucky said.

Jamal shrugged, hopped. "So it's a classic. Belongs to some rich guy who'll give us a reward for alerting him that his car is screwed up."

"If we could find him," Lucky said.

"Or her."

Lucky smiled. "There is that possibility."

The two kids had almost reached the car when a taxi turned at the intersection.

The cabbie saw them and steered toward them, cruising for a fare.

"Here's where we spend some of your winnings," Jamal said.

The cab was veering in to be at the curb in front of them. Lucky took a step. Paused. He was staring at the old gray Bimmer.

"Wha's it?" Jamal asked.

"I heard something knocking."

"I heard a voice said, 'Take this cab.' " Jamal hopped toward the taxi.

"It's coming from that car." Lucky pointed toward the BMW. He glanced around. "Who'd park here, anyway? It's a long walk to anything." He raised a hand, stood still. "There it is again. And look at the car. It's kind of rocking."

"So maybe some couple's in there doing the nasty."

"No. There's nobody in there." Lucky headed toward the BMW again.

Jamal turned halfway and raised his hand, signaling to the cabbie that yes, they wanted the cab, and motioned for it to come on.

Lucky was already at the BMW, cast in red from the blinking taillight, when Jamal reached him.

Jamal stopped and stood still. He heard the knocking, too.

"There's something trapped in there," Lucky said. "Or someone." He moved to where he could see the car's interior. He tried the door and found it locked "There's nobody inside here."

"What I said, man."

"Noise gotta be coming from the trunk."

Jamal could hear the knocking clearly now. Whoever or whatever was inside the trunk must have heard them on the outside. "Somethin's alive in there, bro."

"Let's open it," Lucky said.

"Can't. No handle. And we ain't got no key."

The cabdriver had figured things out, a car parked in a godforsaken place, its lights blinking erratically, two curious young guys, trying to get the trunk open. He got a pry bar from the tool box he carried in the cab's trunk and went over to them. He could go either way with the pry bar, if he had to. But these two didn't seem dangerous. Couple of kids.

"There's something or someone trapped in there," Lucky said, pointing.

"I'd bet on *someone,*" the cabbie said, leaning close with his ear to the trunk lid. "Unless *something's* learned to holler for help." He jammed the iron pry bar's edge beneath the lip of the trunk lid. The metal made a squealing sound.

"That's a BMW," Lucky noted.

"It's an old pile of crap, too," the cabbie said. "And some poor bastard's trapped in the trunk and trying to get out."

"Could be a classic," Jamal said.

"Stand back," the cabbie said, bearing his weight down on the pry bar. "Might be a guy with a gun in there."

The lock gave and the trunk lid sprang open.

It wasn't a guy with a gun. It was a woman. She was nude and bound with duct tape, including a piece over her mouth that she'd worked half off. Her hair was plastered to her face with perspiration and she looked like somebody had beat the shit out of her. Even had what look like knife cuts and cigarette burns on her nude body.

The cabbie began using his pocketknife to cut the tape away.

The woman lay still except for sucking in huge breaths of the night air.

"Bet it was stuffy as hell in there," Jamal said, unable to look away from the abused naked woman. Despite her abysmal condition she was actually kind of—

Weaver glared at him and said, "Look in your pockets instead of at me, and see if you can find a cell phone."

She climbed out of the trunk. She was unsteady at first, leaning on the car, then was able to stand.

"You sure ain't got a phone in any of your pockets," Lucky said.

"I can call in and get the cops here, lady," the cabbie said.

"I am a cop," she said.

Jamal and Lucky began backing away.

"Stay where you are!" Weaver said. "Please."

They continued to backpedal. "It ain't like you got a badge or a gun or anything proves you're a cop," Jamal said.

"They got a point," the cabbie said, heading for his cab with its two-way radio.

"Why the hell are you hopping?" Weaver asked Jamal.

"He just does that," Lucky said. "Hops around. Only sometimes."

"There a cure for that?"

"Heavy stuff in his pockets."

Weaver licked her fingertips, then touched them to some of the cigarette burns on her breasts.

Both boys stood still, staring, mesmerized. Jamal's jaw was hanging open.

"Don't run, but don't stare at me."

They began shifting their weight. They were made for movement.

Weaver put her hands on her hips. "Listen, you run and I'm gonna remember your faces."

"We *sure* ain't gonna remember yours," Lucky said.

Both teenagers hooted. Jamal hopped. Then they ran like hell.

"Little pricks," Weaver said.

The cabdriver was back. He was carrying a light blanket that looked like it had oil stains on it. "Help's on the way," he said. "I thought you might want this."

"Thanks, I do, even though it'll hurt."

He handed her the folded blanket and looked in the direction the two teenagers had run. "They saved your life."

"I wanted to thank them."

"Notice how that tall one's always hopping?"

"Yeah. He should carry something heavy in his pockets."

A hunched-over woman pushing a two-wheeled wire grocery cart had spotted them, seen that Weaver was in trouble, and was coming toward them at a slow but steady pace.

"A good Samaritan," the cabbie said.

"Another one," Weaver said. "I wonder if she's got a cell phone."

73

Quinn pulled the Lincoln to the curb and answered his cell phone. Pearl gave him a look. Quinn said, "It's Weaver."

"Damned right it is," said the voice on the phone.

"I was letting Pearl know." He turned the volume up on the phone so Pearl could hear. "You okay, Nancy?"

Heavy breathing. Gathering herself. Quinn didn't like this.

"Nancy—"

"The bastard worked me over, Quinn. Then he left me locked in a car trunk to die there."

"What did he—"

"Never mind. I survived. But he made me talk. I couldn't help it."

Everybody talks.

"Did he believe what you told him?" Quinn asked.

"I don't know. It might be true. I don't think I could have convinced him otherwise, unless I at least half believed it myself. Anyway, I'm sure he's gonna act on the information."

"Which is?"

"I overheard a phone conversation at the restaurant. Winston Castle was talking about where *Bellezza* was hidden." Weaver's voice trailed off. Quinn wondered if she was hurt more seriously than she assumed. Was she thinking straight?

"Nancy—"

"Shut up and listen, Quinn. Information flows both ways. Winston Castle said *Bellezza* was hidden at the restaurant, concealed inside the birdbath near the garden maze."

"Inside?"

"It was used as the base and core of all that fancy concrete work that even the birds weren't happy about. You ever see a bird take a bath in that thing?"

Quinn hadn't. He thought about the bust inside a layer of concrete, preserved as if encased in a time capsule. "You think the bust might really be there?"

"Question is, does the killer think it might be there. I don't know for sure, but my impression was that he believed what I was saying, considering what he was doing with the burning tip of his cigarette."

"Who was Winston talking to?"

"I never figured that one out."

"Listen, Nancy, this might seem like a dumb question, but—"

"He enjoyed it, Quinn. The bastard loves inflicting pain." She paused. "Is that what you wanted to hear?"

"God, no, Nancy. But it's what I expected to hear. I had to make sure."

In the corner of his vision, Quinn saw the muscles in Pearl's jaw tighten. She was staring straight ahead when he spoke into the phone. "Nancy, I promise you we'll get the—"

"Yeah, yeah. I gotta go now, Quinn. Ambulance is coming for me. And a patrol car, too."

There was a medley of noise on the phone, none of it recognizable.

"I love all this attention."

"Nancy—"

"You be careful, Quinn. I mean that."

"Tell her to lie back down," a male voice said in the background. One of the paramedics. "Ma'am, please—"

"Careful, Quinn," she said again.

And the connection was broken.

The Lincoln didn't have a siren, but there was an old cherry light Quinn had bought at a police memorabilia sale in New Jersey. The kind with the big magnetic base you could clamp onto the car's metal roof. He stuck the round plug, at the end of the wire he was holding, into where the lighter used to be. Then he straightened out in his seat, opened the window, and let in a blast of humid wind and a few raindrops. He crooked his arm and stuck the flashing red light to the car's roof, directly over his head. Then he raised the window as far as it would go without crimping the wire.

"To the Far Castle!" he said, in reply to Pearl's questioning look, feeling a little like a character in King Arthur's Camelot. What he needed was a lance.

"Drive like we've got a siren," was Pearl's advice.

74

The killer worked the flat steel base of the two-wheeled dolly beneath the bulk of the birdbath. He used his body weight to help tilt back the heavy mass of concrete, and perhaps marble, and *Bellezza* was free of the ground.

It was caked with remaining concrete and clods of mud, and it didn't look like a thing of beauty. It looked like the kind of big chunk of whatever it was that Con Edison had to dig and chip around on most of their jobs.

The dolly's rubber tires made ruts in the mud and an impression in the wet grass. The killer shoved with both legs to get the dolly moving. The going was slow. It was imperative to keep the heavy load's forward momentum as the killer found traction and slowly moved the dolly and its burden toward the parked van.

The killer noticed a large black car turn the corner at the nearest intersection. A Lincoln town car.

How could they know I'm here?

But he knew how. The bitch from the NYPD had somehow made it out of the BMW trunk. *You're sup-*

posed to be dead. His mind's eye saw her dead—only she wasn't. She'd contacted Quinn and told him the same story she'd told the cops.

Two figures emerged from the black Lincoln. They were still almost half a block away. Both of them looked as if they were holding guns.

That was all right. The killer had his own guns. A cut-down Kalashnikov automatic, as well as a small handgun strapped to his ankle. If you knew whom to ask, where to look, you could practically buy guns on the street corners in New York.

The killer did a half spin and rolled the dolly back the way he'd come, off the solid, smooth walkway and onto the damp grass. Nothing in his movements or attitude suggested he was anything other than a manual laborer at his task.

"Better stay right where you are!" Quinn called.

The killer drew his automatic weapon from beneath his shirt and laid down a field of fire between himself and his pursuers. As soon as he fired the last shot, he took advantage of Quinn and Pearl's (the woman must be Pearl) temporary fear and disorientation. He leaned his weight hard into the two-wheeler and reversed direction. Another burst of gunfire came his way, but too late. They'd let down their guard for a few seconds and he'd taken advantage of it.

Another three, four, five shots. He heard the bullets rustle the leaves around him and snap a few small branches.

Not even close.

They were using peashooters compared to the Kalashnikov.

"Where the hell did he go?" he heard the woman ask.

"Where else?" Quinn said. "Into the hedge maze."

The killer had taken precautions, both in his surveillance and his preparation for the unexpected. He knew he might eventually be searching or trying to remove *Bellezza* from the Far Castle. He had a place to go.

Nearby.

Close enough.

The trick now would be in getting there.

Abandoning the heavy concrete bust, D.O.A. forged ahead through the thick maze. His meticulous memorization of the maze paid off. He could maneuver through the hedges swiftly and never have to double back. Not only that, he could hear Quinn and Pearl pursuing him and know precisely where they were. Once they were in a pathway directly opposite his own. He kept quiet, knowing they would soon come to a cul-de-sac and have to retrace their steps.

Meanwhile, he knew he was near a spot in the maze where he could break through the hedges and make his way into the street in the next block. From there he could get to the decrepit building where he'd rented the small office to use as an observation post. Once in the building, he could actually watch his pursuers give up the chase. They were welcome to the stolen van and equipment. He even looked forward to watching unseen from above and across the street, as they pored over the abandoned vehicle, searching for clues that weren't there.

If he'd had another few minutes, he might have had the bust loaded into the van.

The only thing that could have interfered with his plans then was Nancy Weaver escaping from the BMW's trunk before heat or madness overcame her.

And obviously she had escaped. She was alive and talking.

75

It was easier for the killer than he'd anticipated to break out of the hedge unseen and get to the building that lay diagonally across the street from the Far Castle.

The door, which the killer had oiled, made no sound as he admitted himself. He took the rickety wooden stairs fast, listening carefully to make sure that he wasn't being followed. That no one had seen him.

Once ensconced in his tiny observation post, he began to tremble. This encounter had been close. His planning, his thinking ahead and superior strategic instincts had saved him again. Luck had helped. No, not luck—fate. His covenant with fate was intact.

They had to believe in each other.

Controlling his breathing, he made himself calm down.

So close . . .

Nancy Weaver had done her best, and here he was, still functioning, still winning the game. More police would soon be arriving, and they'd search everywhere for him, for where he'd left *Bellezza*. No doubt they'd tromp and blunder through the hedge maze and locate the bust. Maybe they wouldn't notice it was no longer a birdbath.

The killer smiled at the thought. He held the police in the lowest regard. If it weren't for Quinn, the game wouldn't be half as exhilarating.

Quinn didn't go to bed that night, because he knew he wouldn't sleep. Not until he learned the results of the lab tests he'd requested be rushed. The microscopic life forms found in hairline cracks of the marble *Bellezza* abandoned near the Far Castle hedge maze would tell him what he needed to know.

At 3:30 A.M. Quinn's desk phone in his den jangled. Caller ID informed him that the caller was Renz.

Quinn picked up. "Whaddya know, Harley?"

"You were right, Quinn. Lab says that bust that was hiding inside the birdbath is no more that ten years old. Possibly a lot younger than that."

"What are the odds of accuracy?"

"Lab says there are no odds because there is no doubt. Science, Quinn. I'd explain the various tests they did, but I wouldn't understand them myself. That bust that came out of the Far Castle garden is a work well done, but it was never so much as touched by Michelangelo. Not unless the restaurant's got an employee who goes by that name."

"If they do," Quinn said, "I bet he's part of the family."

"I been thinking about something," Renz said. "This bust that was in the birdbath under concrete is by all reports a damned good imitation. So suppose—"

Quinn knew what Renz was going to say and said it first: "Suppose what everybody's been chasing—the bust that made its way over here from France—is also an imitation?"

"It does seem that someone would have figured it out by now."

"They say museums are full of great imitations," Quinn said. "But we've got carbon testing to determine age. The birdbath bust wasn't old enough to have come over here from Europe during World War Two."

"True," Renz said. "That's comforting."

"Like DNA is comforting," Quinn said, "even though it leaves us at the mercy of the experts."

"I'll sit on the test results like you asked, Quinn. But tomorrow I've gotta tell Minnie Miner or she'll nail my future career to the wall right next to my balls."

"Sounds painful and unprofitable."

"So you've got your answer on the age of the birdbath bust," Renz said. "And while it's an imitation, it's a damned good one. So if nothing else, we've further established that Michelangelo was a breast man. Now we can go to bed."

"I don't think I will."

Renz knew his old fellow cop and knew the signs. There had been a subtle but profound change in the investigation. A quickening. "We're getting close, aren't we?"

"Closer," Quinn said.

After hanging up on Renz, Quinn went into the office's half bath and rinsed his face with cold water. When he toweled dry and glanced at his reflection in the mirror over the basin, he was surprised. The man staring back at him was the familiar amiable thug he was used to seeing, but tonight there was also a curious lupine quality to his bony features. An intensity.

He knew the look. It frightened some people. It was that of a predator about to close on its prey. There was nothing about it that suggested reason or mercy. The time for conscious planning was past.

The fang was ahead of the brain.

76

Renz hadn't wasted any time in telling Minnie Miner about the imitation bust at the Far Castle. And she hadn't wasted time in making use of the information. Her guest on her morning program was Winston Castle. Quinn watched like a loyal fan.

Castle was wearing a nicely tailored suit and a red-and-blue-patterned ascot with matching handkerchief. He sat calmly in his wing chair, while Minnie sat facing him in a seemingly identical chair that had been made artfully and unobtrusively higher than its mate. There was a small table between the angled chairs on which were glasses of what appeared to be water. Minnie wouldn't have her guests run dry.

"And you had *no* idea that *Bellezza* was hidden in your birdbath?" she was asking Winston. She was bright and incredulous.

"Nor that the bust was an imitation," Castle said. He sounded absolutely British on TV. Quinn was impressed.

He and Pearl were seated at their kitchen table in the brownstone, facing the small flat screen on the counter.

"I'm glad we decided to watch this," Pearl said. "Winston is a really great bullshitter."

"World-class," Quinn said.

"You'd think he just tossed on his post-foxhunt suit and was a guest at a summer lodge. Are you sure he isn't really British nobility?"

As if he'd heard her, Winston nonchalantly crossed his legs and draped an arm over the back of the wing chair.

"I don't think he's sure what he is," Quinn said.

"Are you and your incredibly dedicated family planning to continue the search for the genuine *Bellezza?*" Minnie asked Winston.

"Of course. But I think we'll want to learn more about the imitation that was concealed in the birdbath in the Far Castle garden. We don't want to dash off half-cocked somewhere and have everything go all pear shaped."

Pear shaped?

"No," Minnie said thoughtfully. "I suppose not."

"Even on a noble quest like ours," Winston said, "there come times when the most productive thing one can do is simply nothing. It gives the mind a chance to catch up with all this dashing around we've been doing." He smiled broadly. "I will say the search has become even more interesting."

Minnie smiled broadly, knowing they were going into a commercial. "Thanks very much for being our guest, Sir Winston Castle. Or should I call you Duke or Earl?"

Castle smiled modestly. " 'Sir' will be just fine, Minnie."

Minnie looked as if she might be about to upchuck,

but she held her smile. "Good luck to you and to your fascinating family, sir. Tally-ho!"

Castle smiled thinly and Britishly, not exposing his teeth.

Quinn used the remote to switch off the TV just as a commercial for a product that made computers operate faster was coming onto the screen. An infant wearing a pin-striped business suit and a power tie appeared seated behind a vast desk.

"Did we really just see that?" Pearl asked.

"The baby IT guy?"

"You know what I mean," Pearl said. "*Sir* Winston Castle."

Quinn shrugged and then stood up to leave for the office.

Said, "Cheerio, old thing."

It was priceless, the way Pearl glared at him.

77

Quinn found himself thoroughly admiring Winston Castle's acting ability. So convincing had been Castle that he even had someone as incessantly phony as Minnie Miner frequently off balance. Surely this portly, elegantly attired factory of charm was on some level absolutely sincere. A kernel of sincerity lay concealed in every expression of bullshit. Though this installation of the news commentary program had been Minnie Miner's production, *Minnie Miner ASAP* had been Winston Castle's show.

At the same time, Minnie could seem to be whichever sort of person she chose. A woman with a closet full of personalities. Outward and aggressive as she was, she could also fool people into mistaking her for a naïf. Nature did that sometimes, made the most deadly flowers seem beautiful and innocuous. The ones with the poisonous thorns.

Quinn settled back in his desk chair, thinking about the Far Castle garden, how the concrete birdbath had been hidden in plain sight. Even if it had happened to be noticed and more carefully regarded, no one would have suspected that it might have been the concealment for something remarkable within.

No one would have dreamed that a creation of Michelangelo might lie beneath a crude layer of concrete, or that a much sought after concealed object might be a worthless facsimile.

This investigation reminded Quinn of those Russian dolls, each slightly smaller and hidden within the other, becoming successively more diminutive as they were explored. That kind of concealment tried the patience of any searcher, looking over and over again, finding the same thing, until curiosity, and then hope, finally waned.

It all reminded Quinn of the Tucker-Castle whatever it was—family, or cult, or what was the difference—when it came to finding and claiming a thing of beauty and a fortune? These people weren't as deadly as D.O.A., but they were easily just as devious.

Quinn had his suspicions that it wasn't only the killer who was yanking his chain.

He dragged his desk's land line phone over to him and called Pearl.

She was still at the brownstone, and sounded calm when she answered the phone. Which meant that Jody had probably left. They had begun the day with the two women arguing about whose phone the government had legal and moral authority to tap. Pearl and her daughter could discuss such subjects until they were all talked out and Quinn had long since fled to wherever it might be legal and moral to smoke a cigar.

"Still reeling from the Minnie Miner show?" Pearl asked him.

"Not per se," Quinn said.

"That sounds like something Winston Castle would say. He must have gotten to you with his member-of-parliament persona."

"I suppose that's why I'm calling," Quinn said. "There's something familiar about Winston Castle's act. It reminds me of a magician's patter, designed to get you looking at one hand while he's doing something with the other. Just when everybody's attention is distracted, *Presto!* Out of the hat pops the rabbit."

"Or the right card,"

"Never play poker with them," Quinn said.

"Rabbits?"

"People. Like the ones in Winston Castle's whack-job family, or whatever it is. They have their patter."

"Meaning?"

"Maybe somebody has a real Michelangelo up a sleeve."

"Magicians," Pearl said, not quite understanding. "I've always kind of liked them."

"Their act wouldn't work if you didn't."

"I still like them."

"They cut people in half, you know."

"Only beautiful girls. And it doesn't seem to hurt."

"I wouldn't want to see you proved wrong."

"Where are you going with this," Pearl asked with a sigh. Jody had apparently worn her down.

"We are going to stake out the Far Castle's Garden."

"I thought we were concentrating on D.O.A."

"Maybe we are," Quinn said. "My guess is he's *not*

one of the many people who think *Bellazza* isn't in the garden, just because an imitation has already been found there."

"Are we among the many, Quinn?"

"On one hand, yes."

"But on the other?"

"Presto!"

78

The searcher came by night, as Quinn had suspected he would, and hours after the restaurant had closed.

Quinn was slouching low behind the steering wheel in the black Lincoln. He'd parked where he had a catty-corner view across the intersection and the Far Castle's outdoor dining area. Beyond the stacked and locked tables and chairs loomed the shadowed topiary forms of the garden. Beginning several feet behind the flower beds was the larger garden, wilder and less arranged than the beds, with a variety of bushes and miniature trees. Adjacent to that, the entrance to the hedge maze loomed, a pathway to deeper darkness.

Quinn tensed his body. Had he heard a soft sound through the car's lowered window?

An odd sound. Like a muted clunking followed by a soft scraping noise.

It took him only a moment to realize that what he'd heard came from the direction of the dark garden.

Quinn knew he might have imagined the sound. He sat still, staring into the garden.

A full minute passed. He didn't hear the sound

again, but he was sure he saw something move in the shadows.

Quinn and Pearl were in constant touch with their cell phones. A simple tap of Quinn's fingertip made Pearl's phone buzz softly and vibrate.

"We got something," Quinn whispered, when he knew they were connected.

"I heard something, and there's movement in the garden, kind of repetitive. Could be digging."

"Or a couple making wild passionate love," Pearl said.

"The British don't do that."

"Hah! Isn't that what English gardens are for?"

"We should find out," Quinn said. "Call for backup, but make sure they move silently and don't close in yet."

"You mean backup for the wild passionate love?"

"Pearl! Damn it!"

"What are you going to do?"

"I'll just twiddle and wait. Maybe the butler will happen by."

Quinn waited exactly three minutes. He knew that by the time backup came on the scene, it might be too late. And careful as they were, they might spook whoever might be digging in the garden.

Quinn didn't like this.

Too many mights.

He had the Lincoln's interior lights set so they wouldn't come on when he opened the doors. He slipped out of the vehicle into the night.

In the silence, he could hear the ticking of the engine cooling down, and mentally eliminated that as the source of the faint but undeniable noise he'd heard. As if the night weren't warm enough, heat rolled out from beneath the car, along with the smell of high-octane gas and baked oil.

Staying low, he carefully moved away to approach the Far Castle.

When he got closer, he saw the movement in the garden again. What moonlight there was picked it up. He entered the garden as quietly as possible.

He quickly lost sight of where he thought he'd heard the sound. Crouching motionless, he stared into the darkness.

Again! The sound.

He saw nothing but moved toward it. Took a wrong turn in the maze and then silently retraced his steps.

And there was the sound again. Louder. Closer.

He was sure now of the source of the sound.

The noise he'd heard was what he'd first guessed, that of a shovel blade working the earth.

Now he knew what he was dealing with. He drew his old police special revolver from its holster. There was no safety on the gun, so he thumbed back the hammer.

The sound of someone digging—unmistakable now—became even louder, lending direction. With each *chunk!* of the shovel he could hear an exhalation of breath. With each cautious step he took, the picture gained definition.

He saw a bulky figure with a shovel, facing three-quarters away from him, standing in what looked like the middle of a bush and wielding a long-handled spade.

He was wearing what appeared to be elbow-length brown leather gloves that flared out at the top as if to protect his forearms.

The digger paused and spoke: "Ouch! Damn it to hell!"

Winston Castle. Sounding not at all British.

Quinn kept his revolver pressed against the side of his thigh and stepped forward. "Hurt yourself?"

Castle made a sound that was almost a shriek. Staring at Quinn, he dropped his shovel and held his heart. "Ah, Quinn! I'm glad to see you, but you scared the bloody bejibbers out of me."

He recovered quickly, did Castle.

He flashed his white smile. "This bush is a pyracantha, sometimes called a thornbush because it's full of bloody thorns." He leaned forward, graceful for such a paunchy man, and picked up the shovel handle, planted the spade's scoop, and leaned on the wooden handle. "Not the best sort of spot to bury something," he said.

"Oh? You're burying someone?"

"Some *thing,* old chap. Some valuable papers in a waterproof pouch." Castle shook his head and made a face, as if there were a nasty taste in his mouth. "One can't trust the banks these days. Not anymore." He cocked his head to the side, regarding Quinn. "Say, old chap, can I trust you?"

"Marginally."

Quinn holstered his revolver.

He motioned with his head. "I see a hoe over there. I'll help you dig. Between us, we can keep those thorns out of the way."

"Why, that's bloody sporting—"

"And we're not burying anything," Quinn said. "We're digging up something."

"Ah! You have me there."

"Yes, I do."

The wide, white, BBC smile. "You're sure of that, old thing?"

"I am."

"Well, you're spot on. I assumed this would be the last place where anyone would choose to dig, where there are such wicked thorns. I think that's especially true now, with the other bust already found and established as worthless."

"So what are we digging up?" They both knew, but Quinn wanted to hear Castle say it.

"Hmmph. What I want has been long enough in the ground."

Quinn waited.

"All right," Castle said. "It's *Bellezza*. The real one. Now we both know, and we can bend ourselves to the task at hand."

"You underestimated me," Quinn said, hacking away at the thick branches with the hoe. "You hired me in part so Q&A and the NYPD would scratch you off their suspect lists. You're still on mine."

"Suspect list? Good heavens, you can't be serious! I never killed anyone. I absolutely *couldn't*."

"Don't underestimate yourself."

But Quinn was sure Winton Castle wasn't a psychosexual killer. Certainly not D.O.A.

He warned himself not to be so sure about Castle. It was impossible to fathom somebody with such a tenuous hold on reality. Hard to believe that over the centuries Michelangelo had instilled in Winston Castle a conscience.

"I'm interested only in recovering *Bellezza* for my family," Castle said. "The rightful owners."

"Keep digging," Quinn said. "We can determine later who owns the bust. If it's actually here, where you say it is."

Winston Castle looked him square in the eye. "It isn't something I'd lie about."

Something else, maybe, Quinn thought.

79

It took another twenty minutes before Quinn's hoe struck something solid. Castle, digging next to him, leaned forward eagerly and tapped whatever it was with the point of his shovel. There was a faint hollow sound.

Quinn saw something dark gray in the hole they'd dug. It was cloth. He bent low and touched it with his fingertips. Something wrapped in oilcloth had been buried beneath the pyracantha thorns. He scraped with the hoe while Castle frantically dug around the object with his shovel. Quinn found himself wishing he had a pair of long leather work gloves like Castle's. His bare forearms burned as needlelike points of the thorns lacerated flesh.

"A box!" Castle said breathlessly. "It's in a wooden box wrapped in old cloth!"

He squatted low and extended a gloved hand into the space they'd cleared between cloth and mud. Across from him, Quinn lowered himself to his knees. Then he reached down and was glad to shove his bare hand deep into mud. His fingertips touched oily cloth—and wood.

"I got my fingers under it," Castle exclaimed through a wild grin. "Got you, beauty, got you, beauty . . ." he muttered. Quinn thought that if this was another phony piece of sculpture, or an empty box, and Castle knew it, he was laying his act on awfully thick.

And, Quinn had to admit, convincingly.

Quinn curled his own fingers beneath the bottom edge of the box.

He and Castle looked at each other, exchanging a silent signal, and heaved together to lift the box from its hole.

Castle yanked the oilcloth away and tossed it to the side. What was left was a sturdy wooden packing crate. There was what appeared to be a label on it, long since faded and stained until it was illegible. The acrid smell of aged cedar wafted from the box and from the hole it had been in. Quinn was reminded of graves opened for exhumations.

Castle hurled off his gloves and began frantically prying the box's lid with his fingertips. The lid was stubborn. Castle should have gone slower, examined the box, before laying into it like that. Quinn saw the glisten of blood in the faint moonlight.

"The lid's nailed tight," Quinn told him. "There's a better way to get into it."

Castle struggled to his feet, wiping his wrists across his perspiring forehead. His eyes were glistening like the blood seeping from beneath his fingernails. Quinn realized that for Castle, this was indeed like finding the Holy Grail.

It took Castle only a minute or so to use his shovel

to pry the box's wooden lid open far enough to where he could wedge the shovel blade beneath it, then use his weight to pry the lid open all the way. Feeling some of Castle's excitement, Quinn helped with the hoe.

Tightly driven old nails squealed as they were pulled from ancient wood. Ignoring the rusty nails, Castle tossed the wooden lid aside and dropped to his knees like a supplicant. Quinn knelt beside him to examine the box's contents.

There was something large wrapped in a soft green cloth. Castle's trembling hand lifted a corner of the material. Lifted it higher.

The cloth had concealed the bust of a beautiful woman. In ways not immediately comprehensible, it made the previous, fake *Bellezza*s, look lifeless and artificial.

"Look!" Castle was saying in an awed voice. "Would you *look* at this!"

"I'm looking," Quinn assured him. And what struck him was that *Bellezza* seemed to be looking back at him.

"These, too!" Castle said. "These, too!"

He was pointing at a ribbon-bound stack of letters. When he moved to untie the ribbon, it separated in his fingers.

A cursory look at the letters revealed that they were written by French resistance fighters. No doubt the ones who had rescued *Bellezza* from the Germans. There were also letters composed by Nurse Betsy Douglass, addressed to her married sister, Willa Kingdom. Those letters authenticated the origin of the bust.

In the corner of his vision, Quinn saw a figure cross the street farther down and enter the garden. He immediately assumed it was Pearl, grown impatient in the car. She was probably leading the backup that had silently arrived.

It wasn't Pearl.

Goaded by fear, Pearl fought her way up from unconsciousness. It took her a few minutes to realize the fix she was in. To remember the suddenly moving shadow, the figure that had sneaked up beside the parked Lincoln's rolled-down window.

The knife blade had glinted dully, moved quickly, too fast for Pearl even to cry out.

And now . . . ?

She dropped a hand to her lap, raised it, and was amazed by the amount of blood that she saw. She glanced down and was horrified.

Pearl probed gently about with her fingertips, exploring to find out where she was bleeding.

When she did find out, it scared the hell out of her.

Blood was pulsing from low on the left side of her neck, her carotid artery. Her assailant had reached through the window and drawn the knife blade across her neck, knowing she'd bleed out fast, figuring she'd be out of the game.

But he'd only nicked the artery, she was sure. She'd seen arterial bleeding before and knew this could be a lot worse.

Pearl remembered that Quinn kept a box of tissues in the glove compartment. Keeping her left hand pressed to the slow wellspring of blood coming out of her neck, she reached over with her right and opened the glove compartment.

Damn!

The only tissue was a small, unopened cellophane-wrapped pack.

She removed the pack, then tore its cellophane wrapper and dropped it on the car seat. Using the entire package of folded tissues as a pad, she pressed it to the side of her neck.

It stanched the flow of blood, but she knew the tissue would soon become saturated and the bleeding would increase again. To minimize that, she removed the cloth belt of her slacks and wrapped it at an angle around her neck, pulling it tight so it kept the tissue compressed and in place. She was still bleeding and would become weaker. The world would fade.

It seemed to be fading already . . .

80

"Looks like my timing was perfect," D.O.A. said.

He held a gun in each hand. Quinn recognized one as an altered Kalashnikov. The other was a small semiautomatic handgun. He noticed the killer's unnatural bulkiness and realized he was wearing a bulletproof vest. The vest didn't fool Quinn. It wasn't to save a life; it was to delay a death. Tonight was going to be the killer's grand and glorious exit. His reign of terror mustn't end with a single, inglorious gunshot.

The killer craved a final, glorious achievement, before his meteoric streak to eternal infamy.

Infamy would be his final, precious possession. His goal. Fame would be brief, but infamy had longevity.

It wasn't a live woman that he sought this time, but one who was a beauty of the ages.

"You know what I want," he said to Quinn. "We think the same way."

Castle, eyes popping with fright, glanced at Quinn.

"You won't possess her very long," Quinn said.

"I don't need to."

"He yearns to be famous," Quinn explained to Castle. "More than that, he might have found a way to be the *most* famous murdering psychopath. He wants to possess *Bellezza*."

Castle moved protectively toward the marble bust. D.O.A. laughed and hefted his automatic rifle.

"Cops will hear the shots," Quinn said.

D.O.A. aimed his smile at Quinn. "You mean like with the dead woman in your car? Pearl, wasn't it? I wish I could have had a little more amusement at her expense. You'll be glad to know I made her death a relatively fast one. Though it probably didn't seem that way to her."

Castle couldn't believe what he was hearing. Didn't *want* to believe it. He moaned as his terror bent him forward. He was trembling so violently that he was almost vibrating. His knees gave and he stayed in his awkward, doubled-over position, kneeling like a penitent frozen by fear.

"Your friend seems to have a keen notion of what's about to happen," the killer said, staring for a moment, searching for the fear in Quinn's eyes. He didn't find it, which angered him.

The two men's gazes remained locked. Quinn saw in the killer's eyes a feverish fear and desperation as well as anger. And there was something else, unmistakable and infuriating: It took Quinn a few seconds to realize that riding the crest of the killer's fear was a glint of something incongruous but undeniable: amusement. The bastard was actually amused by what was going on around him. Hell was about to break out, and he relished the coming carnage.

The killer said, "I think I'll save Fatso for last, then strike out for new methods and arousals."

Turning to see the effects of his words on Castle, the killer instead stood shocked.

The paunchy, terrified man apparently hadn't been as paralyzed as he'd appeared. He'd managed to escape silently into the garden's hedge maze.

Quinn took the opportunity to unholster his revolver, but only managed to touch the gun with his fingertips. The killer had quickly swung both his guns to point toward the real and immediate danger. Quinn. Not the bloated phony who had fled in fear into the hedge maze.

The killer had spent hours memorizing the maze from a high window across the street. But he wasn't sure he would know the maze's mysteries better than the man who'd possibly designed them.

Another possibility: Was Quinn bright enough to have misled him? Maybe the terrified fat man hadn't entered the maze at all.

Either way, he was surely free of the maze by now.

As if to confirm the killer's thoughts, there were sounds of activity from out in the street, beyond the garden and maze.

Then, yes, the fat man's voice. Almost surely.

The killer, his gaze and guns still fixed on Quinn, listened intently. He hadn't made out what the man said. Only that someone was really out there. But something surely was wrong.

Quinn, for the first time, saw vulnerability in D.O.A. Something essential had changed. Hunter had become hunted, and knew the heightened senses of the doomed.

Traffic beyond the garden. But not enough. So quiet . . .

The killer understood what the silence meant. Others who hunted him were arriving, arranging themselves strategically. Positioning and preparing.

But they wouldn't be prepared quite yet. Wouldn't be in place.

Opportunity. Limited, but exactly what the killer wanted.

Without warning, he sprinted to the hedge maze's dark entrance.

Quinn, who hadn't had time even to consider taking a shot at the killer, ran toward where he'd disappeared in darkness, and followed him into the maze.

Into blackness almost complete.

And isolation.

The only sound was the faint brushing of legs and shoulders against the hedges, both men moving fast, each knowing the other's mind. It was like a dance where neither partner could see the other.

Both knew where the maze would lead.

81

Quinn ran as fast as possible through the hedge maze. He couldn't build up much speed because of the frequent right-angle turns that required almost complete stops. If he wanted to keep up with the killer he had to dig in toe or heel and pivot sharply with each turn.

He could hear D.O.A. crashing along on the other side of the hedgerow to his right. It sounded as if the killer was directly opposite him, only five or six feet away. But Quinn couldn't be sure enough to take a blind shot through the thick hedges. Even if his sense of hearing provided enough accuracy for his bullet to find its mark, the hedge's thick branches and foliage might be enough to divert it to God knew where.

Quinn ran hard, feeling the pain in his thighs and chest, using his ears to direct his feet. He tried to calculate if he was gaining ground on the killer. Now and then he'd make a wrong turn, and he'd have to try to crash through the hedges to the next pathway. That never worked, but he was lucky enough to gain gradually on the killer, to stay close enough to gauge their respective positions.

But not so close as to chance taking a shot.

Luck. Good for me, bad for the killer. He'll run out of hedgerows eventually.

Then Quinn suddenly wondered if it *was* luck. The killer was younger and should be able to outrun him.

But the killer didn't seem to have gained ground.

Wrong. Something was wrong.

Quinn was being led.

Short of breath, his legs and lungs aching, Quinn realized the killer had deliberately lured him through the maze in a circuitous route, back to where the chase had begun.

He wanted to be sure that Quinn understood. That he'd been led. The killer was in control and had chosen the time and place. He wanted death, and knew he was going to die. And he wanted Quinn to die with him, knowing that he, Quinn, had lost the game.

The game that meant everything. Quinn understood now the keen amusement in the killer's eyes.

Timing was so important.

Both men broke from the hedge maze at almost the same moment, simultaneous to an armada of police and emergency vehicles arriving at the scene. And there were plenty of news media representatives. Vans with tower aerials mounted on their roofs, media wolves already dismounted and on foot, units of camera and lighting professionals, and well-coifed media stars, all running toward police barricades that were already in place. The scene was epic. The night electric.

The killer felt his heart swell. *This* was what he wanted, even better than he'd anticipated. Here was a drama that would dominate every news outlet, every Internet scan, and hold the population in thrall. The finale of the hunt, with the hunted and hunter locked in deadly combat.

Quinn would understand what had happened, even as his life faded. He'd know he'd been outmaneuvered.

Let the fools of the world think what they may. Quinn would breathe his last knowing he'd lost the game.

And the world will be watching.

Quinn and the killer were both clear of the hedge maze now, and through the garden. Uniformed cops advanced across the street toward them, along with darkly clothed members of the Tactical Unit. They were approaching at slight angles, allowing for a cross fire.

The killer thought his bulletproof vest would keep him alive at least as long as Quinn lived.

Quinn wasn't so sure. He raised his police special revolver, dropping to one knee so he'd be a smaller target, and opened fire on D.O.A.

The killer seemed invulnerable in his bulky vest. He was smiling as he leveled the Kalashnikov at Quinn.

That was when one of Quinn's bullets found its way beneath the side of the vest and lodged in the killer's chest. He dropped hard and didn't move, supporting himself on one elbow.

Still without a clear shot, the Tactical Unit held its fire.

Wounded in the same leg that had been shot years before, Quinn limped toward the killer, who had struggled up and was now seated cross-legged on the pavement, his arms and hands hanging limply at his sides.

As Quinn came near, he saw again the madness and amusement in the killer's eyes. The eyes were hypnotic, and Quinn was distracted enough that he didn't see until it was too late the killer raise a handgun that had been concealed beneath his right thigh.

Quinn knew that from this range, he was dead.

The killer hesitated, savoring the moment.

Steadied his aim.

Pearl shot him.

The heavy Glock round slammed into the killer's head, just behind his right ear.

As he lay dying, the killer stared up at the night sky and knew he'd be huge in tomorrow's papers. Where he'd always wanted to be. Above the fold.

Quinn had a round left in his revolver. He stood and started to walk over so he could shoot the killer again in the head. He needed to be sure that D.O.A. was finally and forever dead. There was no pain, but his right leg gave out and he was on his knees again. He looked down and saw that his thigh was bleeding.

He raised his gaze to look at Pearl. She seemed calm, standing there with her Glock still in her hand. The hand and gun were as steady as if they were sculptured stone.

"You never were one to wait in the car," Quinn said.

Pearl looked down at him. "Lucky you."

A uniformed cop walked over and bent low, found the stray gun beneath the killer's body, and slid the weapon ten feet away. He didn't straighten up, but stayed still with his head bowed, listening to something the dying killer had to say. Then the killer turned his head toward Quinn, but his eyes were closed, his mouth half open, as if he'd been interrupted mid-word.

Then, incredibly, the mouth smiled.

The uniformed cop sauntered over to Quinn and squatted down near him. He motioned with his head toward D.O.A. "He's good as dead. On his way out even if the paramedics pump blood in him by the gallon."

"Good," Quinn said.

The cop smiled thinly. "I wouldn't contradict you."

Pearl laid her hand on Quinn's forehead. "Have we got medical transport on the way?"

"We do," the cop assured her.

"He whispered something to you," Quinn said, gripping the cop's sleeve as the man started to straighten up.

The cop nodded. "Told me to give you a message. Said I should tell you *checkmate*. Just that one word."

Quinn looked over and still couldn't be sure the killer was dead.

"I think he's gone," the cop said.

Quinn clenched his teeth against the pain and fought to stand up on his good leg. The cop helped him, even though Quinn pushed him away at first.

"Checkmate," the cop said again.

Quinn ran out of strength and sat down again hard on the pavement.

"Go tell him *royal flush*," he said.

But the D.O.A. killer was dead, in a pool of his own blood, seduced by a woman.

82

Two days after the shoot-out at the Far Castle, Renz dropped by the Q&A office and informed Quinn that tests had established that the *Bellezza* bust found buried beneath the thornbush outside the restaurant was less than ten years old. The letters, which had been artificially aged, were also phony.

Another imitation.

Quinn wasn't surprised.

"Any word on where Winston Castle or Maria are?" he asked.

"Blown in the wind," Renz said, "like the answers to a lot of questions. The Ohio family members—or whatever they are—know from nothing."

"I have a feeling Castle and his wife—if Maria's really his wife—will turn up again. There aren't any warrants out for them."

"There would be if I could think of some charges," Renz said. Not meaning it. Why stir up this mess and make it politically radioactive again?

"What about the restaurant?" Quinn asked. He adjusted his bandaged leg where it was propped on a low hassock.

"The Far Castle is closed. Sign in the window says it's temporary, for remodeling. Doesn't say for how long." Renz glanced around the office. He and Quinn were the only ones there. "Pearl okay?"

"Physically, yeah. But she's got a lot of mental baggage to rummage through."

"Feds?"

"Minor wounds," Quinn said. He smiled faintly. "They seem to have saved his marriage."

"Weaver's out of the hospital already," Renz said. "She's a tough lady."

"Pearl visited her there," Quinn said. "That's probably as well as those two will ever get along. And it won't last."

"Tough ladies," Quinn said. "That's what brought D.O.A. down."

"Poetic something," Renz said. "Justice would have been if we could have let Pearl, Weaver, and Feds's wife, Penny, team up with all the victims and beat the bastard to death." Renz raised both hands. "I know, I know. 'Then we'd all be just like him.' "

"No," Quinn said, "I wasn't going to say that."

This was the second time Pearl visited Nancy Weaver. They were alone in the room, which was on the fifth floor and let in too much traffic noise.

"It's nice of you to come by," Weaver said. She was resting on her back in bed, an IV tube snaking to the back of her right hand. What was visible of her body showed bruises that were every color of the spectrum

"We're on the same floor," Pearl said. "So it's no big deal."

Weaver didn't nod. Didn't move.

"It's not like us to get along this well," Pearl said, for a moment wondering what the hell she was doing there.

"I'm not hurt as bad as I look," Weaver said. "I'll be out of here soon."

"Same for me," Pearl said.

Weaver shook her head. "God, you almost died. You can't just walk out of here after a few days."

"We both almost died," Pearl said.

"Occupational hazard."

Pearl wondered if Weaver was as far along on the recuperative scale as she thought. Like she might disentangle herself from all those tubes, struggle out of bed, and stroll out of here.

"Are you two plotting something?" a woman's voice asked.

Both women looked at a hefty nurse in a blue uniform. She was holding a clipboard and staring over it at Pearl and Weaver. A plastic tag pinned to her uniform declared that her name was Florence.

"Should you be out of your room?" the nurse asked Pearl, fixing her with a Quinn-like look.

"Doctor said it was okay," Pearl lied.

"I'd like for you to step out for a while," Florence said.

Pearl nodded, moved to the bed, and squeezed Weaver's hand. "You're a good cop," she said.

Weaver smiled up at her. "We both are."

* * *

Pearl was in her room, fully dressed, when Florence knocked and then entered.

Florence's eyes widened and became hard. "What do you think you're doing out of your hospital gown?"

"Checking myself out," Pearl said. "Going home."

"You can't do that."

"I can," Pearl said. "I'm a cop. I can do whatever I want as long as it's legal." She pushed past Florence and felt a heavy hand on her shoulder.

"If you impede me in any way," Pearl said, "I'm going to handcuff you to the bed and leave you there."

Pearl felt the hand on her shoulder become lighter. She walked out from beneath it and went out the door.

Florence followed her into the hall. "I know there's something going on between you and Nancy Weaver. Some kind of competition. I could see it in the two of you. This isn't the time or place for that kind of nonsense."

"What kind of nonsense would you suggest?"

"Anything that won't turn relatively minor injuries into something more serious."

Pearl stopped and stood so she was facing the nurse, holding her ground. "You really can't stop me, you know."

"I know. But I should be able to. For your own good. Some of those wounds might become infected."

"Doubt it," Pearl said. "But if they do, I'll come back. I promise."

Florence watched her as she walked down the hall, toward the elevators.

Then the concerned nurse headed for Weaver's room, praying that *she* wasn't dressed in street clothes.

"Lord save them from themselves," she murmured.

83

The week after D.O.A. died, Quinn was at his desk at Q&A, leaning back in his swivel chair and barely keeping it upright by using his new cane. There was a space of about half an inch where perfect balance was achieved with the cane's tip only slightly touching the floor. He was getting tired of that game and wondered if he could remove the cane altogether and remain upright, when his desk phone rang.

The sudden noise surprised the hell out of Quinn, and he and the chair almost went over.

He managed to remain upright, dug the tip of the cane into the floor, and swiveled the chair around to where he could reach the phone, answer it, and identify himself.

"It's good to hear your voice," said Winston Castle.

Quinn sat forward, the cane and all chair legs on the floor. "How have you been, Winston?"

"Fine, of course."

"And Maria?"

"Also fine."

"Now that we're all fine," Quinn said, "let's get to why you called."

"You sound angry with me, Detective Quinn."

"I'm not," Quinn said, surprising himself by realizing that was true. "I'm just befuddled."

"I'm calling from Mexico," Castle said, though the caller ID on Quinn's phone said the call originated in some place called High Wind, Texas.

Quinn decided to let it go. Nothing else was genuine about Winston Castle, so why should this be? "I heard the restaurant's closed."

"Temporarily," Castle said. "I sold the business, though I continue to own the building. I'll simply be renting out restaurant space."

"How does Maria feel about that?"

"She's the reason we're doing it. It's for her well-being."

"Part of the reason, anyway," Maria said. On an extension phone in High Wind. "Winston and I have chosen the life we want to live, and right now the restaurant doesn't fit into it."

"Apparently," Quinn said, "neither do English accents."

"You noticed that, old thing?" Castle said.

"Difficult not to."

"It seems to me," Castle said, "that there was a reason for the substitution of *Bellezza* busts in the restaurant garden. This whole thing was planned."

"What whole thing?"

"Everything from the fake *Bellezza* to D.O.A.'s escape."

Quinn was surprised, then wondered why he should be. "D.O.A. is dead," he said. "I saw him die."

"Somebody in a bulletproof vest was shot and killed."

"Yes. A man named Dwayne Oren Aiken. I chased him for years."

"Can't you admit, Detective Quinn, that there is the slightest possibility that this Dwayne Oren Aiken survived. I mean, wouldn't he *want* to be officially dead?"

"Why?"

"So you'd stop hunting him. And he could sell *Bellezza* to a dedicated but dishonest collector."

"Do you really believe that?"

"I think it's possible. That's why I'm in Mexico."

"You're in Texas."

"Very near the border."

Quinn agreed with Castle that there really were such art connoisseurs, who would be content simply to own but never show such a wonder. Quinn also knew there were people whose joy was in searching for the unattainable. Classics had been written about them. Movies had been made. At least Castle, whom Quinn had come to like, was a seeker and not a hoarder. Apparently Maria was the same. That kind of dogged optimism and persistence seemed to Quinn to be a healthier, happier existence than most people led. So let Castle, and his entire crazy family, the quasi or real descendants of the Kingdoms and Douglasses and Tuckers, roam the world and seek. It wasn't a bad thing to nurture and chase a dream. For some, it was the only thing.

"I understand now how the case became so complicated," Quinn said. "The precious object it revolved around never existed."

"That's a possibility," Castle said. "But you must understand our quest for the art treasure gives our family its raison d'être. Its reason for being. And the family needs me to keep it out of trouble. This is the only family I have, Quinn. And for some of us, our search is the only meaningful thing in our lives."

"I do understand," Quinn said, thinking Michelangelo would be pleased by such a constructive fancy.

"I knew that you would."

"Good luck to you and to your family," Quinn said.

But there was no answer. Winston and Maria Castle were gone.

In the wind again.

Quinn told no one other than Pearl about the conversation. They agreed that Q&A would never be for sale.

The new owner of the Far Castle continued to operate the restaurant under the terms of the lease. Nothing appeared to have changed.

On stormy days, one gargoyle on the building's concrete cornice, shielded from immediate view by the restaurant's canopy, emitted no water but seemed to glory in the rain. It was a bust of a woman with her eyes closed and a slight smile on her face, basking in the downpour. Knowing there would be another sunrise. She was a thing of beauty.

ACKNOWLEDGMENTS

With special thanks to Marilyn Davis.

Don't miss John Lutz's next exciting thriller featuring
Frank Quinn

JIGSAW

Coming from Pinnacle in 2015!

Keep reading to join Frank Quinn and Pearl Kasner
as they are hired to solve a jewelry heist that
leads murder . . .

SWITCH

by John Lutz

Prologue

"There's a finger in her," Nift said, watching Pearl Kasner's face for a reaction.

She didn't show much of one.

Quinn and Pearl watched Medical Examiner Dr. Julius Nift, crouched low near the woman's body, move his shoulders and arms, probe with what looked like long, thin tweezers, then stare and shake his head. Before him, lying between the corpse's widely spread legs, was a small, bloody object.

"What do you mean," Pearl asked, "a finger?"

Nift held up his rubber-gloved left hand, fingers spread. "One of these." He made a fist except for his extended forefinger. "This one, to be exact. Or one like it." He grinned. "It was lodged in her vaginal tract. Wanna take a look?"

Pearl did. So did Quinn.

Quinn said, "Man's finger?"

"Almost certainly. Right size for a man's. Nail's trimmed close. No polish. Lots of stuff under it. Maybe rich with DNA."

"Fingerprint?"

"Should be discernible. Once we get it cleaned up."

Quinn nodded, standing with his fists propped on his hips, and glanced around Alexis Hoffermuth's luxurious penthouse apartment, amazed anew by the vastness of the room they were in and the obvious wealth that showed in every facet of the place.

He had met Alexis Hoffermuth here just two days earlier, when she was alive.

Her body had been discovered scarcely an hour ago after she didn't show up for an eight o'clock appointment (so unlike her), and failed to answer either her cell or land line phone.

The doorman had admitted the woman she was scheduled to meet in regard to a political fund-raiser, and there Alexis Hoffermuth was, in her altered state.

Pearl and Quinn looked at each other, each knowing what the other was thinking: money and murder were such close friends.

"Strange calling card," said Nift, who liked to play detective, "a forefinger in her twat." He glanced at Pearl to see if he'd gotten a rise out of her. "Whaddya make of it, Pearl?"

"If he's a serial killer, he's limited to nine more victims."

"Unless—" Nift began.

"Shut up," Pearl said, and he did.

"She was over fifty," Quinn said, nodding toward the victim. "You'd never know it, even like this."

The dead woman stared wide-eyed back at him, flecks of blood visible in the white around her pupils, the way eyes were after someone's been strangled. In this instance, strangulation appeared to have been caused by the Burberry scarf around her neck. Yet the expression of pain and bewilderment frozen on her face wasn't quite like that of a strangulation victim.

"There are a lot of imitation scarves like that floating around New York," Nift said. "You think that one's real?"

"It's real," Pearl said.

"The boobs aren't," Nift said.

"You would notice that."

"Expensive job, though. But then, it would be."

"No need to wonder about cause of death," Quinn said, changing the subject before Nift and Pearl clashed. They often played this game. Nift seemed to regard making Pearl lose her temper a challenge. Not that she was his only target.

"Don't be too sure," Nift said. "Cause of death can be tricky." Squatted down as he was, he craned his neck and glanced around, as if seeing the upper half of his surroundings clearly for the first time. "Place is big enough to be a museum. Looks kinda like one, the way it's furnished."

"What about time of death?" Pearl asked. She didn't want to talk about décor.

"The victim sometime between midnight and three o'clock this morning. The finger sometime before then."

"How do you know that?" Quinn asked.

"That the finger died before she did?" Nift grinned. "Putrefaction, discoloration, suggest several days, depending on ambient temperature. Also, I gave it the sniff test." He grinned wickedly at Pearl. "Wanna smell?"

"That finger's not the worst smelling thing in this room," Pearl said angrily.

Nift ignored her. He'd gotten a rise out of Pearl again. He was temporarily ahead on points in the game he insisted they play.

Like Quinn, Pearl was a former NYPD homicide detective. Now they were part of Quinn and Associates Investigations—Q&A, as it was commonly called. The agency was formed when Quinn decided to extend his avocation beyond hunting down serial killers, which was his area of expertise. Q&A was more of a traditional detective agency now, and its employees were part owners and had a stake in its success.

Because of Quinn's legendary and well-earned reputation for tracking and apprehending serial killers, the agency sometimes still did work for hire for the city. That work wasn't exclusively serial killer cases; now it included almost any kind of criminal case that was high profile, sensitive, or for any other reason important to the city, or to the political well-being of its police commissioner. These contracts were mainly because the police commissioner, Harley Renz, and Quinn went back a long way.

Not that they liked each other. Quinn lived by his code, and Renz was without a code and enthusiastically corrupt. Still, the two men got along. Frequently they could help each other obtain what they wanted, however different those wants might be.

The techs from the crime scene unit were still going over the vast apartment with their lights and chemicals, cameras and print powder.

"Maybe they'll find something," Nift said, motioning with his arm to take in the activity around him.

"I know what they won't find," Quinn said.

Nift straightened up beside his black bag and looked at him. "You know something about what went on here?"

"Maybe," Quinn said.

Part One

It all started not-so-innocently enough.

Ida Beene from Forest, Ohio, who called herself Ida French, knew exactly what she was doing when she slid into the backseat of the parked limo in her preoccupied manner, pretending it was a mistake and she'd thought it was a different limo, one that was waiting for her.

Craig Clairmont, Ida's current love interest, watched her from a nearby doorway. He could make out her pale features inside the limo's tinted rear window. Watched her mouth work as over and over she said how sorry she was, how she'd made a terrible mistake by entering the wrong car. Her active, shapely form was never still as she jabbered and waved her arms, pretending to be a bit zany but at the same time apologetic. All the while, he knew she was substituting the gray leather Gucci purse on the seat with her almost identical knock-off Gucci bag she'd bought on Canal Street for thirty dollars.

An embarrassing mistake, that was all. She kept repeating that as she reversed her trim, shapely derriere out of the limo, yakking, yakking all the time, overplaying it, keeping Alexis Hoffermuth distracted and confused. Her words drifted to Craig: "Oh, my God! So sorry, sorry. I'm such a goofball. Never did this before . . . should have been paying attention . . . please, please forgive me. Never, never . . . Such an embarrassing mistake." All the time gripping the gray leather Gucci purse by its strap.

Only it wasn't *her* Gucci purse. It was Alexis Hoffermuth's. And inside Alexis Hoffermuth's purse was the little item Hoffermuth had bragged in the society columns that she wanted dearly and was going to purchase at auction. The item for which she'd kept her public word and outbid everyone, including a pesky telephone bidder who kept running up the bid.

Ida slammed the limo door behind her with a solid *thunk!* and strode quickly away, showing lots of ass wiggle, clutching the purse tight to her side. The limo driver, a burly man in a dark uniform with gold buttons, got out and stood on the other side of the car, looking after her. Obviously wondering.

Craig tensed his body, knowing he might have to act. This could go either way. Nonviolent would be best, but Craig and Ida could play it rough if they had to.

Fortune was precariously balanced here.

It teetered, leaned, and fell Craig and Ida's way.

The chauffeur made no move to follow Ida, and lowered himself back into the gleaming black limo, behind the steering wheel.

The limo dropped a few inches over its rear wheels and glided out into Manhattan traffic, like a shark released into the sea.

But the sharks were behind it, on land.

Craig walked down to where Ida was waiting outside an electronics store. She was near a show window, pretending to gaze at the various gizmos: thumb-sized cameras, video game players from China, and cell phones that incorporated every imaginable capability. She looked like an actress who could play a ditsy blonde on TV, maybe missing a card from the deck, barely smart enough to lose at tennis. Craig knew that look was deceptive. Ida was wicked smart. And right now she was thinking hard, waiting for Craig.

He stood next to her, leaned over, and kissed her cheek. "You make the switch okay?"

"This is a genuine Gucci," she said, clutching the purse tighter.

"I'm only interested in what's inside."

"So let's go home. I know you don't want to look at it here on the sidewalk."

"It deserves more careful treatment than that," Craig agreed.

Ida smiled. "Fifty cents on the dollar treatment."

That had been the deal—fifty percent of the bracelet's bid price. It didn't seem like such a good deal, but it was safe and came to almost a quarter of a million dollars.

Craig took Ida French's arm. They made a striking couple, the slim blond woman and the tall, classically handsome man with steady blue eyes and wavy black hair. They both dressed well and expensively. They could afford it. Especially now.

Home, in the small den off the apartment's living room, they rooted through Alexis Hoffermuth's purse.

There was, somehow surprisingly, the usual women's items: makeup essentials; a comb; wadded tissue with lipstick stain on it; a wallet that, disappointingly, held nothing but credit cards; a cell phone (which Craig would get rid of soon, along with the purse, in case it was one of those phones that could be electronically traced if it got lost); a Sotheby's auction catalog; and, of course, the Cardell diamond-and-ruby bracelet, that for a brief time had been the Hoffermuth bracelet.

Craig smiled. Now it was the Craig and Ida bracelet.

They dumped the rest of the purse's contents out onto a tabletop. Not even a dollar in cash. The rich lived large and traveled light.

Craig opened a drawer and drew out a paste bracelet that was a duplicate of the real Cardell bracelet they had stolen. He dropped it in the Hoffermuth bitch's purse then scooped all the other contents in on top of it. Before closing the drawer, Craig got out another paste duplicate of the bracelet and laid it on the table away from the genuine one. The fake bracelet in the purse was for fooling Alexis Hoffermuth for at least a little while. That was the second duplicate Cardell bracelet. A third one, the one Craig placed on the table, was for fooling someone else.

They held hands as they went into the living room. Craig poured them each a flute of champagne.

They toasted each other.

"You'd better get rid of the purse with that cell phone soon," Ida said, placing her glass on a paper napkin.

Craig agreed, but he wasn't worried. It would be a little while before Alexis Hoffermuth noticed the leather of her purse wasn't its usual softness, and the brassware was a bit bright and tacky looking. And the clasp didn't quite hold.

Then, with a plunging heart, she would realize that it wasn't her purse.

But it was exactly like her purse.

She would open the purse and see that it contained only wadded white tissue.

And it would dawn on her like a nuclear sunrise—the Cardell bracelet, for which she'd just paid $490,000 at Sotheby's Auction—was gone.

Spirited away by a thief!

Or had it been?

She would try to recall the features of the woman who looked and acted like a flustered young Lucille Ball. Alexis would realize the woman had switched purses and left her with nothing but wadded tissue.

But there'd be something else in the purse . . . Alexis Hoffermuth's fingers would jab and dance through the tissue, then close on a familiar object and draw it out.

The bracelet!

Relief would course through her. But not without some reservations.

Craig Clairmont smiled. Alexis Hoffermuth wouldn't understand. The bracelet somehow had been removed from her purse and then found its way into the substitute bag. Had the thief made some sort of mistake? She certainly was the type to do so.

Alexis might wonder that again, when her real purse was recovered with the bracelet still in it. A bracelet like it, anyway. It might be a long time, and a lot of wishful and confused thinking, before it occurred to her that the recovered bracelet was yet another not-so-cheap imitation. That the thieves were simply playing for time.

The very clever thieves.

Ida and Craig each took another sip of champagne.

That was when Ida's eight-year-old daughter, Eloise, flounced into the room.

May 6, 4:35 p.m.

They thought at first he'd been struck by the sanitation department truck, one of those behemoths with the huge crusher in back.

But the man in the alley seemed unhurt except for the fact that he was bending over, holding one hand folded in the other.

When the trash truck had left the narrow passageway and turned a corner, Otto Berger and Arthur Shoulders exchanged glances. They were both bulky men in cheap brown suits. Otto was slightly the taller of the two. Arthur was slightly wider. Otto made a motion with his head, and the two professional thugs swaggered toward the lone figure in the shadows. The man looked up at them, and Otto smiled, not parting his lips. This was who they were expecting.

"Bingo, bango," Arthur said.

"Gee, what happened to your hand?" Otto asked.

The man, whose name was Jack Clairmont, grimaced. "I got it caught in the trash truck's mechanism when they used that damn grinder."

"That's a lotta blood you're losing," Arthur said.

"I'm goddam afraid to look."

"What was you doing," Otto asked, "tossing something into the truck?"

"Didn't I see you get something from one of them guys who sling the trash bags?" Arthur asked.

"Like making an exchange," Otto said.

The injured man squinted painfully at them.

Otto, though huge, was quick. He stepped forward and kicked Jack Clairmont hard in the side of the knee. Clairmont yelped and dropped to his elbows and knees on the concrete.

"Don't make no noise now," Otto said

Arthur was holding a knife. "He makes noise and it'll be the last time," he said.

Otto gave Jack Clairmont a wide grin. His teeth were in need of thousands of dollars worth of dental work. "Very good, Arthur. This gentleman can't make noise if his vocal chords are flapping around."

"If vocal chords do that," Arthur said.

Otto kicked Jack in the buttocks, not hard this time. "Crawl over there into them shadows," he said.

Jack Clairmont craned his neck and stared up at them. He looked as if he were about to cry. "Who are you guys?"

"I'm Mr. Pain," Otto said.

Arthur's turn to smile. Perfect teeth. "And I'm Mr. Suffering."

"And you better become Mister Crawl," Otto said. "Right now would be a good time to start— What the hell was that?

"Only a cat," Arthur said.

"Thing was jet propelled. And black."

"Bad luck."

"Not for us, Arthur."

"What'd it have in its mouth?"

"Who gives a shit? We got business here, Arthur."

"Then business it is." Arthur looked down at the injured man and grinned. Sometimes he loved his job.

Otto stared hard at Jack Clairmont and motioned with his head, as he had earlier to Arthur, indicating direction.

Jack Clairmont began to crawl.

Then he stopped. "*Oh, my God! My hand!*"

Otto sighed. What the hell was this about? He remembered the black cat.

"I'm missing a finger!" Clairmont moaned. "That goddam crusher on the trash truck cut off my finger! *My finger.*"

Otto shrugged. "It ain't as if anybody's gonna be asking you for directions." He kicked the man again and pointed with *his* finger.

Moaning, sobbing, Clairmont resumed his crawl toward the shadows, favoring his right hand.

Still holding the knife, Arthur stood with his beefy arms crossed and stared at him. "He ain't very fast."

"Yeah," Otto said. "That missing finger, maybe."

"You think it could affect his balance? Like when you lose your little toe?"

"I never lost a little toe, Arthur."

Arthur said, "Hey, that cat! You don't suppose . . ."

"We ain't got time to look and find out," Otto said. He glanced around. "This is far enough," he said to the crawling Clairmont.

"Yeah," Arthur said. "Time for you to rest in pieces." He laughed. No one else did. "I was referring to the separated finger," Arthur explained. But a joke never worked once you deconstructed it.

"This guy's kind of a wet blanket," Otto said, shoving Jack with his foot so he turned and was leaning with his back against the wall. "We been here too long already. Stick him, Arthur, so we can leave this place before somebody happens by."

"*Happens by*? You must watch the BBC."

"Pip, pip. Do stick him, Arthur."

Arthur stuck him.

May 6, 4:58 p.m.

Ida and Craig were sitting in the living room, watching cable news on the TV with the sound muted. There was no news yet about the Cardell bracelet theft.

"Where's Boomerang?" Eloise asked.

Craig looked at her, this annoying child that came with Ida as part of a set, half of which Craig loved. Loved enough to use, anyway.

"Who's Boomerang?" Craig asked, without real interest.

"Her cat," Ida said. "You know Boomerang."

"Only in the way you can know a cat," Craig said.

"I think he ran away again," Ida said.

Eloise shrugged. "He doesn't *run* away. He always comes back. Like a real boomerang."

"Usually with a gift," Ida said, cringing at the thought of some of the grisly trophies Boomerang had left on the kitchen floor as offerings. Everything from dead sparrows to rat heads. The more horrific the better. Boomerang would reenter the way he'd left, through the kitchen window, always open a crack to the fire escape, and deposit his offering on the throw rug. Then he'd be demonstrably proud. Cats seemed to think that way. At least cats like Boomerang.

"He's probably out doing it to the lady cats in the neighborhood," Craig said.

"Craig!" Ida warned.

Craig smiled. Maybe he and Boomerang weren't all that different from each other.

"Trash pickup happen yet?" he asked.

Ida gave him a stern look. They weren't supposed to talk about this in front of Eloise. Craig's brother Jack was going to make the switch of the Hoffermuth bracelet for cash to one of the sanitation workers. Over $240,000. A bargain for the fence, Willard Ord, considering he would remove the bracelet's jewels and sell them separately for more than twice that much. A steal for Willard. Except for the fact that Jack was going to give Ord's emissary the remaining duplicate paste bracelet patterned on the Sotheby's catalog illustration.

Jack was supposed to call brother Craig on his cell phone when the switch was completed.

Only he hadn't called.

Craig stood up from the sofa. "Goin' out for a smoke."

"Don't let anyone see you," Ida said. "The mayor's given the cops orders to shoot smokers to kill."

"Funny, hah, hah," Craig said. He picked up Alexis Hoffermuth's purse and folded a sheet of newspaper over it. "Might as well drop this in a mail box."

"Not one too close. And bring that damned cat in if you see him."

"He's not a *damned* cat," Eloise said.

Ida pulled a face. "No, honey, he's not. I'm sorry I said that."

"Anyway, he won't go far. And nobody'll think he's a stray, 'cause I put his collar on him."

Craig looked at Eloise. "Collar?"

"That pretty collar with the jewels in it you brought for him," Eloise said. "The one you left on the table. I put it on him and fastened the clasp. It fits perfect." She grinned. "Makes him an even handsomer cat."

Craig and Ida stared at her, comprehending but not wanting to believe, stunned.

"Good Christ!" Craig said. He walked in a tight circle, one foot staying in the same place.

"You put the bracelet on Boomerang?" Ida asked.

"Collar," Eloise corrected.

Craig doubled his fist.

"Eloise, go to your room!" Ida said.

Aware that something horrible was going on, and somehow she was the root of it, Eloise obeyed without argument.

"I wasn't going to hit her," Craig said.

"We knew that, but she didn't."

Craig sighed. "Yeah . . ." He stared helplessly at Ida. "What are we gonna do?"

"Cats don't like playing dress up. Especially tomcats. But if Boomerang didn't work the col—bracelet off right away, it probably doesn't bother him and he'll leave it alone. When he comes home, he should still be wearing it."

"So we do nothing?"

"Seems the thing to do."

"You mean not to do."

Ida looked slightly confused. Still in character from earlier that day.

Craig strode toward the door. "I need a cigarette."

Ida would have gone with him; she could use a cigarette herself. Only there was Eloise. Ida didn't see herself as the kind of mother who'd leave her guilt-stricken kid alone for a cigarette. "Don't light up till you get outside," she said to Craig. They'd gotten the landlord's notice that smoking was no longer allowed in the building.

"I'm not going out only for a smoke," Craig said. "Jack was supposed to switch the other fake bracelet for cash with the sanitation guy, then call me. I wanna find out why he never called."

Ida told Craig good-bye and counted to ten. She knew she wasn't as ditzy as the role she played. And she understood what had to be done in this situation even if Craig didn't. He'd argue with her, and forbid her to do it. That was why it had to be done before he had a chance to disapprove.

The cat, the bracelet, simply had to be recovered. Craig wouldn't understand that there were times when your enemies could become your best friends.

Ida picked up the phone and called the police.

Craig Clairmont walked over to Amsterdam through a warm May mist before dropping the purse in a mailbox. Then he retraced his steps until he was half a block away from the passageway where the switch was supposed to have taken place.

Jack was almost invisible in the dark. Craig had to squint and stare hard to see his brother. Jack was down at the far end of the passageway, sitting on the ground as if he might be exhausted, his back propped awkwardly against the brick wall.

Jack saw Craig, but dimly. He raised his right hand, tried to crook a finger to summon Craig.

Aw, Jesus!

But Craig saw the movement and jogged toward him, fearing the worst.

When he got near his brother, Craig saw all the blood.

Jack had so much to tell Craig. *Things Craig had to know.*

He struggled to speak but couldn't translate thoughts into words.

Craig said something to him he didn't understand.

The light was fading.

Jack was barely alive. He rolled his eyes toward his brother Craig. His face was damp from the mist, his breathing ragged.

"What the hell happened?" Craig asked, bending down next to Jack. He saw a lot of blood, but no injuries, though Craig was holding his stomach with both hands.

"Double-cross," Jack said. "Bastard took the bracelet, then instead of giving me the money he started beating on me. I fought back and he hopped in the truck and it started to pull away. I grabbed onto it and that big trash crusher thing came down. My hand got caught in the machinery and it cut off my finger." Jack hadn't been gripping his stomach; he'd been clutching one hand with the other and keeping them both in close to his body. He held up the mutilated hand. "Cut the damned thing right off, Look at this, Craig! For God's sake look!"

Craig looked and felt his stomach lurch.

Jack whimpered. "You gotta get me to a hospital."

Craig didn't like this at all. Things would get even more dangerous when the thugs who stole the bracelet realized it was another fake, a paste duplicate, like the one he'd slipped into the Hoffermuth bitch's purse before dropping it in a mailbox.

"What're we gonna do?" Jack asked his older brother, who usually had all the answers.

Craig grinned to lend Jack hope and courage. "We're gonna call the police. Get you an ambulance."

When Jack didn't answer, Craig was surprised.

He looked down and saw that his brother was dead. He hadn't noticed the mass of blood around Jack's chest and stomach.

"Christ, Jack! Somebody stabbed you in the heart!"

Of course, Jack still didn't answer.

Craig stood over his brother, emotions rushing through him, over him, anger, grief, fear, panic.

But the panic, and then everything else, passed. Reality had to be faced. Manipulated.

Craig knew he was something Jack never really was—a survivor.

He also knew that now wasn't a good time to bring in the police. For any reason.

There wouldn't be another trash pickup for several days. Probably nobody would wander down this shadowed passageway. Nobody who'd contact the police, anyway, if they came across a dead body.

Still, Craig knew that to feel safe for even a short

length of time, he'd have to at least partially conceal the body.

Down near the far end of the alley a Dumpster squatted like a tank without treads. They didn't empty those Dumpsters very often. And when they did empty this one, there was always the chance Jack wouldn't be noticed.

Craig bent over and gripped his brother beneath the arms. Digging in his heels, he began to pull the dead weight that had been Jack.

If Jack were still alive, he'd understand.

By the time he'd returned to the apartment, Craig thought he was as depressed as possible.

That was when Ida told him she'd called the police. About Boomerang the missing cat, not the bracelet, she assured him.

She thought he took it well.

May 6, 8:15 p.m.

They were in the office late. Pearl and her daughter, Jody Jason, had come by to wait for Quinn to finish up so they could leave together and have a light supper and wine.

But Quinn wasn't interested in only finishing paperwork. He had something to say.

Pearl looked at Quinn, not knowing if he was kidding. "You're serious? This is a case for Q&A Investigations? You want me, personally, to look for someone's missing cat?"

Her jet black hair hung to her shoulders, framing a

pale face and dark, dark eyes. Her teeth were large and white and perfect. Quinn thought, as he often did, that everything about her was perfect. She was a small woman somehow writ large, as vivid as poster art.

He nodded. "Boomerang."

"Pardon?"

"That's the cat's name—Boomerang."

"Is this cat an Aussie?"

Quinn made a face and shrugged.

"I was just wondering if this case was going to require international travel," Pearl said.

Quinn sat quietly. It was the thing to do when Pearl was in this kind of mood. Ignore her. Best not to be in any way assertive. It was pointless to goad her.

Pearl said, "This cat business is coming to Q&A by way of Renz, right?"

"Well, yes." It didn't do to lie to Pearl.

"You regard this as women's work, looking for a missing cat?"

"In this case, yes. Yours and Jody's."

Something in his voice made Pearl understand that she'd bitched enough about this one.

Pearl's long-lost daughter, with whom she'd been reunited only recently, looked like a slimmer Pearl only with springy red hair. She lived with them in the West Seventy-fifth Street brownstone that Quinn was rehabbing. Jody had a mid-level bedroom, bath, and sitting room, where she spent much of her time when she was home. She had inherited a streak of independence from her mother.

"It's your case because you have a cat," Quinn said. "You and Jody."

"Snitch is your cat, too."

"Come off it," Quinn said. "The cat hardly looks at me. Tries to scratch me if I pick it up."

"Cats are like that."

"I don't see Snitch trying to scratch you or Jody."

"We pick him up right. He knows we like him."

"You think I *don't* like him?"

"I'm not so sure."

"Whatever, the job is yours and Jody's. Feds and I are working the Hoffermuth bracelet case, and Sal and Mishkin are doing field work in Stamford on that truck hijacking."

A missing bracelet and a truck hijacking, Pearl thought. Times were hard.

And now a missing cat case.

"I thought *we* were working the Hoffermuth case."

"We are. How much time can a missing cat case take?"

"Did Boomerang just run away, or was he catna— stolen?" Pearl asked.

"All we know is that he's missing."

"A male cat. It figures, name like Boomerang."

Quinn didn't know what she meant by that and didn't want to get into it. "We're not sure yet. He's simply missing."

"Maybe run over by a truck," Pearl said.

"Damn it, Pearl!"

"Okay. But if the cat doesn't return in seven years, do we declare it legally dead?"

"Seven times nine," Quinn said.

"Who's our client? Other than Renz?"

"A couple. Craig Clairmont and Ida French. They're the cat's owners."

"Usually it's the other way around," Pearl said.

Quinn sighed, losing his patience with her, insomuch as he ever really lost his patience. "We'd be wise to keep Renz happy."

"You can't *keep* him happy unless he already is," Pearl said. "And he isn't, ever."

"Except when he's involved in something unethical, immoral, and contagiously corrupt."

"You would stand up for him," Pearl said.

Quinn reached into his top desk drawer, drew out a yellow file folder, and tossed it on the desk near Pearl. "For you and Jody to read."

"The Boomerang file, no doubt."

"Treat this like any other missing person case," Quinn said without smiling.

She rolled the folder into a tight cylinder. "Renz give you this?"

Quinn nodded.

"I'd like to return it to him in a special way."

"Behave, Pearl. Same goes for Jody."

"We will," Pearl said. "How, I won't promise."

"This is weird," Jody said.

She was slouching on the sofa in the living room of Quinn's brownstone. She and Pearl could have waited until morning, or returned to the office after dinner, to study the Boomerang files, but they didn't. That was Pearl's idea, making the Boomerang investigation a home project. Pearl didn't want to defile the office by using it as headquarters for a cat hunt.

Pearl agreed with Jody—the case was weird. Reading the file made that apparent.

The clients, the married couple—if they actually

were married—used different names. The woman kept her maiden name. Ida French. The husband was Craig Clairmont. They lived in the West Eighties with their eight-year-old daughter, Eloise. They had faxed a photo of the errant Boomerang. He was a black cat with long whiskers and a direct stare into the camera that could only be described as haughty.

The clients themselves hadn't yet visited the office (or faxed photos of themselves). It turned out that Fedderman had interviewed them initially. He'd talked to them in their apartment, then phoned Quinn. Q&A had accepted the case, and just like that they were cat hunters.

Thinking about it, Pearl yawned and absently shook her head. The things a tight economy begot.

May 7, 2:06 a.m.

They were here to search.

Otto Berger and Arthur Shoulders carefully approached the passageway where they'd killed Jack Clairmont. Willard Ord, the fence and their boss, had a nose to smell a rat. He also had a multitude of sources, and years of experience in such transactions. A tongue had wagged; a word had been dropped. He knew Jack was going to try to pass off a paste imitation bracelet to them. In Willard's line of work, there was only one way to deal with that kind of betrayal.

Betray first.

That had worked out okay, for the most part.

So here were Otto and Arthur, sent to search the passageway to dispose of Jack Clairmont's body, and to make sure Clairmont's finger went with it. All under cover of darkness.

Clairmont's severed right forefinger was important. It might provide a print, which could lead to trouble. Of course the finger might have fallen *into* the trash truck, where it almost certainly wouldn't be noticed. But there was no guarantee of that.

Their first problem was Clairmont's body. It was gone. Someone seemed to have moved it.

They were secretly relieved. They might be killers, but neither man was fond of handling people once they'd been dead for a while. Otto wouldn't even touch raw hamburger.

There was nothing to do about this state of affairs except find what they'd come for, and let Willard Ord figure out what to do about the missing corpse. Willard would still want the severed finger. Its fingerprint might lead to Craig Clairmont, and then to Willard. It was also possible someone other than the law had taken the body. Like the brother. Craig might do their work for them and dispose of the body permanently. They hoped whoever *had* taken Jack Clairmont had also found and concealed his finger. It wouldn't do for it to turn up someplace when least expected.

They went about their task in workmanlike fashion, keeping their hands cupped over the lenses of their flashlights to direct the diffused beams downward.

Arthur happened to lift the lid of the Dumpster and shine his light into it. Still looking for the finger. And he found the rest of Jack Clairmont.

"What do you think, Otto?" he asked.

Otto was staring at the body, lying barely visible among trash bags, an old baby stroller, and some broken-down cardboard cartons someone had tossed in the Dumpster. It was possible—even likely—that Clairmont's body would be unnoticed and go into the trash truck's compactor to be dumped in a landfill. Then there would be no reason for Willard Ord to know what happened.

Or so Otto convinced himself.

"I think the brother," Arthur said. "He musta known where Jack was going for the money-bracelet exchange, then came and found him dead and figured he had to get rid of him or he'd draw cops as well as flies."

"I have no wish to get in there with all that yuk," Otto said.

"Nor do I," Arthur said. "If we cover him up some more, Jack Clairmont might never be seen again. He'll go unnoticed to a landfill."

"We might as well wish for the best," Otto said. "Safest thing would be to leave Jack right where he is. Pretend we never came across him."

"Willard would accept that only if we find the finger," Arthur said. "That would prove we came here and searched."

Otto agreed.

They searched on.

"This is hopeless," Arthur said, after a while. "If the finger did drop to the ground, some animal could have taken it away."

"No way to know that for sure," Otto said.

"Who knows anything for sure, Otto?"

"I do. You should, too. If we slack off on this job and that finger turns up for the cops, Willard will see that we lose some of *our* fingers. Or worse."

"Worse?" Arthur didn't have much of an imagination when it came to subjects other than torture and assassination, but what he did have was working hard.

Both men knew that someone might have to get in the Dumpster and root around for the finger. They could flip a coin. But even that seemed too risky.

"I believe this is impossible," Arthur said, after a while. "I have a suggestion. Since I thought of it, my belief is that you should do it."

"What is *it*?" Otto asked.

"We satisfy Willard's wishes by returning with a finger. Jack's remaining forefinger."

"Yuk, yuk, yuk," Otto said, but he knew he was going to do it. Willard wouldn't know one finger from another. Arthur had come up with a solution to their problem.

"Easier than rooting through trash and garbage for a finger that probably isn't there," Arthur said.

So Otto used his knife and did *it*. Then he let himself down out of the Dumpster with Jack's newly severed finger. Said, "Yuk!" again—and dropped the finger to the ground.

At the same time, in the corner of his vision, Arthur saw a flitting dark shape, like a moving shadow.

When he reached down for the severed finger, the dark form beat him to it, snatched it up, and whirled. The animal had its teeth and claws bared and looked very possessive. With grave misgivings, Arthur reached for the creature, was hesitant, and got only a brief feel of fur.

The cat shot between his legs and broke toward the far end of the passageway.

Otto was waiting, squatted down like a Sumo wrestler, and his huge, foreboding form caused Boomerang to halt for a moment.

Otto's right hand darted down, and his fingers closed on fur and loose flesh at the back of Boomerang's neck. He didn't like the feel of the animal, but he kept a good grip.

Boomerang thought something like *What the hell?* Before he could react, all four of his feet were off the ground.

The big human had him by the back of the neck. Boomerang hated to be lifted like that. He snarled, spat, wind-milled with his legs, claws extended, tried to bite, to tear.

"Little prick is pissed off," Arthur said. "I'll throw him in the Caddie's trunk and we'll take him with us so he won't come back here and hang around the Dumpster."

Otto kept a strong grip on Boomerang and held him extended well out from his body so the cat couldn't inflict injury. The animal suddenly became still, but that didn't fool Otto.

They started back toward where their black Cadillac was parked.

Otto abruptly stopped and pointed.

"What?" Arthur asked.

"The finger," Otto said. "What we came for. Get it Arthur."

"Jesus!" Arthur said. "We almost forgot."

"*You* almost forgot."

"Oh, no! Don't try to hang that one on me."

While Otto and Boomerang watched, Arthur soon found where the cat had dropped the newly severed forefinger. He stooped and gingerly inserted the finger into a plastic baggie of the sort that held sandwiches.

"It doesn't matter who almost forgot what, Arthur. Just so we give the finger to Willard."

"You know, I always wanted to give Willard the—"

"Don't say it, Arthur. Don't even think it."

They walked on toward the street. Mission accomplished. Confident now in attitude and stride.

Boomerang dangled limply in Otto's iron grip, eyes narrowed, almost shut, biding his time.

May 7, 4:48 p.m.

It hadn't occurred to Ida and Craig that Alexis Hoffermuth not only regarded the police as public protectors; she saw them as her personal servants. Through taxes and contributions, she paid a large portion of their salaries, and she wanted a return on that investment.

Her call to the police had been prompt, distraught, and demanding. When Alexis Hoffermuth spoke, people listened. When she was upset, they listened extra hard.

The bracelet in the imitation Gucci purse had itself been an imitation. Even though it wasn't the *real* Cardell bracelet, it was a pretty good paste facsimile. Some smartass crooks were playing with Alexis Hoffermuth's mind to keep her off balance and buy time, toying with her, toying with the police, making a fool of her and the police commissioner—Harley Renz.

Renz wouldn't have that. Absolutely wouldn't.

Neither would Alexis Hoffermuth.

So here Quinn was with Pearl to see Alexis in her apartment in the exclusive Gladden Tower, an impressive edifice her late husband had constructed.

Rather, paid to have constructed.

An unctuous doorman met them in the marble lobby and interrogated them as if they really didn't belong in the building, but maybe, just maybe, he would permit their temporary presence. Quinn made a mental note of the fact that the marble desk where the doorman usually sat had a brass plaque on it identifying him as Melman. No first name, unless it was Melman.

Quinn would remember Melman.

After they'd passed inspection in the lobby, they were given the privilege of riding the private, walnut-paneled elevator to the fifty-ninth-floor penthouse. They stood side by side, their bodies touching, as they rocketed up the core of the building. The back wall of the narrow elevator was lined with tufted taupe silk. There was no sound.

"Zoom," Quinn said.

"Reminds me of a vertical coffin."

"You *can* take it with you."

Quinn had been expecting a butler, but when the elevator finally settled down, rather than enter near space, its paneled door opened, and Alexis Hoffermuth herself met them.

The widow had the immediate commanding presence that sometimes accompanies great wealth. She was in her early fifties, lean, cosmetically enhanced, and attractive. When twenty years younger, she'd probably been stunning. She was wearing a sleek black dress and black high heels, and looked as if she might be ready for a luncheon date to discuss a million-dollar endowment. Society page newspaper photos Quinn had seen came to mind. Alexis was active in the city's social as well as political life and would usually be on the arm of a younger, handsome escort.

More accurately, *he* would be on *her* arm. Alexis was what the current flock of society journalists called a cougar. Quinn thought she looked the part. She even moved like a—

—*Cat*, Pearl thought. The woman looked and moved more like a cat than any human she'd ever seen. She gave Pearl the creeps.

"Please do sit down," Alexis said, gracefully gliding to the side. She motioned toward a sitting area defined by a large Persian rug, matching cream-colored sofas, and easy chairs. One wall of the vast penthouse was glass, affording a stunning view of the buildings to the east and then the river. The high, high ceiling was also partly glass. Beyond it clouds floated past like lost souls of the city. All in all, the apartment reminded Pearl of an airport terminal. If dirigibles were still in fashion, surely they would dock here.

Looking as if any second she might pause and arch her back, Alexis moved to a small mirrored table. She opened the drawer and drew out a handful of glitter.

Pearl and Quinn were seated side by side on the soft leather sofa facing the glass wall. Quinn thought they must look like the pilot and copilot of the *Enterprise*.

Alexis glided over and showed them the two bracelets.

"They're beautiful," Pearl said, staring at the glinting clear diamonds and gleaming rubies.

"But they're imitations." Alexis pointedly turned her attention to Quinn. He was the power half of the duo that had come to see her. "Good imitations, for sure, but I want the genuine bracelet back."

"Tell me how it was stolen," Quinn said.

Alexis recounted how some blond woman had piled into her parked limo, yammering and pretending she'd made a mistake and entered the wrong vehicle. Black limos looked so much alike. Oh, she was always screwing up. "Bad girl! Bad girl!" she had actually said.

During all the apologies and confusion, she'd switched purses.

"She apologized a dozen more times as she clambered out of the car, and left me with an imitation Gucci purse containing an imitation Cardell bracelet," Alexis said. "Later, my actual purse was returned to me by the postal authorities. Someone had dumped it in a mailbox. Either the person who stole it, or someone who found it after the thief had disposed of it. Miraculously, it still contained all its contents, and something else—what appeared to be the Cardell bracelet. Closer inspection revealed it to be almost worthless paste, yet another imitation."

"Somebody went to a lot of trouble," Quinn said.

Alexis Hoffermuth nodded sagely. "People will do that," she said, "for a lot of money."

"But it's an odd way of stealing," Pearl said.

Alexis stared at her as if offended. "Why? It caused confusion and misdirection, bought time, and by now the crooks might be in some other country, toasting their success and each other."

"Or that might be what they want us to think," Quinn said.

Alexis looked at him not at all the way she'd looked at Pearl. The handsome-homely Quinn filled his space and could inspire confidence and give hope, sometimes just by being present. He gave the impression he'd wandered down from Mt. Rushmore to become a cop.

Alexis smiled dazzlingly at him. Cougarishly, Pearl thought. "Do you really think, Detective Quinn, that we have a decent chance of recovering the real Cardell bracelet before it's disassembled and sold by the stone?"

"It's enough of a chance that it's worth taking, dear," Quinn told her.

Bastard! Pearl thought. *Dear!* Why did women fall for his bullshit?

Why did I?

"Commissioner Renz spoke very highly of you and your agency," Alexis said. "Of course, he's as much a politician as he is a policeman. I would go so far as to say he can't be completely trusted."

"I would go so far as to say you might be right."

Alexis favored him with another predatory smile. "I appreciate the restraint of your reply." She repositioned herself about five feet to her left, slim hips moving like silk, so she was facing Quinn directly and placing Pearl on the periphery. "Shall we talk fee?"

"I appreciate your directness," Quinn said.

And fee they talked, as if Pearl didn't exist.

But Pearl listened, and was astounded by how much Alexis Hoffermuth would pay for the return of the genuine Cardell bracelet.

Pearl didn't look at Quinn as they were shown back to the private elevator, fearing that they both might break out in grins. As the elevator descended she could imagine Alexis Hoffermuth upstairs cleaning herself with her tongue. She decided not to mention that im-

agery to Quinn. Men and women saw the Alexis Hof-
fermuths of the world differently.

When they'd left the elevator and exited the lobby,
both of them did smile.

"I can still smell the money," Pearl said, as they
walked away from the stone and glass tower where
Alexis Hoffermuth lived like Rapunzel with a short and
stylish do. She glanced over at Quinn. "You weren't shy
about asking for our share."

"Alexis is the type who isn't shy about giving."

"I sensed that about her, too."

"I was thinking about her charity events."

"Me, too."

There was a break in traffic, so they jaywalked.

"You've got Jody pissed off now," Pearl said, as they
gained the curb on the other side of the street. "First
you put her on the cat case because it wasn't important,
and now you've got her back at the office doing paperwork and missing cat research while we go talk with
Alexis Hoffermuth."

"The case got more important," Quinn said. "I know
that because Renz is bugging the hell out of me to get
it solved."

They came to where Quinn's aging but gleaming
Lincoln was parked in a loading zone.

"Back in the real world," Pearl said, when they were
in the old car's quiet interior and buckled up.

"You sure?" Quinn asked.

"Never."

She smiled. She liked it when Quinn got all metaphysical.

"Seldom," she amended, hoping to draw him into a complex, philosophical discussion. That was always good for some smiles.

But he drove in near silence, his usual taciturn self. Complicated yet simple in way and deed. Smart enough to be direct and unerring in his aim.

She wouldn't love him nearly so much if she could figure him out.

Part Two

B ut what was time to a cat?

It took so little of it to extend a paw and lift the latch on the metal cage wherein Boomerang had been tossed after the ride in the dark car trunk.

Then, of course, a cat could find a window open a crack, or a door slightly ajar. Easy egress for the sleek and the furred.

And underlying it all, the mission.

Boomerang planned to get back home with his find eventually. He was named Boomerang because, when left to roam, he invariably, sooner or later, came back— and with some kind of offering. He seldom left and returned without having accomplished something important. His proffered souvenirs were a point of feline pride. The object clasped in his jaws now was especially prized.

He peered around a corner with cat elasticity, then detoured into a narrow passageway that was one of his favorite haunts. The dim brick and concrete corridor ran between two apartment and commercial buildings, where trash bags were piled like lumpy pillows.

This looked interesting.

Boomerang paused and struck a pose, alert to traffic and voices and the stirring of garbage-sweetened air in the fetid alley. Nothing unusual. Nothing dangerous.

Temporarily losing interest, he dropped his future offering alongside a dented metal trash can and moved smoothly as a miniature panther to the nearest black plastic bag.

With the delicacy of a surgeon, he extended a claw and made an incision in the bag. Ah! He withdrew a foam take-out container with leftovers that contained some sort of sea food. A real find!

He glanced back at his intended offering, to make sure it was safe, then began maneuvering the take-out container so he could lick its interior.

He was in a secluded place where he wasn't in any rush to finish his meal. The trophy he was transporting could wait until he was good and ready to continue his journey back to where he'd come from. What was the hurry? It wasn't as if he had an appointment; and if he had one, he might not bother to keep it. He was, after all, a cat.

And a handsome one at that.

May 8, 2:02 p.m.

Quinn decided that to mollify Jody he'd go with Pearl for an initial interview concerning the missing cat. That they would do this should send the right parental message.

"You reported your cat missing?" Quinn asked Craig

Clairmont. At least he assumed it was Craig Clairmont. The guy fit the description Fedderman had given him, but Quinn was to the point where he was taking nothing for granted. If he were a cat, he'd find something jarringly wrong with Clairmont. As it was, he felt only a vague unease.

Quinn was standing. Pearl was seated in a stiffly upholstered chair that looked as if it should be behind a desk rather than in a living room. The apartment was furnished that way, mismatched and mostly functional. An interior decorator would puke.

"We only rent here," Clairmont said, as if reading Quinn's mind.

Quinn found that disconcerting. "Your cat," he reminded Ida French.

"Boomerang," she said.

Pearl smiled. "Because he always comes back?"

"Yeah. Only this time he didn't," Ida French said. She was a sleek dishwater blonde, almost beautiful. But there was something about her blue eyes, an intensity that was unbecoming.

Clairmont seemed embarrassed. "I guess you think it's foolish, contacting a private investigation agency to search for a missing cat."

"They can be like part of the family," Pearl said.

As if on cue, a small child with hair exactly the color of her mother's sidled into the room. She was wearing blue shorts and a color-keyed blue and white blouse. Blue socks and jogging shoes. About nine years old, Pearl estimated. Cute, cute, cute.

"This is Eloise," Ida French said. "My daughter." The girl went to her and clung. She completely ignored Clairmont.

"About nine?" Pearl asked.

"Eight."

Pearl smiled at Eloise. "A big girl for eight. And so pretty!"

Eloise smiled back.

"Now I understand the urgency about getting Boomerang back," Quinn said. But he wondered. How many kids must there be in this city with missing cats, and nobody was phoning detective agencies about them?

Pearl must have been thinking the same thing. "If you give us a better description," she said, "we can put out an ACB."

The Clairmont-French family appeared puzzled.

"All Cat Bulletin," Pearl explained, with not a trace of a smile.

Quinn felt like twisting her nose. Maybe he would, in the elevator.

Nobody else seemed to think Pearl was less than serious.

"He's black with three white boots," Ida French said to Pearl. "A good-sized cat. Likes to roam, but always returns. Only not this time. And, oh, yeah, he's wearing a cheap kind of bangle collar. Looks like jewels."

Pearl thought, *Huh?*

"You like to dress up your cat?" she asked Eloise.

"Not much," Eloise said.

"The collar was a gift," Ida French explained.

Craig Clairmont spread his hands hopelessly. "That's about all we can give you by way of description."

"He's a handsome cat," Eloise said defensively.

Ida French patted her daughter's head. "No one says otherwise, dear."

Quinn pretended to write it down in his notebook.

"Handsome cat . . ." Then he looked more seriously at Clairmont and Ida French. "We'll do what we can, send some people around the neighborhood to talk with folks, keep an eye out for Boomerang."

"Cats don't usually go far from home," Pearl said.

Quinn wondered how she could know. Or if she really did know. He wanted to get out of there before she mouthed off.

"We'll be getting busy," he said, and moved toward the door.

Pearl stood up and moved with him.

The Clairmont French family stirred. Craig Clairmont and Ida French thanked them. Eloise said goodbye.

In the elevator Pearl said, "Jesus H. Christ!"

Quinn reached for her nose, but the elevator stopped its descent on the second floor and a woman walking with a metal cane entered.

Pearl started to say something else, but Quinn raised a finger to his lips, cautioning her.

"Renz must have his reasons," he said.

Pearl said, softly, "And Clairmont must have his reasons for wanting Boomerang back."

"Jeweled collar," Quinn said. *Or maybe a bracelet.*

"See it all the time in New York," Pearl said. "Cats decked out like fashion plates. Accessories aren't just for people."

The elevator lurched and continued its controlled fall.

"World like a puzzle," Quinn said.

The woman with the cane ignored them.

* * *

When they got back to the office, Quinn phoned Renz to try to find out more about who and what they were investigating. What was the motivation for this concern about a missing cat?

"I've got my reasons," Commissioner Harley Renz said, when Quinn had finally gotten through on the phone. He recognized Renz's clipped, official voice.

"I need to know those reasons," Quinn said, "if I'm going to waste valuable hours and shoe leather because of a missing cat. Even if he is handsome."

"You need to take this seriously, Quinn. I certainly do."

"I need to have a reason. Probably it would be the same as yours."

"No, no . . ."

"Try me, Harley. I do understand that you place some importance in this. It would make it seem more worthwhile if you'd condescend to share." Quinn also understood that Harley Renz valued information as the currency that bought power. Not to mention more actual currency. "I don't need to know it all, Harley. Just some of it."

There was a long silence on the phone. Quinn thought at first that the call had been dropped. Then Renz said, "Craig Clairmont has a sheet. He's a jewel thief."

Big surprise.

"And Ida French?"

"Nothing on her. But that just means she hasn't been caught yet."

"Eloise?"

"Who the hell is that?"

"Their eight-year-old daughter."

"Oh, yeah. Ida's kid."

"Is Clairmont the father?"

"It's possible," Renz said. "Conjugal visits and such."

"Jewels . . ." Quinn said thoughtfully.

"And we both know some jewels have been stolen," Renz said.

"Belonging to Alexis Hoffermuth. *The* Alexis Hoffermuth."

"What are you getting at, Quinn?"

"The missing cat, Boomerang, was wearing a cheap jeweled collar when he disappeared."

There was silence except for the gears in Renz's brain meshing.

"You're shittin' me!" he said.

"No," Quinn said, "and a cat might slip a loose collar off, even back on again. Over and over. They like to play around with things."

"Like certain people. Mostly of the female persuasion."

"We got some kinda connection," Quinn asked, "between Alexis Hoffermuth and Clairmont-French?"

"It looks like we do," Renz said. "A half-million-dollar jeweled bracelet. And of course, little old me. It's a connection, but it isn't proof. You receiving the message?"

"Received," Quinn said, and hung up the phone.

He wondered if Renz had already known about the cat wearing the bracelet around its neck. Maybe even Alexis Hoffermuth had known. Maybe she'd pressured Renz into using NYPD resources to search for a missing cat, even while she wanted him to pull out all the stops trying to recover a bracelet. Money could addle people's thinking.

Half a million dollars . . .

Pearl was at her desk, staring at him. She knew he'd been talking to Renz.

Quinn looked back at her. Said, "We gotta find that cat."

May 8, 3:32 p.m.

The cat, the bracelet, Alexis Hoffermuth.

Only one of them could talk.

Quinn and Pearl returned to the palatial penthouse where, with Alexis Hoffermuth, they discussed again the day of the theft.

"I only glimpsed the man," Alexis Hoffermuth said. "And it all happened so fast, I'm not sure I could identify the woman."

"You have some sense of their respective sizes?" Quinn asked.

"Average. Both of them."

"Hair or eye color?"

"The woman had blond hair streaked with dark. Blue eyes. The man's hair was dark. I think very dark. I seem to recall that he had blue eyes, too."

"Any distinguishing marks? Tattoos, scars, moles . . ."

"Not that I noticed." Alexis Hoffermuth shook her head in frustration. "It all went down so fast."

"Went down?"

"You know—*happened*. Like on TV cop shows."

"Ah." Quinn shifted position in his chair. Leather creaked. "What about another vehicle? What were they driving?"

"If the perps had a car, it was parked out of sight. And to tell you the truth . . ."

"What?"

"It all went down so fast, I'm not even sure if the man was with the woman. At the time I thought she was this ditsy tourist or something who thought the limo might be for hire. I didn't expect jewel thieves."

"Or thief, singular."

"No, wait! On second thought, I'm certain the man *was* with her. They hurried from the scene together."

"What about the cat?"

"I saw no cat." She arched an eyebrow. "Police Commissioner Renz told me a couple called to report that their cat had run away. I thought that odd. Isn't that what cats do? Run away?"

"My cats always do," Pearl said. She was seated on the sofa, facing Quinn and taking notes. They were both taking notes, making a bit of a show of it.

"Boomerang," Quinn said. "That's what they call this cat, because he roams but he always comes back."

"A tomcat," Alexis Hoffermuth said. "Just like the male human species."

Amen, Pearl thought.

"There's something else interesting about Boomerang," Quinn said. "He's wearing a jeweled collar that might be a bracelet. And he belongs to a professional jewel thief."

"The man *and* the woman?"

"Just the man is a pro, as far as we know."

Alexis Hoffermuth shook her head again. "Men get women to do things . . ."

Quinn nodded. "Keeps us busy."

May 8, 8:12 p.m.

Otto Berger and Arthur Shoulders, sitting across a table from their boss Willard Ord, listened to Willard sum up what he'd told them: They were in Ord's garden-level apartment in the Village. The rest of the brick building, upstairs, was vacant except for storage and also owned by Ord.

"So it could be the fake bracelets," Ord said. "The nonsense with the cat, all or most of it, was to help mislead and convince the insurance company the real bracelet was stolen. It looks like an insurance scam to me, with Alexis Hoffermuth using the Clairmont brother and Craig's wife. Hoffermuth has probably already filed for a big settlement."

"The cat didn't have no bracelet around its neck when we snatched him," Otto pointed out.

"I take your point," Arthur said.

Willard stared at him, disgusted. "There is definitely the possibility that no bracelet was ever stolen, and Alexis Hoffermuth still has it."

"Insurance fraud," Otto said. "Makes a lotta sense."

"We need to find out for sure," Willard said.

"The easiest thing might be to make her talk," Otto said.

Willard smiled. "Easier than chasing a cat."

"More fun, too," Arthur said.

May 9, 10:17 p.m.

"What on earth is the emergency?" Alexis Hoffermuth asked, when her private elevator door slid open and two huge men in cheap suits stepped out. She was wearing blue silk lounging pajamas and a matching top with decorative string ties and a low neckline. Her slippers were fur-lined and matched her outfit. "The doorman phoned up that I should admit you. That it was important."

"Melman," one of the men said. "He sent us up here."

"Yes," she said, puzzled. But she trusted Melman completely. "Why did he let you in? Are you acquaintances of his? Family?" She found both possibilities highly unlikely.

They said nothing. One of them smiled, displaying horrendous teeth. The other blatantly observed the unfastened top buttons on her pajama top.

Alexis didn't like this at all. Tomorrow she'd have a serious talk with Melman.

Fearless as ever, she crossed her arms and stared unblinkingly at both men. If it was a fight they wanted, she didn't mind stepping up out of her weight class. "Well?"

"You actually sleep in that outfit?" asked the slightly smaller man, with good teeth.

"That would be beside the point," Alexis said.

She'd had enough of this. Her evening had been disturbed, and that made her grumpy. She stalked toward the nearby phone to call the doorman's desk and set things straight with Melman.

Alexis was amazed that the two men had entered farther into her domain. They'd even moved apart somewhat as if to block her access to her elevator.

She held the receiver down near her waist and could hear the phone down in the lobby ringing.

Then it stopped ringing, but no one spoke.

Alexis pressed the receiver to her ear. "Melman? Melman?"

The man with the horrible teeth grinned and said, "Get her."

Alexis actually advanced on the man, raising her hand to slap him.

But before she could bring the flat of her hand forward, he punched her hard in the stomach. She made a whooshing sound, then panicked and thrashed around when she couldn't inhale. Her mind was functioning, but not well.

She began a harsh rasping that caught in her throat. The pristine white ceiling with its skylight was in front of her.

How did I get on the floor?

"When she catches her breath, she's gonna wail like a train whistle," one of the large men said.

"I'll find something, Arthur," said the man with the bad teeth.

He disappeared in the direction of her bedroom.

The one called Arthur began to undress her. He worked a few buttons on her pajama top, then lost patience and ripped the top apart, sending buttons flying. Alexis was now able to breathe in a labored way, but she still couldn't muster enough strength or will to move of her own accord, enough air to scream. Someone—*it must be me!*—was whimpering.

Arthur had a wicked looking knife now, and was skillfully slicing material in order to undress her. Except for her pajama bottoms, which he simply yanked off.

Through her terror, Alexis felt a mounting rage.

Who are these animals, that they think they can do this to me? I'll be able to speak in a few minutes. Then I'll tell them who I am, what's going to happen to them, how very sorry they'll be. Damn them! They'll be so sorry!

Breathing was still a great effort, but she thought that with even more effort she could talk—could *scream.*

She attempted to scream but heard only a soft croaking sound.

"Here, Arthur," said the man with the bad teeth. "She's getting her sea legs. Better stuff this in her mouth before she yelps."

"We're not on a ship, Otto."

"This is no time to be a grammarian," Otto said, handing something to Arthur.

My favorite Burberry scarf! Oh, damn them! Alexis managed another moan. Louder.

"Better stuff," Otto said.

But instead of wadding the scarf and stuffing it in her mouth, Arthur wound it tightly around Alexis's neck. "Help me flip her on her belly," he said. "She can try to tell us what we wanna know, but whenever she gets spunky and raises her voice, I'll give the scarf a tug, choke the bitch a little at a time. She can live quite a while that way."

"That sounds productive, Arthur. We are, after all, here to get information."

"No point in stuffing the goose that lays the golden egg," Arthur said.

Alexis felt their hands on her, and her stunned body was rotated onto its stomach. A hand pressed her head against the carpet. The one called Arthur used a pants leg from her pajamas to bind her wrists tightly behind her. Then he made a fist with the hand holding the knife and pressed it painfully into the small of her back. When Alexis cried out, he used his other hand to yank the scarf tight, bending back her neck and choking off any sound other than a strangled gurgle. She kicked hard against the carpeted floor and against Arthur, but he simply ignored her kicks. Seemed, in fact, to enjoy watching her flail around.

"What I'm gonna do," he said, leaning close to her ear, "is what I done plenty of times, so don't think it won't work. I'm gonna ask you a question, then you're gonna lie to me, then I'm gonna insert the point of my knife between two of your vertebraes—"

"Verte*brae*, I think that is, Arthur," said the one called Otto.

"Wouldn't that be singular?"

"No. It's like *octopus* or *medium*."

"What about *stadium*?"

"You got me there," Otto said.

Arthur turned his attention back to Alexis Hoffermuth. "Thing is," he said to her with his foul breath, "I know just where and how to insert the blade between your verte*brae*, and believe me, next time I ask a question you'll be eager to answer it and I'll know you'll be telling the truth."

"I'll still—" The scarf contracted like a vise against Alexis's larynx and her words were choked off.

"You'll be dying to tell the truth," Otto assured her. "Nobody refuses telling the truth to Arthur. He's the best at his job."

"Like a polygram," Arthur said.

"Poly*graph*," Otto corrected.

"Of course!"

"It's a thousand-to-one chance Arthur's not gonna eventually kill you when he knows you've spilled everything you know or ever knew, but at a certain point, you'll think that's a bet worth making. It'll be all you got left."

"Making folks speak the truth," Arthur said, "is a psychological thing. Long time ago, my psychiatrist told me I was the one should be the psychiatrist. He had something there. And I got something here. Show her, Otto."

"Yuk," Otto said. He pulled a plastic bag from his pocket and drew something from it. He held the object out where Alexis could see it. "Know what that is?"

Alexis stared. The thing he was holding was tubular, darkly splotched, with gray and white showing and red and—a fingernail!

My God, it's a severed finger!

"She knows, Arthur," Otto said. "See her eyes?"

"I do, Otto."

"You need some lubricant?"

"She's pissed all over the place. I'll use that. She should feel it go in."

Alexis did feel it. She struggled to scream, her eyes wide with horror. They were inserting the horrid *thing* into her! The scarf got so tight she momentarily lost consciousness.

". . . Like I said, psychological," she heard Arthur say. "While you're laying there—"

"—Lying," Otto said.

"Lying there wishing your back pain would stop, you can also think about that finger. I got nine more of them for you, counting thumbs."

That last was a lie, but Arthur thought the powers

that be would forgive him. He was, after all, seeking the truth.

"I wonder if all those fingers will fit," Otto said.

"Oh, they will," Arthur said.

Alexis felt the knife slide into her back, into her spine. The pain traveled everywhere inside her body. It was electric. It was unimaginable.

When the scarf was loosened she was breathing hard from attempting to scream.

"You got a lot more vertebraes—verte*brae*," Arthur said. "So, are we ready to talk about the insurance scam?"

"What insurance scam?" Alexis asked. "What on *earth*—"

Arthur smiled. She was a good little liar.

He inserted the knife again.

This process might take hours.

He was patient.

May 10, 9:20 a.m.

Melman, the Gladden Tower doorman, was inside his drab studio apartment overlooking a parking lot in Queens, He didn't know for sure if Otto and Arthur were Alexis Hoffermuth's cousins, here from California, who wanted to surprise her. Didn't care, either, once they'd paid him a thousand dollars in tens and twenties to look the other way and let them use the private elevator to the penthouse. As a crooked ex-cop, he'd accepted larger bribes. But considering his present salary, and the state of the economy, this one looked too good to refuse.

Melman saw on TV news this morning that he'd been only half right.

The two men weren't really Alexis Hoffermuth's cousins from California, here to surprise her.

But they *had* surprised her.

That left Melman with two choices—he could run, or he could be implicated as an accessory to murder.

He thought the situation over and decided he'd better not even take time to pack. He phoned in his resignation, leaving it on an answering machine. That might at least slow things down a little. Then he hurriedly grabbed up a few items to take with him in his small carry-on. After a quick glance around, he headed for the door.

He had to get out of here before the police showed up. Or worse still—

Melman had saved time by packing only the carry-on, but there wasn't much time to save, when it was so rapidly running out.

When he opened his apartment door, the two big guys were standing there, the so-called California cousins.

Melman's mind raced. This was not good. The resignation, the hurried getaway. He could easily be fitted for Alexis Hoffermuth's murder.

If the police had been at his door, he at least would know his body wouldn't be buried in a shallow grave over in New Jersey. That would be some very small, very brief, comfort.

"Going someplace?" the big man asked.

"Oh, he's going someplace," the even bigger man said. "He just don't know where."

Melman knew the man was wrong. He realized with a certainty glowing like a star, illuminating his entire mind, that from the time he'd taken his first bribe as a rookie cop in Brooklyn, he'd known where he was eventually going.

May 10, 9:21 p.m.

Renz called Quinn's cell phone that evening when Quinn and Pearl were home in the brownstone watching an early episode of *The Good Wife* on TV. Jody was upstairs studying for a legal exam. Quinn thought maybe she could learn more down here in front of the television.

Pearl glanced at him, curious about the phone call. Quinn pointed to the TV and she used the remote to freeze and mute the DVD picture.

"I hope this is important, Harley," Quinn said into the phone. "Like I'm just about to see a case broken and all the bad guys going to jail."

"Unreality television," Renz said.

Quinn wandered out of the living room, in case Pearl wanted to press Play and watch the conclusion of the *Good Wife* trial. It was about a crooked international pharmaceutical company. The DVD would retain its position on the disk only so long. If the phone call lasted a little while, the TV screen would go blank and they'd have to go back to the beginning and fast-forward. Or choose scenes. Whatever the hell you did with a DVD.

"Okay," Quinn said. "Court's in recess."

"Preliminary tests show we got no record of the DNA left from that severed finger that was found in Alexis

Hoffermuth's vaginal tract. Got something else, though. A fingerprint. A match turned up right away in the FBI database."

Quinn waited three or four seconds, knowing Renz was in love with dramatic pauses. "So tell me, Harley."

"The fingerprint—right forefinger, incidentally—belongs or belonged to John Wayson Clairmont. Goes by Jack. Three arrests in upstate New York for burglarizing jewelry stores. One conviction. Did a three-year stretch behind walls, was released four years ago."

"Tell me he's related to Craig Clairmont."

"His brother," Renz said.

Quinn paced with the cell phone, wondering about this development.

"You wanna send one of your people to talk to brother Craig?" Renz asked.

"No. Let's not tell Craig, or Ida French, about the owner of the finger yet. See how this plays out."

"Jack might not have had anything to do with Craig, and Craig might have nothing to do with Alexis Hoffermuth's missing bracelet."

"Or Jack's missing finger."

"But it isn't missing—"

"Jack would disagree."

"The rest of Jack might be as dead as his finger," Renz said, "tucked away someplace where it won't be found."

"Jack was at one time in that alley where we found his finger," Quinn said. "Unless somebody transported the finger there."

"Always a possibility," Renz said, "somebody running around with a spare finger. Good for counting beyond ten. But where the finger was found is easy walking distance from Craig's apartment. You believe that much in coincidence?"

"No," Quinn said. "You got anything else?"

"Ida French. Real Name Ida Beene. From Cincinnati. Used to be a hooker, one conviction, then went to work as a hotel maid in Cleveland. Seems to have cleaned up her act."

"So many people go to Cleveland to start over," Quinn said.

"Craig's real name is Lester," Renz said. "Not much about that couple is real."

Quinn waited, then said, "That it for tonight?"

"Not quite. Nift's postmortem on the Hoffermuth woman is in. She died of a heart attack."

"I thought the scarf—"

"Probably it was only used to choke off her screams when the knife was applied to her back. There were a lot of knife wounds along her spine, very precise, between the vertebrae. Nift said whoever wielded the knife was skilled. The insertions must have produced incredible pain. She had her heart attack simultaneous with being throttled to keep her quiet."

"Hell of a way to die."

"There are a few good ways, but hers wasn't one of them."

"Any other cheerful news?"

"That's it for now," Renz said. "You can sleep on it."

"But not very well," Quinn said, trying to hang up on Renz. But Renz had already broken the connection. Renz liked to do that. Thought it made him the dominant party.

When Quinn returned to the living room, he saw

that the DVD had timed out and Pearl was now watching a Yankees game with the TV on mute.

Quinn told her about Renz's phone call.

"Sounds as if Craig was in on stealing the Hoffermuth bracelet with his brother," Pearl said.

"And maybe the cat has the bracelet around its neck. Eloise thought it was a collar."

"Which is why Craig and Ida Bee—French—are so hot to find Boomerang."

"But what's the deal with Jack's finger?" Quinn wondered aloud.

"Maybe Jack told somebody something he shouldn't have," Jody said. She had come downstairs and listened at the living room doorway to Quinn's account of his phone conversation with Renz. Her springy red hair was flat on one side from reading lying down. "He might've fingered somebody, and the severed finger's a mob message to anyone else who might have similar ideas."

"Sounds plausible, but I've never heard of the mob doing that," Quinn said, "cutting off somebody's finger because they fingered someone. They usually cut off more than that."

"But it's his forefinger," Jody said. "His pointer."

"Wouldn't they cut out his tongue?"

"You ever try to cut out somebody's tongue?"

"Well, I—"

"She might have something there," Pearl said, mostly to defend Jody.

Jody glanced gratefully at her mother.

These two were about to gang up on Quinn. He could feel it.

"Let's all sleep on it," he said, echoing Renz's suggestion. "What's the score on that ball game?"

"Detroit's winning eleven to two in the eighth inning," Pearl said.

"Let's go back to the DVD and see if that international pharmaceutical company gets convicted of testing that dangerous drug on kids in third world countries."

"What pharmaceutical company?" Jody asked, her ire obviously up.

Quinn loved to do that with Jody.

"Have you ever considered," Jody said, after the pharmaceutical company's entire board of directors were successfully tried in the Hague for murder, "that Alexis Hoffermuth might have set up this whole thing? She might still have the genuine bracelet."

"And all this running around and bracelet switching is to deceive the insurance company," Pearl said. "Everyone's so curious about where the bracelet is, they're beyond questioning whether the thing was ever stolen in the first place."

"I've thought about it," Quinn said, though he had only briefly. With Alexis Hoffermuth, you'd better be damned sure you have something before opening that particular door.

Jody, whose thirst for justice hadn't been quenched by the downfall of Big Pharma, looked from one of them to the other.

"We shouldn't rule it out," Quinn said.

Pearl's cell phone chirped, and without thinking to check who might be calling, she answered it.

"Pearl!" her mother's voice said, from Golden Sunset Assisted Living in New Jersey. "I have been trying to get in contact with you in regard to an outrageous change in dining room seating in this nursing home hell—"

"Assisted living," Pearl corrected, as she often did.

"Anyway, to continue my diatribe—and I know that is how you regard it, unable to conceptualize as you are that nefarious things do go on in this purgatory of pain that reasonable people . . ."

"Is that Grandma?" Jody asked, her face lighting up. "Let me talk to her!"

Pearl tossed her the phone, and Jody snatched it from the air and walked off into the next room, yammering.

Pearl and Quinn smiled silently at each other.

May 11, 1:19 p.m.

"Jack is dead?"

Ida seemed astounded.

Craig Clairmont looked suddenly out of breath and sat down hard enough in a patched vinyl wing chair to move the heavy piece of furniture six inches across the hardwood floor.

"We don't know that for certain," Quinn said. "We only have the finger."

Ida French went to stand at the back of the chair, over Craig's right shoulder. She appeared ill. "And you know it's Jack's finger?"

"Yes," Pearl said. "Fingerprints. Print."

"Jack would never harm anyone," Craig said. "Not physically, anyway."

Quinn thought that an odd thing to say but let it pass.

Jody was seated off to the side, observing. She'd wanted to come with them, actually meet these people. She viewed it as research for her own fledgling career in criminal law. You couldn't know too much about the criminal mind.

"It could be theorized," Quinn said to Craig, "maybe even proved, that you stole Alexis Hoffermuth's bracelet and were also implicated in her death."

Craig appeared to have been struck a glancing blow. "Wow! That's wild."

"Jewel theft and homicide are wild."

"First Jack, then that poor Mrs. Hoffermuth," Craig said, pacing. "Or maybe it was the other way around." He seemed unable to sit down.

Jody looked at Quinn and smiled slightly, appreciating the performance.

"Mrs. Hoffermuth was a number of things," Quinn said, "but not poor."

"I meant, what she must have gone through."

"Do you know something about it?"

"How she was tortured. It was on the news. It—"

There was a scratching on the door to the hall. Craig exchanged glances with Ida French.

More scratching. Insistent.

The kitchen window must be completely closed.

Both of them leaped toward the door, bumping into each other. It was Craig who wrestled the door open.

A large black tomcat strutted in, arched its back, stretched, then continued toward a hall leading to what Quinn assumed were bedrooms and a bathroom. It had

three white boots and the slightest touch of white between its eyes.

On the welcome mat behind him the cat had left a
glittering jeweled bracelet.

This time Ida French managed to elbow Craig aside
and snatched up Boomerang's offering.

"Boomerang?" Pearl asked, to make sure.

"There isn't any doubt," Craig said, staring at the
bracelet in Ida's cupped hand. "But that bracelet looks
like an imitation."

"Sure does," Ida French said, after a slight hesitation.

Quinn and Pearl got up and went over to examine
the bracelet. Ida never offered to release her grip on it.
The jewels might have been fake, but then no one there
was an expert.

"It has to be imitation," Ida French said.

"Unless Alexis Hoffermuth was trying to pull off an
insurance scam," Craig said.

Quinn guessed that Craig, inspired, was trying to set
up a scenario wherein he could convince everyone the
bracelet was paste jewelry and it might as well stay
with him and Ida French. But if that didn't work, blame
might be shifted to Alexis Hoffermuth, dead and unable to defend herself.

"You would know about scams," Quinn said.

Craig looked at him, surprise on his handsome features. Then he smiled. "Part of your job, I guess, looking into people's unsavory pasts."

" 'Fraid so," Quinn said.

He saw that Jody was leaning forward in her chair,
the only one in the room more interested in what was

being said than in the half-million-dollar bracelet. She was a people person.

"Where is your daughter, Miss Beene?" Pearl asked.

Ida French seemed not at all fazed. Pearl had to hand it to her.

"Eloise is with my sister in Queens." She gave a wistful smile. "I didn't think you set up this appointment for just a chat."

"You planned the theft of the bracelet from the limousine," Quinn said to Craig, "executed when Alexis Hoffermuth was being driven home from the auction. Ida is the one who actually stole the bracelet, using a confusing exchange of identical purses and a paste copy of the real Cardell bracelet. You and your brother Jack planned to turn the bracelet over to a fence in exchange for cash, only you were greedy. You were going to slip the fence a second worthless replica of the bracelet. Double crossing somebody like that got Jack killed, after his killers amputated his finger."

"It didn't happen exactly like that," Craig said.

"The details will be tended to later in court," Quinn told him. "Ida, here, judging by the expression on her face, didn't know you and Jack were going to take the money from the sale of the second replica and disappear with that and the real bracelet. Boomerang upset that plan when he ran away after Eloise had mistaken the bracelet for a cat collar and put it on him."

Quinn exchanged a look with Jody. *Divide and conquer*.

"Everything was going to be split three ways!" Craig said.

Ida French appeared dubious.

"The fence spotted the makeshift cat collar at the

pickup point, as Boomerang was running away. It looked exactly like the bracelet he'd just bought. That was when Jack ran afoul of the lawless. The fence also came to wonder what we wondered—was Alexis Hoffermuth working an insurance scam from the beginning?"

"Maybe we can work a deal as to who that fence was," Craig said. "Who killed my brother. Along with whatever else you need to know."

Ida French stared at him in disgust. She knew he'd give her up in a minute. Even a New York one.

Pearl's phone played its four musical notes from the old *Dragnet* TV show theme.

She checked to see who was calling.

"That Grandma?" Jody asked.

Pearl nodded, furious at her mother. She could pick the damnedest times to call.

"Can I talk to her?" Jody asked.

"You don't have—"

"I *want* to," Jody said. "You never know when it might be important."

Pearl tossed her the cell phone. Jody caught it and went out into the hall.

"You can do your plea bargaining with the prosecutor," Quinn said to Craig. "As can you, Miss Beene."

"My daughter—" Ida said in a choked voice. But not before Quinn had seen the calculation in her eyes. Eloise was a bargaining chip.

"The people we want—and are going to get—are the ones who killed Jack Clairmont and Alexis Hoffermuth."

"I can tell you who they are!" Craig said.

"Don't be an idiot," Ida said. She'd apparently thought

this out. "We didn't kill anyone. Didn't have the real bracelet for very long. There might not even be enough evidence to convict us. Especially if I keep quiet and don't testify against you. They can't make a wife testify, you know."

"You two are really married?" Pearl asked.

Ida grinned. "In Las Vegas, two years ago. We did it so we could file jointly and not pay so much tax on some gambling money we won." She glared at her husband. "Alexis Hoffermuth can't identify that woman who got into her limo; she's dead. And we don't know where the hell that cat got that bracelet. Or who killed Jack or cut off his finger." She laughed, staring directly at Quinn. "They don't even have enough evidence to arrest us."

Quinn wasn't sure if what she said was true, but he didn't have time to give it the test of reasonableness.

Boomerang strutted into the room, and when Quinn and Pearl were looking at him, Craig and Ida broke for the door to the hall. Boomerang got in the spirit and dashed with them. Caught up with them in two large bounds. Quinn and Pearl followed.

The door to the hall burst open. Jody was there, still talking on Pearl's cell phone with Pearl's mother. She extended her foot daintily and tripped Craig Clairmont. Ida tripped over Craig. Quinn tripped over Ida. Pearl managed to leap over them all but fell and skidded to a halt near the stairs. She caught a glimpse of Boomerang streaking down the hall toward God and cat knew where.

She quickly struggled to her feet, and staggered over to help Quinn handcuff Craig and Ida before they could gather their senses.

Jody took several steps backward, the phone still pressed to the side of her head.

"So now you can go back to sitting with the same people for dinner?" She was asking her grandmother.

She grinned at the obviously affirmative answer on the other end of the connection.

If a person was persistent enough, things had a way of working out.

"The insurance company has agreed to let the heirs cancel their claim and place the bracelet in a vault," Quinn said to Ida Beene and Craig Clairmont in an interrogation room at the precinct house. "We won't make any media statement about that."

Craig and Ida silently nodded in unison. They both looked small and pale.

"It's possible that we haven't enough to charge you, or to get a conviction, but the people who cut off your brother's finger and killed him in an attempt to make him talk, probably the same ones who tortured and killed Alexis Hoffermuth, are still out there. There isn't enough evidence against them, either, to trigger an arrest."

"Damned legal system!" Craig said.

"You want some advice?"

Craig shrugged. "Why not?"

"You and Ida should make arrangements for the kid, maybe with Ida's sister or Social Services, and then move far away."

"Arrangements?"

"I'm thinking long term," Quinn said. "You wouldn't want Eloise to talk about what she might have overheard. You need to cut ties completely to guarantee her safety."

He didn't say Eloise would be better off with a family that didn't deal in jewel theft.

"My sister's place in Queen's is no good," Ida said. "I have an aunt back in Ohio."

"That'd work," Quinn told her. "And there's one more condition. Eloise takes Boomerang with her to Ohio."

"Done," Craig said. "But the damned cat will probably find its way back."

Later, in the brownstone, Jody questioned whether the deal Quinn had made was entirely legal.

"Maybe the outcome isn't exactly legal," Quinn said. "But it's just. And it gives the kid a chance."

Jody looked to her mother.

But Pearl was as impossible to read as Quinn.

Jody shook her head and grinned. "You two!"

"Three," Pearl said.

Epilogue

Jody wasn't along on this one. Fedderman and two uniforms had the front door of Willard Ord's house in the Village covered. The back door was being watched by two more uniforms and a plainclothes detective from the nearby precinct house. In the front and back of the building were also Emergency Service Unit sharpshooters, the NYPD equivalent of a SWAT team. In dangerous situations, the safest strategy was to overwhelm the suspects.

Pearl and Quinn stood to the side, and Quinn reached over and rang the doorbell.

Within a few moments, floorboards creaked softly inside the old brick building in the Village. A yellow porch light to discourage bugs flickered on, and the door opened.

Willard Ord stood in the doorway. He was wearing what looked like a white bathrobe and glossy black wing-tip shoes with black socks.

"You're police," he said with a smile. "You don't need any identification other than your eyes."

Quinn could see beyond Willard a table covered with cards and poker chips. There were three chairs at the table, and three beer cans on it.

"Are you alone in the house?" Quinn asked.

"Yes. In fact, I'd just gone to bed when I heard the doorbell."

There were shouts from around the back of the house, and several gunshots. Most of the shots, and the last of them, sounded as if they came from ESU sniper rifles. ESU snipers always hit what they aimed at, and they shot to kill.

Quinn and Pearl both had their handguns aimed at Willard, who shrugged.

"I'm alone now," he said.